Praise for *Strangers in Budapest,*
a December 2017 Indie Next Pick

"Jessica Keener writes about post-communist Hungary with the heart and specificity of someone who's lived it . . . Her writing sparkles when she alternates between detailing her characters' motivations and describing their new home in all of its volatile, foreign, scaldingly hot charm. She demonstrates a masterly touch in the way she drops dashes of bleak Hungarian history into marital squabbles, family meals, and morning jogs . . . fusing emotion to setting and past to present with cutting brevity. As the novel progresses, its focus tightens, with stories of the dead and oblique warnings of the soon-to-be-dead jointly creating a haunting atmosphere . . . Well-executed . . . twists keep the pages turning fast . . . *Strangers in Budapest* doesn't exoticize or patronize its location; rather, in a rare achievement for an American novel of this international emphasis, it revels in the complexity of its appeal."

—*Entertainment Weekly*

"Full of seduction and intrigue, this thrilling novel is a perfect homage to a city in transition." —*Real Simple*

"With chills lurking around each corner, this second novel by author Jessica Keener is the perfect page-turner for late autumn."

—*Boston* magazine

"A slow burn of an international psychological thriller. Recommended for fans of Chris Pavone." —*Library Journal*

"Annie and Will, a young American couple with a new child, repair to Budapest to forge their future and escape their past. What they find is a city smothered by heat and tangled in history. When their paths cross with a mysterious elderly man named Edward Weiss, Annie discovers that she's caught up in a life of tragedy that forces her to confront the losses in her own past. *Strangers in Budapest* is a beautifully written mystery propelled by well-crafted and fully imagined characters. Atmospheric and ominous, this novel asks us what we're willing to do to start over in a new world when the old world won't let us go."

—Wiley Cash, *New York Times* bestselling author of
The Last Ballad

"In the Budapest of Jessica Keener's gripping new novel, menace lurks down every street and infuses every interaction, until the city itself becomes a brooding, sinister presence. With lyrical prose, Keener examines grief and guilt, deception and hatred, and the search for an elusive redemption. *Strangers in Budapest* is a remarkable novel that continues to haunt me, weeks after I reached its powerful, unexpected conclusion."

—Lauren Belfer, *New York Times* bestselling author of
City of Light, *A Fierce Radiance*, and *And After the Fire*

"From the first pages of *Strangers in Budapest*, the words 'You must not tell anyone' made me feel as if a hand had reached out from the shadows to pull me under, and I was swept away inexorably by this hypnotic plot, these dark scenes, relentless tension. *Strangers in Budapest* is a riveting, beautiful book that throbs with plot and sparkles with excellent prose."

—Lydia Netzer, author of *Shine Shine Shine*

"Jessica Keener's *Strangers in Budapest* is a provocative novel about the power of the past—and our interpretations and misinterpretations of it—to haunt the present. A wonderful book."

—B. A. Shapiro, *New York Times* bestselling author of
The Muralist and *The Art Forger*

"What do we run away from? And what do we run toward? Two American expatriates in Budapest, a lonely young mother with a devastating secret, and an old man desperate to discover the truth about his daughter's death, forge a shattering connection. Gorgeously told and deeply moving, Keener's brilliant new novel is a bold, brave, and dazzlingly original tale about home, loss, and the persistence of love."

—Caroline Leavitt, *New York Times* bestselling author of
Cruel Beautiful World

"Keener immerses the reader in Budapest's postcommunist period in all its tumultuous glory . . . The author combines strong characters and a riveting plot to craft a memorable novel."

—*Publishers Weekly*

"Keener's second psychological novel, set in modern Hungary, dramatizes both national and personal outcomes of harrowing past events. Budapest becomes a powerful symbol of past horrors, lush culture, and an uncertain future. Reminiscent of Hilary Mantel's *Eight Months on Ghazzah Street* . . . and similar in tone and theme to Kim Brooks' historical novel, *The Houseguest*." —*Booklist*

"In Keener's *Strangers in Budapest*, the city is as much a character as any, and as Annie and others begin to cave under its crumbling weight, what's revealed where East meets West is a story about the implacability of the past—present, progress, and denials notwithstanding." —*Foreword Reviews*

"A mesmerizing story of love and loss, Keener probes the depths to which grief and disappointment can drive a person away from those who only wish to love them."
—Karen Dionne, author of *The Marsh King's Daughter*

"This exquisite novel draws the reader in from the very first pages and refuses to let go. Not only did I feel like I was in the exotic, beautiful city of Budapest, but every emotion felt by the young mother at the center of this ominous tale became my own. In *Strangers in Budapest*, Jessica Keener proves once again that she is a brilliant, lyrical writer with a true understanding of the human heart."
—Ellen Marie Wiseman, internationally bestselling author of
The Plum Tree, What She Left Behind, Coal River,
and *The Life She Was Given*

"Jessica Keener has written a gorgeous, lyrical, and sweeping novel about the tangled web of past and present. Set in a richly detailed Budapest, an American couple and their newly adopted son, there for the promise of building a business, become entangled with an irritable World War II vet hoping to settle a score. A story of confronting truths, acknowledging old wounds, and stepping into the present. Suspenseful, perceptive, fast-paced, and ultimately restorative." —Susan Henderson, author of *Up from the Blue*

"In *Strangers in Budapest*, Jessica Keener's riveting novel of conscience and suspense, multiple strands of fate and guilt, cultural memory and private trauma overlap and tighten into an ethical knot of compelling, hypnotic design. An enthralling read!"

—Melissa Pritchard, award-winning author of *Palmerino*

"A taut, elegantly written, magnificent novel. I can touch, taste, smell, hear Budapest. Even the car alarms are rendered with beauty and precision. Jessica Keener turns pain and redemption into a masterful work of art."

—Risa Miller, author of *Welcome to Heavenly Heights*

"*Strangers in Budapest* is both lyrical and propulsive, capacious and rich in detail. The characters will stay with you forever. A courageous, compassionate, and deeply wise novel."

—Patry Francis, author of *The Orphans of Race Point*

"Moody and captivating . . . Past events—from the liberation of the concentration camps after World War II, to the Hungarian Revolution of 1956, to more personal tragedies—haunt all of the characters in this novel in different ways, and Keener does an excellent job of tying these threads together into an emotional, unpredictable, and often riveting story. Most impressive, however, is Keener's Budapest, a rough-edged, darkly beautiful city rushing into the future. It makes for an ideal place in which to explore themes of loss, love, and the courage required to come to terms with the past."

—*Jewish Book Council*

"Masterful . . . Fans of slow-burn suspense novels who also enjoy fish-out-of-water situations will find much to love here."

—Bookreporter.com

"A fabulously complex and mysterious tale that is full of atmosphere and suspense. The plot moves quickly and Budapest of 1995 is the perfect backdrop with its picturesque location, tragic history, and political complications. From the very first pages the reader is bombarded with an air of danger that seems to permeate almost every scene and conversation . . . A powerfully provocative psychological thriller that combines engaging characters with a gripping and darkly atmospheric plot. This novel's gut-wrenching discussion of how our past actions often affect our present is both poignant and thought provoking. Within its pages, Keener masterfully examines sorrow and remorse, dishonesty and loathing, and the ultimate search for unattainable redemption, truth, and love."

—*New York Journal of Books*

"A genuine love letter to a little-understood city, where even outsiders with the best intentions will always remain strangers."

—*Manhattan Book Review*

"Keener expertly weaves together a story that not only showcases an expat life, but also shares the tragedies, memories, and grudges of strangers in a beautiful city who are more connected than they have come to believe."   —*BookPage*

"Keener's writing is unquestionably skillful. Her ability to render multidimensional characters through sophisticated description and dialogue is excellent."   —*Chicago Review of Books*

"Jessica Keener focuses on an expat couple's ever-darkening adventure in a way that sucks you in."

—*Campus Circle* (Los Angeles)

"This is a fictional thriller that captivates the reader in the first few pages. *Strangers in Budapest* has an engrossing storyline . . . Guilt and murder brings a morality into focus while choices about rights and wrongs are discussed openly. The characters are full bodied, personable, and believable. The setting is described thoughtfully and with care. The author includes history lessons on the city of Budapest through her characters, mainly Will. It is a fast-paced page-turner that will leave the readers deep in contemplation."

—*Portland* (OR) *Book Review*

"Full of suspense . . . Keener depicts Budapest as its own character, with beauty, suffering, and colorful revolutionary attitudes."

—*The Improper Bostonian*

STRANGERS IN BUDAPEST

STRANGERS

in

BUDAPEST

———•— A NOVEL —•———

Jessica Keener

ALGONQUIN BOOKS
OF CHAPEL HILL
2018

Published by
ALGONQUIN BOOKS OF CHAPEL HILL
Post Office Box 2225
Chapel Hill, North Carolina 27515-2225

a division of
WORKMAN PUBLISHING
225 Varick Street
New York, New York 10014

First paperback edition, Algonquin Books of Chapel Hill, October 2018.
Originally published in hardcover by Algonquin Books of Chapel Hill
in November 2017.
Printed in the United States of America.
Published simultaneously in Canada by Thomas Allen & Son Limited.
Design by Steve Godwin.

This is a work of fiction. While, as in all fiction, the literary
perceptions and insights are based on experience, all names,
characters, places, and incidents either are products of the
author's imagination or are used fictitiously.

LIBRARY OF CONGRESS CATALOGING-IN-PUBLICATION DATA
Names: Keener, Jessica Brilliant, author.
Title: Strangers in Budapest / a novel by Jessica Keener.
Description: First edition. | Chapel Hill, North Carolina :
Algonquin Books of Chapel Hill, 2017.
Identifiers: LCCN 2017021078 | ISBN 9781616204976 (hardcover)
Subjects: LCSH: Aliens—Hungary—Budapest—Fiction. | Parents of murder
victims—Fiction. | Budapest (Hungary)—Fiction. | LCGFT: Thrillers (Fiction)
Classification: LCC PS3611.E344 S77 2017 | DDC 813/.6—dc23
LC record available at https://lccn.loc.gov/2017021078

ISBN 978-1-61620-864-6 (PB)

10 9 8 7 6 5 4 3 2 1
First Paperback Edition

For Barr and Sam,
and Susan Keith

This is where we are in history—to think
the table will remain full, to think the forest will
remain where we have pushed it; to think our bubble of
good fortune will save us from the night—a bird flies in
from the dark, flits across a lighted hall and disappears.

—STEPHEN DOBYNS, "Where We Are (after Bede)"

Oh I'm sleeping under strange strange skies

—THE ROLLING STONES, "Moonlight Mile"

One

She'd grown used to calling the Danube by its Hungarian name—Duna. In fact, she preferred it over the American version. The whimsical sound—Duna—felt light on her tongue, fanciful and upbeat, a spirit rising. But, like all things in this city, the river that glittered at night concealed a darker surface under the day's harsh sun. The water looked sluggish and dull from this high point on the bridge.

"How much farther?" Annie asked. They had walked a mile, but it felt longer to her.

"Almost there," Will said, waving his well-worn map. "A few more blocks."

"Good, because this whole thing feels crazy."

She pushed their son, Leo, in the baby jogger across a crowded Árpád Bridge—one of eight bridges spanning the river that divided the city into two distinct parts, Buda and Pest. In her running shoes, T-shirt, and shorts, Annie nudged the jogger between couples and families seeking relief from the excessive heat, many of them heading to Margaret Island and the kiddie sprinklers, woods, and shade the park offered. Today they would bypass the park and its entrance from the bridge. She tried to hurry on, but throngs of people strolling in front of her forced her to slow down.

"Think of it this way," Will said. "We finally get to see their apartment."

"I know. I'm glad about that."

She did not feel good about it, though. The day had begun with an unsettling fax, an urgent request from their neighbors back home in the States. The strident beeping from the machine in the living room woke her early, before dawn, while Will lay immobile beside her in bed, undisturbed. She sat up, trying to locate the unpleasant sound.

On the bridge, she turned her attention back to the riverbank below and the ferry boats boarding day-trippers for a journey to Vienna four hours away.

"We should take that ferry to Vienna sometime," she said.

"I agree. We'll do it," Will said.

She pushed harder, the humid air dragging on her T-shirt like a heavy coat.

"Up and over," she said to little Leo, tilting the baby jogger back and hiking it over a curb. Leo loved the sudden movement and let out a joyful screech.

She and Will both laughed at the happy sound. How little their son required—sleep, food, a ride in a stroller—to make him feel loved. She wished she could say the same for herself. After eight months of living here, things were not turning out as they expected.

At last, they reached the opposite end of the bridge and stepped onto the Pest side of town—pronounced *Pesht*—otherwise known as the flat industrial section of Budapest, where streets, arranged in gridlike patterns, fanned out for hundreds of blocks. Buda was the hilly side.

"Look both ways," she said as they crossed a wide avenue ringed with trolley tracks.

"There's the street," Will said. "Károly utca. Number 647 should be on the left." He closed his map.

They entered a serene residential street, empty except for parked cars and deeply shaded by maples and oaks, grand as any she'd seen back home in Massachusetts, limbs reaching high into the moist atmosphere. The trees offered a soft feeling of relief from the sharp-edged, intractable sun reflecting off the main boulevards. Leo bent his head back to take in the quilt of greenery overhead. His auburn curls matched Will's exactly, a coincidence that seemed more miracle than a stroke of fate. How else could she explain it, given that their son had come to them via an adoption agency in North Carolina?

"Ap, Dada." Leo pointed to Will's map.

"Map, that's right," Annie said. "Daddy needs to hold on to it."

THE THREE-STORY BRICK building lacked classical architectural adornments. She guessed it to be late 1930s modernism. Old newspapers littered the entranceway, where a panel of buzzers listed residents' names. Annie stepped closer to the panel, scuffing a roll of newspapers out of the way, and rubbed her finger across the handwritten letters.

"Just as Rose said. Here it is, number 2F. Rose and Josef Szabo." From her hip pocket, she unfolded the piece of thin fax paper.

Dear Annie and Will,

    We are concerned about the heat you are having. Please go to our flat, no. 2F at 647 Károly utca. A man named Edward Weiss is living there. Edward is in his seventies and not in good health. He has diabetes and a heart condition. We are worried about him.

It was true. Temperatures had turned lethal these past weeks. The summer of 1995 was breaking records for the longest stretch of days over ninety degrees, according to Radio Free Europe, the station she listened to every morning since coming here eight months ago. Already a dozen elderly had died. *More deaths expected, no end in sight*, the announcer had warned in that Euro-British broadcaster's accent she'd grown accustomed to.

"Ready?" Will said. He stood next to her, a good half foot taller than she, blocking a ray of sun poking through the trees. He wore his usual summer attire: madras shorts, collared shirt, tennis sneakers.

"Wait. Her instructions are very specific," Annie said. She reread them aloud: "'This is important. You must not tell anyone that he is living there. We are trusting you. The buzzer to the apartment is broken, but the front door to the building will be open. It is never locked. Go to the second floor. Knock loudly. Tell him we sent you. He will not like this. Call right away if you find a problem. Hugs and kisses to Leo.'"

Rose's handwritten consonants curled in the same Hungarian style of script Annie had seen on store receipts here.

"It's odd Rose never mentioned this Edward Weiss," she said. She hoisted Leo from the jogger to her hip.

"I know. Let's go." Will easily lifted the aluminum baby jogger and carried it through the doorway.

She loved entering buildings for the first time. She attributed this pleasure in part to her father who owned a real-estate company in Portland, Maine, where she grew up. He taught her that buildings were meant to be inspected, surveyed, and assessed. But for Annie, it was more than that. Unknown buildings held secrets, possibilities, surprises—a peek into other people's hidden lives.

A center staircase greeted them.

"There's an elevator," Will said, pointing to a dark corner behind the stairs.

"Let's walk up."

The open stairway turned three times around a shaft shimmering with dust and sun from a skylight above. Leo grasped strands of her short hair. He tightened his plump legs around her waist, the sweat on his soft skin indistinguishable from hers. On the second-floor landing, they found the apartment midway down a dark hall, the last name, SZABO, on a tag beneath a peephole.

She knocked, then looked into the peephole, but it was covered up and she could only see black. Leo reached out to touch it.

They waited.

She knocked again. Louder.

"Mr. Weiss?"

She pressed her ear against the door. "I hear something."

The peephole lightened and after some jostling the door was unlocked. An elderly man with a large forehead stood in the doorway.

He eyed the jogger without the usual surprise that Hungarians exhibited.

"Yes? What is it?"

He spoke perfect American English and wore a pajama set: thin navy-colored pants and matching short-sleeve shirt hanging loosely, as if he'd lost a lot of weight. The dark material accentuated his pale liver-spotted skin. Annie took a step back, struck by his bedraggled appearance. The old man's eyes followed her, two dark lights quivering with nervous energy. She wondered if he were feverish.

Will said, "I'm Will Gordon. Our old neighbors in the US, Rose and Josef Szabo, asked us to come by. This is my wife, Annie. We used to live across the street from Rose and Josef."

"In Massachusetts," Annie said.

"Yes. Yes. I know about you. What are you doing here?"

Annie looked at Will, then said, "Rose was concerned about the heat. She asked us to stop by."

"Why didn't you ring the buzzer? What were you planning, a break-in?" He looked behind her, his dark, burning eyes scurrying up and down the length of the hall.

"She told us not to use the buzzer," Annie said. "She told us to knock." She shifted Leo on her hip. The baby was focused on the old man, taking in his appearance and behavior.

"Thank you. I'm fine. Is that it?"

"Rose was concerned about the heat," Will said.

"What about it? It's hotter than hell."

The old man's gray hair, matted from sweat and grease, gave off an odor like burned toast.

"That's all," Annie said. "We didn't mean to disturb you. Rose was concerned. We can come back another time." She turned toward the stairs. He reminded her of men she'd served at the home-less shelter in Boston. Sometimes it was better to feign disinterest.

"Door," Leo said, pointing at Mr. Weiss. The baby squirmed in her arms, wanting to get down and walk.

Mr. Weiss swatted the air. "Hold on. Don't get dramatic on me. I've had enough of that in my life. Never mind. Come on. Bring your child in." He patted Leo's arm, and in that moment of contact, she saw something soften inside him.

"What's your child's name?"

"This is Leo."

"He's the one who matters. Come on. Bring in that stroller or whatever you call that thing." He waved them inside.

Sensing they had passed some kind of test, Annie looked at Will, then stepped across the threshold into the apartment and put Leo down. Edward shut the door behind them and locked it. A standing fan rattled the air in the living room, making unflattering noises.

"You've been here since January, have you not?" Edward said.

"That's right." She was stunned to learn that he knew this. Did this mean he had been here all this time? The apartment didn't look lived in. It lacked furniture except for an orange couch parked in the middle of a large living area, another standing fan next to an easel, and a small television propped on a suitcase.

"When did you arrive?" Will asked.

"Not important. Listen closely, please," Edward said, raising his voice and facing them. "If you care about an old man, and I believe that you will, based on what Josef and Rose told me about you, you'll honor the understanding I have with them. I don't want anyone to know I'm here. If you violate this confidence, we're done. Understand?"

"Yes. Absolutely." Annie nodded but didn't understand at all.

She kept her eye on Leo as he wandered toward the windows on the opposite wall.

"Don't mention to anyone that I live here. Not one person. Not your babysitter. Not your American friends, or your family back home, or the taxi driver, or the person who cleans your apartment. Understand?"

"Sure," Will said, nodding.

Leo blew air, imitating the sound of the fan. The room smelled of oil paint. On the easel by the windows, Annie saw a small unfinished painting of a mountain scene. Leo was heading toward the easel but had stopped to inspect a scratch on the wood floor. Still bewildered, she tried to reason out the facts. Until this morning, Rose and Josef had not mentioned anyone living in this apartment. All those times Josef referred to his flat, he bragged only about its real-estate value, heightening its importance with jabs of his stubby hands. Not a peep about an old man living here.

"We thought the apartment was empty," Will said.

"It was."

Annie looked down at the wooden parquet floor and noted the same herringbone design she had seen throughout Budapest, including the flat they rented. This zigzagging floor pattern had lost its shine long ago, worn down to an unvarnished layer. But the room was spacious—she guesstimated twelve hundred square feet, enormous by Budapest standards—and in that way she understood why Josef raved about it. It would have worked well for the three of them had Josef rented it to them. But he hadn't. Perhaps this Mr. Weiss was the reason why.

Leo came back and tugged on Annie's hand.

"What else did Rose and Josef say about us?" Will asked.

"Josef thinks you're a nice couple searching for something. Doesn't know what for. Says you had more than enough to satisfy you in Boston. Big house, yes? Nice neighborhood in the suburbs. Good jobs. Americans are never satisfied. We always want more, am I right?"

"I suppose so," Annie said, wanting to be agreeable, though she wasn't sure what she wanted at this point. This friend of Rose and Josef's did not look well. She allowed Leo to steer her back toward the door. She was hungry and hot, and it was obvious that Edward, as Rose had warned in the fax, wasn't thrilled about this unexpected visit. "We're sorry we disturbed you," she said. "Rose and Josef were worried."

"Worry. What a waste of time. What does it get you? Nothing. I assure you."

"I suppose you're right," she said. On a table next to the couch, she saw an empty glass and a small framed picture of a woman in a wheelchair. The photo in the frame had been torn in half. "You have a lot of room here," she said in an effort to be friendly. "Josef often talked about this apartment. It's nice."

"Come on. You're thinking why doesn't he fix this place up, put it on the market, and turn a good profit. Am I right? They don't live here anymore. It would make sense. What are you trying to accomplish in this godforsaken place?"

"I'm here on business," Will said.

"Yes. But for what? The big killing. The big deal?"

"We're hoping to build communication networks in outlying towns."

Annie was proud of Will. Though Hungary was not the slam-dunk moneymaking opportunity her husband had imagined it would be, he had a philosophy. She took a step closer to Will, hooking her free arm around his.

"Will has a theory that communication networks can prevent wars."

"Theories." Mr. Weiss snorted. He held up his hand to stop her from saying any more. "Don't talk to me about theories or war. Good luck to you both. Hungarians have been traders for a thousand years. Traitors, too, if you know your history."

Annie wanted to protest. Dismissing an entire country was harsh, but she kept silent. Instead, she nodded to let Mr. Weiss know she knew her history. She knew that Hungarians supported Hitler, had decimated a million Jews. She knew the country had been taken over by Russia following the war and had only officially freed itself four years ago, in 1991, when the last of the Russian troops finally vacated the country. It was a new day here, a new era. Communist statues had literally been toppled. Now Russian watches decorated with communist symbols were sold as mementos on street corners to tourists. It was a new time of hope, wasn't it? Couldn't people and countries change?

"May I ask what kind of business you were in?" Will said, crossing his arms.

"Sales. Medical equipment. Sold large expensive machines to hospitals and clinics. Did it for thirty-five years. The truth is, it was a racket in the guise of helping, like so many things—and people."

"I'm sure your machines helped people," Annie said, thinking of Tracy, her older sister. She wished someone would invent a machine that could eliminate Tracy's seizures. But no. So far, nothing had worked. Tracy had undergone surgery after her brain injury, but the seizures hadn't stopped. Now she took pills and wore a special helmet, and used the latest electronic wheelchair to help mitigate her deteriorating circumstances.

"What about early detection?" Will said. "MRIs have been a great service."

Edward shrugged. "Sure. It's old information in new, fancy packages, telling people what they already know or don't want to hear. Is that helping?"

Annie wanted to ask him what his machines revealed about his own obviously deteriorating health. But the room was stuffy and the fan next to her wasn't doing much of anything except tossing around hot air and making noise. She wondered about the picture of the woman in the wheelchair, but Leo had wandered back across the room and found Mr. Weiss's tubes of paints and was trying to unscrew the top of one of them. Annie hurried over and gently took his hand. He protested, squealing.

"Come over here, sweetie."

"He's a curious child," Mr. Weiss said, nodding.

He didn't seem to mind Leo's shrieks, and for that she was grateful.

"Does your boy want something to drink?"

"Thank you. We're fine," Annie said.

The old man grunted and started toward a tiny kitchen area, an alcove off the living room. He turned on the tap, poured himself a glass of water and drank it in one gulp. He was gruff, rude, then polite. What was going on here, she wondered.

Will called to their son. "Leo, come over here."

Annie scooped him up. On the easel, the picture of a mountain on a canvas the size of a book charmed her and revealed an able hand. On the floor, a small stack of similar-size canvases caught her eye. "Beautiful paintings," she said, but she wondered how could he paint in this low light. The living-room windows, tall and wide, needed cleaning. Street grit dulled the sun pressing through. A set of old-fashioned velvet curtains framed the windows. She didn't want to imagine how old they were. The part of her that liked things neat and in order wanted to dust and clean up this place.

She turned to Will. "We should go." It was time for lunch and Leo's afternoon nap, but Leo pulled away from her again, wanting to touch the paintings.

Edward shuffled toward her. Despite a slight stoop, he was nearly Will's height.

"Let the boy look. He's fine. He can't hurt them. Go on. Pick one up."

Leo grinned as he slid from her grasp and plopped down on the floor. The canvases were small enough to manipulate with his chubby thumbs.

"They are lovely," she said.

Edward almost smiled. Encouraged by this, she said, "Are you from Boston, too? Do you have family here?"

As soon as she asked, she regretted it. The old man's body locked up. His eyes flogged her as if she had insulted him.

"No. No family here."

"Pains," Leo said, picking up a brush.

Mr. Weiss turned to Leo and the burning in his eyes cooled down. How sudden these changes, she thought. She'd seen this sort of thing at the shelter: emotional squalls in grown men, erratic behavior flip-flopping, the way Leo acted when he needed something. She'd seen it with her brother, Greg, when he started drinking in high school.

"You have a nice boy," Edward said, his voice tender. "You trust your babysitter? I assume you hired a Hungarian. You trust her?"

"Yes. She's wonderful," Annie said.

"You did a background check?"

"Yes, another American family referred her to us," Annie said.

"People can fool you."

He looked stricken again, as if a sharp object had stabbed his stomach. He leaned over and squeezed his eyes shut.

"Mr. Weiss?" She reached toward him.

"Sir, why don't you sit down?" Will put his hand on Edward's elbow. "Is it your stomach?"

She wondered if they should call a doctor.

"No. Look. Please. You'll have to excuse me now." The old man started for the door, his body tilting as if his legs were not the same length. "I'm going to have to cut this visit short."

Annie picked up Leo and settled him on her hip, but he resisted, reaching out first toward the easel, then Edward.

"Honey, no. It's time for lunch."

"Sorry for the trouble," Will said.

"Everything in life is trouble, haven't you learned that yet?" Edward said, breathing hard.

Annie paused at the door.

"We're happy to run an errand for you. We have a car. If you have a doctor's appointment—anything. Please call us. Our cell phone number is on Will's card. Did you bring a cell phone with you?" She quickly scanned the room for a landline, not expecting to see one. Very few Hungarians had phones in their homes. Or, if they did, it meant they had waited five, even ten, years for one and paid too much money or had some special connection to someone higher up in the food chain of favors. Only a select group had cell phones—the nouveau riche, state and city officials, politicians, and of course, Americans. She spotted Edward's cell phone on the couch. "Please call us if you need *anything*," Annie said.

Will handed him his business card.

"Look, I knew you'd show up eventually."

"Call anytime," Will said. "We don't live far from here. We're down by the river."

"The river, you say?"

"Yes."

Annie watched this information ricochet inside the old man's throat. He swallowed and straightened his back, seeming to engage in something, then looked at her with new intent and interest.

"Any other Americans in your building?"

"No. No other Americans. Just us. The rest are Hungarians," Annie said. She shifted Leo onto her other hip, but her son had become a body of twists and twirls. "Please, call us."

"I will. I will do that."

He nodded and opened the door, his surprisingly nimble fingers grabbing hold of the doorknob. "Keep an eye on your boy there. Watch out for thugs. Don't let him out of your sight."

Two

He needs a doctor," Annie said as soon as they stepped outside. She let Will take the stroller so she could call Rose on their cell. "He is not okay."

"Maybe not. We caught him off-guard. He wasn't expecting us."

"That's true, but did you see how he walked?"

"Arthritis is my guess. He's old."

"How do they know him? Why is he here?"

Annie dialed Rose's number and listened to the echoing wires connecting overseas to the States. It would be very early morning in Massachusetts. "You've reached the Szabo residence. Leave your name." Click. Rose's message made no attempt to sound friendly. In this way, her old neighbor's Hungarian roots, despite nearly fifty years of living in America, revealed itself. Earnest, serious people, Hungarians didn't put on cheerful pretenses or offer gratuitous smiles the way Americans did.

She spoke slowly into the phone in an effort to sound calm and clear. "It's Annie. We're fine. We just left your friend, Mr. Weiss. Honestly, he does not look well. Does he have a doctor here? Maybe it's nothing, but I'll feel better when I've talked to you. Call when you get this message. We miss you."

As soon as Annie hung up, the cell rang.

"I was in the bathroom," Rose said. "What happened?"

"Your friend doesn't look well. He looks feverish."

"He's not well," Rose said. "You are suffering terrible heat, yes?"

"Yes. I think he should see a doctor. He was in pain. His stomach or legs—he limps. How do you know him? Why is he here?"

"I can't tell you, dear. You will have to trust me. He has a good doctor. I know this. There are good doctors in Budapest. Did he talk to you?"

"Yes. He let us in. We saw your apartment. It's nice. He was sweet with Leo."

"He's a good man," Rose said.

"He wasn't happy about our visit."

"No. But now you are friends?"

"I wouldn't call it that, but he said he would call us."

"Good. I knew he would like you."

"When did he get here?"

"I can't tell you. Maybe he will tell you. Listen. You know you can trust me, Annie. Remember what I used to do. You did the right thing. How is little Leo?"

Annie remembered quite well what Rose used to do, and she

thought back to the first time she learned of Rose's involvement in the Jewish underground during the war. "I know how to keep a secret," Rose had said, sitting across from Annie in a booth at a neighborhood restaurant in a strip mall. Rose had sounded stern, but her hazel eyes had filled with tears. Annie didn't press. At the time, she was just getting to know Rose and wanted to respect the older woman's privacy and the memories that clearly and understandably upset her. From then on, Annie felt conscious of Rose's role as a Jewish woman from Hungary who had managed to make it to the States after the war, and how Rose responded to life in general, as if everything mattered intensely—whether it was sharing a recipe for a chocolate cake or the name of a landscaper or her husband's uncertain health. Now, with an ocean between them, in different time zones, Annie accepted Rose's authority on keeping confidences and followed her lead by detailing the list of Leo's new words. But after she hung up, she couldn't shake her uneasiness around Rose's insistence on secrecy. And, yes, she understood in an abstract way what Rose had done during the war. But that was fifty years ago. A half century had passed. What did that have to do with Mr. Edward Weiss *right now?*

"Bizarre," she said to Will, catching up to him. He had continued down the block with Leo while she was on the phone. She repeated what Rose had said and waited for Will to offer some insight. "So what do you think?"

"My advice? Don't get caught up in this, Annie. We did what Rose asked us to do. We don't have to do anything more."

It wasn't the answer she wanted to hear.

"He needs a doctor. He looked feverish."

"He's a grown man. Do you want to go to Luigi's for lunch?"

"Yes. That's fine."

They turned back onto the main avenue. At the very least, Annie thought, the Italian restaurant that catered to American expats would be air-conditioned. But the old man's voice kept echoing: *Keep an eye on your boy there. Watch out for thugs. Thugs*—what an old-fashioned word. Of course she would. Of course she would watch her son.

"Strange man," Annie said, leaning over to give Leo a kiss.

"Chew, chew," Leo said, pointing to his shoes. He kicked the footrest, clapping it with his heels because he liked the sound of his new shoes tip tapping on the metal frame.

"Yes, sweet. I'm glad you like your shoes."

She smiled and took a deep breath in an effort to lighten up. Innocence and oblivion in one refreshing package. Why not do what Hungarians do on summer weekends? Stroll. Eat. Stroll some more. If only she didn't feel so restless amid the crush of pedestrians, which if viewed from above, looked like a giant organism undulating up and down the sidewalk. Again, she tried to put the visit with Mr. Weiss out of her mind, but his voice had found its way in. *Traitors, too, if you know your history.*

"But aren't you the least bit curious?" she said to Will, who, she could tell, was back in his own world, most likely thinking of all the meetings he had to set up, the money he needed to raise to launch his venture.

"I'm sure he has his reasons. We don't need to know what they are."

"Could explain the real reason Josef didn't rent his flat to us," she said, remembering how Josef had steered the conversation away from talk of Will and Annie's renting his apartment. "If Mr. Weiss was living here, it would explain why Josef told us he didn't want to rent it in case he needed it. Remember?" Annie said.

"I remember. Or it could be simpler than that. He said it needed repairs. And he was right. Our place is much nicer."

They both laughed.

"True," she said. "It definitely needs a face-lift."

Back home in Stow, Massachusetts, Josef and Rose lived in a brick ranch that needed repair—Monet-like ripples stained their foyer's ceiling from roof leaks. Josef probably knew his place wouldn't be right for them. Annie and Will lived across the street in a white colonial—the contrast between the two homes like polar opposites, yet she grew to love her elderly neighbors with their sharp Hungarian accents. She and Will lived on that street before selling and coming to Budapest.

Many a time Annie had stood in their foyer exchanging gardening tips, borrowing eggs, and listening to the older couple's stories about Hungary. Josef talked about his apartment in Budapest, about World War II, about his escape from the Nazis by wearing a German uniform. He went on and on, rhapsodizing about Hungary like a possessed lover, his voice husky from years of smoking cigars, while Annie listened with fascination and sorrow.

It was Rose who connected them with their Hungarian landlady and their lovely rental apartment located mere blocks from the Duna. The apartment was furnished, the wooden floors polished and shiny, and the price was cheap—75 percent less than what they would pay for the same space in the States.

Annie felt her chest flattening again, her arms rubbing against walls of heat. She wiped the sweat from her forehead and remembered the glow on Mr. Weiss's face, his peculiar intensity that she sensed had nothing to do with the summer heat wave. He reminded her of the men at the shelter in Boston where she'd worked. They had the same fevered expression from suffering too many heartbreaks and disappointments, all of them limping from injuries in their pasts, unable to escape addiction, mental health, war traumas. Hadn't she come here to escape her past, too? She was a new mother who wanted to get away from the adoption agency that gave them Leo, and of course it all coincided with Will's desire to escape corporate life and go out on his own. Again, she heard Mr. Weiss's parting words: *Keep an eye on your boy there.*

Three

Edward listened through the door until he could no longer hear the baby chattering in the stairwell as the family descended the stairs. He returned to the kitchen to drink another glass of lukewarm water. As long as he stayed hydrated and didn't exert himself, he would be okay. He took the blood sugar kit out of the drawer next to the sink and pricked his finger to measure his levels. He would be okay. He was fine right now. Hot. Christ. It was hot, but he would manage that. The digital numbers acceptable. For now, anyway.

He avoided stepping on the spilled coffee grounds on the floor. The girl, Annie, was concerned about him—he could see that—but he would leverage it. She could help him.

It was inevitable, their visit.

Rose told him. She said they needed to know about him. "It is my job to look after you. You will have to trust me." Trust. He didn't trust. Nonetheless, he agreed.

Look. He knew he could move into that new hotel downtown. Rose told him about that, too. Told him about the air-conditioning. Told him the hotel met American standards. She said their flat would not. Damn right. But he wanted anonymity. That was number one. He couldn't get that at a hotel. He'd have to register at a hotel. He'd have to show his passport. He'd have to tell them how long he planned to stay—no, not what he wanted. He wanted this. What he had right now.

He turned back to the living room to sit down. It was too hot to paint. The interruption, it rippled through the big room like a muted siren, sound waves disturbing the air. He needed to rest. Quiet things down, stop the motors running in his mind. Always the looping thoughts about his daughter and wife. This would do for now until he got situated. That was the thing. He would get himself in order.

As soon as he sat down with the glass of water on the table next to him, the fan blowing hot air across his chest, he let his head nod, easing into the sound of the fan growing louder like an airplane taking off. He felt the air lifting underneath him, his body hovering, floating on top of waves.

I'm not going to let this slide, he had told Sylvia.

And where am I in this equation? she'd asked him.

What equation? Who's talking math?

Me. I am.

Sylvia wanted it to go away. All of it. The questions about their daughter Deborah and the pills. Vicodin. Miracle pain drug. What the death certificate said. Overdose. No. He didn't believe it. No. Something wasn't right.

The sound of the fan and the soft cushion on his back disappeared into darkness. The sound of blowing fans, wing motors, plane engines. That was it. The plane. All of them wounded. He was the only one sick. The only noncombatant *unwounded*, yellow-sick with hepatitis. Yellow-eyed. Fatigued. Worse than now. His body jerked and he woke—saw the parquet floor, his easel and half-finished painting. Back here in Europe. Not war. Deborah. His daughter.

He let out a groan. He knew about sick. This didn't compare to that. In that field hospital for a couple of weeks or more. There with the American 106th Infantry Division, the ones captured by the Germans. Those men starving and wounded and everything else you see in war. He had been the only sick one. White defecation. Took months to get rid of it. Not wounded. And they moved him to Paris by air, that hospital just near the tennis courts. What the hell was the name of that place?

He put his hand on his chest, sweat soaking into his shirt. The whirring of fan blades, the afternoon hours whirring, too. Edward lay on the couch, the whole planet spinning, sinking into time's shadows shimmering in his mind, the whole room, the whole strange city of people, and that scum who married Deborah was in Budapest, somewhere close to the river, so close he could feel him. *Found a place by the river. Wish Deborah could see how beautiful it is here.*

Four

A block from Luigi's restaurant, they approached a pushcart florist on the corner selling roses and carnations. Good prices. Super cheap. Two dollars—two hundred forints—for an entire bouquet. The American dollar went a long, long way here.

"Ower!" Leo leaned out of his canvas seat and pointed to flowers in vases on the pavement. Will stopped so Leo could look. A petite dark-skinned woman sidled over to Annie.

"You want? Flower?" The Gypsy woman spoke in broken English, her dark eyes shining like moonlight.

"No. *Köszönöm.* No thanks," Annie said.

Annie smiled, but the woman persisted, yanking a bouquet of

pink carnations from a plastic pail and swinging it under Leo's nose. Annie nodded.

"Bell-ah. Yes?"

"Yes, they're lovely."

Leo reached out to touch them and the Gypsy woman zeroed in, holding the flowers for Leo to touch.

"Dollar." The woman raised two fingers.

"Okay. All right. *Igen.*" Annie pulled out two hundred forints, but the woman shook her head.

"American."

"While you get the flowers," Will said, "I'll check out that phone booth." He pointed to a red phone booth a few blocks down a side street.

"Please don't be long," she said. Phones were the reason Will left his job at Fendix. The majority of Hungarians didn't have phones, neither landlines nor cell phones, so they used public phones owned and run by the state, located in colored booths on street corners like the one Will was off to inspect. Red phone booths were wired for long-distance calls only, silver for local calls, and blue for both. Will wanted to make private phones affordable.

Annie fished through her wallet again. Everyone wanted American dollars here. The Gypsy rushed back to her stand to prepare a small bouquet when two young Gypsy girls appeared at the woman's side and handed her money. Annie guessed the children were the flower women's daughters.

"Ower," Leo said, stretching his arms toward the Gypsies. Annie repositioned the jogger and sat down on the curb to wait.

"Hold on. She's getting them ready for you," she told Leo.

The Gypsy girls looked like twins. Both had dark shoulder-length hair, sleeveless blouses, and long skirts sweeping the tops of their bare feet. The older one, a few inches taller, couldn't have been more than ten, Annie guessed. The younger one, maybe eight, saw Leo and skipped over to him to touch his reddish curls when three skinheads—young men with shaved scalps, wearing black clothing and boots—emerged from the crowds and shoved the little girl out of the way. "Gypsy steal American baby," one of the skinheads said, spitting on the sidewalk.

Intimidated and upset, Annie whirled the stroller around to distract Leo, who had gone silent before bursting into tears. By then, the skinhead and his two buddies had crossed the street, running and laughing. Their disgusting mission accomplished.

Annie stooped to calm Leo, scanning the sidewalk for Will, but she still didn't see him in the crowd. She moved to the side of a building.

"Look, Leo."

The Gypsy woman handed Leo his flowers, and in that one moment, he was back in baby heaven, burying his face in the petals, captured by their smell and beauty. The two girls ran back over to his side.

"Thank you. He loves them. Your children?" Annie asked the woman, and gestured toward the bridge.

"No English."

She asked the question again in Hungarian.

"Children? *Gyermekek?*" It was one of the few Hungarian words Annie knew.

The woman nodded, then turned to a couple who had stopped to look at the flowers. Leo flutter-kicked again. "Nice." He blew air between his teeth, breathing in the flowers' scents around him, his nose wrinkling in glee.

The Gypsy mother gave her daughters several roses wrapped in cellophane and pointed to the bridge. The sisters held hands, the older one with her long, skinny arms leading the way, the younger one compliant, following behind as they both reentered the streams of pedestrians converging at the busy intersection. Right away, the taller one began tugging on the skirts and pants of men and women passing by. A few people shouted and flailed their arms at the girls to shoo them away. Annie was horrified, yet the mother appeared indifferent, hardened by the rude and violent behavior toward her children, treating it as if it were normal. The older daughter persisted, pulling her sister deeper into the center of the masses on the sidewalk, burrowing into the crowd until Annie couldn't see them anymore.

Where was Will? Leo was hungry. He needed to eat. There. Annie spotted her tall husband in the crowd, heading back toward her. She stood up.

"Carnation. Can you say it? Tell Daddy." She pointed to Will.

"Nation, nation!" Leo screeched, holding out the bouquet for his dad.

Will laughed and Annie smiled despite an odd pressing feeling in her chest. She looked back to see if she could find the Gypsy girls, but they were gone. Why weren't they wearing shoes? She felt uneasy in the swirl of people and heat, disturbed first by her meeting with Mr. Weiss and now by the sight of those young girls in their dirty bare feet and those horrible skinheads.

"What is it?" Will took her hand. "What's the matter?"

"A skinhead pushed a little Gypsy girl. It was awful. He said Gypsies steal American babies. That's just a racist lie. Plain and simple. I honestly couldn't believe what I was seeing. Where are the police when you need them?"

"Are you sure you're okay? I'm sorry I wasn't here. Those skin-heads are scary. They really are. They're trouble."

"Horrible," Annie said, shaken and disturbed. She tried to settle herself.

"You know what? I'm going to see Mr. Weiss again. Something's wrong. I know it is."

"Something might be wrong, but it's not our business. He doesn't want it to be. Let it go, Annie. The guy wants to be left alone."

"I don't know about that."

They walked alongside the stroller, neither of them saying anything. Will's response was not what she wanted to hear. The skinhead's violence lingered like a bad smell, and she found herself searching for a way to cleanse herself.

"I hope he calls us if he needs something," Annie said. She didn't think she could leave it alone.

"I hope so, too. Let's try to enjoy the rest of the day." He stopped and brushed her bangs aside, then kissed her on the lips, which surprised her. "This heat is getting to us," he said. "I'm sorry I wasn't here when that happened. Leo seems okay. I'm sure we'll all feel better after we eat some lunch."

She appreciated his attempt to cheer her up. They had come here to learn what it was like to adopt a new culture, to step into something unpredictable and disorienting. Prior to coming here, she had barely traveled outside of New England, had tried to be careful and measured in her decisions. Coming here had been any-thing but certain.

"It was awful. They're like Nazi brownshirts."

"You are exactly right. No different."

Will held open the door to the restaurant for Annie and Leo

to enter. She paused to take in the broad view around her. Trolleys sidling across wide avenues—the oldest metro system in mainland Europe. The streetcars reminded her of Boston, and in that way, Budapest felt familiar to her. Boulevards sectioned the city into twenty-three districts, rippling out in rings from the center of town to ancient ruins of former Roman settlements in the outskirts. All in all, Budapest was a lovely, walkable city, the newest darling of capitalism and the Western world. A city full of promise. Now, after fifty years of communist rule, the Russians had finally left. Hungary's cultural revival had begun. The country was striving to become modern after decades of war and a long history of failures, reopening its rusty gates to Western businesses and entrepreneurs, like Will.

The threesome walked into Luigi's restaurant with its welcoming wafts of air-conditioning. Bright ceiling lights hung overhead. Annie looked at Leo, covered in petals, a beautiful sight, and yet an ominous sensation still nudged her like a beggar's insistent and lonely hand. What about those two Gypsy girls? Were the gates opening for them, too? Where did they live? And Edward, what in God's sake was he doing here?

Five

The room was packed, busy with Americans eating lunch, escaping the heat.

"There's Dave. I had a feeling I'd run into him here," Will said. "Order the penne for me. I won't be long."

"Take your time."

Relieved to be out of the heat, she headed for an open table next to the picture window. What good luck. The table would give Leo entertaining views of pedestrians walking by, pigeons, and trolley cars.

"You order now?" A slender woman began clearing the tabletop of pizza crust and crumpled napkins. She didn't bother to fake a smile, which Annie appreciated. None of the annoying "Hi, my name is so-and-so, and I'll be your server today" silliness you got back in America.

"Yes. Could you bring some bread right away?" Annie looked at Leo. "It'll keep him occupied. My husband and I will have the penne."

"*Persze*—of course." Dressed in a short black skirt and white blouse, the young woman surprised Annie by breaking into a smile. "What is his name?" she said, looking at Leo.

"Leo."

"*Kicsi baba*. I get you bread." The waitress smiled again and left.

A Hungarian smiling? It was the only time Annie observed Hungarians acting effusively—toward children. She learned this when she and Leo first arrived in the airport last January. After she got her luggage, she stood in a long line to pass through customs, Leo asleep against her chest. She was settling in to wait, but then men and women in front of her kept turning to her and waving, pointing to the front of the line. She hadn't understood at first. She thought she had done something wrong until a woman came over, gently took her arm, and with a big smile ushered her to the front of the line. It was a lovely gesture, one Annie would never forget, especially after so many hours of traveling, and she was anxious to see Will, who was waiting for them in the next room. He had flown ahead two weeks earlier to secure their flat.

The waitress returned with a basket of rolls, handing one to the baby.

"Lee-oh. I like."

"*Köszönöm*," Annie said.

Leo laughed, reaching out his hand for the bread.

They named him Leo after the sun. Naming their son had

turned into an effort not to offend either family. On her side, the Episcopalian side, it would have been natural to name the first-born son after the child's father—William—but on Will's side, the Jewish side, it would have offended his parents, who had hoped Leo would be named after a dead grandfather or dead somebody in the Jewish tradition of honoring the dead.

But then Annie would have felt left out and she wanted something that would bridge the differences in their upbringing—a name that would hold equal meaning for them. So they agreed on Leo. Will joked that Leo was also the name of James Joyce's fictional Jew, a wanderer, a seeker, and that association hit a right note for Annie as well because she had felt that way, too: a wanderer from an early age, searching for something she couldn't find at home, drifting through the rooms of her family's impeccably restored, historic Maine house late at night when everyone was asleep. In her childhood home, every piece of furniture had its proper place—not so for her family who lived in it. Her parents worked hard to keep her sister Tracy's brain-damaged life and, later, her brother's alcoholism and death, out of public sight. These things were not talked about. Instead, Annie, who was the youngest, simply took on the role of doing things right.

"Eep, eep." Leo pointed to a pigeon stabbing crumbs on the sidewalk outside.

"That's right honey. That's what the birds say."

A year after Greg died, she met and married Will, a Jewish man from Miami. Her parents didn't know what to think of her decision, or how to respond—they'd lost that ability once and for all after her brother's death—so they said nothing. When she and Will moved to Hungary with their infant son, her parents couldn't understand that either. Why Hungary? her mother had asked.

Why Hungary?

As soon as Leo arrived in Annie's arms via an adoption agency, something burst open inside her, some dormant seed awakened. Will felt that way, too. And once Leo was legally theirs, Annie couldn't wait to leave the country, couldn't wait to leave her old life, couldn't wait to get out from under the adoption agency's watchful eyes in the name of one particular case worker, a Mr. John Calloway. Calloway was a tall man with big ears who had insinuated himself into her and Will's life six months leading up to Leo's adoption, which was finalized and officiated by a Massachusetts judge.

To be fair, Calloway did what adoption case workers were supposed to do. He visited their home every two weeks to check, probe, and question them about baby care. But she resented the process. During his visits, Calloway inspected their house, smiling and nodding as he perused their downstairs rooms, the living room, and kitchen before climbing upstairs to Leo's bedroom in search of clues of misconduct. Of course, he found none and signed off at the three-month mark, which allowed the judge and lawyer to proceed with the finalization of Leo's adoption. Thank God for that glorious day.

Beside her, Leo handed her his smooshed roll, and she took his fingers and kissed them. Coming to this foreign city had taken her far, far away from that particular worry about her beautiful son and the constant, unmentionable burden of who she was—a girl who'd lost both her siblings to tragedy.

Few Americans traveled to Budapest, yet the feeling of Calloway crossing their personal boundaries lingered; the real possibility that a stranger could have cut her heart with one disapproving scratch of his pen on his agency report made her shiver. It touched a raw nerve in her. She knew how a lifetime changed in an instant.

An errant baseball. A sudden glint of sunlight, and her family's life was broken forever. First her sister, then her brother.

Thank goodness Leo was solidly and completely theirs now. Annie reached into the jogger and pulled out Leo's powered milk, his formula that she mixed with water. She shook the bottle then handed it to her son.

With a new *baby?* her mother had asked.

Yes. She and Will thought it was a perfect time. Why not? Leo was four months old. He wouldn't care where he lived as long as he was with his parents. When she told her friends, Annie discovered that Americans, her friends included, had a hard time imagining that babies lived—let alone thrived—anywhere outside the States. She looked out Luigi's big windows and wondered where the little Gypsy sisters slept at night. In a dingy apartment in the outer reaches of town? In a tent? She didn't know anything about the Gypsies and decided it was time she did.

ACROSS THE CROWDED restaurant, Will stood at a table talking to a bald man who Annie guessed was in his fifties, presumably Dave, and a younger man with longish brown hair. Will must have mentioned her because Dave raised his chin toward her and waved. She responded in kind, lifting her hand, thinking it comical the way Americans in Budapest gravitated to the same restaurants, read the same newspapers—the *New York Times*, the *London Times*, the *Wall Street Journal*, and the city's expat paper, the *Budapest Reporter*—as if they had all joined the same traveling circus. And, in fact, they had.

Women in sleeveless summer dresses, men in shorts, their hairy legs stretched out under cafe tables; corporate officers like Dave in their summer uniforms of polo shirts and khaki slacks—an all-American expat crowd at this hour. A few couples with their kids. What was the point of coming to a foreign place to hang out with one's own? So far, she'd gone out of her way to avoid befriending Americans—those few thousand who had come to meld with this city of several million. Yet here she was, doing just that.

Will walked toward her, the older and younger man following him.

"Annie, this is Dave Johnson. Remember I mentioned him a few weeks ago? And this is his translator, Stephen Házy."

She shook their hands. Dave's hand felt meek, his palm bent as if to say, I'm not much of anything. By contrast, Stephen's palm was open, his handshake confident and firm.

"Annie, nice to meet you," Dave said. "You'll have to meet my wife when she gets back from the States. Stephen here is from Boston. He came over several months ago. Great find for us. He speaks fluent Hungarian."

"Really? How did you learn it?"

"Grew up with it. My parents are Hungarian. Anyone would learn under those circumstances." He tipped his head in a deferential way, engaging her. "I understand your husband took lessons before coming over. Commendable."

"Most people don't try," she said, proud of Will's efforts. Except for Stephen, she had not met one American who spoke more than a few phrases of Hungarian. They assumed it was too difficult a language and didn't bother, relying on Hungarians to speak English, which many did, though haltingly.

"Are you enjoying your time here?" Stephen asked her.

"It's a fascinating place."

"You mean difficult? Not easy for Americans to adjust here, is it?" he said to her as if he could hear her deeper thoughts, his green-gray eyes taking her in. He spoke softly, the way Hungarians did, but he didn't have a trace of an accent. "Nothing to do on weekends, right?"

"It's a different pace." She decided he looked more European than American, wearing sandals, and an open button-down shirt that revealed his chest hairs. Or maybe it wasn't European but some kind of upgraded hippie look.

"There's plenty to see, you know. Day trips. Little villages you should check out. I like those flowers your son has there."

She looked at Leo consumed now by his bottle, the shredded flower petals scattered around him.

"Where did you grow up?" she asked. He was classically hand-some—balanced features—as tall as Will with bangs that fell in a careless, offhanded way. Approachable was the word that came to her.

"Originally? New Jersey. But I left there long ago." He spoke as if New Jersey were a faraway, imaginary place, his eyes gazing out the window at the crowded street. "You see, my mother was preg-nant when they left Budapest. Came over after the '56 uprising. I was conceived here. So, technically, I guess you could say I began here. I was born in the States."

"A terrible battle," Will said.

"Blood under the bridge," Stephen said. "I didn't have to live through it. My parents did. My father, especially. Rest his soul. He never recovered. That's the truth."

"I'm sorry," Annie said.

She watched Stephen's face as his eyes circled around the room and back to her. She wanted to ask more.

"Stephen's been a great help to us," Dave said, patting Stephen on the shoulder. "Will, I want you to meet the mayor of Székesfehérvár. It could lead to something. It's a nice town. I believe it used to be the capital."

"Yes. It was the City of Kings. Dozens were crowned there. The name means 'royal white castle,'" Will said.

"Interesting," Dave said.

"Will is full of interesting facts," Annie said.

"Most Hungarians call it Fehérvar, or White Castle," Stephen said, smiling at her.

"Good to know that," Will said. "Town's got one hundred fifty thousand people."

"If you sign on a town like that," Dave said, "other towns will follow. It's a good opportunity. What do you think, Annie?"

"That would be good," Annie said, making an effort to sound enthusiastic. She didn't know why Dave would ask her. Probably his way of trying to include her.

Stephen raised his eyebrows. "You look skeptical."

"Not really." She shrugged. He was an observant one. She wanted to be hopeful about this lead, but a shadow in her heart dulled her feelings. This whole endeavor was proving far more difficult than Will or she had anticipated. She had arrived with her own foolish belief that they could come here, leaping across an ocean, and just make things happen without experiencing delays or duress. So *American* of them. She put her hand to her chest and took a deep breath as if something were pressing against her.

"Well, I'm happy to help out. Sweet-looking kid," Stephen said.

They all looked at Leo sucking on his bottle, his eyes closed, oblivious to all but milk and sleep.

"He is. Thanks. What about you? Do you have children?"

"No. No. No." He shook his head as if such a thing were completely out of the question.

"Not easy being a mother here," Dave said to Annie. "Took my wife a year to settle in, but she did. You'll see."

Annie appreciated Dave's effort to keep things positive. But she knew that working for the large utility company meant Dave got paid an American salary and it wouldn't matter if he succeeded here or not. Corporate types like Dave got perks for transferring overseas: their rent, health insurance, travel expenses, and cars paid for by the parent company. Not so for Will. He was on his own, and so was she.

"It's a complicated city," Annie said.

"It's a lot of things," Will said.

"It's not what Americans think," Stephen said. "We Hungarians are hardier, more intelligent, than Americans understand." He shrugged. "Of course, I speak the language. That makes all the difference in how you experience it here. I'm sure you know exactly what I mean." He opened his palms as an invitation to believe and trust his perspective.

"Will manages to speak pretty well—for an American," she said. "I only speak a few words and phrases."

"I'm terrible at languages, I don't even try," Dave said. "Hungarian? Forget it."

Stephen shook his head again.

"It's like everything else. You have to put the time in to learn it," Will said.

"Americans don't put in the time," Stephen said.

"What do you mean by that?" Dave said, pretending to look offended.

"Oh, I don't mean to sound critical of Americans," Stephen said, tossing his bangs, and lifting his head back to put Dave at ease, but Annie could see that he was withholding something.

"Would you like to sit down and join us?" she said. She was curious to hear more, to learn what it was like for Stephen to be back here. Maybe he could offer some tips. Tell her about how the Gypsies lived.

"No, no. Thank you," Dave said. "We'll let you two enjoy your family time. Stephen and I need to finish up. Good to meet you, Annie."

Stephen hesitated, took a business card from his shirt pocket, and slid it on the table toward her.

"If you need a translator or assistance for anything, here's my number." He held his hand out for her to shake and they shook hands once again. "Don't hesitate to call. I mean that."

"Thank you."

The two men returned to their table and Annie slipped Leo's bottle from his mouth. As expected, he'd fallen into his deep afternoon sleep.

Will sat down opposite her and began to eat the food that had just arrived.

"Stephen's an interesting guy," Annie said.

"He was definitely interested in you."

She shrugged. "They're both nice. How is General Electric doing here? Are they making a profit?"

"They got in early. Some other big companies are here. Alcoa took over a plant. They're investing big dollars. Dave's a decent man."

"Yes. He seems so. Stephen could be a great help to you, don't you think? He's fluent. How long have you known him?"

"Met him today."

"Oh, he acted as if he knew you longer."

"I think that's his way. Maybe Dave told him about me."

"Dave has financial security. It makes a difference," Annie said.

Will focused on scooping up a forkful of pasta, but she could see he was frustrated by her comment.

"Look, Dave's got a good attitude," Will said. "I think he's that way and that's probably part of why he's been successful at GE. He fits in. Doesn't make waves."

"What you're doing is harder," she said.

Entrepreneurs like Will did not have the financial security that Dave enjoyed. It was a sticking point for her. Will might insist it didn't matter to him, but she knew it did. Golden handcuffs. Retirement plans. Then again, entrepreneurs had the hope of making huge profits, much greater than what Dave earned, plus the creativity to make their own decisions. She'd accepted this as part of the risk and reward of starting a new venture. It was part of the freedom, too. Will was his own boss and he liked that. But she didn't feel as confident about his prospects anymore.

She was committed to being with their son this year—had quit her job at the shelter two weeks before Leo was born—and to giving Will a chance at his venture, but Hungarians, it turned out, weren't easy in business. They took their time—time that Americans couldn't fathom. Hungarians changed their minds at the last minute, sabotaging deals at the eleventh hour. Recently, the *Budapest Reporter* featured a story about a hotel deal that had fallen through. Why had that happened? The Hungarians had upped the purchase price when they learned of others' interest in the property. The buyers got upset and backed out. She was beginning to wonder who, indeed, was making a big killing here in Eastern Europe?

Finally, she said, "I wonder what deals are going on right now. Do you think anyone is successful here?" She scanned the room abuzz with loud American chatter.

Will laughed. "Sure, Annie. We need to give it more time."

One thing she did know, everyone was talking huge amounts of money. Here, money was like confetti. Everyone had an idea. Losses or gains, tax write-offs? What did it matter? It was all a game, pieces of paper falling out of the sky. It created a sense of unreality, a kind of money high. Part of the circus mentality. But it wasn't just here in Eastern Europe. Back home, before they'd left, stories of instant millionaires and billionaires had begun to show up on the front pages of newspapers and the living-arts sections in the Sunday magazines. The new rich. Their amazing McMansions decorated by high-priced designers. Instant antiquity. Private jets. Palm Beach and the islands. It was all blather and banter. Eastern Europe was America's new corporate pet. But what if it all crashed? Then what?

She finished her pasta and said, "Is Stephen on GE's payroll, too?"

"No. Independent contractor."

"He could be useful. Have you thought about taking him with you when you meet with the mayors?"

"He's expensive. A day trip adds up. I'm sure he's useful. You don't need to worry about me. Focus on yourself. I know I've said this many times, but try to meet some of the American women living here. They're smart, well intentioned."

"I know they are."

From the first days, Will had urged her to join one of the expat groups like the International Women's Association. Still, she resisted because she wanted to immerse herself in the country's culture.

"I didn't come here to live an American way of life." She pushed her plate away.

"I'm not asking you to do that."

"I know you're not."

From day one, she had been determined to mimic what those Berlitz language courses did, immerse herself in the strange sounds around her the way Leo did.

The waitress came by and refilled their water glasses. Annie reached for Will's hand and knit her fingers through his.

"Maybe I could help the Gypsies?" Annie watched the surge of pedestrians passing by, wondering where the two girls had gone. Across the street, ornate stone buildings with elaborate rooftops loomed over the sidewalks, simultaneously breathtaking and depressing, their gray facades still pitted with bullet holes from World War II. It made her heart leap, then sag, with the thought of all that carnage.

"What would you do with the Gypsies?"

"I don't know. I don't know what they need. I'd have to find out."

Will scraped the remains of his lunch. "The expat community might know where to steer you."

"True."

The idea appealed to her. Maybe the Gypsies would lead to something new, something unexpected. Hadn't she come here to learn something different about herself? Get off her well-worn path of safety. She resolved to do something.

"Those buildings," she said, pointing across the street. "It's a shame what's happened to them." She took another exaggerated breath. "Bullet holes everywhere. There's no escaping the past in this country. No wonder Hungary has the world's highest suicide rate."

Will put his fork down and crumpled his paper napkin. "What can I do to help you get out of your funk?"

"Ignore me?"

Will laughed. "I don't think I can do that!"

At the far end of the room, she saw Dave talking with Stephen, who like some person with a sixth sense turned his head and smiled at her. Embarrassed, she looked away. She could ask Stephen about the Gypsy population. Surely he would know. She could do something meaningful in the community while Will figured out his work situation.

They had been here eight full months—plenty of leads but no closed deals. Week after week, Will attended meetings, joined the American Businesses in Hungary group. A few dozen corporate types, like Dave from General Electric, plus entrepreneurs like Will, got together for coffee and networking at the Hilton up on Castle Hill. One man from Illinois had started a T-shirt business. Someone from Florida had opened a laundry. A couple from New Jersey ran a New York–style deli.

Maybe her mother was right to ask, why Hungary? Eight months ago Annie had come here with arms outstretched, eager to take in whatever this new Old World wanted to show her. The architecture offered so much grandeur rising from the city's renaissance in the 1870s, and again in the 1920s, but the buildings looked downtrodden, their facades soot-covered, pockmarked by decades of neglect. Splendid arched doorways were chipped and weather worn, no money for repair.

What did this country offer her? Maybe she was no different from Dorothy in *The Wizard of Oz* trying to get to Emerald City, then, once there, realizing the glittering city wasn't so shiny after all.

Budapest was covered in a century of grime. Annie had followed the yellow-brick road, and now she couldn't help but wonder if the Wizard—in this case, the promise of making money, the promise of change—was actually a false god.

"You can't save an entire country, Will."

"What are you talking about?"

He looked at her in a way that let her know she was making an unfair and unfounded statement.

"What I want to do with phones is one piece of a much larger global shift," he said. "I'm a small part of that. You know that."

"I know. I'm sorry. I thought it would be easier."

"Me, too. Patience. Dave's been here two years. We have to change our expectations."

"To what? No expectations?"

They both laughed, releasing tension. She leaned toward Will and placed her hand on top of his on the table. "I think countries are like families. Hungarians don't want Americans barging in and taking over like the Russians did, like the Germans did, like the Americans are trying to do."

"Hungarians don't expect things to go well because they have a long history of failing."

"Like my family," she said, slumping, feeling sad.

"Come on. We made a choice, remember?" Will gathered both her hands in his, and in that moment she was grateful for his love.

The waitress returned to refill their water glasses and placed the bill on the table. Annie noted how the other Americans at Luigi's were smiling away, their white teeth advertisements of good health and cheer—so unlike Hungarians' more serious, subdued expressions. She pulled her husband closer, kissing him.

"Okay. Let's go," she said. "Are you ready?"

"Yep."

She looked at Leo still sleeping, not a worry on his sweet face, and felt a stab of emptiness, the missing element of grandparents not here to enjoy and dote on him. Again, she heard her mother's incredulousness: *You're going now? With a* new *baby?*

Certainly Leo didn't care, but Annie was glad to be far, far away from the adoption agency and that meddling social worker who presumed he could intrude in their lives at any time. With that thought, she felt a renewed sense of sympathy with Hungarians trying to forge a new way of life.

Will stood and reached into his pocket for his wallet, then patted his hips, front and back. "My wallet," he said. "Do you have it? I had it with me." Will checked his pockets again, then looked in the pocket of the jogger.

"Slow down. Don't panic," she said. "It's somewhere."

"No. No. I distinctly remember taking the wallet with me because I didn't want to leave all that cash at the apartment."

"How much cash?" She rechecked the jogger pocket, digging her fingers past an extra diaper and wipes for Leo, starting to feel Will's concern.

"Nine hundred dollars." He patted his pockets. "I bumped into two men when I was walking toward the phone booth. I didn't think anything at the time. You saw how crowded it was."

"Yes. But I wasn't paying attention because of those horrible skinheads. What did the men look like?"

"They stole it. They took my wallet. They set me up."

Six

He awakened on the sofa and looked up at the white ceiling until his mind focused and made sense of the room. The ceiling had crackles in the dull paint. Sylvia would be appalled. His pajama top was soaked through, the towel he placed underneath his back damp and stale with sweat. He looked down at his feet and wiggled them. All intact. He remembered the day. It was August. Sunday. 1995. Day seven. He wasn't crazy. It was like the old days when he traveled to Europe for work, moving in and out of small hotels, getting the packing down to a science of saving space. He was a good traveler. His whole life he'd learned to adjust to hotel rooms. First things first—he'd find the emergency exit. Sometimes it was down a long hall. Here on the second floor, he'd go out the kitchen window to a fire escape if he had to. The building had an elevator and that wide set of stairs.

He sat up, a slow movement of sliding his legs around to the floor. There was an adjustment time. You got the lay of the place. This was no different. He had his dictionary, the one with common phrases. His daughter Nan, born practical, her years as a nurse second nature to her, asking, *How will you communicate your needs, Dad? You don't speak the language.* But he knew how it worked. They had good doctors here. He did his research. So did she. He still had his old contacts in medicine. She had her current contacts. Hungary was a smart population. Smart and poor. That was all.

"Hungarians are intelligent. The medicine is good," he told her. "You know that."

"But they don't have money for equipment," she said. "Promise to call me every day. Every. Day. Will you?"

"Yes. I can do that. I promise."

He finished the glass of water and refilled it from a pitcher on the floor, thinking back fifty-two years. Just about this time in August and just as brutally hot in Alabama, where he went for boot camp. He took that train from New York that day. Said good-bye to Sylvia and his parents. What a crazy thing, to get engaged and then go off to war. Youth is stupid and brave.

Was he brave now? He didn't know, but he wasn't as stupid. He had his backup plan. He had the number for a cab, the new hotel downtown with air-conditioning. He had options. Choices. A way out. A way to survive. The war taught him that. Until you put yourself to the test, you can't know what you're capable of. That was the attraction of war. Caves, jungles, woods. Hills. He sat taller, pushing the cushion behind his lower back, surprised by the comfort of it. The bottom cushion, a single long orange mattress, was good and hard, good for his back. The human body knew how to manage these basics. He had learned that because he made it through the war.

He reached for his cell phone on the floor, where it had dropped from his hand. He promised he would call Nan. Thousands of years the race had survived this heat. Humans were animals. Worse than animals. He'd seen it all in the war. For now, he would shower, put on some fresh clothes, and study the map. Having settled on a plan, he perked up.

Edward shuffled to the kitchen and refilled the water pitcher, pouring himself another glass and returning to the sofa and the fan. It took a few minutes to settle back into a pool of solitude to nurse his source of pain. But there it was. His older daughter's death certificate said accidental overdose, but he knew that was wrong. Deborah took painkillers for her multiple sclerosis. Of course she did. She didn't want to die. She was a fighter. It was her lousy husband who killed her with too many pills. Seven months ago. Edward grew more certain of this fact each day. He went over it again. One month after they buried her in Boston, the lousy scum moved to Budapest. Said he wanted to return to his Hungarian roots.

Bullshit. Edward didn't believe a word of it. Van Howard wanted to disappear. He came here thinking he could live like a king with his daughter's insurance money—ten times a king with the exchange rate—and Edward had no doubt he would. American money went far in this country.

Edward pressed into the couch, his shirt still wet. If he could weep, he would. Instead, his heart held back. At seventy-six years old, he still had a chance to make things right, even if the rest of his life had gone wrong.

The cell phone rang—there on the table. It would be Nan, his younger daughter and only remaining family, calling from the States. Nan lived north of Boston. The phone vibrated a third time. He fumbled for it.

"Did Ivan come?" she asked, her voice strong. Steady.

"Yes. He did. Yesterday."

"Good. How are you managing the heat? The paper said it was almost one hundred there. Can't you buy an air conditioner?"

"I don't like them. They stuff up my sinuses."

"Dad, that's ridiculous. You can take something for that. That kind of heat is debilitating. It's dangerous for someone your age." Nan was a surgical nurse, had seen the worst—head injuries, fractured spines, blood, guts.

"I appreciate your concern. How about a pill to find your sister's killer?"

"Are we having a conversation? You sound tired."

"Did you hear from him?"

"No." She sighed. "I seriously doubt he will contact me again. I'll call you if he does. You know I will."

"He'll write again. His conscience will do him in. That's how it is with these types. Time is their enemy."

"We've been over this. I don't think that's going to happen, Dad. You told him to stay away, remember?"

Again she spoke a painful truth, and it silenced him.

Get the fuck out of my house, he had said to Howard after the funeral. Howard, who was tall and lean as a vaulting pole, and ten years older than Deborah, bowed to him, spoke politely, and said,

"Sorry I've upset you," on his way out the door. Edward hadn't heard from or seen him since. How many times had he been over this in his mind? Too many. He knew that. He wasn't insane. But he didn't understand that what he said to Howard was the final straw for Sylvia. That she couldn't take it anymore. That she couldn't or wouldn't put up with his mouthing off anymore. That she had lost the will to fight. How many months ago now?

"Christ! What a stupid fool I am!" he said aloud to the fan, and to the heat and the dusty sunlight that came through gaps in the window shades, and to his surviving daughter on the phone four thousand miles away.

"Dad, give yourself a few more weeks, and then will you let this go? She's gone."

"No. I won't. Not in my lifetime."

"You can't prove anything. There's no evidence."

"I'll take care of it."

Nan sighed. "Listen, I called to tell you someone's interested in your house."

"Interested or ready to write a check?"

"It's a couple with two children. They're coming back to look again."

He got on a plane to Budapest before the realtor put the For Sale sign in the yard. He didn't want to see it. Instead, Nan took care of the details. Her enormous strength surprised him. All those years of worry and fretting about Deborah while Nan carried on. She had his business sense. A solid head on her shoulders. He pictured Nan sitting at her kitchen table. Pale face, dark eyes, hair short as a boy's crew cut. The smell of low tide a few blocks from where she lived in a two-family house that she and her partner,

Patricia, bought as an investment. He saw her wearing a loosely fitting man-tailored shirt to cover her large breasts, breasts like her mother's, his Sylvia. Sylvia dead four months after Deborah. Three months, three weeks, three hours. What difference did any of it make? Time was laughing at him.

"Dad? Are you listening?" Nan, the practical one, the opposite of Deborah, whose voice used to rattle with emotion.

"What's that?"

"I'm coming to see you. I've booked a flight after Labor Day. Mark it down. Don't tell me not to. I've made arrangements at work."

"You'll have to stay in a hotel. There's no room here."

"I know, Dad."

"You won't change my mind about leaving."

"No kidding. Like changing rock to water. Did it ever occur to you that I may want to see my father? I'm your daughter and I'm alive."

Her words punched him in the throat. She was right. In the silence of that truth they both didn't say anything. He knew he should apologize. What had he done? He looked across the living room at his easel, his paintbrushes, his pile of *London Times* on the floor under the window, a smaller stack of the *Budapest Reporter*.

"I'm sorry, Nan. It will be good to see you. How are you?"

"Fine, thank you for asking. Weather's hot here, too. I'll call you tomorrow, Dad."

He put his cell phone back on the table. She was a good, solid girl. He didn't worry about her. Never had. He stood and waited for his body to balance, then scuffed across the parquet floor to the kitchen for something to eat. In the refrigerator, he had a large block of cheese and salami. He made a sandwich and ate it standing at the counter.

When he told Nan he was moving to Budapest, she called the chief of medicine at her hospital and got a referral for a young physician in Budapest who practiced out of a house in the hills. So far he hadn't needed him. As long as he stuck to his diet, kept off cookies, stayed away from pasta and beer, remembered his daily shots of insulin, he kept the diabetes in check.

Back to the sofa, he sat down in front of the fan. "What are you looking at?" he said to the whirling blades.

Nan, in her straight-talking way, was the person who handled him best. Maybe it was the training she got as a nurse—all those years working in critical care units. Nothing fazed her. Or maybe it was the fact that she was a lesbian and had to deal with living a secretive life that hardened her. No, it preceded all that. She was born that way. When she fell off a bike, she got right back on.

Deborah, on the other hand, came out of the womb with a wandering eye, literally and figuratively. The surgeon fixed her eye at six months. Later on, in her teens, she couldn't walk past a beggar without handing the man or woman a coin. At seventeen, Deborah showed up with a homeless poet she met in Cambridge—cracked front tooth, hair tangled, smelling of oil and metal, stunk as if he slept in the subway, and probably did. Edward walked into the house after a day on the road selling, saw this drifter holding hands with his daughter, looked at her with her brown hair down to her waist, hippie skirt, ruffled blouse, her dark eyes wide open to the injured, and told the man to get the hell out of his house.

Get the hell out of my house. Get the hell out now!

Dad! What are you doing? How dare you? Deborah ran off and didn't talk to him for weeks. It was just one of many blowups about her choice of boyfriends.

In college, Deborah moved in with another doozy—a pot-smoking, hippie bicycle mechanic who finally went on a cross-country bike trip and left her with three months' unpaid rent, which he—Edward Weiss, the father and fool—paid. And now he had to deal with Howard. Worse than a boyfriend. Her legal widower.

Seven

"What do you mean, they set you up?" Annie asked.

Will was kneeling on the restaurant floor, looking under their table for his wallet.

"It's probably at our flat," Annie said, turning the jogger and pointing it toward the door. She paid for lunch with cash she had on hand and was ready to leave when she saw Stephen coming over to her.

"Everything okay? I was just heading out."

"Will seems to have misplaced his wallet."

Will stood up. "Or someone stole it."

"I'm sorry," Stephen said. "If it's stolen, you should report it to the police."

"I doubt it was stolen," Annie said. "It's probably sitting on his desk at home."

"You won't be the first," Stephen said. He gave her a look of confidence as if to say he knew about these things.

"What do you mean?"

"I know it's upsetting when it happens, but it happens, especially to Americans."

"What do you mean?"

"Ukrainians. They target Americans. Americans are easy prey. Call me if you need help. Was your license in it? That could be a nightmare," Stephen said. "But I can help you with that."

"What kind of nightmare?" Annie surveyed the crowded room.

"The license. You'll have to go to the police and get something to replace it. You've got my number there." He pointed to his card on the table. "If it's not at your flat, call me and I'll meet you at the station."

"We'll manage. Thanks," Will said. "We should go, Annie."

"Thanks very much," she said. She released the brake on the stroller.

"Hold on. Let me talk to the waitress in case it shows up." Stephen flagged their waitress who came over to him. He spoke rapidly in Hungarian, his words soft and fluid, spilling out without hesitation. Annie was impressed and comforted at the same time. The waitress frowned, shaking her head. Stephen said something else and the waitress walked away looking irritated.

"She thought I was accusing her," Stephen said. "You have to speak firmly about these things. Let's hope you left it at home."

"Thanks. That's likely where it is," Will said.

Stephen bowed and headed toward the door. Annie looked at

his card. It was bare bones. Black lettering on white: his name and cell phone number with country and city codes for Hungary and Budapest. No company name. No address.

STEPHEN HÁZY
c. 36 1 438-5629

She put it in her shorts pocket. Everyone in Budapest had a business card to hand out, including Will. Everyone was looking to cash in or make a deal or a connection.

"That was nice of him to want to help."

"I can handle this, Annie."

"Of course you can."

She watched Stephen exit. He walked with a sure, balanced gait, his hair tousled in an appealing, friendly-dog kind of way. Despite what Will said, part of her wanted him to stay to help them.

"Let's go," Will said.

Outside, they retraced their steps from the flower stand, which was now closed for the day, to the phone booth four blocks down the side street. Will opened the folding door of the phone booth, which she now resented and blamed as the cause of their current trouble and which looked very much like the ones in the States except for its bright red color. He searched under the seat. Nothing. They headed back toward the bridge and home.

"Don't you think we should go back to Mr. Weiss's to see if you left it there?"

"I think he would have called," Will said. "It's either home or those men fleeced me."

"But what if you dropped it on the way? Mr. Weiss was so out of it, it could be on the floor next to the door. He may not have seen it."

"I didn't drop it. I either left it at home or it was stolen. Call him if you want to."

"We didn't get his phone number."

"He has ours. If he finds it, he'll call."

"Why don't I run back to his building, check the sidewalk where we walked, and rule it out. I'll catch up with you."

They arranged to meet on the other side of the bridge. In her heart, she hoped Will had left it at the apartment. When she reached the brick building, she hesitated, then pushed open the exterior door with the broken lock and quickly ran up two flights into the dark hallway. If Mr. Weiss saw her, if he was walking out for any reason at this moment, she would stand tall and tell him the honest, embarrassing truth. As it turned out, no wallet appeared in the hall or on the steps or on the sidewalk. She chided herself for being rash and ran out to the street again, feeling more foolish than disappointed in the heat and sun. If the wallet had fallen inside the apartment, she hoped that Mr. Weiss would call like Will said, but her greatest wish was that Will had simply left it in his sock drawer. The fax was so disorienting this morning. They had rushed out . . .

Running back toward the bridge, she kept her eyes on the sidewalk, passing clothing stores, appliance stores, offices —all of them closed on Saturdays for the rest of the weekend. Since the spring, however, more convenience stores had opened, another sign of free enterprise taking hold. Restaurants and cafes—that's where the crowds went. Still, after all these months, she *expected* all the stores to remain open—her American psyche lunging out like a hungry child, demanding access to the toys she was used to back home.

She spotted Will with Leo standing on the other side of the bridge under the shade of a tree.

"Nothing," she said.

They resumed the trail back to their flat.

"Who were those men? What did they look like?" she asked.

"Two tall guys with dark hair. It happened so quickly I didn't see their faces. They bumped into me on the sidewalk. I didn't think anything of it, except that it seemed odd because they were holding a bag between them and that's what I knocked into. Instead of slackening their grip, the bag caused me to fall forward. They didn't say anything, no apology. That's what bothered me. Now I get it."

"You didn't say anything when you came back."

"I brushed it off as being rude or the craziness of the crowds and the heat. It didn't occur to me that they were trying to steal my wallet."

Now she felt irritated and angry. As they walked away from the river toward their street, Annie reminded herself that this would not be the first time Will or she had left something behind: a key to the apartment door, the battery charger for their cell phone, and now, she hoped, his wallet full of cash.

Back home in the States, Will would never think of carrying that kind of cash in his wallet. But here everyone dealt in cash, expected cash, except for the better hotels and restaurants, which catered to tourists and took credit cards. It made sense to keep a stash of money on hand. In fact, it was prudent. In Hungary, cash was king. No one wrote checks. Banks didn't use credit cards. And ATM machines didn't exist here. It was hard to believe but true.

They walked into their dark, smelly foyer—the one aspect about the building that repulsed her—and passed their building superintendent sweeping the entrance. The super looked the same every day: a bony, chain-smoking middle-age woman who Annie guessed was in her forties. Here was an example of Hungarian resistance to outsiders. Even after eight months, Annie, who had tried to be friendly from day one, did not know the woman's name because the super refused to talk to her.

"Hello," Will said.

The bony woman averted her eyes and pulled on her broom.

Annie smiled at the bad comedy of it and said hello, and as usual, the super turned away—sentry to her broom and rum and angry-looking teenage son who lived with her on the first floor. Annie smelled liquor now, an odor like wet pennies in the stale air.

Will headed for the elevator and hit the call button.

Twice a day, sometimes more, the super swept the foyer's entrance. Once in the morning; once at night, occasionally midday like today. Those first few weeks, Annie had tried to make a connection, but the woman with cropped dyed-red hair would not allow it. With each hello, the super shook her head to indicate she didn't understand a word Annie was saying. After that, she turned her back when Annie appeared. Annie, out of some perversely American impulse to be liked, insisted on saying a perfunctory hello. Every time. It felt like a game at first, but now it had become a source of irritation.

The elevator was taking a long time. They waited for the doors to open.

Despite the super's twice-daily sweeps, the entranceway remained grim—dull cement floors weathered by grit, no windows, and those smelly garbage barrels stacked in a little storage room to the right of the entrance that emitted the foul odor of rotting food.

Their modern apartment building—modern for Budapest—was seven stories high, three units to a floor. The building itself, tall and narrow, was tiny compared to those behemoth concrete complexes the Russians built just outside the city center, ugly blocks of gray with tiny windows and flat facades, nothing at all warm or welcoming. By comparison, she had come to think of her building as a pretty good find. A small garden next to it gave them something green to look at from their bedroom window on the top floor.

Finally, the elevator doors opened and they went in.

"I bet she could use the money," Will said, meaning the super. "Her son, too."

"Are you thinking they took it while we were out? I don't think so. That's paranoid."

"*Shhh*. Lower your voice, Annie. She has a key to our place."

"The wallet could be in your underwear drawer."

"My theory is that she's a leftover brick."

"A communist informant? I don't believe it," she said.

"She hates Americans. That's clear."

"Fine. But she's been harmless all year. Why now? It's too risky."

"Why not?"

The elevator made its slow, steady way to the seventh level and shuddered to a stop.

"If it's not here, then it was those two men outside Luigi's. The money's gone. I'm sure of it. We won't find it here."

Annie had a feeling Will was right.

The elevator doors slid open and they walked out into the small hallway outside their door, Leo heavy in sleep in the jogger, his ragged carnations resting in his lap.

"She could use the money, but I doubt it's her," Annie said.

Sometimes she thought of leaving money in an envelope and slipping it under the super's apartment door—an anonymous gift. But the woman looked nervous, even paranoid. Annie was convinced she was an alcoholic. That would explain her behavior—using Coke cans to hide daily rations of cheap rum. Once, Annie thought her face looked bruised. Her teenage son appeared as miserable as his mother. The son, with his short orange-dyed hair, wore straight-leg jeans and black thick-soled shoes. It was a kind of punk/car mechanic/rebel-skinhead look. A possible skinhead. Right here under her nose. The son also avoided looking at her whenever Annie ran into him in the hall. She had wanted to help their sorry, miserable lives, but after so many rebuffs and what she had seen that skinhead do to that little Gypsy girl, she couldn't summon up any feelings of sympathy for his empty, twisted, repressed life right now.

Annie wheeled Leo inside their flat. "I'll look in the front rooms," she said. A shaft of bright sunshine greeted them. She thought of Mr. Weiss, again wishing she had his phone number, wishing the wallet were miraculously lying on the old man's floor.

Will hurried down their long, sunlit hallway, which linked Leo's room and the kitchen to a living room and their bedroom at the opposite end. She could hear Will shuffling papers, opening drawers.

She loved the apartment—practically stole it for a few hundred dollars a month, including utilities. The herringbone floors, shiny as glass, the corner unit with so much light, and windows in Leo's room that looked out to distant but spectacular views of Castle Hill, an old section of Buda. At night the castle glowed like a Disney World postcard. Spotlights lit up the castle's stone walls casting long, elegant shadows under the stars.

Annie searched the bathroom off the hall, checking pockets in their pile of dirty laundry. In the living room, nothing on the couch or the desk with the fax machine. She felt her throat closing up, the apartment stifling and thick with heat.

"Not here," Will said, coming down the hall again. "It's lost. They stole it. God damn it. I'm reporting it to the police."

"How will you do that?"

"We'll walk over now."

"Do you want to call Stephen?"

"No. I can manage it. If I need him, I'll call."

"I guess he was right."

"Right or not, the wallet's gone."

Once more, they stepped back into the hall, baby asleep in the stroller. Two other tenants lived on their floor: an elderly woman, frail and stooped, who Annie had seen twice in eight months, and a middle-age man who lived by himself with his beer. She saw him more often, several times a week in the hall lining up empty beer cans on his door mat next to his shoes. The super collected the cans once a week.

Today Annie counted fourteen beer cans.

They went back down in the elevator and passed the super again, standing at the door finishing a smoke.

"God, she's miserable," Annie said once they stepped outside.

"So am I right now."

"I know. I'm sorry."

Will pulled out his street map. "We need to cross the river and then it's just a few blocks from there."

She felt bad for him, but the super's misery had gotten under her skin.

"Seriously. Can you imagine living her life?"

"That's a rhetorical question."

"Not really."

"Worry about your life. Worry about mine right now."

"I do. I'm sorry."

Outside, seeing the road and the cars heading toward the city center, she thought of the many thousands of people living their lives, hauling hidden stories. Hundreds of thousands. Millions. The entire planet was full of people hauling secrets, struggling to come to terms with them, like her brother. Like her sister.

"Where to now?" she asked.

Will pointed toward the river.

"I think the super got divorced when her son was a toddler. Maybe her ex beat her and knocked out her side tooth. She has terrible teeth. I'd be an alcoholic if I lived her life."

"If all those things are true, what can you do about it?"

"I don't know," Annie said. "That's what bothers me."

"She has her life. It's not a happy one, but it's hers. Start with your own life, hon. Promise me you'll meet some of those American women. Give it a chance."

Will took her hand and squeezed it. "I'll get over this. Anyone would be upset."

"I know."

What she didn't say is that the super reminded her, daily, of what her family didn't discuss. Her alcoholic brother's death five years ago in central Florida. Thirty-one. Unmarried. She was twenty-eight at the time. Newly married. The last time she saw him, Greg had been at her wedding, but even then her mother left the reception early to take him back to the hotel, embarrassed by his drunken behavior. Greg was stumbling on the dance floor, had knocked over a chair. It made Annie sad. It was summer. At the time, her mother had felt hopeful. Greg had landed a six-month contract to work at the university. Some new science facility. Maybe Greg would settle down there, her mother said before the wedding. Then the wedding revealed that nothing would stop his drinking. Annie stopped hoping for her brother. So she retreated from him. She stopped trying. During high school and college years, he disappeared for months at a time, then reappeared working construction somewhere on the East Coast. One wild throw of a baseball and their lives split off forever—her brother, her sister, her family—damaged for life. And, for Annie, she too buried a part of herself that fateful day.

She stroked Leo's sweaty head.

THE POLICE STATION, or *rendőrség*, was located in a 1920s deco-style white-stucco building. Its preserved exterior hid a dark, rundown interior—beauty and ugliness coexisting, each one vying for dominance. It was a familiar aspect of the city and it unsettled her again. She sat down in one of the plastic chairs in the main room, Leo by her side, asleep for now and hopefully for at least another hour. Will went to the service window and explained the situation in Hungarian, speaking well enough to get by.

The woman behind the window pointed to another door.

"We need to fill out a report," Will said.

Annie followed him into a small room where a large-bellied policeman sat at a metal desk.

"Sit down, please," he said. "I speak little English."

Will explained what happened, talking slowly in Hungarian, looking up words in his pocket dictionary. The policeman hunched over his desk, his shoulders lopsided and bulky.

"I write paper but"—the officer shook his head and shrugged—"we find American wallets in Duna, on street. Every week. Empty. Gypsies. No good." The pen looked tiny between his thick fingers. He grimaced then dropped his pen on the table.

"You're saying this is a scam?"

Will flinched, then squared his shoulders.

"I don't know this word, *scam*."

"Criminals?"

"*Igen*. Yes. They are Gypsy."

Will pointed to the papers. "I don't think they were Gypsies. They looked different. I'll fill out those forms."

The policeman leaned toward them. "Gypsies. This is the way."

Annie thought of the flower woman and her two girls and those disgusting skinheads. She didn't believe it was the Gypsies. Will would know. Tomorrow she would go back to the flower stand and follow the mother home, see for herself. She watched Will write his name and address, the make of his car, and his passport information. Did Will look that obvious in the crowd? That *American*?

Of course he did—*they* did. Her husband's dense curls, his tall, muscular posture—no, that wouldn't have singled him out, though the men in Budapest tended to be shorter, smaller-boned. With Annie in her American running shorts, their *American* jogger that no one in Budapest had seen before, the three of them together were a walking pronouncement of their absolute Americanness.

"Impossible," he said, looking at Will. "Nothing we can do."

"What do you mean, *impossible*? How many like me?" Will asked.

Annie knew that Will was annoyed by that favorite Hungarian expression: *impossible*. It was the antithesis to their American way of thinking.

"Will. Forget it. He's saying there's nothing he can do about it."
She was sickened, too. This theft sucked the air from that shrinking
balloon of optimism that floated around her when she first arrived
in Budapest.

The officer nodded at Leo and smiled.

"How old?"

"Almost one year."

"I'm sorry. Wallet. Every week somebody."

She looked at her child, who mixed Hungarian sounds with
English words because he spent every day with Klara, their Hungarian babysitter, and Klara's boyfriend, Sandor. Another convenience:
babysitters cost nothing compared to what she would have to pay
in the States.

"Do you know who these Gypsies are? Where they live?" Annie
asked the officer.

Will repeated what she asked in Hungarian.

The policemen shrugged. "Pest. They do this after Russians
leave."

The policeman left the room to make a copy of his report.

"Why don't we call Stephen, have him look at the forms?"

"I can read them, Annie."

"Just trying to be helpful."

Above them, a 1920s chandelier seemed oddly out of place—
intricately etched crystal glass and brass—hanging in this ugly utili-
tarian office. Annie considered the life of the chandelier, guessing it
had hovered in the wings of history, bearing witness to horrors. Possibly lifted from a Jewish home during the Nazi occupation. Probably stolen from one of those Gothic stone-and-wood estates lining

the big avenue that led to the hills of Buda and to Leo's pediatrician and the green region of the city where most American expats lived.

"Do you think they targeted you because you're Jewish?" she said.

"Doubtful." Will went over to the windows—two French windows that might have been beautiful except for the bent metal blinds defiling them. "I'm American. I have big American dollars. Pretty simple and obvious. There aren't many Jews left in this city. I don't think anyone's thinking about Jews here. The city's making a grand gesture of restoring the big synagogue downtown, but that's about it."

"Well, I'm not convinced."

At the end of the war, the city was emptied of Jews in a matter of months—more than a half-million Hungarian Jews rounded up, sent off to be gassed at Auschwitz and Bergen-Belsen death camps, an orgy of murder when Hitler saw the end coming.

The policeman returned and handed another form to Will.

"This is for car. If police stop, you show." The policeman shook the paper at them both. "You must have. Okay?"

Will's cell phone rang.

"Hi, Stephen. Yes. Filling out the forms right now."

She listened as Will told Stephen where they were.

"No need," Will said. "Thank you. Sure."

He hung up.

"What did he say?"

"He offered to stop by. I told him not to."

"That was nice of him to offer, don't you think?"

She felt relieved to know that someone American, someone able to cross the language barrier, was so available to help them. Will managed, but he wasn't fluent. On the form, she read Will's birth date, their address back in the States, their address here in Budapest, and Will's bank number.

"What are they asking for?" She pointed to a long paragraph that Will had written in Hungarian.

"An account of what happened."

"You keep in car," the policeman said, handing Will several copies. "One copy for you. Understand?"

"*Igen.*" Will gave the policeman his business card. "Call if you find the wallet. It's got a pen mark on the front. The baby wrote on it."

They all looked at Leo, asleep in his stroller, impervious to it all. The prospect of finding a waterlogged wallet with an ink scribble mark on it was ridiculous. The officer nodded, but it was clear he didn't think he would ever make that call.

"I'm glad I reported it," Will said. "Even if they never find it. Maybe it will motivate them to do more."

They stepped outside, Annie manipulating the jogger over the threshold, Leo's limbs shaking gently from the movement.

"Stephen!" Will said. "You didn't need to come."

"I know." He shrugged apologetically. "You're not mad I did, are you?" Stephen smiled at Annie.

"Of course not," Annie said, glad to see him again. "How are you?"

"I was a block away when I called. Did you get those papers?"

"All set," Will said.

"That's good. You'll be fine with those papers."

"I still can't believe he was robbed," Annie said.

"It happens to the best. Don't take it personally," Stephen said.

He leaned over and took hold of the front wheel of the jogger, helping her lift it over the stairs onto the sidewalk.

"I'll try not to. Thanks."

She wanted to feel optimistic and not discouraged. She reminded herself that these mixed, uncertain sensations were common to expats and that getting robbed would upset anyone, expat or not.

Stephen tapped the wheel of the bike with his sandal. "Nothing bothers this guy, does it?"

"Not usually."

"Thanks for your concern," Will said.

"Have a good rest of your day." Stephen took a step back, his moss-colored eyes drawing her in. "See you soon."

"Thanks, Stephen," she said.

They watched him walk away. Annie didn't want to go home to their suffocating apartment and it was too warm to stay out. The heat's constant presence was a wall hemming her in. She couldn't climb over or get around it, like the thought that they had actually been robbed. It stirred up waves of homesickness. Yet, she still held on to the stubborn hope that Mr. Weiss would call and tell them he had found it.

"That was nice of him," she finally said. "Why were you unfriendly?"

She waited for Will to say something, but he was lost in himself, his shoulders rounding inward, his mouth stiff with annoyance, silent and grim. He looked miserable.

Finally he said, "I wasn't unfriendly. It's very simple. I didn't need his assistance in handling this. It's personal. That's all. Let's go to the hotel and cool off in the lobby. It's too hot to do anything else."

Eight

Every day, so much. You will have knee problems," Klara said to Annie.

"I hope not," Annie said. She finished tying her sneakers and stood up. "I'll be fine." Her babysitter was young, but she worried over things, which cast a permanent shadow of doubt across her face except when she was talking to Leo.

"Today we go to the park, okay, *kicsi baba*?"

Leo rested comfortably on Klara's hip, his hand reaching around her neck to hold her long brown ponytail. She was more than a babysitter to him. They loved each other and it showed.

"Perfect. I'll meet up with you in an hour or so, after my run."

Annie kissed Leo and went out to the hall elevator. Most

weekday mornings she went for a jog along the river or to Margaret Island and back, but today she planned to head across the bridge to see Mr. Weiss. She would go to the island to meet up with Klara and Leo afterward.

The elevator dropped smoothly to the foyer and opened its doors to the stink of garbage baking in the heat. Will had already left for a downtown breakfast with Dave to discuss the City of Kings connection. Outside she passed the super, who was smoking a cigarette. No surprise when the woman turned away, pretending not to see her.

Another too-hot day in August. She ran with a bottle of water in hand, her cell phone in the other, the sun slicing through her exposed skin. She was the only person running this morning. She jogged past women hurrying to work in heels and summer skirts. Most of the men wore short-sleeve polyester shirts, long pants, no ties. Later she would take Leo to an air-conditioned hotel up on Castle Hill to cool off.

The distance from her flat to Edward's seemed shorter today as she crossed the bridge, then slowed to a walk, her arms, legs, and face slick with sweat. She didn't want to show up as a dripping mess in the hall outside his door. Toweling herself with the bottom of her T-shirt, she turned onto his street and there, several blocks down, she saw Stephen Házy standing on the sidewalk next to a tree trunk, smoking a cigarette.

"Hello there!" she said, waving to him.

It surprised her to see him there, but he looked even more startled to see her and made a motion to toss his cigarette behind the tree, as if she had caught him at something, then changed his mind. He shrugged good-humoredly, exhaling a stream of smoke.

"This is a pleasant surprise," she said, stopping in front of him.
"It certainly is."

She was glad to see him. It wasn't cooler under the maple tree,
but less bright, easier to see. His clothing looked similar to what
he'd worn the day before: dark pants; white corporate shirt with
sleeves rolled up to his elbows; and sandals. "Do you live here?" She
gestured at the low brick buildings behind him.

"No. No. I'm meeting a client."

"What kismet. Thanks for coming to the station yesterday. You
didn't have to, but it was nice of you. I really appreciated it."

"I hope Will didn't mind."

"No. He's okay. Upset to think he was targeted, you know? It's
weird."

Stephen took a long, finishing drag of his cigarette, then
dropped it on the sidewalk, snuffing the smoky stub with the bottom of his sandal before putting the dead filter into his pocket.

"That's considerate," she said. "I'm impressed."

"I've tried to quit, but as you can see, I failed. I hope you'll
forgive me." He tilted his head until his bangs fell over his eyes in
a mischievous tangle. He nudged them in place with the back of
his hand.

"Worse than quitting heroin, I hear."

He laughed. "What would you know about heroin?"

"Working with homeless. In my old job."

"Is that right?"

He raised an eyebrow, absorbing this new information about
her. "I would not have guessed that about you."

"What would you have guessed?" She reached up to a lower
branch and pulled on a maple leaf, curious to hear how he would
answer.

"Lawyer, maybe?"

"Nope. Why'd you think that about me?"

"You seem like someone who follows rules."

"I follow good rules. Is that so bad?"

"I didn't mean it to be. So, is this your running route?"

"No. I run different places. Margaret Island. Little side streets like this one for a change of pace or for the shade." She looked up at the treetops. She felt funny lying about Mr. Weiss, but that was one rule she wouldn't break. A promise was a promise.

"You won't see Hungarians running in this heat. You Americans are nuts."

He sized her up in a way that didn't feel offensive to her. His half-closed eyes and the humidity gave him a glazed, distant look. Everyone was suffering in this heat.

"And you're not American?" She was joking of course. She took another swig of water, letting the water spill over her chin.

He laughed, showing white symmetrical teeth. "I'm as American as they come. I'm as Hungarian as they come, too. There's no denying both sides of me."

"My old neighbors are Hungarian—Hungarian American. They came to the States after the war."

"Yep. We're everywhere. You can take the Hungarian out of the country, but you can't take the country out of . . . You know what I mean."

"Sure." She tasted salty drops sliding into the corner of her mouth. "You know, you were right. The policeman said that the wallet stealing was a racket. How did you know? Did you hear about it?"

Stephen bent over to pick up a twig, then twirled it in his hand, considering. "I read about it in the paper. Listen. Money is replaceable. You have identification papers. That's the important thing around here. Whatever you do, don't lose those." He flicked the twig into the air. They both watched it arc then land in the street.

"You're well informed."

"I know the drill. My uncle and a few cousins still live south of here. Near the Yugoslavian—now Croatian—border."

"Things are bad there, aren't they?" She'd been reading about the increasing number of refugees crossing the border into Hungary.

"It's a sad situation." He made a gesture toward his shirt pocket to light another cigarette, then changed his mind. Instead, he sighed a long, heart-heavy sigh. "I need to go down there. Have you traveled the country outside of Budapest?"

"Not much. Not yet, anyway. We will, I'm sure."

"I'll take you and Will sometime. Show you the country the way the natives see it."

"That would be great. I'll tell Will."

She reached up and tugged on a leaf stem again until it broke off. Even in the heat, the soft, green membrane felt cool between her palms.

She handed him her leaf. "Feel this. Ever wonder how leaves withstand the sun beating down on them all day?"

He said something, twirling the leaf and letting it fall, but his words got lost in the noise of a truck rumbling past them, its brakes screeching, before entering the main boulevard. They both laughed simultaneously at the raucous sound.

"Don't get stuck behind one of those on the highway," he said. "Take it from me. It will drive you insane."

"What made you decide to move here?" Annie asked.

"I didn't decide." He narrowed his eyes and shook his head. "The truth? I came for my dad. My parents fled after the '56 uprising, but it was hard on them. Very hard. Dad took his life when I was six." He closed his eyes, summoning something inside, and said, "I came back here for him."

"I'm sorry."

He opened his eyes, his whole face inviting her to be with him in his sadness. "Thanks. I don't know why I'm telling you this. We've just met. You're easy to talk to, but it's not a great way to endear myself to you."

"It's okay. I understand. I lost my brother that way."

She felt his hand on her arm. "Sorry, Annie."

She let out a short breath thinking how differently Stephen and Mr. Weiss had responded to the same two words: *I'm sorry.* Stephen soaked them in. Edward repelled them. For a moment, she allowed herself to share an exchange of silence under the tree. She scuffed a pebble with her sneaker, the street quiet except for dull sounds of traffic and horns rising from the boulevard.

"I have a theory," Stephen said. "People like us, we have a kinship. I sensed something in you at Luigi's. The moment I met you."

She shifted her stance and took another swig of water. She wanted to say that she felt comfortable, too, when she met him but instead said simply, "Thanks. That's sweet," and let the moment settle between them before directing the conversation to what was really on her mind. "I have a question. What do you know about the Gypsy population here? They can't all be thieves."

"They're not. But you need to be careful. They live by a different set of rules."

"What about the children? I'm sure they need clothing, money, books?"

"They're cut from a different cloth. What are you thinking?"

"They're terribly poor. The other day I saw two little Gypsy girls without shoes. They couldn't have been older than six or eight or ten. Maybe I could donate money for clothing."

"I'll look into it and get back to you."

"You have our number."

"I sure do."

Stephen straightened his stance and waved at someone behind her.

"Excuse me, Annie. There's my client. I'm afraid I've got to get going. Thanks for listening to my sidewalk confessional. I think I did most of the talking."

She turned and saw a tall, dark-haired man walking toward them. The man stopped about a block away.

She shook her head. "Not at all. It was mutual."

"Good." Stephen tipped an invisible hat, offering a half smile, his eyes sweeping over her in a gentle, beckoning way.

"See you soon," she said.

"I hope so."

He hurried down the block to join his client.

She stayed under the tree, bending over to tie her sneakers, which didn't need tying, but she didn't want him to look back and see her heading toward Mr. Weiss's building. Did it make her a liar to be deceptive in this way? She had promised Mr. Weiss. So she waited and watched as Stephen and his client kept walking toward the main boulevard in the direction of Luigi's. Another block and they veered toward the center of town, crossing a wide intersection over trolley tracks, then disappearing down a side street. Only then did she proceed down the remaining three blocks to Mr. Weiss's building.

This time she didn't hesitate to enter the foyer and start up the center stairway. She had little hope that Mr. Weiss had found

Will's wallet on the floor, but it would be the reason she would give him, the excuse, she decided, for showing up once again unannounced. And it wasn't a fabrication. The wallet could have fallen out of Will's pocket when he was lifting the jogger up the stairs. Or maybe someone found it and turned it in to the building super. Every building had a super in Budapest.

She stood in front of Mr. Weiss's door and knocked twice. The peephole in the door lightened.

"It's me."

She lifted her now-empty water bottle to say hello and listened to the metal chain sliding off the track, the double locks unbolting.

"You again? What is it? Where's your boy?"

"Home. I'm sorry. I would have called, but I didn't have your number. I won't stay. Will lost his wallet Saturday. Did you happen to find it? I was hoping it might be here."

He grunted. "No. But come in and look. See for yourself. You don't think I would have called you?"

He had on a different set of pajamas—she was glad to see that. But he didn't look well, though she saw he had made an effort to comb his hair, and he smelled of fresh paint, not burned toast.

"Thank you." She stepped inside. Will was right in presuming Mr. Weiss would have called. What did she really know?

"What kind of businessman loses his wallet?" he asked her.

She felt provoked but ignored the comment and glanced at the floor. Everything looked the same—the long electric cord leading from the fan to the wall socket, the standing fan buzzing and turning, some magazines and those paintings in a stack on the floor by the easel. She saw that he'd opened the curtains wider for more light.

"We think someone stole it, unfortunately." She stood near the door, ready to leave. "May I have your phone number? That way I won't worry about disturbing you. I see you're painting." She turned toward the easel.

"Never mind that. You're here. Why are you running in this heat? That's not smart, is it? Drink some water. Fill up your bottle. Go on. Help yourself. Then I'll give you my phone number."

She went into the kitchen.

"Let it run a minute," he said.

She stood at the white ceramic sink and waited for the stream of lukewarm water to cool. The man's paternal manner surprised her. She couldn't remember the last time her own father expressed such a simple concern for her well-being.

"Thanks."

She walked back into the living room and stood, not sure whether to sit down or to leave. She remained standing. He sat on the couch.

"What did the police say to you?"

"Thieves go after tourists, Americans. We went to a restaurant after we left you. Well, first we bought some flowers. Will said two men bumped into him on the sidewalk. I didn't see it happen. I guess they set him up."

"They spotted an easy target. I can see that."

"What do you mean by that?" She felt offended. *Easy target*— those words again.

"Come on. You're a neon sign. Americans with money. What are you doing here? You've got a life. A baby."

"The baby's happy here."

She sipped her water, insulted now by his goading. Why couldn't he simply say, "I'm sorry that happened," and let it be?

"Look, you're floating, that's what I think. You're here with your kid and your husband, but what about you? What are you doing here? You don't want to be one of those women following her husband around. What did you do before you came here?"

She couldn't believe he was saying these things to her. How could he possibly know what she needed or who she was?

"I worked with homeless men in Boston. At a shelter. Maybe Rose already told you."

"Ah. Perfect." He grinned a little too gleefully. "You're a social worker, is that it? A helper type. You know what I say to that? What for? Who are you helping? My daughter was that way. I could never understand it. Maybe you can give me an idea."

"What did you daughter do?"

"She helped vampires. They sucked on her until she got sick and then she kept helping them anyway." He gritted his teeth.

"What is she doing now?"

He shook his head, his face twisting. "Dead. Gone."

"I'm sorry."

He swatted the air.

She glanced at the framed torn photo of a woman in a wheelchair and assumed it was his daughter.

"Enough with the apologies. Look, you're too young to waste your time here. You have a family. Your son. Go home and make a life for yourself. You're wasting your time here."

He spoke as if he heard her private, nagging thoughts, and it made her want to cry. She felt her eyes watering.

"I have to get back. Could I have your number?"

She tried to steady herself by focusing on his neck, wrinkled, with stray gray chest hairs poking out of his V-neck shirt.

Edward squirmed on the couch. "Don't cry. I've upset you now.

Don't get mad at me. I'm an old, decrepit man, but I've lived longer than you, remember? You'll be old one day. I don't have time for BS, I told you that. I'll tell you what I see. Social workers, people like you, they make it their business to help other people, but let me tell you, if you dig a little, you'll find you're trying to help yourself. It's about you, not them."

She didn't know whether to pursue this talk any further. Yet something inside her nudged her to be direct and uncensored with him. It felt like the only way.

"I find comfort in helping people in need. They open up in ways others don't. Not always, but often. Like you, they cross lines. They talk about how they feel." She looked at the windows facing a view of another brick building across the street, and at his painting—dark, simple shapes of hills and a sky. "There is something honest or real about people who have suffered. I'm drawn to that."

"The question is why," he said, his eyes searching her face. "My daughter took in strays. Couldn't resist them. Drove me nuts." He covered his mouth with his palm. She remembered noticing his hands yesterday, his nimble fingers.

Again, she turned to go. He was all over the place. Nice. Mean. Direct. Secretive. Provocative. What was his game? What would he throw at her next? It angered her, too. "My sister," she finally said. That's why. My sister is brain-damaged from an accident. I grew up with that."

She watched him take in this information, surprising herself with her own directness about a topic she usually avoided. She didn't tell people, let alone strangers, that her sister had brain damage. Her brother had asked her long ago not to talk about it, and now he was gone. He couldn't forgive himself for that day his base-ball changed the whole family. From that early age of four years old, she learned to be careful and quiet, and to help, do what she could to prevent accidents from occurring, but in the process, she dug a hole for herself, buried some living part of herself there.

She didn't say those things now. Instead, she felt the weight of the memory pressing on her neck, choking her. She put her hand on her throat and said, "Why are you here?"

"I'm here to find someone."

"Why the secret?"

This startled him. He leaned forward, breathing, as if deciding on something.

"I'll get to that. But, first, you offered to help me and I think I know how you can. You said you lived by the river. Where exactly? Do you have a car?"

She nodded. "We live on the Buda side, a few blocks from the river, about a mile from here. Not far from the center."

"I would like to take a ride along the river to look at the build-ings. The apartment buildings."

'It's a long river," she said. "What part?"

"Not far from you—but on the Pest side. Can you go tomor-row? Early. I tire easily. I'm getting tired now."

She thought it through while the fan head swiveled toward the windows, stopped midarc, then shifted toward her again. "Yes. I have to make sure Will doesn't need the car. I'll call you."

SHE LEFT WITH his phone number in her pocket, a scrap of paper torn from a grocery ad, feeling energized as if she had sealed a pact, earned something from him—something like trust, a sense that she had a mission to accomplish even if she had no idea what that mission would be or where it would take her or what it meant. She moved quickly, jogging back over to Margaret Island where she knew she would find Klara and Leo at the sprinkler in the park. The city felt different today than it had on the weekend. The workday was under way, which meant fewer crowds on the sidewalks and more cars jamming up the streets—the ubiquitous small Ladas from Russia, noisy cars with their smelly blue exhaust smoke. Buses and trolleys pushed through, following well-established routes. At times she could almost pretend that she belonged here, was living a normal life, and maybe that is what Mr. Weiss gave her today—a sense of purpose.

As soon as she walked through the park gates, the air felt different, the sounds from the streets hushed by trees and expansive lawns. Margaret Island was a two-hundred-acre refuge of green in the heart of the city. A parkland with meadows, formal flower gardens, a spa, a small zoo, playing fields with swings, hidden paths in the woods for lovers, grassy knolls for Frisbee throwers. There were ancient ruins, too.

She spotted Leo swinging high, Klara and Sandor standing guard near the swing. She waved at her son, who shrieked when he saw her coming.

"Hello, pumpkin!"

Leo pointed to the sky. "Wing!"

"He is happy today," Klara said. "Every day he is happy." Klara held a daisy in her hand, then said, "We have our anniversary today. Me and Sandor. Four years we are together."

Klara wore a yellow ankle-length skirt and white cotton blouse. Sandor wore a formal white shirt and brown pants, his lean height accented by a fedora. How sweet that they had dressed up for the occasion.

"Congratulations. That's a long time. How did you meet?"

"In school," Klara said, looking at Sandor.

"Take the rest of the afternoon for yourselves," Annie said. "Go enjoy."

"No. That is okay," Klara said.

"Go on. I'll pay you the same. Don't worry about that."

The couple looked at each other and, in the serious manner of Hungarians, nodded but didn't smile. Klara gave Leo a kiss and Annie took her place behind the swing. She watched the couple walk away, arms down at their sides, withholding any public display of their affection.

Nine

Her chest felt heavy with pent-up energy as Annie put the Saab's stick shift in gear. Maybe this was a mistake to go to Edward's. She would tell Will tonight. Why was she doing this? She settled her feet on the clutch and gas pedals and pulled out of their parking spot in front of their building. The drivers here won the prize for worst ever, worse than Boston drivers. Here, they cut in front of you without apology. They honked ceaselessly. They drove too close to get an edge on the traffic. And the exhaust had a peculiar spoiled-egg smell from cheap petrol. Awful. Yet she felt compelled to go, to follow her gut urging her on, though she didn't understand why or what. Nothing was adding up. Nothing.

She crossed Margaret Bridge and managed to get through tangles of traffic before turning onto Edward's quiet street. There he was, waiting outside by the mailboxes. She parked, and before she could get out of the car to help him, he was shuffling down the short walk. Once again, she worried about the heat of the day and its obvious effect on him—his slow, listing walk. Thankfully, their Saab was air-conditioned, though the sun scorching the windshield caused the car to fill with sticky moisture.

She pushed the electric control button and waited until the passenger window was halfway down before calling out to him. "Are you all right?" What a sight he was in those pajamas—another set of them. He wore sneakers and every few steps stopped to catch his breath. He clutched a rolled-up paper in his hand.

"I'm not dead yet," he said, his voice both strident and friendly. He stopped midway on the walk, looked up, and smiled at her, his face changing to something open and inviting as if they had known each other for years, a lost uncle found.

"Take your time."

She forced herself to watch him take the last halting steps to the car, open the door, and slowly lean in before landing safely in the leather bucket seat. His balance was off. The bad knee, or whatever it was, caused him to lean to one side. He yanked on the door handle and lifted himself to get his legs in right.

"If you can believe it, I used to be pretty athletic." He grunted and settled in. The effort caused him to break into a sweat.

She closed the window, then reached around and pulled the seat belt so he could snap it in.

"Thank you, miss," he said.

He was dripping with sweat.

"Before we go, let me show you," he said. He unrolled a map and pointed to the road along the Duna.

"I believe a good many residential buildings are on this end," he said, pointing to the fifth district. "Drive along the causeway and then you can turn around and take me back."

"That's it?"

"That's it."

"All right."

She put the car in gear and inhaled the odor of his cinnamon-scented aftershave and his coffee breath.

"I appreciate this," Edward said, nodding. "I won't take up more than an hour of your time. Assuming your son is with the babysitter? She comes every day?"

"Yes. He's fine. They have a great time together." She wanted to close the door on any suggestion of doubt around that. What was his issue with Hungarians, anyway?

"What do you do, then? You have a lot of time on your hands."

"I do," she said, nodding, clenching the wheel. She needed to concentrate on driving. She was entering the boulevard again and the crowded intersection, loud with trucks and Ladas, and stinking with the smell of petrol and exhaust, overwhelmed her senses. She shifted gears.

"There's a lot of traffic this morning."

Finally, she got in line and turned onto the road that ran alongside the river, moving slowly, wedged between cars ahead of her and behind, until the swarm of traffic came to a complete stop.

"There's an accident ahead. See it?"

"Take the next exit," he said, pointing to a street a few blocks ahead. "Mission aborted."

He swiped his face, then dried his hands on his pajama pants.

"Bad timing," he said, more to himself than to her.

"You sure?" She looked at him.

"Sure."

The traffic began to move again, advancing slowly up the block, so she said, "Can you tell me who you are looking for? You said no bullshit, remember?"

"Fair enough. I'm looking for someone who lives in a building on the river. I don't have his address, only a PO box number."

"I'm confused."

She signaled to turn and finally got out of the jam.

"My daughter Nan told me the return address is in Budapest."

"Your daughter?"

"Nan, my youngest, lives in Massachusetts. Deborah's dead. I told you."

"Yes." She stopped herself from saying sorry again. She didn't want to agitate him. She nodded sympathetically but said nothing. She was even more confused with the mention of Nan and the PO box number.

"A parent's worst nightmare. Thank your stars you don't know." He flinched in his seat, and grabbed the inside handle on the car door. "This was a terrible idea," he said.

"I kind of do know," she said.

"What's that mean?"

"I lost my brother. It's different, but not really."

He didn't say anything, which surprised her. His silence felt louder than his sharp retorts.

"When was that?"

"Five years ago. Suicide."

"My condolences."

"Much good that does, right?" she said, feeling both angry and sad. She could feel him looking at her. Maybe now he wouldn't give her such a hard time. She felt almost smug as she turned onto his street.

"Here we are." She parked in the same spot in front of the brick building and shut off the motor, relieved they'd made it safely back, her shoulders and arms tense from the drive.

He sighed and fumbled for the door handle.

"I'm walking up with you." She would not take no for an answer and braced herself for a rude response. She didn't care. She would ignore it.

"Okay, Miss Annie. Thank you."

She almost laughed.

"Good. I never know what you're going to say."

She got out and walked around to open the car door for him. He let her take his arm and together they pulled him out of the car. All of it took enormous effort.

He shook his head. "My body doesn't do what I want it to. You can't imagine the frustration. Aging is a crock of shit, I can tell you that. You lose things. People die on you. What's the point?"

She nodded, deciding again not to engage or pursue this philosophical argument. She wouldn't win and it wasn't about winning. If only she understood what this was really about. "Take your time. That's all I ask," she finally said.

Inside, they took the elevator up two floors. It opened up around the corner from his apartment door.

"You did a good thing for an old man today," he said, pushing the key into the lock. "Come in and get yourself a glass of water before you leave."

She followed him back inside as if they were old friends. It was much darker, the brown curtains drawn shut, the only light coming from a small window in the kitchen area. The fan was on, rattling and turning.

"That fan works hard at nothing," he said. "I need to take these damn shoes off. They're too tight." He moved toward the kitchen. "I'm thirsty. You thirsty?"

"Yes. I'll help myself." She started to follow but stopped when she heard a cell phone ringing, the bell extra loud for his bad hearing.

"That's your phone," she said. She saw it on the sofa. "You want me to answer it?" He was in the kitchen downing a full glass of water, so she picked it up and in the process saw the framed picture of the woman in the wheelchair lying faceup on the sofa. His daughter had a big smile on her face, open brown eyes. The picture was missing its other half, but she could see a set of man's hands on the daughter's shoulders. She pushed the answer button and handed him the phone.

"Hello? Hello? That you, Nan?"

He held the phone awkwardly to his ear.

"Let me call you back in just a minute, okay? I need to sit down. I'll call you right back."

He clanked the phone on the countertop and it fell to the floor. "Christ." He leaned over to get it, but she rushed in and picked it up and put it on the counter.

Enough was enough.

"Mr. Weiss, my son and I go to the hotels and sit in the air-conditioned lobbies to cool off," she said. "Would you like to come with us today? You can't stay in this oven. It's dangerous."

"Look, I appreciate your concern. I'll tell you what. You call me later this afternoon. Call me in a few hours. Can you do that? I'll be fine. I'll take a cold shower and then I'll sleep. I need to do that now."

He became overly polite again and pointed to the door. This aroused her anger. But other than lasso and drag him with her, she could see he was determined to stay.

SHE LEFT IN a private huff, mad at herself more than anything. Will was right. She had allowed herself to get caught up in someone else's business, and for what? Edward was impossible to pin down. She wanted to help because Rose asked her to. Like Will said, they had done their job. The old man had their phone numbers. They had his. He knew to call if he needed something. Here she was doing what she herself despised: insinuating herself into his life. Didn't she hate it when people did that to her? She was done with this silliness. She needed to focus on herself.

She got back into the hot car and rolled the windows down for a breeze while she drove to dispel the feeling of being trapped. She wanted to get back before Will showed up or needed the car. She didn't want him to know she'd wasted a morning with this aborted errand. Will might think someone stole the Saab if he noticed it was gone. Car thefts were a huge concern in Budapest. This was one scam they did know about. They'd read about it in the travel books before they came over. "They weren't that innocent"—she said aloud in the car—responding to Mr. Weiss's provocative remark he'd made earlier. In fact, they'd purchased a special antitheft lock for the steering wheel for that very reason and with good results. No one had stolen it in these past eight months. The wallet scam was a quirk. A fluke. Or too new to make it into the travel books. They hadn't read or heard anything about it.

In the parking space outside her apartment, she locked the steering wheel in place and made up her mind to meet those American women. Enough of this self-imposed isolation. Enough.

Ten

Wearing a long summer skirt and sandals, she walked into the small restaurant downtown and heard their loud American voices before she saw them waving at her from a round table in a corner. After eight months, the banter and quick smiles hit a hungry spot in her chest. She hurried over, feeling starved for American conversation.

"Terrific! You found us! This is Annie," Betsy said, then pointed to an empty chair beside her. "Sit down. We're glad you made it."

"Thanks. Hi, everyone."

It was Betsy's ad in the *Budapest Reporter* that Annie had clipped out months ago. *For newcomers and old*, the ad said. *Sharing expat stories, laughs and a few drinks. Call Betsy.*

Valerie and Lisa said hello from across the table, and next to her, on the other side, was Jane—all of their names, so easy on her ears.

"Homesick yet?" Betsy asked. "It helps to know a few people. Believe me. It will save you time." Betsy was pretty in a petite, perky kind of way, her brown hair boyishly short. On the phone she told Annie she'd moved to Hungary from Washington, DC, several years ago. She was a diplomat's wife. "We've all been where you are. I'm glad you finally decided to give us a try."

"I'm sorry it took me so long. Where's home for all of you? I mean, before here?"

"Home? Who has a home? That's a loaded question, my dear." Valerie shook with silent laughter as she reached for her Bloody Mary and drained it, her high forehead and long dark hair smoothed back with a yellow headband.

"You don't have a Boston accent," Betsy said. "Didn't you say you were from Boston?" Betsy worked in marketing before she had three kids and moved overseas. She wore a white sleeveless dress splashed with carnations.

"I grew up in Maine. I moved to Boston for graduate school."

"Your husband, too?"

"No. He's from Florida. We met in graduate school, in Massachusetts."

Valerie lifted her arm to flag the waiter.

"Maine has a beautiful coastline," Betsy said. "Bet you miss that."

"Sometimes I miss everything American."

This spawned an outburst of hilarity around the table, except for Jane who was noticeably quiet.

Across the table, Lisa, her face freckled from the sun, reached for the salt and sprinkled it into her Bloody Mary. "I grew up in

Maryland. Lived in England, then Pennsylvania, England again, now this." She shrugged. Her blonde, shoulder-length hair was almost metallic-looking.

"Annie, what do you drink?" Valerie asked her.

"I'll have a beer. Hungarian. Any type is fine." Annie unfolded a cloth napkin, draped it over her lap, and settled in.

"You drink that?" Valerie asked, surprised.

"Sure. I like it."

"I can't drink that stuff anymore," Lisa said, agreeing with Valerie.

"To each her own," Valerie said. "I'm so done with Hungarian drinks. We'll have another round of Marys. How about you, Jane?"

Jane shook her head and cupped her water glass. "I'm fine, thanks."

Both Lisa and Valerie looked crisp and coiffed in similar-print cotton dresses and gold necklaces. Annie was surprised by how quickly she disliked them. She guessed the two best friends shopped together, did everything together.

"Michael Jackson is in town," Lisa said, shifting the topic. "He's at the Kempinski. Did you hear?"

"Right. He married Elvis Presley's daughter? Now that's got to be fake," Valerie said.

Betsy said, "I heard the security over there is impossible."

"I agree. That marriage is a sham," Lisa said. "I don't believe it for a second."

Annie shook her head. "I think it's real. Why not? He's misunderstood, a musical genius. I don't see how anyone can know him."

"Just like this place," Valerie said. "Misunderstood. You'll see. You're still new at this. Trust me."

"I don't feel new." Annie tried to smile. She wanted to be pleasant, but her sense of annoyance was growing as she sat in the pseudo American Grille, so she turned to Jane, who she guessed was in her fifties.

"How long have you been here, Jane?"

"Three years, but we're leaving next month for Turkey."

"Lucky Jane," Valerie said.

"I hear Turkey is beautiful," Betsy said.

Everyone nodded to that.

"Are you looking forward to moving?" Annie asked.

The others howled.

"If it were me, I'd be beside myself," Valerie said. "You are so lucky, Jane. I cannot wait to get out of this place!"

"Valerie, your day will come," Betsy said. "We're leaving at the end of the year and now that I know that, I'm feeling a little sad. No. I am." Betsy creased her napkin. "Okay. Not that sad. Is everyone ready to order?"

Jane smiled at Annie.

"Welcome to the expat community."

"Thanks."

"I haven't seen you at any of the gatherings."

"I haven't attended any until now."

"Wanting to get the real experience?"

"Yes! Exactly that." Annie couldn't believe that Jane understood this. She turned to face her, relieved to be sitting next to her. "How's it been for you?"

"I'll get to that. But, first, good for you for trying. What do you think so far?"

"Harder than I expected. Hungarians seem depressed, have you noticed? But you've been here three years. That's a long time. Does it get easier?"

"You adjust," Jane said. "And you're right. They are depressed. It's not an easy place. Then there's trailing-spouse syndrome, or TSS, as I like to call it."

"What do you mean?"

"The wife goes along with the husband, trailing his job placements. It makes it hard to grow roots."

Bothered by this, Annie straightened the fork next to her plate. She guessed Jane suffered from TSS given the tired, resigned expression on her face and the limp way her hair framed her face.

A young waiter dressed in black pants and shirt placed a large mug of beer in front of her. Annie took a long drink while Lisa and Valerie continued debating Michael Jackson's marital life. She thought about TSS and decided it didn't apply to her. She and Will had come here together because they chose to. It was a joint decision.

"Who's your husband working for?" Jane asked.

"Himself," Annie said.

"Venture funding?"

"That's right."

Jane half-smiled in a wistful way and reached for her glass of water. "Good luck."

"I guess I'll need it." Annie took another long drink of beer. It was a soft, sweet beer that she much preferred to German beers. She wondered if Jane saw signs of TSS in herself?

"I think Michael Jackson's coming here is good for business," Betsy said. "It puts a spotlight on Budapest. Now everyone will want to come."

Valerie guffawed again. "They'll come, tour a few days, think it's cute, then hightail it out of here to Vienna."

"Vienna is the place for shopping," Lisa said, returning to what was obviously her favorite topic.

"I'd like to go there," Annie said, wanting to be agreeable—but determined not to become like these women who were tired and jaded, worldly yet parochial, in their opinions. Except for Jane. Jane was different.

"You'll have to write down your recommendations," Annie said.

"The museums are wonderful," Jane said. "Truly spectacular."

"And the opera," Betsy said. "You can't miss that."

"And what would you like, please?" The waiter stood ready to take orders for food. He spoke English well, his soft, gentle Hungarian inflection reminding Annie of a French accent, though Hungarian bore no relation to romance languages and was, in fact, a linguistic mystery of sorts. There were theories about the origins of Hungarian, but no one knew for sure.

The menu at the Grille included an American grilled cheese sandwich, a Texas burger, and a California Cobb salad. She ordered the grilled cheese. "I'll have another beer, too."

"Persze."

Persze—this favorite Hungarian expression. Every Hungarian used it and it meant "of course," with all its incantations of attitude: arrogance, intelligence, impatience. *Of course, we are a smart people, smarter than you think, smarter than the world understands. Of course—our country is loaded with PhDs, brilliant mathematicians and doctors who are experts in every subject. Persze—of course—we are one notch above everyone else, didn't you know? And if you didn't,*

why should we bother with you, another foolish foreigner with money,
passing through?

Jane ordered a Cobb salad and turned to Annie.

"Should be fun to see their interpretation of a California Cobb
salad."

"Might be your last in a while," Annie said. "You'll have new
foods to explore in Turkey."

"True." Jane nodded and smiled that wistful smile again.

"So how do you manage trailing-spouse syndrome?"

Jane sighed. "I've never quite settled into it, but giving it a
name helps. You know, once you've identified something, it makes
it less powerful."

Annie wondered if after eight months of living in Budapest, her
own smile had grown wan like Jane's. She drank more beer. God.
She hoped not.

"Give it more time," Betsy said to Annie.

"I'm not sure how long we intend to stay. Has anyone taken
that ferry to Vienna?"

"Never done that," Betsy said.

"We drove once," Valerie said. "Took us six hours. The traffic
near the border was horrendous. Those two-lane roads in Hungary.
Horrible."

"Valerie, you're giving Annie a terrible impression of this place."

"Does this feel like home to you?" Valerie asked Betsy.

"It's where I live. I do my best."

"And you're leaving."

Annie looked around at the coterie of woman laughing and chatting, exchanging barbs and witticisms. They sounded desperate and
worldly. Strange combination. She didn't know how to contribute.

"Do you all live in houses?" Annie said, trying to take part. She knew the question sounded naïve—almost silly. She figured they all lived up in the Buda Hills where the houses were.

Valerie hesitated long enough to convey surprise and slight irritation at Annie's question. "Of course, why?"

"We're renting an apartment near the river," Annie said. "I guess I'm missing our house. I've almost forgotten what it's like to be in a house, although our apartment is nice."

"If you stay awhile, you should get into a house," Betsy said. "You'll feel more settled."

"There are some good ones in the hills," Lisa said. "Modern conveniences. We all live pretty close to each other."

Annie nodded, regretting her question. "I'd heard most Americans lived there."

"The air's cleaner, too," Betsy said. "The air in the city is pretty bad."

"High rate of asthma," Valerie said.

"That's why we're on the seventh floor," Annie said. "The air is better higher up. That's what I read, anyway."

Listening to all this talk of houses, she felt a sudden longing for her beautiful white colonial house in Massachusetts, the one they'd sold and left without a second thought, happy to be on their overseas adventure, flush with a new baby and sense of purpose for their life moving forward. Eight months later, she was missing it, missing what she had taken for granted—as Edward pointed out—wondering why they had not been content with owning more than enough. She drank the rest of her beer. Thinking like that was akin to trying to catch those white lines on a highway while you're speeding ahead, the lines slipping behind you into the past. That was her old life. She didn't know when they planned to go back or when they would return to the States to visit. As for furniture, they had put theirs in storage, in one of those air-conditioned lockers in Boston. Annie nodded again as the women talked about their houses, how their small front-loading washing machines worked better than they expected—superior, in fact—to their top-loading American ones.

She ordered another beer, catching the waiter's eye and pointing to her empty mug. Then she turned to Jane.

"What do you know about the Gypsies?"

"Be careful," Betsy said, overhearing. "They'll rob you."

"Did you read about that wallet scam?" Valerie asked everyone. "Watch out for Gypsies. They're professional thieves."

Annie thought about mentioning the skinheads and what happened to Will, then changed her mind. Valerie would tell her, again, how horrible it was here, and she didn't need to hear that one more time. But it did bother her that people assumed the scam was run by Gypsies. Even Stephen said the two wallet thieves were Ukrainian. Not Gypsies.

"Isn't that a stereotype, though?" Annie asked. "Not all Gypsies are thieves."

"Of course not, but many are," Betsy said.

"Gypsies are second-class citizens here," Jane said. "Worse than that."

The others nodded out of what seemed like respect or tolerance for Jane. Unlike the others, Jane spoke without sarcasm or irony.

"They're like any group of people who are treated as second-class citizens," Valerie said. "Except they're not interested in assimilating."

"I believe the American Women's Club tried to start a tutoring program for some of the Gypsy children," Betsy said, trying for a more serious tone. "It never got off the ground."

"What happened?" Annie asked.

"The woman who started it left for South Africa. From what I heard, a few Gypsies showed up once but didn't come back."

"I used to work with homeless men," Annie said. "It takes time to build trust."

The woman stopped talking and looked at her.

"You can start anything you want here," Valerie said. "That's one thing. You can be queen if you want to be."

WHEN THE HOUR ended at the Grille, the women exchanged farewells, some making reference to future plans to visit the Herend Porcelain factory, a two-hour trek west of Budapest.

All of them, including Jane, jangled car keys for the drive back up to the Buda Hills, those American neighborhoods Annie had been so determined to avoid. She was still relieved that she had listened to her intuition about that. What other secret whisperings did she need to attend to?

She started her walk home along the river, a bit drunk in the middle of the day, thinking, *You can be queen if you want to be.* Oh, yes. She was queen of her own private queendom. Queen of Leo. Queen of her cell phone and fax machine and Hungarian babysitter, which reminded her that she should check—she fished her cell phone out of her bag. A missed call from Mr. Weiss. No message. Over an hour ago. She hoped he was all right. Concerned, she pushed the redial button and waited for his number to ring.

Eleven

He heard three knocks on his door, the same three knocks he heard yesterday when Ivan, the Hungarian boy, came to deliver his air conditioner. Today he came with groceries.

"*Egy pillanat!* One minute." The language wasn't as hard as everyone made it out to be. He'd learned a few useful phrases. Edward knew the boy was coming but had dozed off on the couch after his lunch, his glucose levels rising from too much sugar, his diabetes rebelling.

"*Egy pillanat!*"

He pushed up on his elbow slowly. And if he couldn't blame his sugar intake, then it was the heat, clinging still to ninety-five, -six, -seven degrees. His ragged crescent of silver hair was damp

against his neck. He checked his watch: twelve thirty. The standing fans—he'd added a second one—plus a small air conditioner,
which Ivan had mounted in the kitchen window, kept the place
tolerable. Yes. He'd conceded to his daughter's pleas, but the air was
stale because of it, with moisture dripping on the sill.

The boy knocked again.

"I heard you. *Christ. I heard you.*" He looked down at his swollen feet and lifted his torso off the sofa, leaning forward on his
thighs to balance himself and give time for his blood to find a steady
level in his head. When he reached the door, he unhitched the chain
and yanked on the handle, the door swollen from humidity. He let
the boy in, shut the door, and slid the chain back on its track.

"Over there, please. I cleared off the counter."

He pointed to the kitchen, then shook his head at himself. He
had the unfortunate habit of overdirecting people. The boy knew
what to do.

"Yes. I know," Ivan said.

"Thank you," Edward said, his voice conciliatory.

He liked Ivan, had liked him the instant the boy extended his
long arm to shake hands at the airport. Rose had made the arrangement. A lean young man with a gentle demeanor. "I am Ivan. You
are expecting me. Let me take those."

"Good. Thank you."

"I take you," Ivan had said. "The bus is here."

Edward had stood on the sidewalk while Ivan mounted his
three suitcases into the back of the bus, then scurried back to help
him get into the bus. The steep stairs stole Edward's breath.

"You are tired? Trip is too long," the boy had said. "Sit here."
He said something to the bus driver.

"Long wait in Frankfurt," Edward told the boy once he was seated next to him on the bus. "You understand my English?"

"Yes. Quite well." Ivan nodded. "I studied English in school."

That layover in Frankfurt had been tough on his arthritic limbs. Couldn't sit in one place, so he paced the long hallways, perused the duty-free shops. There were no direct flights from Boston to Budapest.

"How far to the apartment?"

"Not so far. Forty minutes."

Edward was satisfied. The boy's kind demeanor appeased his physical pain. He settled in for the ride.

"IT'S WORKING WELL," Ivan said, heading for the kitchen. The boy carried several meshed bags bulging with groceries and mounted them on the countertop.

"Yes. Thank you." Edward followed him. He watched Ivan unpack the goods.

"This heat not good but the air conditioner helps, yes?"

"Can't stand the damn thing."

"But for old—"

"Yes. Yes. I'm old. Seventy-six times the sun has circled the earth in my lifetime. Insignificant in the big picture. You understand what I'm telling you?"

"*Persze,*" Ivan said, nodding.

He was wise, this young kid. Edward could see that in his eyes— a curious green gray. Not spoiled, like young Americans. He stopped to consider this fact. "Tell me," Edward said, pouring glasses of water for himself and Ivan, "what is that? What do you call this sausage?" Edward pointed to a package wrapped in wax paper.

On the counter, Ivan lined up a kilo of cheese, two loaves of dark rye bread, bananas, three tomatoes, a carton of milk.

"Debreceni. You will like it." Ivan was about his height—six feet—friendly and serious. "They run out of Gyulai sausage. *Run out*—that's what you say in America, yes? Run out?"

"That's right. Smart boy." Edward laughed. "We run out. Americans run out of everything." He looked at Ivan with appreciation.

"Debreceni is good. You tell me next week if you like it best. The cost is same." Ivan took the glass of water and drank it.

"Okay. I'll tell you." Edward handed Ivan a wad of money. He paid the boy each week to shop for him—three thousand forints, about thirty dollars, to shop and deliver groceries, plus another two thousand for the boy's time. Everything was so damn cheap in Hungary; it was ludicrous. He gave him an extra two thousand forints to deliver the air conditioner. Resourceful and smart, the kid carted the air conditioner across town with a dolly, knowing he had hit the jackpot. Working for an American meant good money—a week's salary for a few hours' effort.

"What are you going do with all that money I give you?"

"I am saving it."

"For what?"

"To buy a flat, after I go to university."

"Good. Good for you."

The boy lived with his mother across the street from Edward. Ivan's father had died suddenly of an aneurysm when the kid was six. *I don't remember it*, he told Edward. He had one older sister, married with two kids, who lived in the countryside where it was more affordable. His mother never remarried.

"Twice in one week," Edward said. "I haven't scared you away yet?"

"*Nem*. No. Of course not. I enjoy knowing you. It will be hot again tomorrow. You have to stay inside. It's the only way."

Edward shrugged him off.

Ivan looked at the door. "Someone is here. Are you expecting?"

"No."

Then Edward remembered he had called Annie earlier. He wanted to ask her to come over again—not to drive him along the river. No. He decided that was a stupid idea. He headed for the door, stopping to look through the peephole.

A man he recognized. No.

"It's Van," the man in the hallway said. "Van Howard, sir."

Edward's arms became numb. He leaned into the door.

"How did you know I was here?" He talked into the wood.

"Mr. Edwards?" Ivan said behind him.

He waved Ivan away.

"Nan gave me your address but not your phone. Did she tell you?"

The door was old and thick. Howard's voice came through like dull thuds. The peephole gave Edward distorted glimpses of an ear, his eyes, his nose as he shifted to make out his whole face.

Him.

Edward unlocked the door but kept the chain on, opening the door wide enough for a man's foot. "You know I've been here several weeks."

"I should have written. I'm sorry. Would you like me to come back? Is this a bad time?"

"You don't live far, isn't that right?" Edward blocked the door opening.

"Yes."

In the wave of heat from the hallway, Edward smelled something sweet—a strong aftershave.

"Tell me," Edward said, lowering his voice. "Do you think you can get away with it?"

"I don't know what you're talking about." Howard shook his head. "Please not that." He turned to leave.

"Just a moment," Edward said. "I'll unchain this." Edward stepped back. The boy was behind him. The idea that Howard might try to harm them crossed Edward's mind. He was an old man. But Ivan was young, lean, and strong. "Where in Pest do you live exactly?"

Howard, his blond hair swept back, looked scrawnier than last winter after the funeral.

"By the river. Downtown. Why don't I come back another time and we'll talk." Howard glanced toward the stairs. "If Nan had given me your—."

"You're not a talker. You're a liar."

Liar propelled out of his mouth, pent up in his throat for too long. Oh, he had a long, long history of this. His mouth vomiting words, stinking up the whole goddamn place.

"You won't get away with this! Do you hear me?" He yelled, but by then Howard was leaping down the stairs to the street.

LATER, AFTER IVAN had left, Edward went through this scenario for the rest of the day, his mind looping like water in a circular sluice, round and round: how he had asked Ivan to chase Howard, how Ivan returned to tell him Howard had disappeared, out of sight by the time he had reached the sidewalk. Round and round, for the rest of the afternoon and into the night, he went

over this scene, berating himself for his stupidity. He should have
invited Howard in, befriended him. Caught the liar in his lies. Another round and he'd called Nan and insisted she read the letter
again—how many times had she read it to him?—ignoring her request to *please, please calm down. Dad. Dad.* What was the postmark
on the envelope? A PO box number for a return address.

He had it memorized now. Every word.

> *Dear Nan,*
>
> *I am writing to you because you of your kindness to me
> at Deborah's funeral. How does life go for you? I moved to
> Hungary. There are opportunities here that distract me from
> the pain of losing Deborah. Everything about Boston reminds
> me of my wife and the future we planned together. Every street
> has a memory. I can't believe she is gone. I wonder if it was
> God's way of sparing her from her worsening condition. Who
> knows? You're a nurse. Maybe you know what I mean. I hope
> your father will come to understand that there are more sides
> to her story than he has imagined. Thank you for letting me
> know where to find him. I live near the river, and the beauti-
> ful views of rocks and statues offer comfort.*
>
> *With sorrow,*
> *Van*

He was paying for his stupid impulses. *You and your stupid
mouth*, Sylvia had said.

Why hadn't he talked to Howard calmly? Time would undo
the wrong. Sleazeball shows up with his slimy, polite face. Unannounced. Funny how Howard failed to give him his phone number
or exact address. "Live near the river," Howard had said.

Edward grunted. Couldn't bear it. Wanted to shoot him on the spot, but the boy was there. Besides, that was not his plan.

Get the hell out!

I don't know what you're talking about.

Howard ran. Of course he did. Disappeared like an ant into the sprawling nest of Budapest. Afterward, Edward told Ivan to leave, too. He needed to calm down. Jesus Christ. Liar knew precisely what he was talking about.

When the phone rang, he told Annie he couldn't talk to her right now. He would call her back. He promised. A day or two. He shut her off. "God help me," Edward groaned. He turned on the couch, weeping, at last. "What have I done?"

Twelve

Bernardo wants you to do what?" Annie wore black heels, a black pencil skirt, and a sleeveless white blouse for the occasion, but she was not looking forward to this dinner with Will's former boss at the Kempinski Hotel downtown. Will strode beside her, his face taut, his eyes squinting the way they used to when he worked at Fendix. It was twilight and the city crowds had shifted to nighttime activities. Thankfully, the heat of the day had surrendered to more comfortable temperatures. Everywhere, she saw couples like herself and Will, plus singles in their twenties, all scurrying to meet friends for dinner or drinking, for a performance at the Liszt music academy—something she and Will often did—before they went out to the clubs. Gallery openings and summer street musicians added to Budapest's thriving night life. There were no children on the sidewalks at this hour. Leo was back at their flat under Klara and Sandor's care.

"He's involved with a group of venture capitalists," Will said. "They've got software that lets you log into your computer anywhere in the world. He wants someone to cover the Eastern countries. It's an opportunity. I'll hear him out."

The word *opportunity* made Annie suspicious. Will's telephone venture wasn't exactly speeding along. She was learning that Hungarians could take years to decide whether they wanted to engage in a business transaction.

They crossed the Duna—over the Chain Bridge—a gorgeous sight at night with its looping chains lit up like a roller coaster at a fancy amusement park.

"How do you discern between reality and all the marketing hype?" Annie asked. She wanted to believe in those über–buzz words that Americans binged on with unabashed, boundless, unquenchable greed: *opportunity, venture money*. But she was losing her taste for them. A breeze rose up from the river below. Decorative lights on the tourist boats twinkled. The city glittered in darkness, became magical. She reached for Will's hand.

"You don't. You have to see who's behind what. See what kind of money is invested, that sort of thing."

"And what about your mayor?"

"He's thinking."

"Which means?"

"Not much, I'm afraid. But he hasn't said no."

"I'm starting to wonder if the newspapers know what they're saying." Annie said. "Is anyone having success here?"

Will nodded. "A few. Possibly. I don't know."

"Not that bagel place," Annie said. "The *Wall Street Journal* got it all wrong."

"Agreed."

A New York–style deli launched by two Americans got a rave in the *Wall Street Journal*, but Annie knew for a fact it was struggling. She'd met one of the owners. Apparently, bagels, lox, and cream cheese weren't must-have foods for Hungarians. Yet a story profiling the "successful" venture made the front page of the *Wall Street Journal*. Front page!

"And that American-style laundry," Will said. "A bust."

"I know. But they wrote a full-length column in the business section touting its success. I don't get it," Annie said.

"They need to do their research."

"That's why Bernardo misses you." At Fendix, Bernardo once told her how Will excelled at research, found obscure data that no one else could uncover. "This is going to be strange to see him here," she said.

"Yup," Will said, sounding tense.

They stepped onto the Pest side and headed for the luxury hotel in the city center a few short blocks away. Bernardo was staying there. How typical of him. He didn't scrimp on material things. He went for the best. The Kempinski was Budapest's newest top-of-the-line and only five-star hotel.

At the hotel's entrance, a doorman in uniform opened one of several glass doors, raising an eyebrow at her, nodding approval. Will pointed to a door off the main lobby that led to a smaller bar and dining area. They walked into a darkened, air-chilled room with contemporary blond wood and wall-to-wall carpeting. She had been here before with Leo on one of the summer's many sweltering afternoons.

"Annie, Annie, Annie," Bernardo said, embracing her. Short and muscular, he squeezed her just a little too hard and kissed her on the lips as if she were his old, trusted friend, which, of course, she wasn't.

"Can you believe we're here in this friggin' place together? Sorry, Annie. I can't believe it myself. Jesus, it's cheap here. A person can live like a king. I can see why you came here. How are you? What can I get you? Glass of wine? Beer?" Bernardo flagged the bartender.

"Never expected it," Will said, shaking Bernardo's hand.

"Neither did I, man." Bernardo grinned at Annie. "You sure look good as ever. How's motherhood?"

The thing about Bernardo, he could be your best friend: personable, asking all the right questions, handsome with lively expressions and flushed complexion. He knew how to break through to people, especially when they resisted him.

"Motherhood's great. Amazing. Thanks."

The bartender looked expectantly at Bernardo. Bernardo grinned and swiped a lock of hair off his forehead. "A bottle of that Hungarian red wine I've been drinking. Great stuff."

Will pulled out his new wallet to pay, but Bernardo refused him. "No, no. This is on me."

"Egri Bikavér. Bull's Blood, they call it."

"What's that again?"

"*Eg* like *egg*, and *re* as in *re*finance," Will said.

Bernardo shook his head, laughing. "Got it. It's imprinted in my brain forever. Eggs refinanced. I like that."

Bernardo *was* handsome. She'd give him that. Square, balanced face, thick black hair, and eyes that zeroed in on her with precision and intensity. She could feel him wanting to know what she was really thinking about him, about his being here.

"I know. I know. You can't believe I'm here either," he said to her. "I left Fendix last month. Opportunities are too good to pass up, but you already know that."

He looked at Will, eager for affirmation.

"Plenty of it," Will said.

"Annie. You talking Hungarian now?"

"No. Hardly. I point a lot," she said, smiling.

"It's not a third-world country, as you can see," Will said.

Annie smiled. She and Will were used to this misperception of Hungary by Americans.

"Yeah. Man. Mea culpa. Love the power of the dollar here, though," Bernardo said. "Unbelievable."

"It sure is," Will said.

"That's what I want to tell you about. Sonny's got a start-up."

Sonny was Bernardo's former boss who took a retirement package two years ago, then bought land in the mountains of North Carolina.

"Go on," Will said, slipping his arm around Annie's waist.

Start-up was the other buzz word. Annie was sick of hearing about start-ups.

"This one's going someplace," Bernardo said, looking at her, noticing her resistance. "Sonny's got twenty investors. Most threw in half a mil. You should see his place. Beautiful. House on a lake, woods, fields. Works from home. Got a computer, a few phone lines. What else does a person need these days, you know? Called me for months. Wouldn't let up. Seriously. Finally offered me half a mil up front, plus monthly bonus incentives. I'm good for a couple of years even if nothing works out. The deal's going down right now. Couldn't refuse it. Could you?"

"That's serious money. When did he get this going?"

"Spring. Not even six months."

"Nice plans," Annie said. "They're moving quickly."

The money was impressive, yet something in her recoiled. As Bernardo talked, she couldn't help thinking of his duplicitous behavior at Fendix. She had liked Bernardo when she first met him at a company function soon after Will took the job, but over time she grew disenchanted with his magnetism. Was he sincere? She couldn't say. Sometimes yes, sometimes no. He was a climber, of that she was sure. He liked to put his arm around you, then step on your shoulders on the way to higher corporate levels. Annie remembered how Bernardo had befriended one of the marketing directors, a gay man named Harrison, then fired Harrison to please the higher-ups who despised Harrison because he was gay.

"I didn't get it when you left. It confused me, I admit it," Bernardo said to Will as the bartender filled their glasses from a newly opened bottle of Bull's Blood. Bernardo passed the bartender a rolled-up American dollar.

"Whatever happened to Harrison?" Annie asked.

"Poor bastard," Bernardo said, taking a long swallow of wine. "Hardest thing I ever did. Hardest thing. I heard he took a job in Miami. He landed on his feet. Look, maybe it was for the best. I liked him personally. You know I did." He looked at Annie for affirmation.

Annie tasted her wine. He was convincing. But she decided not to believe him.

"I know you did," she said, looking away.

She finished her glass, wishing she had eaten something before coming over. Already, the Bull's Blood was surging through her limbs.

Will placed his palm in the small of her back.

Annie wondered about Bernardo's wife. Where was she in this new mix? There were rumors about that, too. "How's Eileen?" Annie asked. "And the kids?"

"Unstoppable. Taking care of the kids. Great kids. She's a brick. Unbreakable."

"Tell her hello," Annie said.

"Absolutely I will. I want her to come over here. If I'm going to do this and do it right, I want the family to move here. Like you."

As she leaned against Will's arm, Annie remembered how Bernardo's urgency could either annoy or charm, depending on his need at that moment. Did he need Will to do his dirty work, or was he simply looking for a drinking companion, someone to keep him company in this lonely country? And then there was Bernardo's life story, which he liked to tell—how he came to America from Venezuela when he was six and how he grew up with his aunt and uncle in New Jersey. He never spoke about his parents. It was a story he told when he first met you: how he had to fight to fit in, how kids made fun of his accent, how he went to Stanford on scholarship. It was an admirable story—she recognized that—a true American success story.

"Bernardo, you know better than anyone what it's like to move to a foreign country," she said.

"I was a kid. Sure. I'm ready, but Eileen has questions. She's on the fence." He shrugged. "You're living like kings, right?" He seized the menu and started reading: "Bottle of wine: two dollars and fifty cents. You got to be kidding! Can't get a single glass of wine for that in the States. What do you pay for your place?"

"Practically nothing. Couple hundred a month," Will said. "We got lucky. Our old Hungarian neighbors back in the States had connections. If you go through American channels, you'll pay three times as much, but it will still be cheap."

"Listen, Will. I want you in on this. Money's not an issue. Seriously. I need you to help me out here."

"What are you suggesting?"

"Come on board full-time. We can talk details tomorrow. Meet for coffee in the morning."

"No promises, but I'll be happy to talk," Will said.

"That's all I'm asking. Now let's have some fun. Shall we eat? What do you recommend for dinner?"

THEY ATE AND drank at a table in the bar. Will and Annie sat on one side of the table, Bernardo across from them. Will ordered chicken *paprikash* for Bernardo, a classic Hungarian dish and a favorite of Annie's because of its tender meat. Gnocchi-like pasta floated in a light sauce of garlic, paprika, onion, and a dab of sour cream. That was the Hungarian palate—a weave of subtle, quiet spices that drew you in.

"I feel like I'm with family," Bernardo said, polishing off another glass of wine. "When you told me you were hauling over here with the baby, I couldn't believe it. Couldn't believe it," he said, shaking his head. "But I gotta tell you. I envied you. I thought you were crazy, but I envied you. I admit it."

"Most people thought we were crazy to come here, especially with a new baby," Will said.

"Crazy is good. It's good," Bernardo said. "You take risks and it pays off."

"You hope so," Will said.

Annie, of course, knew the full story. Risk meant endlessly waiting for mayors to decide. Lots of promises, nothing concrete, no tangible money in hand. It was all starting to look and feel like smoke and mirrors, like the bagel and laundry stories. Promising? Yes. But, so far, no more than that. Worse, it was starting to feel like a secret she didn't want to keep. The initial capital would soon run out and neither of them wanted to dip into their savings. God. She didn't want to think about that.

"I admired you and I hired you." Bernardo laughed at his silly rhyme. "I got that right."

"Yes, you did," Annie said. She smiled, acknowledging that, indeed, it was Bernardo who had courted Will, hired him at Fendix, and given him a solid financial start. "What's new in Boston?" she asked.

"Real estate's starting to move. I mean, really move. You could sell your house for twenty percent more now. And it's not stopping anytime soon."

"Is that so?" Annie said. Real estate was in her blood. She grew up listening to it, so it galled her to think she could have made more in such a short time, but then, that was Bernardo goading her a little, looking for her weak spot.

"Timing's everything," Bernardo said.

"We got a good price," Will said. "A good profit."

"We did," Annie said, smiling. They sold their house quickly because of the renovation and got all their money back and then some. Of course, they could have sold it for more if they had been willing to wait longer, but once Will gave his notice at Fendix, he wanted to leave ASAP. Everyone was talking about Eastern Europe. Budapest was hot. Prague was hot. Will wanted to start right away.

"If I sell my house, I'll make fifty percent above what I paid for it. But I've got to get my wife to agree."

"You don't have to sell it. You could rent it," Annie said, feeling momentarily bad about his marital struggles. "We thought about doing that," she said, turning to Will.

"We sold it. We made money. We're here," Will said. "We'll buy another house."

"Buy something here," Bernardo said.

"Absolutely not," she said, laughing, knowing Bernardo was prodding again, looking to see where she really stood on this matter of relocation and, additionally, how long she was willing to stay. She didn't want to give Bernardo any hint about that. Let him wonder. "Why don't *you* buy something here?" she said, prodding him back.

He grinned, taking her bait. "Maybe I will. Why not? What would it cost you for a place on the river?"

"Nothing. Twenty thousand American dollars. Can you believe that?" Will said. "But it's hard to say how long you'd need to wait to get a return. Could be decades."

Under the table, Annie felt Will's hand on her thigh, reassuring her.

"What about Eileen?" Annie wanted to shift the focus back to Bernardo's problem. "Does she want to move?"

"Eileen's tough. That's why she married me."

He grinned, letting her know that he knew he was evading her question.

• • •

AFTER DINNER, THEY took a cab to Club Z, a punk rock bar that Annie and Will discovered by accident one night on one of their meanderings through the city. In the cab, Annie sat between Will and Bernardo, the wind fanning them through the car's open windows.

"Don't they have air-conditioning?" Bernardo said. "Ask him."

"No work," the driver said.

Bernardo pulled off his tie and unbuttoned his collar, then turned to Annie. "When in Budapest, right?"

"I'm watching it," Will said to the driver, pointing to the taxi meter. "No games."

The driver, a gray-haired, skinny man, shrugged.

Annie was glad Will was asserting his authority, letting the cabbie know he knew all about taxi scammers who ran up the meters on clueless foreigners. Again, she found herself needing self-affirmation that they were not as naïve as Mr. Weiss had said they were. Unnerving man. She wondered if he were bipolar or something. When she had called him back after her women's luncheon, he had been abrupt, said he couldn't talk, had practically hung up on her, then surprised her by calling her the next morning, sounding perfectly calm and asking her to stop by. He told her that he had something he needed to tell her. *Not on the phone. Stop by, will you? Come in the morning.* She promised she would, tomorrow. She was flattered and intrigued. What could he possibly need to tell her?

"Annie, you with us?" Bernardo said, nudging her knee with his.

She turned to him, smiling. "You'll fit right in. You're a natural chameleon, right, Bernardo?"

"Not sure how to take that. Hey, Will. Your wife's giving me a hard time."

The cab swerved down a narrow road. She grabbed onto Will's thigh and laughed. The good food and wine, maybe the easy American conversation, had relaxed her. Maybe it was the warm summer breeze jostling them. She didn't care. She felt freer than she expected. How cool that they were in Budapest at this exciting, historic time.

"She wants you to feel at home."

Bernardo laughed loud and hard. "For chrissake, Will. I hired you because you weren't the typical Fendix type. That and your beautiful wife. Didn't you read one hundred classics or some crazy shit like that? You stood out, man."

"Come on, Bernardo. You doubled in Spanish lit and advertising. That's quite a combo."

"Spanish lit? Hey, man. I'm Spanish. Those are my roots. The thing I love about you, Will. You want technology to improve communication between cultures. I like that. You want to help the world. It's noble. It comes from the heart. I admire that. I don't think Fendix folks understood that about you. Me, I'm in it for the money, right, Annie? You know that about me."

Annie smiled. It amused her to watch Bernardo once again courting her husband by courting her, pulling out all the stops—honest and full of shit in one big mouthful.

"He likes to do the right thing," she said.

THE CAB STOPPED on a side street in front of Club Z where a small crowd of twenty-somethings milled outside the door, smoking cigarettes. Girls posed in black fishnet stockings, black miniskirts, hair henna-dyed an orange-red, which Annie saw everywhere in Budapest, all of them wearing that Hungarian expression of disinterest that hid deeper emotions of distrust mixed with even deeper cravings to connect. Annie identified with those feelings. Growing up, she held back, played it safe, avoided getting noticed. At the same time, she knew that something was missing, but until she met Will, she didn't realize how isolated and separated she had become from herself.

A group of boys leaned against the brick wall, smoking. Even in summer, they wore tight, punk-skinny jeans, metal-studded belts. These were not the scary, violence-prone skinheads who rambled the city in small groups. These kids were the young artists trying to break free from history, detach from communist Russia's recent debilitating hold, to create something new and positive for themselves. She felt attracted to them. She, too, wanted to break out of some vague repressed feeling in her life, the one that began on that day on the driveway when her brother threw a wild ball.

"I love this place," Annie said, getting out of the car, eager to enter the club. She didn't care that she looked out of kilter in her conservative dress. She loved the rawness of these kids, their hips angled, their obvious discontent and nervous energy. It touched something in her, made her wonder about herself. Maybe that was really why she had come to Budapest, to understand, like the Hungarians, what it meant to be a witness to tragedy, to break from the paralysis of the past.

At the door, she gave her hand to a bald, fat bouncer who stamped it with ink. Inside, she moved through the confusion of bodies and heat. Music below was as loud as a hurricane vibrating in her ears. Boys milling around gave her sidelong glances as she turned down a narrow, circular stairway. Couples shared cigarettes and held bottles of cheap Hungarian beer. She followed the exposed brick wall of the stairwell down to the basement, stepping over legs, bumping into a boy's shoulder.

"Sorry." A boy glanced sideways at her with his beautiful green eyes.

"Annie!" Bernardo shouted. "What the hell is this?"

She kept going down, the red wine in her making her not care about the smoke, which she normally disdained. At the bottom, the basement looked like a bomb shelter. Exposed brick walls, a few round tables, a crowd of three, four people deep at the walls watching a live rock show, African Brazilian rock fusion mixing with American rock. The lead singer swaggered on the stage, imitating Jim Morrison's thick-lipped seductive stances. Behind him the drummer and two more guitar players leapt and gyrated.

"Beer?" Bernardo shouted to her.

She nodded and turned. She saw Will behind Bernardo. The sound in the main room exploded. She felt her shoes humming. Bernardo pointed to the bar at the back and returned with three bottles of beer. Annie took a long, thirsty sip, her sweat soaking her bra, the sweat of others rising like steam. Will put his hand on her back. They danced slowly together amid the crowd of twenty-something rockers. She felt them watching, knew the Hungarians were watching the American couple as she watched them.

With both arms around Will's neck, she turned and saw Bernardo take a young woman's hand, a tall, slim woman with red lipstick and black-rimmed eyes, fishnet stockings and a thigh-high skirt. Instantly, Bernardo was dancing close, his face nuzzling the Hungarian's earlobe, talking into her ear, laughing.

Then Bernardo was beside her, clapping a hand on Will's shoulder, kissing Annie distractedly on the mouth. "Taking off. Great night. Talk tomorrow."

Annie pressed her chin into Will's shoulder and watched Bernardo leave, the woman in fishnet stockings following him up the narrow stairs.

Thirteen

Dear Annie,

   Thank you for checking on Edward. How is little Leo? What new words is he saying? Josef's heart is worse. I want him to see a doctor, but he refuses. You know how he is. Stubborn. How is Will's business? We are anxious to hear from you. The man who bought your house, the horse breeder? He travels a lot, and he wasn't very friendly when I introduced myself. I don't talk to him.

   Here is a letter from the agency. I hope it is nothing.

   Love,

   Rose

Across the bridge to Margaret Island, Annie jogged into the park before heading to see Mr. Weiss and breathed the sweet scent of manicured, watered lawns and trees. She turned onto the running path alongside the river. Following the loop, she passed a mother pushing her child on a swing, couples strolling along pebbled pathways, and clusters of seniors on benches facing the gardens. The river looked brownish today under the hazy sky. She passed the park's small barnyard with horses, goats, and ducks, which Leo loved. All looked peaceful, but she felt shaken inside from the agency letter.

Dear Mr. and Mrs. Gordon:

I have a note here on my calendar reminding me that little Leo will soon be a year old and per our phone conversation last winter, you promised to send his birth mother a report of his progress at year one with a picture or two. I hope you have not forgotten. I will write again if I don't hear back from you. Please respond at your earliest convenience.

Kind regards,

Mr. John Calloway, MSW

First, she couldn't stand the formal way he addressed her—Mrs. Gordon? He'd called her Annie from day one. Second, she felt irritated by his endearment of Leo. While not unexpected, it felt intrusive and insidious—polite in a demanding kind of way.

Little Leo. What did he know of her son? Leo was a mere four months when they left the States, freed from Calloway's smarmy control over their lives. His biweekly visits for three months—yes, she fully understood that the state required it—seemed excessive and insulting; his authority over her felt cloying, as if he enjoyed her dependence on him for the ultimate approval of their adoption. They'd already filled out an exhaustive questionnaire, underwent a lengthy interview by Calloway, got multiple references from friends who wrote the agency praising her and Will's ability to be loving parents. The anger she felt toward him, anger she thought she'd let go of after leaving the country, after leaving their old address and escaping Calloway's prurient interests, throbbed in her head. It's why she put Rose in charge of their mail so that Calloway couldn't track them down. She knew Rose would never disclose where she and Will had moved to. She ran harder now. She needed to calm down.

The adoption papers had been signed, judge-approved, and delivered. The adoption itself was a closed deal, something she and Will welcomed and Leo's birth mother required. Until Leo was legally theirs, Calloway, with his self-serving polite demeanor, had stopped by their house unannounced just to see how things were going—all in the name of social work and his job. It was his responsibility to inspect and sign off on papers certifying her parenting skills; his authority to decide if they were good enough to love a child. What about those drug-addicted parents? Biological parents who abused their kids? Who was coming to their houses to inspect their babies' limbs for hidden bruises? No one.

But then . . .

Annie slowed down again to maintain an even pace. After the adoption was finalized and Calloway was no longer required—legally—to show up, he did anyway. He wanted Annie and Will to meet a young unwed mother. He had an agenda and asked if they would mind meeting with her for an hour. It was as if he couldn't let go of his control, his mission to decide a family's fate. They said yes the first time, still afraid that Calloway might change his mind or rewrite his papers or somehow manage to pull the plug on the adoption. He couldn't. She knew that—in her head, that is, but not in her heart, which was still scared and recovering from years of waiting and yearning for a child. Years of waiting to conceive and failing; years of waiting for that moment of luck or fate, then waiting for lawyers and judges and social workers to sign off on papers—and even then, at first, she still didn't quite believe Leo was theirs, completely, irrevocably, all theirs. So they said yes to Calloway, and a few days later a teenager rang their bell, a sixteen-year-old mother with her two-month-old son. Annie and Will sat in their newly renovated living room smiling, asking inane questions of this young stranger who sat across from them rocking her baby, looking as tense and unsure as they felt, and equally determined to keep her son, too.

"I'll manage," she told them. "I live with my mother and she watches him when I go to class. I'll get my diploma."

"He's beautiful," Annie said to this young mother who, if Annie had been pregnant at sixteen, could be her daughter. Finally, after an hour that felt like half a day, the girl ambled to her car still carrying postpregnancy weight. Annie and Will stood in the doorway watching as she reached the end of their long front walk, put her infant in the car seat, strapped him in, and got herself behind the wheel and drove off.

When she closed the door, Annie turned to Will. "That's it. We're done. We don't have to please that man anymore. How conniving. That poor girl has no interest in giving up her child for adoption. That's why he sent her here, isn't it?"

"I'd say so. It's not our responsibility."

"He wants her to see that her baby would go to a nice couple like us. He's pressuring her," Annie said. Leo lay heavy on her chest, asleep. She walked upstairs and placed their son in his beautiful new gleaming white crib. Will had painted the room yellow and hung cheerful pictures of animals and balloons on the wall. The bedroom was cozy and neat and felt safe—except for her lingering worry that Calloway would attach himself inappropriately to their life.

The next day, when Calloway called to see how it went and ask if the "young gal" could come for another visit, she told him politely and slowly that she felt it was in Leo's best interest to focus on their own family right now. "John. I'm sure you understand our need for privacy and bonding right now." She used the word *bonding* on purpose, knowing it was a parenting buzz word, one that Calloway would embrace. John was silent but then in a quiet, sad voice said, "I understand." But, then, sucker that she was for the wounded, she felt sorry for him and offered a kind of emotional bargaining chip, a way to stay thinly connected by promising to send him pictures of Leo when he turned one, which John could then pass on to the birth mother via the agency.

THAT SEEMED SO long ago. Now that time was near—next month would mark that important landmark in her son's life—and Calloway hadn't forgotten. She knew he wouldn't. That wasn't his way. This thought spawned an old feeling of insecurity, a sense that even with adoption papers signed, her new role as a mother didn't guarantee bulletproof protection from the limitless things that could go wrong, including meddling people like a so-called well-meaning social worker named John Calloway. It made her wary. Becoming a mother opened up new possibilities for disaster.

Her skin broke into a sweat and her heart settled into a strong, pulsing beat as she jogged past the now-familiar thirteenth-century stone ruin of a Dominican convent. A marble plaque marked the burial place of Princess Margaret, the island's namesake. Margaret's father, King Béla IV, sent his daughter to a nunnery when she was eleven years old, fulfilling a vow he made to rebuild his country devastated by the Mongols. Giving up a child to save his child's country and keep it safe? She couldn't imagine it. Maybe the king thought he was keeping his child from harm, sheltering her from predators. It was a different world back then, or was it? How far would she go to keep her Leo safe?

The answer was obvious: five thousand miles, across an ocean, to a country whose language she couldn't speak.

Fourteen

She knocked three times on Mr. Weiss's door. The peep-hole in his door opened and shut. Relieved, she listened to metal scraping and a clickety-clack of the lock chain swinging free.

"How are you today?"

"No different from yesterday."

He gestured for her to enter.

"That doesn't sound too good."

"Who's talking about good?" He waved the air. "How's your son today?"

"Good. Excellent."

Leo was easiest in the morning. Today, as usual, he'd been happy to see Klara, who planned to take him up to Castle Hill.

"Adopted? Is that right?"

"Yes." Obviously, Rose had told him.

"Next time, bring him with you."

He almost smiled at her, an almost smile that hinted of another man, a livelier, happier man. She smiled back and stood in the middle of the room, surveying. Everything looked identical to her last visit—the dusky light, the small piles of paintings, the same picture on the easel—no fresh oil paint scenting the room.

"Feels much cooler in here," she said, spotting the air conditioner in the kitchen window. "How did you get it up here? Those things are heavy."

"I have means. Get yourself a glass of water."

She did as instructed, then came back in and sat on the chair opposite him.

"I'm old. Let's not waste time with small talk."

"At your service," she said.

"Tell me," he said, looking at her, his eyes softer today and more open. "Why did you come to this banged-up city?"

"To support Will's business venture."

"That's it?"

"We had just adopted our son."

"What has that got to do with Will's venture?"

"I wanted to be with Leo, not worry about adoption agencies watching over us—everything was legal, of course. Stamped by the judge. But I wanted to get away from all that. Not worry about it. The process felt intrusive."

"*Hmmf*," he said, then coughed. "Not worry? You're a parent. You'll never stop worrying about your child."

Annie agreed with this simple and overpowering fact. She felt it to her core the moment she held Leo for the first time. "I didn't expect it to be so powerful."

"Life's not what we expect. Your husband. How does he like it here?"

"He likes it well enough."

"Sounds lukewarm. What's the problem?"

She hesitated, shifting in her chair, wondering what this interview was about. But Edward seemed earnest enough.

"Success isn't what everyone says it is here. The *Wall Street Journal* doesn't know the full story."

"Agreed. Success is a phony word as far as I'm concerned."

"If you're happy, that's success. Don't you think?" She leaned forward, cupping her glass.

"I don't measure life in degrees of happiness. Telling the truth, finding the truth—that's success. If you're not happy, what does it matter? You're not happy here. Admit it. I can see it in your face."

She wasn't sure how to respond to this. Tell him the truth? She put her empty glass on the floor.

"Maybe."

"Come on. Don't hedge with me. I don't have time for that, remember?"

"Okay. Maybe I'm not happy here."

She felt the hidden tide of unhappiness rising inside her, her eyes watering. For the first time since her arrival eight and a half months ago, she felt relieved to admit how she truly felt. She'd been trying so hard to push it back down. She looked at the windows, how the sun was straining to get through a sieve of dust and shadows.

"I need more water." She rose and went into the kitchen, feeling confused and conflicted. What was she doing here? What was he? He had no time for bullshit? Well, neither did she. The tiny sink was filled with dishes, as it had been on her first visit. The air conditioner was working, though it made the air feel stale and used. Again, she was tempted to clean up but instead filled her glass with tap water and returned to the chair.

"Rose told me you had diabetes and a heart condition. Do you have a good doctor here?"

He tilted his head. "I do. My daughter Nan set me up. She's a nurse. You don't need to concern yourself with that."

"Then why are you here? You said you needed to tell me something."

"My daughter."

"I thought you said you didn't have family here."

"I have two daughters. My elder daughter was murdered." He pointed to the framed picture next to the couch. "That's what I needed you to know."

She opened and closed her hands. The word *murdered* pummeled her ears. She didn't know how to react. She had never met anyone whose family member was murdered. "My God. I'm so sorry."

He grunted and swatted the air, the swatting almost a physical tic. "I told you I've had enough sorries. Sorry doesn't bring her back. And God? *Pffft!* Look, when Deborah turned fifteen, her troubles began. That's the sorry part."

Annie bit her lip and heard a familiar humming sound—the fan, turning its sorry head back and forth.

Edward swatted the air again.

"Deborah liked saving people. Drug addicts, alcoholics, gamblers. She couldn't stop. I got angry with her. We didn't speak for years." He shook his head. "I couldn't understand it. Why did she pick these types? You're close to her age. You're a helper, like she was. Explain it to me."

"I suppose she wanted to improve their lives, give them something they didn't have." She clasped her glass in both hands. "Or maybe she didn't judge them like most people do." Judgment, she had learned while working with the men at the shelter, was the single most devastating response. It shut everything down. She drank the rest of the tepid water.

"You mean, like her father judged her?" His eyes rocketed upward, his thoughts swerving through an internal map of his body causing his shoulders and face to twitch.

"I didn't mean to imply that."

"Look, she was a hippie. What a pile of crap that was. Peace and love." He made a spitting noise again. "Bunch of lies, phony baloney is what that was. More screwed-up people from that generation. Then Deborah got sick. You know what multiple sclerosis is?"

"Yes. I know someone who has it. A volunteer at the homeless shelter, where I used to work."

"There are different types, you know. My Deborah had the worst of it."

"My colleague tired easily and it affected her balance when she walked," Annie said. "She started using a cane, even on the days she didn't need it, because she said people treated her as if she were a drunk." Annie noted privately how the woman's name was Tracy, same as her sister's, an odd coincidence.

"In six years, my Deborah went from walking to a wheelchair," he said. "And she still managed to find another loser. The last one married her. He drugged her with her own prescription pills. Murdered her, understand? Stole her insurance. He's here in Budapest."

She felt her eyebrows rising. She couldn't fathom this.

"You don't believe me?"

"Not that. I've never—" She felt stupid and clueless.

"My kid's dead, but I haven't stopped worrying about her. Her killer is free. Somewhere in this city. Near the river. I'm here to find him."

"And that's why you wanted me to drive—"

"Bloodsucking off my daughter's life," he said, interrupting her, his cheeks reddening. "You're here to find what? Happiness? You should go home. Raise your son in a good school. Get the hell out of here. It's a depressing place." He paused for a second. "But since you're here, I believe you can help me. It's up to you."

Annie shifted in her seat, uncrossed and crossed her legs, and set her empty glass on the floor. She had cooled down, the sweat gone from her skin. Only her shirt felt clammy.

The word *murdered* scared her, but she felt the pull of "helping" drawing her toward him, like air sucking into a vacuum. It was true what Will said. She wanted to get involved, comfort people, fix what wasn't right, dive into their struggles, get beneath the surface of things. Will said other people's tragedies gave her license to feel her own buried discomforts and pain around Tracy's tragedy, her brother's, her family's wreckage.

"How can I help?"

Again, the shadow of that day on the driveway in Maine, a shriek, her father jumping from the car he was backing up. Was that it? Tracy's brain injury dominated everything from that point on.

Annie was pushed aside. Greg bore the guilt. Her father removed himself. Her mother devoted everything to Tracy, to make the impossible seem right.

"You come to this country, you think you're far away from home, but you're not, Annie. It comes with you."

"When did you get here?"

"Some weeks ago. That's not important."

"When did your daughter—Deborah—die?"

"Murdered. She didn't die."

She looked at the windows again, at the fan, trying to make sense of what was incomprehensible. What kind of unsafe territory was this? She saw him watching her reaction.

"You're scared," he said.

She started to shrug it off, but she couldn't.

"Yes. I don't know."

"He's here. I have to find him. I will find him."

"Does Rose know about this?"

"That I'm here to find him?" He flicked his eyes away, a hesitation. "Yes."

Surprised, she felt confused, unbalanced by this new information.

"You're involved in the expat community, aren't you?" he said.

"Will is, much more than I am. I've been lax about it." She spoke slowly. "But I know a few women. I had lunch with some recently. Why?"

"I understand it's a pretty small group—a few thousand at most. Maybe you've run into him?"

She felt exposed. The sparseness of the room. The ridiculous fan creaking as it turned. The air conditioner shuddering on and off. The old man in his pajamas. She felt a moment of insanity, the wrinkle in consciousness when you wonder if you are awake, making sense. What was she doing here?

"I've scared you," Edward said again. "Tell me the truth. I'll stop right now."

"Yes, but I'm okay." His acknowledgment calmed her, even emboldened her. "Please. Go on." She came to Budapest to live a full life, a genuine life, to get out of her shell of fears. "What is it you would like me to do?"

"Look, I've done my research. The expat community is a small group. It's easy to find Americans. You could help me locate him. He lives by the river."

"I see."

She crossed her legs, thinking of their aborted drive by the river the other day, his eyes burning—the way he looked at her when they came to the apartment the first time. Maybe he was crazy. Or maybe she was paranoid. She didn't know. She swallowed. Her tongue felt dried up.

"Let me get some water."

She went back to the kitchen, refilling her glass, telling herself that if Rose knew about it, something about this would be all right. She felt her phone in her back pocket. She could call Will. The white porcelain sink held three saucers, a fork, a pot. Simple, lonely objects. Should she leave or stay? Only the thought of Rose centered her. She returned to the living room and sat on the edge of the chair thinking Leo was safe with Klara. She was glad she hadn't brought him here.

"Look, forget it. I've scared you. The hell with it."

"I'm trying to make sense—"

"There's no sense to it! God damn it! None."

He pulled himself up from the chair, agitated, his face twisting in pain. Should she run? Was he having a heart attack?

"I need to rest," he said.

"I'll help you," she said, the words spilling out of her before she understood what she was saying or agreeing to.

But instead of calming him, he grunted and walked to the door, and unlocked it.

"Look, I don't have time for fakers and liars, understand? Think it over. You want to help me, fine. If not, *que sera*. We can both agree to leave each other alone. Make up your mind. My daughter was murdered, understand?"

She stood at the door, her heart speeding.

"I'll talk to Will. Maybe he's heard something. When should I come back?"

"I'm here."

She opened the door and let herself out.

Fifteen

Outside, she walked away from the plain brick building but not from the impact of Mr. Weiss's words still expanding in her chest, stretching her lungs to something thin and taut. She sucked on the thick, warm air, thoughts of his murdered child filling her mind. His daughter. Now it was coming together, the picture of him. She needed to think logically. She would talk to Will. No. She wouldn't talk to Will. He would advise her to step back. *Don't try to save him. You can't save him*, she could hear him saying. *Take care of yourself.*

Will wouldn't like it. Maybe it was better to say nothing. Delay telling him. That's it. She wouldn't say anything. Not yet. Getting herself entangled when they had their own concerns? What had she walked into? Why couldn't she resist?

She started to cross the street when a tiny red car honked and startled her, the woman driver skidding toward the next traffic stop. Annie stepped back on the curb to collect herself. She should go home, but she was too upset, disoriented. She turned and headed for the flower cart to see if the Gypsy woman was there. Maybe she was part of the wallet-theft racket. Everything felt elusive as she moved through the crowded sidewalks in her jogging shorts and sneakers. She did not fit in.

Nor did Mr. Weiss. Edward. Strange man.

And murder.

She bumped into a man on the sidewalk who had stopped to light a cigarette.

"Pardon," she said, that word that cupped the universal sound of apology. *Pardon.* The man nodded. He was middle age, dressed in a business shirt and dark pants, his thinning hair sweaty from the hazy heat. What deaths lay hidden in his family chest? she wondered. Annie took in the crowds passing her—professional, all of them, with indifferent, secret eyes. What had they seen? What did they know? She imagined that every Hungarian who had lived through the wars knew of bloodstains hidden somewhere in their lives. And every American? She saw a flicker again, a shadow of Greg hurling his white baseball, a white flash in the air, and screaming her name. *Annie! Get out of the way!*

What was it? She shook her head and looked around her. She felt dizzy. She purchased a bottle of water from a corner store and moved into the shadow of a stone building. The city was swirling.

Trolleys dinging their bells, sliding along circular paths from one crowded district to the next—odorous minicars skimming like oil drops on water across avenues, exhaust smelling like sulfur. It's because they run on two-cycle engines, Will had explained. You have to put oil in with the gas. Look it up, he said.

When the traffic light turned, she crossed the boulevard and walked alongside the river. She needed to get home to relieve Klara, to see her Leo, to center herself. But her tears spilled over, soaking her cheeks. She needed to calm down, stop crying. She wiped away more tears.

The river smelled rusty and let off a cooler draft. A ferry heading for Vienna flushed up white foam, a widening trail of bubbles. She paused to watch it. She and Will should take that boat. Leo would like the ride.

MURDER AND BLOODSHED stained this very river decades ago, this river of history running alongside her, deadly and silent, its brown, swirling surface hiding bloodied dreams and despair. She thought of Will. His mother or father might have been one of those children, a Jew protected by nuns, but fate placed them both in America before the war, not here, where fifteen thousand Jews were hacked down on the banks of this river, shot by sick, pro-Nazi vigilantes. How could Hungarians stand it? How could she? How could Will, a Jew, live here, too?

Her mind sank into a pool of bitter feelings. The truth was: Mr. Weiss was right. She wasn't happy. She was afraid. She didn't want anyone taking her child. What place was truly safe?

Murder and Mr. Weiss. He had come all the way here looking for a killer. What would she do in his situation? A bloodless murder.

How many hundreds of Hungarians walking on this very street had been deadened by the murder of their loved ones?

Annie felt for Mr. Weiss, understood that hope was no longer in his vocabulary. She'd seen it in her parents after Tracy's injury. For years, they tried to cure her sister's seizures, the ones that came after the accident. Experimental surgeries slowed but didn't stop the downward turn of her life. Medications dulled her mind. Tracy became wheelchair dependent. The worse she got, the worse Greg got. Their brother drank. He couldn't hold jobs longer than a few months. And then there was Annie, the witness, the one who lived through her family's private grief, who listened to her mother cry behind closed bedroom doors—her father not there, too busy rambling through empty buildings, assessing them, buying and selling them, obsessed with converting them to usable space. All these memories glutted her mind.

Up ahead, an elderly woman and her tiny dog meandered along the stone wall next to the river. The dog hunched over to poop on the pavement. People didn't pick up their dog waste here. Piles of it corroded the hot air. Did people not care? Had they simply given up? Is this what had happened to Mr. Weiss? Is that why he came to this city: to chase after some crazy notion in the rest of his empty life?

SHE KEPT GOING in pursuit of a positive thought. She needed to right herself. She was late, past her promised time of return to her flat. Surely this city had more to offer. Even the King of Pop, Michael Jackson, had come here to film his newest music video. Another American leaving a territorial mark, another male dog pissing on a tree?

Will was having yet another meeting with Dave from General Electric, and with Bernardo. A lot was riding on these meetings, or maybe nothing was riding on them. If only one of these rendezvous would lead to something concrete. If only Will or somebody could convince the mayor from that City of Kings to sign onto his cable business, his venture could get some traction. If only. If only. She almost didn't care anymore. How bad was that?

Next to the Duna, she stopped again, surprised by the beauty of flowering gardens bordering the Parliament, a massive gray building inspired by Britain's Westminster Abbey. Two football fields wide, it looked like the fortress it was, built a hundred years ago to protect Hungary's constantly shifting borders. Hungary had been through so many regimes over so many centuries.

Over by the rose hedges, she spied three dark-skinned Gypsy girls—Roma, she remembered Jane correcting—crouching as they pulled and snapped off roses. They were thin-limbed, with dark, round eyes, wearing the same long skirts and cotton blouses as the two girls at the flower stall. She recognized the taller one, who spotted Annie and walked directly up to her. The Roma held out her hand, offering Annie the stolen flower for sale. Annie noticed a small mole on the girl's lip.

"Dollar," the girl said.

Annie hesitated. She wanted to give these girls money, but the rose was taken from public property, so she shook her head. *"Nem."* She made a disapproving face and pointed to the rosebushes. "You shouldn't do that. *Nem.*"

The other two ran over and the three girls giggled and started to dance in a circle in front of her. Annie was spellbound, confused, and captivated by their persistence as they danced in a ring around her—all of them barefooted. Even as Annie began to move away, they followed, pumping their hips and twirling in an effort to entertain her. The tallest girl smiled, showing big white teeth, looking right into Annie's eyes, daring her with her hand held open for money. Annie knew she was the same girl she had seen outside Luigi's. Maybe the third girl was a sister, too—all of them too young to be running about without an adult in this city of millions.

Annie refused to take the flower from her. Instead, she gave each girl one hundred forints—one dollar each—a fortune for them. The girls shrieked and ran off.

Tired of wallowing in self-pity, Annie headed toward the main boulevard and hopped a number 2 trolley. The tram ran along the river and offered a full view of Castle Hill across the river. She walked to a window seat and sat down. The bus was mostly empty this time of day except for a small clique of young men sitting at the far end. They dressed like the super's son: black pants, black heavy boots, black leather jackets, a crazy thing in this heat. But this group had shaved heads. Skinheads. Metal chains dangled from their jacket pockets. It was a look, all right, and a scary one. She made the mistake of looking directly at one of the boys, who shouted something at her. She turned away to view the river again. Someone banged what sounded like a stick against the seat. "Fuck American! Fuck American!" This brought on an explosion of sinister laughter.

She refused to turn, her body stiff against the insult. The man driving the trolley car up front didn't move. Maybe he was scared, too. She didn't know. She walked to the front and stood next to the driver for protection. When the trolley stopped and the doors flipped open, she forced herself to slowly walk down three steps to the pavement. She made herself wait until the trolley sidled past her, until she saw the boys' ugly faces pushing against the window glass, their tongues flashing. And then she ran. She sprinted down the pavement toward home, away from those angry young men.

Sixteen

In the elevator, no super in sight, thank goodness, she rode up to her floor. *First Germans come, then Russians, now you Americans,* her Hungarian neighbor had said as a joke some weeks ago when she shared the elevator with him. His shoulders shook with laughter. He avoided direct eye contact, observing her from a sidelong glance as she'd seen so many Hungarians do. And though she knew he was trying to be friendly, his humor struck her as a backhanded way of telling her—albeit nicely—to go home. She had smiled at him because that's what Americans liked to do. Smile. Act like the world was theirs to do as they pleased. Behave like winners.

Today she counted seven beers on the welcome mat in front of his door as she wiggled the key to open her apartment. Klara was in the kitchen, handing Leo pieces of cheese as he sat in his high chair. "Hi, sweet pea." She kissed her son, then poured herself a glass of water and stood by the window fan. "Sorry I'm late."

"*Nem probléma.*"

Maybe it was time they succumbed and bought an air-conditioning unit. If Edward could get one, so could she. Hadn't she had enough of her "when in Budapest, do as the Budapestians do" silliness? She stroked Leo's head.

The kitchen was a cheerful, tiny room with grand views of the Duna and Castle Hill on the hilly side of Budapest. White marble floors and pretty golden pine paneling on the kitchen walls gave the small space an alpine feel: light and airy.

"He is hungry today," Klara said.

"Another growth spurt, pumpkin?" Annie kissed him again.

"*Igen.* I think so." Klara looked apologetic when she smiled, as if smiling were indulgent or dishonest or not cool. She usually braided her hair in two pigtails, but today she wore her brown hair in a single ponytail.

"Where do the Roma live?"

"Gypsies? In the seventh and eighth districts. They are very poor."

The lower-numbered districts were closest to the center. Higher-numbered districts expanded outward from the center like the arrondissements in Paris. The eighth was about a forty-five-minute walk from the flat.

Klara lined up another battalion of cheese squares on Leo's plate. He tried picking one up with two fingers, but the cheese slipped away, dropping to the floor, his fingers not yet able to follow his mind's instructions. He was on track, though. All developmental milestones met on time or early.

"Do you know any of them personally?"

"No." Klara stooped to pick up the cheese and placed it in a trash can under the sink. "Some Gypsies live in Sandor's building."

"He lives in the eighth?"

"Igen."

Victorious, Leo held up a piece of cheese. "Jeeze, jeeze," he said, putting a piece in his mouth.

"Why are they treated so poorly here?"

Klara shrugged again. "It is the way. They are Gypsies. Not Hungarians."

"I don't understand. The Gypsies have lived in Hungary for hundreds of years."

"But they are not pure Hungarian."

Annie looked at Klara. "Did you say *pure*? You know that's how the Holocaust got started, with talk like that."

"Nem. I don't think so," Klara said, shaking her head. "It is not the same."

"Up up," Leo said, stretching his arms out. Annie removed him from his seat to the floor, and she and Klara followed him down the hall to his room, which stayed neat and clean because of Klara's efforts.

"Well, it doesn't sound right to me," Annie said, her anger rising. "Think about what you are saying." She adored Klara but this "pure" talk upset her. She couldn't get a handle on why Klara didn't question her attitude about Gypsies—Roma.

"I am sorry. Maybe my English doesn't explain it. Talk to Sandor," Klara said. "He explain better."

Leo flopped on the floor and began playing with his favorite wooden puzzle.

"Eye-ger," he said, putting a tiger-shaped piece in the correct slot.

"Tiger. Good, sweetie."

They heard Sandor knocking on the door. He came most days to walk Klara home. Leo hurried to the door, reaching his arms up when Annie let Sandor in.

"Hello, *kicsi baba*."

Sandor lifted the baby and set him down again. "I will spin for you."

They watched Leo walk back to his room and return with a spinning toy, which he handed to Sandor. Annie laughed. Clearly this was a familiar game between them.

"He is good today," Sandor said.

She nodded and said, "Klara told me Gypsies live in your building."

"*Igen.*"

"Do you know the family?"

"*Nem.* They stay separate. That is their way."

"Are you afraid of them?"

"*Nem*, not afraid, but they are from different world," Sandor said, tipping his head. "It is worse since Russians leave. There is more stealing. Sorry about Mr. Gordon's wallet."

"The police said it was a racket."

"*Igen*," Sandor said. "I think so."

"Are you saying you want the Russians to come back?"

"No, no!" Klara and Sandor said simultaneously.

"But it is a *probléma*," Sandor said. "The old way and the new way."

"Who knows if it's the Gypsies? That's an assumption."

Sandor smiled and shook his head. "Gypsies are a *probléma*."

"But they are not treated well here," Annie said. "I saw skinheads attack a little girl."

Sandor knelt down and set the toy upright for spinning. "It is a long way why they are in this situation," he said.

"Yet they've been here a long time. A thousand years! That's why I don't understand it."

"I will try to tell you."

Sandor twisted the toy, winding it up and releasing it until it spun, making gentle bell sounds as it twirled. Leo shrieked. He loved it. They all watched the toy until it fell on its side. Sandor spun it again. She could see he was trying to organize his thoughts to explain the Gypsies to her, so she waited.

When she first met Sandor back in the spring, he reminded her of a soft-spoken, lanky folk singer who might have lived in a yurt in Vermont had he been born in America, not someone raised in an orphanage in Budapest, the son of an alcoholic mother. Klara told her that Sandor had never met his father, had no idea who he was.

"The Roma are a special group who moved from Asia to Europe to Hungary," he finally said. "It is typical for Gypsies to be moving. They are with horses. They didn't have houses. They collected what they could. It is what you say an attitude, a life mode not to work and to try and live. It is a problem from the past."

"You mean it's a philosophy," Annie said. "A belief system."

"*Igen.* There are three groups: The first group lives here for generations in Hungary. They are the best. The second group comes from Romania. They are the worst. They live in the woods. They are dirty. And the third group have no social place. Gypsies are not educated. They cannot find good jobs. For example, Gypsies love the children and if the children don't feel well or want to sleep late, they say, okay. You don't have to go to school."

Leo sat between the talking adults, playing with his spinning toy, trying to push the top to make it turn, not succeeding but not giving up.

"Is it true that they steal?"

"*Igen*. They steal." Sandor pushed the top and showed Leo how to hold the handle. "They live in a culture where it is easier to steal than to work. They are looking for the easiest way. They have a problem with rules. They don't follow the rules. They keep their own way. There is very much prejudice against them. *Gypsy* and *thief* in Hungary—it is the same word."

Seventeen

Edward positioned his easel so that it formed a triangle in front of the window. He was alert this morning—as he was most mornings before the weight of his life and the sadness that infused it moved down through his body. He sat with legs open on the chair and dabbed blue paint on the canvas, working quickly, not one to repaint and fiddle. Attack the canvas with an image in his mind or picture from a magazine photo. Get it done, impatience working for him, working faster than his critical thoughts. The view out his window looked like crap—*was* crap. Decrepit buildings. No money to clean and repair them. The air, the curtains, not red but a muddy brown. They called this city the Pearl of the Danube. Bull. Bloody Danube is what it was. He coughed. He knew the history of this place. Night ghosts barfing up Jews murdered on the riverbanks. Bodies pushed pell-mell into the water. Made them take off their goddamn shoes. *Shoes.* Bloodied shores. That's what he saw when he went outdoors once in the evening and stood on the path under the trees by the river. He couldn't stomach the sight of it. Pearl of cruelty.

He rubbed his leg to help the blood circulate, to prevent thrombosis. One more ailment to add to the others—his heart palpitations, which started after Deborah's murder. He had pills for his heart and insulin now to keep his diabetes under control. What difference did it make?

All sensations of belief or hope or faith in something had long passed, gone since Deborah, his Deborah, had died and left a hole in his heart. He lived with fatigue, the emotional sludge of rage. Except when he painted: he dabbed his brush and made quick strokes until a mountain emerged in the distance under a sky that seemed empty and full at the same time. The sky a free place. His flesh untethered, until the mental image of his daughter unmoving on her bed resurfaced. Jesus. His chest clenched. He shut his eyes against a swarm of self-hate, a sensation of his body listing. He opened his eyes again and looked out the window at a fruit truck, the Hungarian lettering familiar to him now.

He saw Deborah lying there when he walked into her basement apartment in Boston, a late January thaw. No snow. A bright, cold sun. January 23. The fucker standing in the hall to greet him, to comfort him, the fake husband, the piece of lying shit, his blond bangs and those greenish eyes. He had called to tell him she was gone.

"I thought she was asleep," the liar said. Edward bent his fingers into his palm. He'd strangle him if he could.

Deborah had said, "We'll be gone four nights. It's one of those deals to Nassau. I need to get away. Don't worry about me, Dad."

But that's not where she went. He killed her instead.

After Howard's call, Edward sped to Boston, down Commonwealth Avenue. Sylvia was getting her hair done. He couldn't get hold of her. Didn't know the name of the damn salon. He called Nan on the North Shore. She headed down.

Outside Deborah's building, a young policeman stood on the sidewalk—guarding what? The truth? The secret? The policeman went into the kitchen, looking dazed. Fresh out of the police academy: buzzed hair; smooth face; lean, straight legs.

Deborah lived in a two-room studio in Back Bay. A garden apartment, she called it. Garden of lies. Garden of death is what it was.

Dad, I told you. It's fine, it's great.

What about safe?

It's Back Bay. It's safe. Totally fine. Stop already.

He swatted the air. He didn't stop.

The policeman sat down and filled out some crap police papers, using Deborah's kitchen table to get it all down. Deborah sprawled on her bed, her limbs awkward, her lips caught in a grim line.

Trying to shake the memory, Edward leaned over between the legs of the easel and with effort picked up his coffee mug from the floor. Cool now, he finished it off. The prospect of getting out of the chair again unappealing. Can a heart feel like an anchor? Sure. Dead weight but not dead. That's how he felt.

Months ago. Minutes ago. It was all the same. And he would

find Howard. He screwed up, let him get away. But he was here. Howard was here and that American girl. She could help him if fear didn't stop her. She had looked scared when she left. Maybe her husband would interfere. But now he saw the error of trying to do it alone. He could use their help. He would plan this. He would wait a few more days.

He leaned forward in the chair, studying the picture forming: a musty-blue sky with a dark cloud congealing in one corner. He smeared tears from his eyes, his thumb across his cheek. Jesus. The images didn't fade. They grew worse. His Deborah's murder, her memory forever a part of him. It killed Sylvia, too.

Sylvia would agree with him on that. No amount of time would make it right. Like the war. Like those bones piled up when he walked through Dachau's gate and saw them—logs, logs with faces, legs, feet. Bones. Gone fifty years. Gone yesterday. Thirty-five years of selling medical equipment in his downtown Boston office didn't bury those skeletons of murdered Jews. Sticks, elbows, femurs, skulls, eye sockets. Bone hell.

Deborah lying on her back in bed, her mouth turned down. Her flesh still the color of the living, but lifeless.

He reached for his glass of water on the floor and drank, then sucked a fist of air into his mouth. He had to keep on.

First time he saw Sylvia, she'd worn that blue dress, tight on her hips and those breasts she couldn't hide. Great smile, that Sylvia. He married her right after the war. When he came home, they bought a ranch in Newton. New Jewish ghetto, highfalutin suburb west of Boston. They joined a temple. Had gotten engaged during the war and married right after it. Where was the sense in that? None. But that's what they did back then. Everyone did it. Stupid. Practically strangers. Racing to begin a new life at home.

Deborah came eleven months later. July 3, 1947. She was born at two in the morning and was trouble from day one. Colic. Then a wandering eye. At two years old, running onto a main highway while they vacationed in Vermont. Oblivious. Her oblivion continued. She struggled at school. Bright but disinterested, she sought out troubled friends. She liked the streets, the real world, the troubled world. At twenty-one, she graduated from Northeastern University in Boston, a miracle in itself, barely passing, and she moved to the South End. Everyone talked about Boston's South End, how it was changing. She rented a studio in a renovated brownstone. Next door, heroin addicts slept in the doorway. He'd practically stepped over one the first time he visited.

"What are you doing? Trying to ruin your life? Get yourself killed?" he asked her. "This is crazy. I don't get it."

"I didn't ask you to."

She had her mother's chin, and when she had something to fight for, she led with it, stretching her neck as if to see better.

Murdered in a garden apartment, a basement, a below-street-level room. Back door opened to a brick patio the size of a king bed. "Perfect for the chair," she told him. "We can park the car in back."

We. Her favorite word.

Deborah bought the apartment using the twenty-thousand-dollar gift he'd given her for graduating college. A mistake. If he hadn't done that, she wouldn't have bought that basement place. Maybe it would have delayed something.

And then her sister, Nan, born four years later. The opposite.

Nan didn't run out into streets. Nan liked school. Nan avoided trouble, just as her mother had.

But not Deborah. Deborah approached the world as if it owed her something. He coughed again. Leaned over in the chair, grabbed the ledge of the easel for balance. He and Deborah were more alike than he understood.

Deborah picked boyfriends who mumbled, who felt the world owed *them* something—boys who didn't look at him when she introduced them. They didn't talk. They had problems. Every six months, someone new, her mission of the month: help the nobodies in the world; excuse the miscreants. Offer a reason why boyfriend number 19 went to jail for stealing a car.

"His father beat him up every day," she said, as if that made stealing acceptable.

Bullshit.

Nan had friends, lots of girlfriends. Studious, never out of line. Nan went to nursing school in New York, then took a job back in Boston, moved to the North Shore.

"You should see the marshes in spring, Dad. The colors are glorious."

Spring. What did it matter? Nan was a surgical nurse at Children's Hospital in Boston, married to the emergency room, while Deborah worked at drug rehab facilities and rape intervention centers in Boston. Then the back pains started. First, she thought the slip on the stairs caused it—those stairs to the beach in Gloucester near her sister's house. But rehab didn't help. Chiropractor couldn't fix it. After that: back surgery. A few months of rehab, she still hurt.

Numbness, then weakness in her legs. Another doc thought it was Lyme disease. Antibiotics for six months. Didn't fix it. Finally, the diagnosis: multiple sclerosis. White female in her late twenties. Aggressive type.

After the funeral, Sylvia lit a cigarette and started smoking again. First one, then straight to a pack a day. Maybe the smoke set off her heart problems. She started sneaking smokes in the basement at night, then spraying the place with perfume. Between his cigars and her cigarettes, what did it matter? Bah. She was funny that way, laughably funny.

He smiled and ached at the memory. Sylvia dead, too.

Deborah's death wasn't on the books as murder. Her death certificate said overdose. Vicodin. A lie is what that was. How many certificates recorded these lies? Thousands. Hundreds of thousands. The world turned on lies.

Deborah found a new mission: how to change the world from a wheelchair. "People don't look at me," she said. "They talk to Van as if I'm not there. They think I'm a mute or stupid because I'm sitting down. Makes me burn."

"People are stupid. People don't know crap," he told her.

He knew war vets that came home in wheelchairs and they wheeled themselves into oblivion. Might as well have been a death sentence. Some took their lives when they got home. What did the world know about these people? He despised humanity. There were a few good people, yes. But they were aberrations. Josef. He was one exception. One in a billion. He had Josef to thank for the apartment.

Sylvia was good, too. Too good for him. After forty-nine years, she walked into the den. He was smoking his after-dinner cigar when she said, "Edward, I've had enough. I'm moving out. I want my own space."

"What are you saying, Sylvia? What are you saying?"

"You heard me. I need peace. Time for me. Myself."

"What? I give you time. You've got it. Here." He waved his hand in the air to show her, his cigar smoke emphasizing his point. "What did I do?"

"I can't explain it," she said. She stood at the door dressed in black slacks and a red blouse. "I don't need your permission. I don't need to report to you or anyone. I don't want to have to be anyone anymore. I've lived my life for other people. I'm done with that. Done. You think it's selfish? So be it. From now on, Edward, I'm done. You'll have to do your own laundry. Shop, cook. You'll figure it out. My life is passing, Edward. I've made up my mind. I don't hate you. I just can't live with you anymore."

He knew it was about Deborah. Their Deborah. When you lose a child, you fail forever. There's no getting out of that. No fixing.

"What about this house?" He looked around at the dark wood-paneled room that smelled of his cigar smoke. He looked at the worn plaid couch, the one they bought on sale two decades ago. Furniture. Like it mattered. The family room.

What family?

"We'll sell it," she said. "I've looked into it. We'll split the money."

"Then piss it away on separate apartments? What's the point?"

"I'm going to work at Harriet's store."

Harriet was Sylvia's best friend from the temple. She owned three clothing stores: Harriet's, Harriet's Too, and Harriet's Three.

Sylvia stood at the doorway, hand on her hip—she was thicker in the waist since menopause, but she worked out at the gym a few times a week. She looked good. She still liked sex. How could she leave him?

"Doing what?"

"Selling clothes. It's doesn't matter. I'll earn commissions. If I do well, I'll manage the store."

That night, she moved into Harriet Bloom's garage apartment, one town over. God, he hated that. His Sylvia living in a maid's quarters.

He tried to put the brush on the easel and missed the ledge. The brush dropped to the floor, a blue smudge, one of many that had dried in spots on the floor, like bird crap.

"Christ almighty."

He leaned over and rubbed the paint, a streak blending into other streaks, telling another story at his feet—the colors of previous paintings, more images from the past collecting at his feet. What did it matter? Dirt. Grime. That's what it all came down to, not the bull-crap decorum that most people shoved into their lives—fake Louis XV bureaus and pressed-wood bedroom and dining-room sets.

Deborah kept her place spare. It surprised him every time. One double bed. One lamp. One table. Except for her candles. Too many candles. Candles on the windowsill, on the floor, in the tiny bathroom where guests could slip and kill themselves on the porcelain ledge of the sink.

When he walked in that day, he knew she was dead, he saw her through the bedroom door. She lay on her back, her face tilted toward the window, her dark bangs oddly neat as if someone had combed them straight. Deborah looked up at the ceiling toward the window: not answering him, sun shining in. What was the sun telling him, that the world didn't care?

Oh! he called out, his voice failing him, his chest falling through the sky, the one that filled his mind.

He dabbed the canvas again, pushing dark blue into the top

corner. He'd painted these landscapes over and over, as if painting them again might open up something he couldn't get at, needed to get at, but . . . What was he looking for? A way out of life? A way to find that piece-of-shit Howard? The man was a fraud, and now Edward was certain he would find Howard again, one more time in his lifetime. He'd made it here. He would do it. He was an ass for losing his temper, but he'd get another chance. Howard was somewhere near. So close he could feel him. He clenched his face and grunted. Then wept.

Outside the Budapest apartment, a fruit truck backed out of a parking space. It was a dirty city, this Pearl of the Danube. Dirty. Smutty. Loud. Nothing got filtered here. Everything did. A city of contradictions. A city of waste. He fit right in.

Eighteen

The following morning, after her disturbing visit with Edward, she still hadn't said anything about it to Will. Instead, she finished her morning run around the park and then headed over the bridge to the Kempinski Hotel to see if Michael Jackson, the King of Pop, had indeed arrived as the Radio Free Europe station had announced. On her way out the door, Will had offered a disinterested response: "That's good. Have fun." Klara was also blasé about the superstar, but that was Klara.

Annie needed the distraction. And now, as she approached the hotel, she saw that her wish would be granted. A boisterous crowd had filled the sidewalk in front of the building, chanting, "Michael!

Michael! Michael!" She couldn't believe it. Hungarians screaming with enthusiasm? Annie joined them at the back of the crowd. She stood higher on her toes for a better view. There! The crowd roared approval and then she saw the real Michael Jackson emerge onto a balcony ten stories above them, looking ethereal, his new wife, Lisa Marie, calmly standing beside him, holding his hand. The pop star wore a red military jacket with gold buttons. He waved and smiled, then turned to the daughter of Elvis, his beautiful petite wife. The crowd roared. And even though Lisa Marie's pale face was half-obscured by her thick dark hair, she commanded equal attention, looking regal in a black double-breasted jacket. The crowd roared again as the couple stepped back into the hotel room, out of view. And then she heard, "Annie! Annie!"

She turned. Bernardo Lopez raised his hand and waved wildly at her, weaving through rows of people to reach her.

"I can't believe you spotted me."

"Who else is in jogging shorts?"

She let him hug her and then she said, "Did you see him? Can you believe it?"

"You like that freak, Annie? I would not have guessed."

"I think he's fantastic. An absolute genius. A music god."

Bernardo shrugged. "A freaky genius. Guy's got a weird obsession with kids."

"He does a lot of good. People forget that. He has a skin disease. Did you know that?"

"Sure. Look, we all have our tastes. He just doesn't do it for me. Hey, I wish him the best. I bet that marriage doesn't last a year."

She shrugged at the comment.

"They've got people standing guard at the elevators," he said.

"It's a zoo. If I'd known, I would have stayed someplace else. I had to get out of there. Where you heading?"

"Home."

She saw him give her a quick approving once-over from her T-shirt to her jogging shoes—and wondered if he was comparing her to the woman he picked up at Club Z? She knew how he operated, which both flattered and repulsed her. At Fendix, she remembered how he was constantly assessing other women at the business conferences she attended with Will, in restaurants, in hotel lobbies, in nightclubs.

Annie offered him a polite, disinterested smile. She also knew that he probably planned on changing her view of him since he'd left abruptly with that woman at Club Z. Bernardo needed her to like him. If he managed to sway her, get her back on his side, Will would stay to help him. Bernardo recognized the power of wives. If a wife resisted an executive move, it screwed things up every time.

"How did Will get so lucky?"

"How did you get so lucky with Eileen? Last night you'd started to tell me how she was." She liked Eileen. His wife possessed an innate charisma and a winning smile like her husband. And she wasn't shy about showing off her huge breasts and curvaceous figure, a trait Annie admired about her. No other women could beat that, certainly not Bernardo's Club Z conquest.

He raked his fingers through his hair as if he were trying to straighten his thoughts. "Truthfully, it's a complicated question. She's fine. She's hard-headed. Like me, I guess." He walked alongside her. "Where did you say you were heading?"

"Back home."

He frowned. He wasn't looking happy this morning.

"Deals with the kids, does it all." He took her elbow and turned to her, his cheeks flushing. "Join me for a drink or a Coke? How about it?"

She wanted to decline, but the curious part of her, the part that wanted to know who he really was, said, "Sure. But it's Coke for me today. I had my fill at Club Z."

"Sorry about that. Listen, Annie, I took the girl home and crashed at the hotel."

Annie squinted. "I don't know what to say. That's your business. But you're not subtle."

"Don't say anything more. You're right. I'm sorry, for what it's worth."

She presumed that meant he had sex with the woman before he went back to his hotel and now regretted it. She'd heard rumors about him from other wives at Fendix, rumors that Bernardo had affairs on the road. Did everyone know except Eileen? She doubted it. Eileen wasn't clueless.

"When is Eileen coming over?"

"In a few days. So she says."

They stopped at a crosswalk and waited for the light to change. "What will you do if she doesn't want to relocate? Commute back and forth? How long do you plan to be here?"

"Don't know that either."

Bernardo steered her into a small cafe a block from the river.

"Looks decent," he said.

"Looks new. Every week another one opens up." Dark wood paneling, black granite tabletops, cafe-style, and a sleek bar with stools gave it a hip vibe. They sat at the bar.

Bernardo ordered a beer.

"Coke," Annie said.

"Sure?"

"Yes."

"You sure are looking beautiful as ever. Tell me the truth. You like it here? Between you and me, I've got marriage troubles. What can I do?" Bernardo looked at her in a pleading way. "Boom boom boom," he said, chopping his hand on the bar. "We have three kids and it gets worse with each one. Not the kids. I love my kids. But Eileen's changed. She's angry. So she gained weight? I don't care if she's overweight. I told her to join a gym. She can diet." He drank half the glass and put his hand up to order another.

At the shelter in Boston, Annie had listened to so many broken men confessing about their failed marriages—not unlike Bernardo's unloading to her now. They told her how they had screwed up. If only they'd paid more attention. If only they had stopped drinking. *If only.* There were so many variations of that. She grew up with it. If only Greg's errant pitch hadn't destroyed Tracy's life . . . or Greg's.

"People change. Life changes," she said. "I guess that's the tricky part." She wanted to say, *Bernardo, messing around with other women won't convince Eileen to hurry over,* but she knew that was the kind of thing people always wanted to say but never did to people who had affairs. She was thirsty and drank her Coke too quickly, the fizz burning the back of her throat.

"Yeah. Things change and you don't even know it," Bernardo said. "I can't tell you when it started to go bad. Maybe the kids? Maybe that's an excuse. I don't know. Question is whether we can repair the damage."

"Do you want to repair it?" She finished her soda and noted with approval how the cafe's decor hit the right notes for her.

Modern and hip, it made her like Budapest again, and for some reason, she liked that Bernardo was confiding in her. Maybe it made her feel more in control.

He started on his second beer.

"Problems snowball. You know what I'm saying? Pregnancy was hard on her. She gained weight. Then the next one, and the third. She went through a lot. I give her that. You know she used to play tennis. She was in good shape. She swims. The pool helps." He looked at her. "I'm talking too much."

"Talking can help."

"You know Eileen. You know how she is."

"She's strong, I know that." Annie knew that Eileen was athletic, muscular, and held her big breasts proudly, and how she admired his wife for that. She carried her breasts like trophies. In a bathing suit, she had an attitude, a woman's swagger that countered her husband's, who, to Annie's mind, acted as if life were a swimming pool filled with naked women dying to screw him.

"Can I get you another?"

"I'm good." She held up her hands to tell him she was fine, but she wasn't fine. She was talking to a married man who had picked up a woman at Club Z, right in front of her, and here she was trying to minimize his infidelity. He was lonely? So what. She was lonely, too, for friends, for a feeling of direction. Who was she to judge?

"How long are you staying?"

"Maybe a week. Eileen said she'd come—without the kids, of course. She's booked a flight. I spoke with her this morning. Told her about you."

"Great. That's a start."

"So what makes you happy, Annie, besides Leo and Will?"

She cupped her chin into her palm and leaned toward him. "Lots of things." She wondered herself about happiness because she did not feel happy in this city, but she would never tell Bernardo that. "Good people. Good weather. Good conversation. I don't know. Why?"

"Well, I'll tell you what makes me happy. Money makes me happy, healthy kids and a good woman." He nodded to the waiter for the check. "You like it here? Tell me the truth. You've been here—what? Almost a year?"

"Forever," she said, then sat back and caught herself.

"Feels long, does it?"

His eyes locked with hers, not missing a beat or a moment of vulnerability as he lifted his beer and finished it off. "Not sure that's a good sign." He had that predatory gaze that she remembered from Fendix, his eyes flicking restlessly around the room, seeking to fill something, seeking answers, seeking a way up his private ladder to success.

"Long enough not to feel like a visitor anymore."

"That's why I need you. You can show Eileen around. Would you do that?"

"I'd be happy to. She'll like it in the hills. That's where the Americans live, except us."

"Why not you?"

"We liked the idea of living away from Americans, but that's us. Your kids will go to the international school. We don't have that concern yet."

Bernardo tore his napkin into small pieces.

"The people here don't smile, have you noticed?" he said, pushing the pieces toward her. "They don't look you in the eye."

She laughed. "Yes. Observant of you. They slide their eyes. Like this." She moved her eyes sideways and they both laughed heartily.

"Jesus. I thought I was the only one. What's with these people?"

"There's subtle stuff you can't see or feel unless you live here."

"Sure. But you like it?"

"Sure," she said, but the word felt forced.

The older waiter placed the bill in front of Bernardo. "You take American dollars?"

"*Persze,*" the waiter said.

"Tell me, how did Will convince you to come over?"

"He didn't. I wanted to come. We both did. And Leo is not in school. He doesn't care where he lives as long as he's with us. That makes it less complicated. Easier." She finished her Coke, the glass half the size of a typical American serving. "I've been told the American school isn't bad. I haven't heard anyone complain about it, but then, I may not be the best person to talk to about that. I could get you some names, though. Eileen should call one of the mothers who have kids in school." Annie thought of Betsy from the American women's lunch.

"She used to love traveling, before the kids," Bernardo said, rolling one of the napkin pieces into a ball.

"She'd have plenty of help here. Super cheap, too. How old are your kids now?"

"All under ten. Two in school. One heading for kindergarten. I don't know what she's afraid of—not your problem, is it?" he said, standing up to leave. "Thanks for indulging me, Annie."

"I'll see you next time with Eileen, okay?" she said.

"You bet."

Bernardo gave her a bear hug and this time she didn't resist. It felt genuine enough. "See you." As he left the cafe and hurried across the street, he raised his hand in a backward wave.

Annie decided that was how he had sex. A quick backward wave of his hand, a flourish and then off. She looked at her watch—almost noon. As Annie crossed over to the Buda side once again, she recast her opinion of Bernardo. Was it that he had decided to present her with a kinder, less certain side of himself? He looked miserable, lost in thought, his eyebrows pulled low.

The air was hitting its peak temperature, hot and moist. As she headed down the *utca* toward her apartment building, the pavement smelled of warm tar. She wondered if Bernardo were testing her, the way he'd been prodding her about happiness and all of that, hoping she might be lonely enough to sleep with him on another afternoon while Will was off on his mayoral hunts.

In front of their apartment building, she saw their Saab parked and felt relieved that Will was back.

"Hey!" Will called to her from the doorway.

He looked tall and handsome as ever, but weary.

"What's wrong?" she asked, kissing him. "You're not smiling."

He tilted his head, thinking of something. "Wish I had good news."

She knew she ought to probe further and ask Will for more details. At the same time, she felt empty of cheer. What could she say to him at this point that would change things for him. The only concrete prospect was Bernardo's offer and that was not something she wanted Will to pursue. Yet Bernardo was persuasive. She felt herself weakening.

"I ran into Bernardo near his hotel. He bought me a Coke. I actually felt bad for him."

"He's a lonely man."

"Lonely and ambitious. He apologized for his behavior at Club Z."

"That's Bernardo. The charmer."

"Right. He wants you to sign that contract."

"You sound like you're changing your mind about it," Will said.

"No. But I felt sorry for him. I really did. He says Eileen doesn't want to come over with the kids, but she's coming for a visit. I think his marriage is in serious trouble."

They entered the dark foyer, passing the garbage bins. The sound of the super's television tinkled through the thin door.

"Who knows where the truth lies between those two," Will said, pushing the elevator button.

Truth. That was another one of those words that tripped her up. At the shelter, she had heard so many versions of it.

Nineteen

Dear Annie and Will,

How are you? We have been busy. Josef got a letter from Steven Spielberg. That's right. The famous movie director. He started an organization called the Shoah Foundation. You remember his movie *Schindler's List*? Mr. Spielberg wants to record survivors' stories. They want to film Josef. Josef is excited and agitated. You can understand. The memories it brings up. We'll see. How is business? And most important of all, how is our little Leo? He must be getting big. Send us a picture. We are waiting to hear from you.

Love,

Rose and Josef

PS: Did I mention that your house was repainted? It is dark green. You would not recognize it.

Annie put the fax into the stroller's back pocket and headed out with Leo to meet Will for lunch at one of the state-run cafeterias, then on to the ferry to Vienna. She needed to write Rose but kept avoiding it, not wanting to write about the shadows of loneliness and disappointment trailing her, or about Edward and his daughter—his murdered daughter—and his request for help and, worse, whether she believed him or not. A trip to Vienna offered a mini-escape as she struggled to make up her mind. For eight-plus months, she'd been holding her breath in this city of contradicting currents.

"You can't save him," Will had said again in the kitchen before leaving to meet Bernardo for a breakfast meeting. She had finally told him about Edward's daughter and how Edward had straight-out asked her to help him, and how she had, without thinking it through, said yes.

"I'm not trying to save him. He asked for help because he believes his daughter was *murdered*."

"You don't want to get in over your head."

"And you?"

Will turned to her. "What's wrong, Annie?"

"Are you in over your head?"

"No. I don't think so." He spoke slowly, looking at her, waiting for her to say more.

"Maybe I'm not either." She went into Leo's room to get him dressed and ready for their trip.

On the way to the cafeteria, she called Edward.

"It's Annie. How are you?"

"You know the answer to that."

"I wanted to let you know that we're going to Vienna today for one night. I'll see you as soon as we get back."

"What's the reason for your trip?"

"We've been talking about going for a while."

"I tell you about my daughter and now you're running off to Vienna. I told you not to waste my time."

"I'm not running off. We'll be back tomorrow night."

"I see what I see." He hung up.

Stunned, she felt nauseated, punched in the stomach by his accusatory words. Leo was oblivious, waving a stick, happy to be in the jogger. She considered calling Edward back to tell him the timing wasn't related—her trip and his daughter. Or was it? She walked faster, tears rising, her anger stirring with confusion. His voice jabbed at her, poked at her soft spots, hurting her. That was how he operated, wasn't it? Provoke and conquer. Why did she let him get to her like this? Her wiser self understood he was in pain, inconsolable pain. That was all he could see. But that didn't excuse his rude, abrupt behavior, did it? Working at the shelter, she learned not to judge. It was her number one rule. What did Mr. Weiss expect of her? He nudged and prodded her to act, take a stand. What did she need to prove?

Her family came first. Even Edward would agree with her on that. And what was Edward doing here? If he found his son-in-law, then what?

SHE PASSED THE Király Baths with the enormous green domes, the jogger practically driving on its own, the large wheels rolling over the sidewalk. How alien the domes looked to her last winter, hovering like spaceships above dark-limbed, bare trees. The city was known for its cleansing baths—*famous* for it—another favorite Hungarian word. She could use a cleansing bath for her own murky emotions. Was she losing her sanity? What was right?

She slowed down again and soon came to a memorial statue of Bem József, where demonstrators gathered during Hungary's 1956 uprising—that bloody, brief explosion of hope for freedom. Almost every day she passed this statue, never stopping until now. She let Leo out of the jogger so he could touch the giant concrete figure dressed in an ankle-length coat and helmet. The statue of Bem József looked stern and defiant, one arm raised, a long finger pointing at the sky. As Leo started up the small steps to touch the base of the statue, Annie spotted Stephen smoking a cigarette on a bench nestled behind a small fir tree.

"Hello there," he said.

"I run into you in the oddest places," she said, parking the jogger next to the bench.

"I come here a lot." Stephen took a long pull of his cigarette, this time not making any attempt to hide his habit. "It's my sanctuary, you could say. A place where I come to honor my dad."

"I'm sorry," Annie said.

"Sorry doesn't bring them back, does it?" A wrinkle of bitterness passed over his face.

"No. But I'm still sorry." That's how she felt about Greg's death. Sorry for her brother's sad, unfulfilled life. Sorry that she couldn't bring him back for a second chance.

"That's fair." Stephen tilted his head back and blew a long

stream of smoke at the blue sky, then tossed the dying butt into the trees behind him. "Where are you heading on this hot day?"

"Vienna. We're taking the ferry and staying overnight. Do you have any recommendations?"

"The museums. There's no denying their greatness." He twisted his mouth as if he'd eaten bitter flakes of tobacco and were trying to spit them out. "But to be honest, the city doesn't do much for me. You'll enjoy the cafes. The pastries. When you get back, you can tell me what you think about it. Just don't forget how rich countries like America and Austria are blind to the needs of countries like Hungary. Isn't that right, Leo?"

"Up up."

They both looked at Leo stretching his arms to get a better look at the statue looming over him.

Before she could tell him to stop, Stephen lunged toward Leo and scooped him up onto his shoulders so that Leo could touch the statue's supersize shoes.

"Careful," she said, standing behind Stephen, holding her arms out ready to catch her son if he fell back.

"He's fine." Stephen flipped Leo over and placed his feet gently on the ground.

"Again!" Leo said, thrilled with his new friend.

"Next time, little guy. I've got to get going. Happy travels. I'm sure Leo will love the boat ride."

Stephen bent his head in that way that she had first found appealing at Luigi's, friendly yet offhanded. Except this time, she saw how his carefree manner was an endearing attempt to lighten the gravity of his father's memory that she had unexpectedly interrupted.

With Leo back in the jogger, she started to run again to shake off her own unsettled memories. Yes. Taking this trip would be a welcome change, no matter what Mr. Weiss said.

When she first came to Budapest, she couldn't comprehend Hungary's widespread commemoration of battles lost. Slowly, she was beginning to understand that the country needed to celebrate courage, the simple yet monumental act of standing up for a belief, regardless of the outcome. That's what mattered—that people did not die in vain. In 1956, innocent men and women were gunned down by Russian tanks, a few thousand brave souls risked their lives for justice, freedom for all, and the power to make choices. They got no help from the American troops who were a mere four hours away in Austria. In the end, their deaths released two hundred thousand Hungarians—a massive exodus west to dozens of countries—some walking into Austria, others flying to America, like Stephen's family, escaping years of terror, years of silent witness to fathers, neighbors, friends disappearing in the night, tortured by secret police inside plain brick buildings. The insanity was everywhere in this city of lost dreams and failures. What had Stephen's father seen? And what disturbances had he passed on to Stephen as a young child?

Where were the informers—the "bricks," as Will had informed her they were called? How many of them were like her super, hiding behind innocuous jobs, living with vectors of those dark days circling inside their heads with no place to escape except inward, into the caverns of the mind. It was madness.

Was Mr. Weiss right? Was she *running off*? She had her son to think about. He had his daughter. If she tried to help him, what would she be getting herself into? A murder? And what about her son's safety?

Yes. Yes. She was afraid. She was a mother. She had a responsibility now. She felt tested. The idea of summoning courage was easy to ponder as long as you didn't have to do anything about it. *Doing* something made all the difference.

She approached another small neighborhood park they often visited, one of many such parks scattered throughout the city, and saw their friend Katya sitting on a park bench. She and Leo had befriended the older Hungarian woman from many morning visits to the swings.

"Katya!" Annie called out. "*Hogy vagy?* How are you?" Annie slowed the jogger but didn't stop.

Katya waved and blew Leo a kiss. She was a short buxom woman with gray hair pulled up in a bun. She didn't speak more than a dozen words of English. Annie couldn't speak more than a few dozen Hungarian words, yet the two women had learned to talk to each other using their hands, facial expressions, and a traveler's dictionary. Annie had even managed to explain to Katya that Will was here for work and how her parents couldn't visit because her sister was sick. *Beteg.*

"Sick. *Nem* good." The older woman had put a hand over her heart in sympathy and with gentle, warm eyes conveyed without words her full understanding of life's complexities. It's why Annie was drawn to older people like Rose and Katya, even Mr. Weiss.

Annie felt a connection with this woman who had a heart condition, its treatment hindered by the expense of medicine in the new noncommunist world that Katya couldn't afford. Katya told Annie her pension didn't cover her living costs anymore.

"*Nem* good for old people," Katya said.

Annie wondered if she should offer Katya money to help her out but feared offending the older woman's pride.

• • •

REACHING THE CAFETERIA, she found Will sitting at a long metal table, waiting for them with a tray full of food—roasted chicken breasts, quartered potatoes, and vanilla pudding.

"How'd it go with Bernardo?" she said, kissing Will and giving him a hug. "Thanks for getting lunch for us."

"He wants me to come on board. Nothing's changed."

"What about you? Are you tempted? It's a lot of money." She immediately set upon cutting the chicken into smaller pieces for Leo.

"I'm listening to what he has to say. He's staying another week. Eileen is coming over to check things out. The money's hard to ignore."

"When do you have to decide?"

"Soon. Don't worry. I won't make any decisions without you. We'll decide together."

"I know. I'm glad we're going on this trip. It will give us some perspective."

"I completely agree."

She ate quickly, excited that they had finally decided to take the ferry, her mood lifting with the prospect of a four-hour boat ride down the famous Danube. In the cafeteria, an elderly man shuffled over to them, stopped to smile at Leo, then pretended to grab his nose. Universal baby trick. Leo giggled, encouraging him, so the old man leaned over and gave Leo a gentle pinch on his cheek. *Kicsi baba.*

Both she and Will smiled politely. The man bowed to them and left. These state-run cafeterias around the city were some of her favorite places to eat. Housed in large old buildings with big windows, fifteen-foot ceilings, industrial ceiling fans, and scuffed-up linoleum floors, no tourists came here, and for that reason Annie felt privileged, as if she had gained access to a country's secret space where history and people converged in a way that most outsiders never experienced.

"We should go," Will said, standing. "We don't want to miss our boat."

Outside, Annie wanted to cry when she saw the same old man begging for money on the sidewalk. He turned to them and opened his palm. She felt ashamed for him when he looked at her without recognition, as if he hadn't seen her just minutes before, had never stopped to pinch their son's cheek, and she felt effectively slapped by her own stupidity and arrogance. She understood that he had a job to do out here on the street, that begging for money had no connection to who he was a moment ago inside. In this way, he put her in her place, humbled her. Who was she to judge? Who was she to imagine his shame? Presume his pride? What did she know of his life? She heard Mr. Weiss telling them how Americans were never satisfied. Always wanting more. *Am I right?*

She put a ten-thousand-forint bill into the man's palm. More than a day's pay for some. The old man nodded, a hint of delight in his eyes, a triumph of good fortune before he turned away from her to beg from someone else.

Twenty

On board the ferry, she sat by the window so Leo could get a good view. Will sat on the aisle. It wasn't a large boat. She guesstimated it could accommodate about sixty people. Rounding the river away from Budapest, they passed Visegrád Castle, a thirteenth-century stone structure perched high on the ledge of a steep cliff.

"Look at that," she said, pointing up so Leo would notice.

Leo slapped the window with his palm, batting at the spray frothing up from the hydroplane's motor.

"That was a cultural hub in Europe five hundred years ago," Will said.

The boat moved past the cliff.

"It looks so fragile."

From the river, the castle looked as if it might crumble, the stones barely clinging to the cliff.

"That's where Hungary, Poland, and Czechoslovakia signed an agreement to cooperate. That was in 1991, I believe."

"An agreement to cooperate . . . that almost sounds funny."

"To show solidarity among nations."

She sighed and leaned back in her seat, gingerly readjusting Leo's shoulders. He leaned into her, nestling his head against her breast.

"Not much in the way of cooperation around here, is there?" she said.

"What's eating at you?"

"I called Edward today."

"When?"

"Before lunch."

Will nodded.

"How is he?"

"Mad that I'm taking this trip."

"Why did you call him?"

"I called to tell him we were going away and that we'd be back tomorrow night. I felt that was the right thing to do."

Will marked a place in his book, then draped his arm around her shoulder. "Good thing we're getting away. I worry about you."

"I worry about you, too," she said.

They were the only Americans on the boat. She presumed most of the other passengers were Hungarians or Austrians. She heard strands of sentences, those rich, gentle undulations in Magyar—the Hungarian word for Hungarian—and an occasional German-sounding word. To her American ear, the rhythms and consonants of Maygar sounded like soft-clicking *k*'s and *t*'s and the vowels like gentle hushings and chortles from the back of the throat. Behind her, an older Hungarian couple unwrapped sandwiches, the wax paper crackling. In front of her, a man was reading Hungary's main newspaper.

Why Hungary? Her parents had gasped in disbelief when she told them of their plans to move there. Why Hungary? What's in *Hungary?* She no longer had a good answer.

They sat for a while watching the shoreline pass by, a bare, treeless shoreline. The dark water bubbled from the ferry's engines, a rocking that eventually put Leo to sleep.

"Annie, I need to talk to you about our money situation."

She turned to Will, taken aback by his tone of voice.

"What do you mean? What's wrong?"

"We may have to break into our savings."

"I don't want to do that."

"I know."

"Why are you bringing this up now?"

"It's as good a time as any." Will shifted his legs and stretched them under the seat ahead of him. "To keep going, I'll need additional funding."

"You haven't said anything about this before. You didn't say anything at lunch when I asked about your meeting with Bernardo."

"I've got investors writing ten-thousand-dollar checks, but it's not enough. I need someone willing to put in half a million or more."

"What do you suggest we do? I don't want to touch our savings." She shifted again in her seat, moving away from him to dispel this uncomfortable news.

"Neither do I."

"Is this about Bernardo's offer? Are you saying you want to go with Bernardo?"

"It's a good offer."

"But do you want to go with Bernardo? What about your own company? That was the point of being here, wasn't it? I'm confused." She didn't want to argue, but she didn't know what to say without sounding irritated. Was this another disappointment, another wrong turn? Another reason to leave this disturbing place?

They passed a concrete embankment, the result of a controversial dam that was half-finished and still under dispute between Hungary and the neighboring countries of Slovakia and the Czech Republic. The shoreline was not pretty; there were no quaint fishing villages or other sights she expected to see on a river tour.

"The water is polluted," she said.

"It's not clean." Will stood up. "Do you want a beer?"

"Yes."

The motion and sound of the water had lulled Leo into a deep sleep. As he lay heavy and limp in the crook of her arm, she felt her misery growing, and her confidence in their decision making draining away. Will's leaving Fendix had been a risk. She knew that. But was it stupid? Had they thrown their whole life away? Why was Will here? To satisfy an independent, creative streak? Was he really just a suburban cowboy, chasing a Wild West dream? Going for that gold rush feeling? Others were doing it, therefore, so could he? Will Gordon—WG TeleVenture—the name on his business card. She had encouraged him to come here, to strike gold like the newspapers claimed others were doing. Make a pile of money—on his own. He wanted to help a country eager to embrace technology. Months had passed. What did he have to show for it?

Will handed her a beer. She took a long sip. "I don't know what to say."

"You don't have to say anything. I'm sorry I didn't say something before. I was waiting for a good time, I guess. We were rushing at lunch. There's Bernardo's offer. I've got a few investors circling. We have options."

"Then let's not worry about it for the weekend," she said, touching his arm. "Let's try to have a good time."

In Vienna, they took a cab to their hotel, but she could see they would not be able to let things go. The room Will booked over the phone was supposed to have a king-size bed, but instead the room had twin beds with a night table separating them. A child's crib was folded up in a corner.

"Don't unpack. I'm going to change rooms," he said, walking out.

She followed him back down stairs, Leo on her hip, and waited in the lobby as Will spoke to the concierge, a short man with slicked black hair. She guessed the hotel was built in the 1970s. The lobby's black-and-white interior looked dated.

"I am sorry. We are full tonight," the concierge said. He stood behind a counter and riffled through a book of reservations. "There is nothing I can do about it until tomorrow."

"I asked for a king bed. I'm not paying for twin beds."

"Perhaps we could put the beds together? We will help you do this." The man spoke English with a British accent. "It is the same as a king bed. We have tried this."

It didn't happen often, but Annie saw a wave of fury tightening Will's shoulders, his face flushing with anger.

"Come on. I'll deal with him later," Will said to her.

They went back up to the room. Annie unfolded the crib and began putting her toiletries in the bathroom. Leo toddled at her side, enthralled with the tiny soaps on the sink and miniature bottles of shampoo.

In the mirror, she saw Will lifting the night table over the bed, pushing the beds together.

"What are you doing?" Annie said, coming out of the bathroom to watch.

"I'm moving the beds. I'm not paying money to sleep without my wife in my bed."

"It's just a bed, Will," Annie said. "Leo, be careful. Daddy is moving the beds." They watched Will struggling to push the beds together. The platform beds were solid wood and hard to move.

"Aren't you being silly about this?" she asked.

Leo kept trying to walk over to Will. She kept pulling him back.

"No. I'm not." After several more tries, he broke into a sweat. He gave one twin bed a final push and stood back to look at the beds wedged against each other. "I'll call for king-size sheets." Breathing hard, he lay across the conjoined twin beds and put his hand between the dividing line. "It's not perfect, but it will do."

Leo squirmed in Annie's arms and pointed to Will. "Up up. Bed. Up." She handed Leo over to Will.

"Up you go, bud," Will said. She saw how the touch of Leo's body—fleshy and firm—calmed her husband. Will lifted their son onto the bed and watched him crawl across the dividing line, but Leo's hand slipped into the crevice and got stuck. "Up bed. Up bed." Will rescued his son, picking him up and bouncing him on his knees. Leo shrieked gleefully, flinging his head backward.

"Watch him, honey," Annie said.

"You don't need to tell me."

He raised Leo high over his head.

THE NEXT DAY they walked around Vienna's historic town center, avoiding the topic of money and the poor sleep they both had due to the crack in the middle of the two beds. Leo slept fine in his portable crib, but Annie kept sliding toward the crack then waking up each time she felt herself falling in. To compensate, she kept repositioning herself back on the opposite side of the bed. Will, in order to stay close to her, stretched his leg across the dividing line every time he sensed her moving away. By early morning, the two ended up squeezed together on one twin bed. As a result, Will's back ached and Annie's neck hurt.

An umbrella of clouds cooled the morning air as they walked across cobblestones soaked in gold-plated, invisible ether. Not a speck of litter anywhere. Annie couldn't get over the enormity of the buildings and the opulence. No beggars or Gypsies—Roma—on the streets. Even the rooftops in the buildings surrounding the old square gleamed with glass that fronted striking penthouse residences she guessed cost multimillions. All this opulence a mere four-hour ferry or car ride away from Budapest. She thought about what Stephen had said and wondered what he was doing today.

Free of the Russians after the war, Austria had prospered. In Vienna, trolleys circling on metal tracks didn't squeak. They swished like ladies dancing in fancy ball dresses. Oddly, the city's perfection felt antiseptic, as if it were missing something alive and breathing— as if the gestalt of energy and art had passed through the town years ago and moved on to somewhere else—possibly to rundown, messy, torn-up Budapest. In Austria, remnants of greatness left imprints like fossils: Mozart's old residences, the State Opera House, grand museums. It gave her a different perspective of Hungary.

"It's so mixed up," she said, thinking about how Budapest was once again trying to make a go at something, trying to get into the game of freedom and choice. She stopped to view a private three-story residence, the multiacre estate enclosed by an elaborate wrought-iron fence. A paved driveway circled around to the front of the house where two stone lions flanked a grand columned entrance and porch. She saw thick drapes framing French doors on the first floor.

"Budapest is stretching out its neck, you know?" she said, turning to Will. "It's taking a risk. It's trying." The realization about the disparity between the two cities and their own unsettled situation put her in a more forgiving mood. Thankful for this shift, she reached for Will's hand.

Twenty-one

The molecules of air popped into light. On his bed, lying on his back, he watched as darkness moved like silt, draining from the ceiling, trailing silver across the room, the blue morning light drifting in from the window. This shifting of the earth and sun was the only mechanism in life that seemed to click into place. It made sense—like the wristwatch his father gave him for his bar mitzvah, the hands still circling after sixty-three years. He sat up on the double bed. Dazed. The foam mattress on a hard wooden platform felt good on his back and aching hips, the small night table with its convenient drawer and a reading lamp on top with a torn pink shade orienting him.

He thought back to day one when he had walked around the

three rooms with Ivan. The bed looked primitive to him, but he deemed it sufficient. What did a single man need? Running water. A stove. Ivan unpacked the groceries, filling the refrigerator as Rose had instructed. Coffee. Milk. Cheese. Bread. Eggs. Hungarian sausage, cold cuts. The basics.

"Thank you. Thank you. I'm all set now. Take this."

Edward put an American twenty in Ivan's hand.

"But that is too much," the boy had said.

"Take it. I'll see you in two days. I appreciate the help."

Then he had called Nan.

"I'm here. Getting settled in," he told her on the phone.

"Give me the lay of the land," she said to him. "All the details." Did you check the stove? Is the refrigerator working?"

"I've got all I need." Except for truth and justice, he thought.

"I'll call you tomorrow," she said.

"Good. Okay. Thank you."

"Dad?"

"What."

"You don't have to thank me. I'm not a stranger."

THIS MORNING, EDWARD thought he smelled rain in the air. He stood, felt himself keeling, and found the wall for balance, pulling back the shade to peek at the dull gray sky. Patience. It was tricky. Hold on to something. This was the moment every day since Deborah's death when the enormous tide of his battered life returned to him—a turgid river carrying the weight of all that went wrong. He would find the sleazeball who had killed his daughter. Lord knows he had stopped believing in anything after Deborah died, after Sylvia died. Except what was right. No one wanted to talk about a murdered child. His friends, the ones still living, the ones who had retired to condos in Florida, patted him on the shoulder, called him a few times a month. *Come down for the winter, Ed. Spend a few weeks in the sun. It will do you good.*

Waiting.

They waited for him to come around. Nan waited. But he had no intention of giving up.

In the tiny bathroom, he uncapped his vial of heart pills. They were supposed to help his arrhythmia, but they made him sluggish, too. Jesus Christ. He'd survived a war. But this—he fumbled with the tiny bottle, pitched two capsules into the back of his throat, then swallowed and went to the night table drawer for his cell phone. The gun lay there, too, at the back of the drawer. Resting.

GETTING TO THE doctor who prescribed his pills, Dr. Zoltan Igor—last name first in this backward country—was a royal pain in the ass: a bus ride up those steep Buda hills to the stop on the corner in front of the doctor's mother's house, a one-story stucco building, neat and clean, with trimmed hedges on either side of a pathway, an examining room in back of the house.

Zoltan checked him out the week he arrived, wrote prescriptions. Next visit, if he needed it, Edward would take a cab. He was through with buses. The last visit put him out of commission for days. No. He shook his head at himself. Too angry to die—that's what I am. God's little comedy. Making him work for his death like it was something he wanted but couldn't have.

A WEEK AFTER shooting holes through a can of chicken soup that he had placed on a tree stump in his backyard, Sylvia told him to stop. What was he doing with a gun? she wanted to know. Who was he? She didn't know her own husband anymore.

"*Sylvia, I'm still the man you married, but if that bastard shows up at my house again, I'll shoot him in the neck.*"

"*And what will that do for us, Edward? Get her back? You'll end up in jail.*"

Edward lumbered across the living room and headed for the kitchen to make coffee. He knew he was mentally in the danger zone now, careening down those highways of thought that drove him across bleak, empty plains, deserts of nothingness.

After the funeral, that shit of a husband held his hand out to Edward, his eyes looking like soggy pools of gray-green mud. This, in their kitchen in Newton. Too many people crowding the rooms. Edward ignored Howard's hand.

"I'm shattered," Howard said. "I don't know what to do. She was my life." He bent over and started crying, sobbing.

"Sit," Sylvia told him, pointing to the kitchen chair.

"I'm sorry," Howard said. "I can't believe this."

Edward heard the words, but his skin still itched. Something didn't add up. This stranger who was ten years younger than his daughter. Deborah hardly knew him, and within months she was married to him. No wedding ceremony. No announcement. Just married. A phone call one day telling them.

"Married? You're married?" Sylvia said over and over.

But, then, that was part of the problem: Deborah's adult life was a secret. She'd had so many boyfriends, they'd stopped counting. How many fights had he had with her over this? *Why can't you settle down? What's the matter with you?* Then came the weakness in her limbs that turned into multiple sclerosis. After that, the medications and prescriptions. Expensive, too much money for her. But it seemed to sober her up. She called more often, asked him to come visit. He sent her a check once a month to help out. He put aside money. She took a new job at an insurance company down-town, one with benefits, paid vacation time. They didn't mind her wheelchair, she said. They let her work at home sometimes.

She said.

Edward crossed the living room again, past the couch and the fans and into the bedroom, the shades pulled to the sill, the light still coming through, unstoppable.

He sat on the bed and took the compact gun out of the drawer. Good and light, made for personal protection, easy to conceal. That's what anyone would think of an old man alone in the world, a man who had been robbed of his daughter. He told Sylvia he'd gotten the gun because he didn't trust Howard, but she didn't be-lieve him. *Ach.* He put it back in the drawer. He'd shot a round in the backyard, into the woods behind his house where Sylvia never liked to go. Shooting came back to him like riding a bike. Easy. Automatic. The army had trained him well. Those twelve weeks in Alabama. Started off fat as an overripe pear when he left home, took the train from Boston and headed south. Three months later, his clothes fit another man twice as big. He was lean. All muscle.

Edward got up again and went back to the kitchen; scoops of coffee grounds had spilled onto the countertop. Christ. What a mess. He was a mess. He looked down at himself. Soft. Gangly legs. A belly, from bread and years of overeating: deli sandwiches, Chinese food, butter. He sponged the black specks of coffee into the sink, poured himself a glass of water. Always, the water.

In the living room, he shuffled to the window and tilted his easel, pulling up the shade for a full view of the redbrick building opposite his and of the wedge of sky above a break in the trees and, farther down, a glance at gray, pitted buildings, a memory of what was once grand like everything else around here. Memories of disaster, loss, stunted dreams. Even the boy, Ivan, only sixteen, looked old and serious.

He turned to his half-finished painting of a landscape, the thin handle of the brush smooth, easy to maneuver, the stiff bristles jabbing grays and blues, creating his version of the sky and then the dark hills, adding a dip of cream into the mix and merging the edges, because nothing was sharp. The sky shaped itself into a silken surface—fuzzy and distant, the smell of oil paint rising, taking him away.

Twenty-two

While he painted, he waited for Annie to come. She would be back from Vienna now. It was early, but she would run here. He was confident of that. A few days and she would forgive him for getting angry. Damn words. He was done with words. Standing at the window, the fan blowing, he shifted the easel just so—to make the day's humid light splay evenly across the small canvas. Already, the sun was pushing through. He believed she would come. He knew she would.

He painted because it took words away. He painted landscapes because they took him away from people. Landscapes spoke the truth. A hill was a hill. A sky was a sky. A cloud was a cloud. Simple. Goddamn truth.

He dabbed the upper corner of the canvas, the stiff brush dipped in steel blue now. The gun safely stored in the bedroom drawer. No words for that.

Dad. Please. Give it more time, Nan had said when he told her he had to go to Hungary. She didn't know about the gun.

You come to the end of your life. Time ends. *Pffft.*

He began painting again after Deborah died. He had been a dabbler in high school. After the war, he'd settled into the serious business of getting married, making money, raising a family—two daughters. He didn't have time for paints. Now time was all he had. Time was all anyone had in this life. That was the goddamn truth.

And then Sylvia had a heart attack, and his wife gone, too, within minutes. Never got to the hospital. Now he was deaf to the world, his heart screaming. His mind unable to sleep.

You lose a child, you blame each other. Sylvia left him, then she died. They hadn't planned on that. Married forty-nine years. Jesus.

After he buried Sylvia, he went to the rabbi to talk. He couldn't make sense of it. What kind of curse is this? My older daughter and my wife?

"Edward, this will sound like pabulum, but in times like these, what you've been through, you have to reach inside yourself and forgive. It will lead you through your terrible pain."

Pain? What did this young rabbi know of pain? Edward sat on a wooden chair in the rabbi's study, the gun in his pocket a satisfying weight. A simple transaction at a gun show. Unbelievable. Easy as buying a mouse trap at a hardware store.

No effort at all.

Forgive?

This man, this rabbi in his forties, pontificating. Words. Forgive? Forgive whom? God?

Bull crap.

Just then he made up his mind. No time for waiting. You take action. He'd learned this from his business. Sales taught him that. You picked up the phone, you made that cold call. If the person on the line said "no thanks"—and most did—you hung up and dialed a new number. You didn't think, now what? You made another call. You didn't wait.

He put his brush down.

Fatigued and only midmorning. He considered the idea of going out. He could walk by the river. Sit on a bench. Wait. Watch for a chance to spot Howard. Howard lived by the river. He lived by the river. He lived by the river.

Foolishness. He knew it. He shook his head, exhaling. The circulation in his legs. Dangerous. Stupid. He knew this. He had to come up with an alternative plan. These things happened in business. You get a flash of what you need to do, and then you realize it's too expensive to implement or you don't have enough manpower. So you regroup. You come up with something different. Another approach. Often, a better one.

Edward felt his heart. He took his glass of water, tipped it, stared into the clear reflection of liquid, the thick line rimming the top, draining it.

And the vision repeated itself.

He slid open the peephole cover and saw him standing with his hands at his side. The boy stood in the kitchen. Edward waved at him to be still.

"It's Van. Van Howard, sir."

Edward opened the door.

"What are you doing here?" He talked over the chain holding the door, blocking the opening.

"*I'm living here. You know that. In Pest. Near the river. Nan gave me your address but not your phone. Did she tell you?*"

"*Yes, she did. What took you so long?*"

Edward leaned his shoulder against the doorframe.

"*In her letter. A few weeks ago. I wanted to give you time to settle in.*" *Howard looked behind him in the hall.* "*Could we talk inside?*"

Edward stepped aside.

"*What are you doing, Howard?*"

"*What do you mean?*"

Howard gave off an odor of sweet aftershave. It infuriated him. Edward said, "*Do you think you can get away with it?*"

"*I don't know what you're talking about.*"

Howard shook his head, then opened and closed his hands. Edward stepped back into the room, glad the boy was still in the kitchen.

He wished he had said, *Ivan, come here.* He wished the boy had come to his side and held out his hand to Howard. He didn't expect to act out of fear.

"This is Ivan," Edward said now, then watched Howard shake the boy's hand.

The idea that Howard might try to murder him stunned Edward; the thought bolted through his body. He didn't expect that. He was an old man. Howard could strangle him and no one would notice. He could slip drugs into his coffee. But Ivan was there. He acted in fear. Blew it.

"*I'm afraid I've upset you. I'll come back another time and we'll talk.*"

Howard turned.

"*You're not a talker. You're a liar. Get out!*"

The words propelled out of his mouth like a mortar, exploding.

Bang. Oh, he had a long, long history of this. Words. Stinking up the whole goddamn business.

"You won't get away with this! Do you hear me?" he yelled at Howard as he watched him run down the stairs, out of sight.

He went through this scenario again and again. Hating himself. Days went by. Six. Then a miracle. Nan called to tell him: another letter from Budapest. PO box. Zip code. A clue.

> *Dear Nan,*
>
>   *As I wrote previously, I hope your father will come to understand that there are more sides to this story. Thank you for letting me know where to find him. He was not receptive.*
>
> *With the best intentions,*
>
> *Van*

Outside, trucks were moving down the street, making deliveries. He heard the brakes, the shifting gears. It was the noise of the city, the urban machine cranking into operation for another day of commerce. Time passing. Time he didn't have. *Maybe you didn't know Deborah the way I did*, Howard had said to him when Edward questioned him after the funeral.

Edward headed back to the kitchen for another cup of coffee, his last for the day, his heart skipping and skidding without brakes. He waited for the fluttering to stop, then turned toward the window and set the dial on the air conditioner to high. It dripped a small pool of water on the kitchen floor. Leaning over, he wiped it up, his body an axis around which the universe swirled and pivoted. She would show up soon. After her run.

Back in the living room, he took in the larger view of things, his paintings stacked on the floor. He took a step toward them, then stopped and went over to the couch. The apartment fan blew warm air across his neck, its motor making a dull, clattering sound, a sound he liked. It was part of his silence. Still, he could hear Nan's voice. *Dad. Please.*

What?

He turned his ear toward a sound of knocking, a gentle knocking on his triple-bolted door.

Twenty-three

Through the peephole, she lifted her hand in greeting.
"One minute."

He unbolted the chain, opened the door, waited for her to enter, then locked the door. She was a pretty young woman, a good six inches shorter than his Deborah, who slumped because of her height.

"I'm here to help," Annie said.

He nodded. "Good. I thought you would."

He pointed toward the kitchen. "Help yourself to coffee. Sugar. Milk. It's all there."

She looked at him and smiled, not moving. "I'm all set. Have you been out today?"

"No. Why?"

"I wondered if you ever went out."

She shifted her weight onto one leg.

"Sometimes. How was your trip to Vienna?"

"It was okay."

"You don't sound excited."

She shrugged. "Seemed like a caricature of itself. Like every-thing had already happened there. Anyway, I'm glad to be here to help you. I had time to think about our conversation. If I were in your shoes, I'd want someone to help me. Not be afraid. Isn't that the point of all this? Not to be afraid?" She put a hand on her hip. She looked almost girlish—not a wrinkle on her face or neck. "I tried to imagine if someone took my son."

"You can't."

"Yes. Of course." She crossed her arms. "You said this man lives near the river. Do you have a picture?"

"Just a minute."

He went into the bedroom and took the ripped photo from the night table drawer. When he returned, she was looking at the framed photo of Deborah.

"Here."

He sat on the couch and watched her. She had the smooth skin of youth,—that time in his life, long vanished, as if he'd never lived it. A picture. Yes. He had a torn picture. It serrated his thoughts, but he forced himself to keep it in view, imprint the bastard's plain face in his mind. Light hair, square forehead, greenish brown eyes. Small chin. He might see him somewhere. A sidewalk. A street.

"He's tall. Tall as your husband."

She kept staring at the torn picture, shaking her head, disbeliev-ing. "I know him. I've met him." She handed the photo to Edward but didn't look him in the eye.

"What is it, Annie?"

"It can't be." She swept her hair back behind her ears and turned toward the kitchen. "Stephen Házy. He's American. A translator. His hair is short with longish bangs. But his face is the same. The color of his hair. We have his phone number on a business card at home." She shook her head. "How can this be?"

"He's a liar. I told you that." Edward felt his blood charging into his chest, a rise of anger. "Get that number for me, will you? How old are you, Annie?"

"Thirty-three. Why?" She took a seat in the chair across from him.

Always in those running shorts. Americans and their exercise regimes. Where did it get them?

"He's about your age."

She unclasped her hands. "Yes. That's what it seemed. Is it possible? You said he was here? You really think it's the same person with a different name?"

"I told you. He's a liar!" he shouted. "You're no different. You don't believe me. No one believes the truth when it's in their goddamn faces."

"I'm trying," she said.

"Please. Annie. Listen to me. He's here. I'm telling you. He's near the river. Near a statue on the river. He'll show up again. My younger daughter, Nan, got another letter from him."

She leaned toward him. "He was very nice to us. Helpful." She sighed and rubbed her eyes.

"Polite. You see? Just what you said. You've met him. But you're thinking he couldn't possibly be . . . Sylvia, my wife, she thought that. Deborah obviously did. Nan, she's not saying."

"He was polite. He seemed genuine. I liked him."

"Jesus. You see? Didn't I tell you that?"

"I'm trying to understand. What about the letter? What did he say?"

His blood tide subsided. He gulped another half glass of water. "Said there were more sides to the story than mine." Edward snorted. Huffed his hot breath. "Liar. Nothing worse than a liar. Listen. You may not think he did anything to my daughter. Drug overdose, my ass. That I know. You may decide that I'm crazy. That's your prerogative."

He looked at her, waiting. He was tiring of this, but he had to keep going—she could help him. He needed that phone number. He would get the number and, from there, the address.

"I'm confused. It's confusing." She put two fingers on her lips, thinking. "I don't think you would have come this far if you didn't believe it was true. But . . ."

She crossed her legs. She had beautifully toned legs. No veins or imperfections scarring her calves or thighs. Youth. Such a waste. The light from the window outlined her body and she seemed for a moment to be floating in front of him, hovering in his gray apartment on a saucer of air.

"I trust Rose," she said.

A feeling of fatigue. Sudden. Like a wind dying down to nothing. Flat. Stillness. He needed that number, but he'd scared her again. The police back home didn't want to investigate. Case closed. It was black and white. Simple. Why screw up their lives for an old, fart, an old *Jewish* fart?

"What about your husband? What's he say about all this? Your coming here."

She squirmed in the chair, uncrossed and crossed her legs.

"Oh, I get it. He thinks I'm a crazy old bastard, too."

"It's not that."

"What, then? Come on. Spit it out."

"Nothing. He'll be fine. He worries, that's all."

"You're not telling me everything. Come on, Annie. Be straight. Get it out. Say it."

She turned her hands over, both palms lifting something invisible toward him, like a plate or gift.

"It's mostly that he thinks I sometimes get overly involved in trying to help."

"Like my Deborah. We talked about that, and about your sister."

"Yes. My sister and my brother."

He waited, but he needed to know more. Nan had a sick sister. Nan spent her days helping sick people. What made these helpers tick? What was the attraction? Annie had everything a person needed and yet she was here in this crippled city.

"You told me your sister's name."

"Tracy. Her brain injury happened when I was four. A long time ago." She stopped and looked at the floor.

"Where is she now?"

"In a group home."

"A life wasted," Edward said.

"No, no—" She looked up at him, her mouth grim. "Please don't think of it that way. Please. It's not fair to her or my brother."

"Point taken," he said. "Tell me about them."

"Tracy's in a wheelchair. She needs round-the-clock care. She was normal before the accident. I don't talk about this." She paused to fidget with the bottom edge of her T-shirt. "I told you my brother died five years ago. Took his life. He jumped from the scaffolding of a building. He was thirty-one."

He began to see that what she presented was not at all who she was.

"Was he married?"

"No. He never married. He was alone," she said, glaring at him. "Like you, I don't want pity from people. I don't talk about these things because it scares people."

"So you help others because it's safer."

"Maybe. Something like that. It depends."

"Why don't you help your sister? She's alive. Your brother is dead. You can't do anything about that."

She flinched, let out a muffled yelp, her head in her hands. Goddamn it. She was crying. Jesus.

"Annie. I told you I'm an old fool."

"It's okay, it's okay," she said into her hands. She lifted her face and wiped her eyes, sucking in an exaggerated breath to calm herself.

Would he ever learn? He looked at the worn floor, a pattern of wood zigzagging like the mind of this godforsaken place. He looked up. He'd pushed too far. What else was new? He expected she would take off.

"I'm sorry, Annie."

Instead, she pressed her lips together, almost smiling. "It's okay. It feels good to cry. I thought you hated that word, *sorry*," she said, propping her elbows on her knees, placing her chin in her cupped hands.

He almost smiled back. "I do."

"Well, I like it. *Sorry* is a good word. It travels far."

"Tears make you live longer," he said, remembering his grandmother's words. She had lived to 102.

"How old are you?" Annie asked.

"Seventy-six."

She used the back of her hand to dry her cheek. "And you? Do you cry?"

"Every day."

She looked at him, her blue eyes pale and soft, the color reminding him of hydrangeas on Cape Cod when he and Sylvia and the kids used to go for a week every August. Those mild, salty days. Deborah flapping her arms, heading out into the ocean too far, too deep, and Nan, the sensible one, the younger one who kept close to the shoreline.

Annie's voice brought him back to the living room.

"Mr. Weiss? Do you think he could harm me or you?"

"Or your son?" he said.

She nodded. "If he's what you say he is, he probably knows where we live. I ran into him on your street a week or so ago. He was meeting a client."

"He's a liar."

He looked down at his watch, the gift from his father that had survived everything. Her beautiful son. No. No. This was wrong of him. It was dangerous. He couldn't let her help except in some remote way. He wouldn't put her sweet boy in danger. Out of the question. No. Her husband was right. He had no business asking her for help. No. No. This was wrong of him.

"That's it. We need to quit this."

He pushed himself up from the couch.

"What are you doing?" She stood also.

"Annie, I was wrong." He moved toward the door to let her out. "I thank you for coming, but I've changed my mind about this." He reached the door, unbolted it, and gestured for her to leave.

"I don't know what to say. I don't understand." She moved toward the door.

"It's not you, Annie. It's me. You need to understand this. You have to leave right now. Don't come back here. Don't come to my street. Your husband is right. You've done enough. I thank you for that. You've helped me. You've helped me see something I should have seen before. I'll call you or you call me. Give me that number, but don't come back here. Keep your son away, too. Understand? I've made a terrible mistake."

As soon as Annie left, he went to the living-room window and looked out to watch her walking quickly down the sidewalk. He scanned the shadows of the buildings as she passed them on the way to the boulevard at the far end. His quiet road looked empty right now. He could only hope that Howard wasn't hiding somewhere, watching her.

Twenty-four

Yes, definitely, Stephen Házy resembled the man in the photo, yet she didn't want to believe it could be him. Maybe Edward was crazy. But pictures don't lie, do they? Sometimes they did. It was an old, crumpled photo. The man in the photo had shoulder-length hair pulled back in a ponytail—no bangs. Stephen's hair was short with only those untamed strands that drifted over his eyes. How could these two men be the same? Was she crazy? She felt the tremors of second-guessing herself, the two disparate descriptions of the same person colliding in her head. She hurried home, dripping with sweat and upset with herself. Will would be waiting for her. They had planned a trip to the country to meet that mayor.

"Where have you been? Have you been to Mr. Weiss's again? We need to get going or we'll be late."

"Yes. I was there. I'm sorry. I'll shower and change quickly."

IN THE CAR, she and Will started on the drive west to the small town of Inota. Will was silent, angry silent—she knew by the way his face looked frozen in concentration. She wanted to go with him today so she could meet one of these small-town mayors. Bernardo's job offer was on the table, and though they hadn't talked about it since the ferry ride, she knew Will was considering it seriously. But accepting the offer would mean staying here for another year or two or more. The reality of that was feeling impossible to her. And, now, there was this issue about Stephen, or Van Howard, or whoever he might be.

"Will, what do you know about Stephen Házy?"

"Dave hired him. He's been useful at meetings. You met him. You liked him. He certainly liked you. Why?"

"Mr. Weiss says he's his son-in-law and that his real name is Van Howard."

"Come on, Annie. What are you talking about?"

"This morning. He showed me a photo of his son-in-law. It's the same man. I'm telling you. I saw the photo. Does he know where we live?"

"Probably. He has my card."

"It's the same man, Will. He's using a different name. Why?"

"I don't know. And I don't care. People come here to escape. Maybe he wanted to start a new life. I don't know. You see what you're doing? You're getting wrapped up in it. How is that helping anyone?"

"I don't know." She looked out the window at the huge Russian block apartment buildings. Ugly gray structures with tiny windows. She didn't have a good answer for Will. "I don't know."

"Let's just say it is the same guy. Maybe he wanted a clean break. Maybe it's his business name. He's a translator. He makes good money doing that. I gave his name to Bernardo."

"Okay."

She liked this explanation. Mr. Weiss didn't want her help, anyway. She would give him Stephen's number and leave it at that. It was true what Will said. People came here to get away from their lives. Hadn't she come for a fresh start? Maybe it didn't matter. Maybe Edward was a desperate man. Yet she was unable to dismiss the unpleasant implication of Edward's haunting words. *Keep an eye on your son.* Leo was with Klara. He was napping. Safe in their flat. The door to their apartment locked. Maybe she was losing her sense of sanity. What was she doing here? She didn't want to live here the rest of her life.

Ahead of them, the sky was gray and dull. Inside the car, the weak wafts of air-conditioning smelled like plastic.

"I should have stayed with Leo today."

"You're all over the place. Call Klara if you're worried. She has our number. Calm down."

"Right."

She shifted her body away from Will and took in the long view of the M7 highway. They passed beat-up Ladas—cars the size of scooters with their stinky diesel smell. She knew that Will was right, but she could feel her faith leaking out of her. She wondered where faith came from. If it leaked, could it be replenished? She dialed their landline.

"How's Leo?" she asked Klara when she answered.

"Everything is fine. Something is wrong?"

"No. Please don't let anyone into the house while we're gone. That's all. I got worried."

"Persze," Klara said.

"Annie. You need to calm down," Will said when she hung up. "You've been listening to Edward. Whatever he said to you today, it's eating you up. I can see it in your demeanor. I know you."

"I'm not going there anymore. Okay?"

"I hope you're not just saying that."

"I'm not."

Life here was feeling impossible. *Impossible*—how un-American of her to think this way. How Hungarian. And another thing: she refused to become a trailing spouse, a woman without purpose. A lost soul. She had to think positively. If she pretended that everything were all right, then it would be. The power of intention. Seize control of her circular thoughts.

Will glanced at her. "We'll be fine."

How she wanted to believe him.

"Are you excited about meeting this guy?" she asked.

"I wouldn't call it excited. Anticipatory."

"It must be frustrating, day after day, like a traveling salesman. Knocking on doors. Getting nos all the time."

"That's the nature of the beast. What are you getting at?"

"I'm just saying it's hard."

"I didn't say this would be easy."

"Of course." *Persze.* Not easy was an understatement.

They settled into their separate, private thoughts, the stretch of highway flat for miles ahead, an occasional tree rising like a shadow in the dried-out landscape. She remembered one pivotal morning in October, before they moved here, when Will had awakened from a bad dream. They lay in bed, in the luxury of their gorgeous re-designed bedroom with trey ceiling, moldings, Palladian windows, French doors leading to a new deck, and a master bath the size of another bedroom. Everything appeared perfect on the outside; but on the inside, something else was deteriorating for Will. Leo's arrival sealed the deal for them, urging them both to make a bold move. Life was for living, not waiting cautiously for a better future.

Was this her better future now? It wasn't looking good. She scanned the dull Hungarian horizon for an answer.

On that morning, Will woke up and said, "I don't want to be an old man looking back, wishing this and that." He had just turned forty. She was thirty-two. He gave his notice that week.

She had encouraged him to make a change, to come here. *Do it*, she had said. *She* was the one who insisted he have faith. Dare to follow his dreams. Now she herself was confounded with doubts.

Will slowed as they came up behind a fruit truck—the truck re-minding her of Stephen's cautionary story about this exact highway scenario. So informative and accommodating. She couldn't believe what Edward was saying about him. Except even Edward admitted that most people thought Stephen *was* nice, but that he was a liar. Was it possible that Edward was wrong? Was his pain distorting the truth? Did he have actual proof that the man in the picture had killed his daughter?

She didn't have answers.

"This is why I wanted to leave earlier," Will said. "We're going to be late because of this truck."

"Sorry. I'm sorry."

She stared at the monotonous fields ahead. Again, she tried to keep her mind on the present. If they got stuck behind this fruit truck, it could double their travel time. Inota was twenty minutes outside Székesfehévár, that famous City of Kings. *Famous* was a word that Hungarians overused when describing themselves—famous goulash, famous paprika, famous Herend porcelain—yet it was a word that was justified in many incidences, as with Bartók, the *famous* musician. Well, why not. They deserved world recognition for the good things, didn't they? Most people knew little about this landlocked country called Hungary.

"What did this mayor say?" she finally said.

"Not much. But he's willing to meet. It's a solid town. You never know what it might lead to."

"Right."

But it felt wrong. This wasn't Will. He wasn't a salesman. He was a researcher, a strategist. Bernardo knew this about Will, too, and would do whatever he could to convince him to accept his offer. It was beginning to feel inevitable.

Finally, the fruit truck exited, and so did they a few miles later, onto a small, country road, more gravel than pavement. Picturesque, serene, no cars in sight—gentle hills appeared, more trees, and then she saw them: a few dozen Gypsies—Roma—walking in single file along the road. Men, women and children, pulling wooden carts, carrying bags.

"What in the world are they doing? Where are they going? Slow down!"

"I'm going slow, Annie. I'm not going to stop. That's the town dump over there, where they live."

"Are you serious? How do you know this?"

"I read about it."

The car scattered dust as they drove past the dark-skinned men, women, and children, all of them looking weather worn, their clothes dull with dirt. Then, quickly, the Roma were behind them, growing smaller again, inching toward the dump.

"That was depressing," she said.

"You're making a judgment."

"They didn't look happy. Maybe we should turn around, give them some money," Annie said.

"I'm not going to turn around. I have an appointment. If you're that concerned, why don't you look into volunteer opportunities? You want to help the Gypsies? Good. Do it."

"Roma," she corrected him. "By the way, Mr. Weiss doesn't want me—us—to go his apartment anymore. *At all,*" she said, blurting it out. Angry.

"When did he say that?"

"Today."

"Good. I guess that finally settles that."

"For you, maybe."

"Annie?"

He reached for her hand, but she eased it away.

She needed to calm down. Mr. Weiss had changed his mind. A sudden reversal at the end of her visit. Even an apology. At first she felt relieved, but now she felt hollow, unfinished, unsettled. The issue of Stephen Házy. None of it was adding up. What was the truth? Stephen was nice. She couldn't shake the fact that he had been kind to her, considerate, helpful. He seemed genuine. But why would Stephen change his name? As for getting involved in volunteer work, it would mean taking another step toward attaching herself here in Hungary when in truth she wanted to *get out.*

They drove in silence until Will turned onto another road, this one paved. It led to a small town square. They parked in front of a redbrick one-story building, which looked closed. Even the maple tree next to the building looked forlorn, withered with thirst.

"Sure it's today?" she finally asked.

"This is how they all look."

Inside the building, she followed him across a clean linoleum floor to the mayor's office where a middle-age woman with short dark hair sat at a desk, smoking, guarding the entry. Will introduced himself and asked for the mayor.

"Nem itt," she said. Not here. She turned back to her work.

Will looked across the hall into a large room and an empty chair behind a desk.

"I have an appointment," he said, then struggled to say it in Hungarian.

The woman took a plain piece of typing paper and began to draw a map with arrows. She handed it to him, glancing at Annie for the first time. Annie made an attempt to smile, but the woman ignored her.

"You find him here. His house," she said. "You go. It's okay."

Will took the paper, but Annie could see that he was annoyed by this.

"Does he have a cell phone?" Will asked the woman, his tone insinuating that he knew owning a cell was the ultimate status symbol.

"Igen. Persze." The secretary wrote the numbers on another piece of paper and gave it to him.

Back in the car, Annie waited as Will dialed the mayor, speaking into the phone in halting but serviceable Hungarian when the mayor answered.

"Okay. We're set." Will turned to her and started up the car again. "He's a few streets away."

"Did he forget?"

"No. He's expecting us."

They followed a curved dirt street a few blocks up a hill without trees to a square stucco building at the top of another small hill. She guessed it was a half mile from the town center. Easy walk. Will parked on the road. Together they climbed a dirt driveway. At the top, a backhoe was stationed behind a huge mound of dirt at the side of the house.

"Someone's putting in a new driveway," Will said. A path had been carved out, but more work needed to be done.

A stone walkway led to the front door. Will knocked. They waited. He knocked again. She felt irritated. The mayor knew they were coming. Finally, they heard the lock turning inside. An overweight short man opened the door.

"Hello. Come in. Please. I am sorry. I was on phone."

The familiar Hungarian accent.

Will shook the man's hand and introduced Annie. The mayor nodded and led them down a dark hallway across herringbone-patterned wood floors. He wore an eggplant-colored polyester suit.

"Sit, please," the mayor said, directing them to a brown vinyl couch. The mayor pulled up a chair. An Oriental rug hung on one wall in typical Hungarian fashion. In their own flat, two small Oriental rugs also hung on the living-room walls, like tapestries.

Will took out his pocket dictionary and began to speak in both English and Hungarian. He explained that he wanted to bring cable to the small town.

"Good, but this is impossible," the mayor said. "Who will do this?"

Impossible. The classic Hungarian response. So predictable, Annie thought. The room was dark. Drapes covered the windows.

"I will need permission from official. You understand?" the mayor said.

"I have it right here." Will said, opening a leather folder. He pulled out several papers with embossed seals the size of silver dollars and several signatures in blue fountain ink at the bottom of the pages.

To Annie, they looked like award certificates. Will had explained to her that these seals took weeks to get.

The mayor bent over the papers, picking them up, one by one, and held each to the low light, looking for the watermark. Slowly, he ran his finger over the signatures, back and forth. Clearly, it was a method, a ritual the mayor had learned years ago, like rolling a cigarette. She expected him to spit on the paper to see if it would stand up to the test, but he didn't. She guessed the mayor was in his fifties because of a balding spot in the back of his head.

Then, as if something in him clicked, the mayor accepted the official seals as authentic. He smiled and took a pack of cigarettes from his shirt pocket, offering one to Will and Annie in confirmation.

"*Kérem,*" the mayor said. "Please."

"*Nem köszönöm.* But please help yourself," Will said, opening his palms like a book. My wife and I don't smoke."

"*Persze.* Americans."

The mayor lit up and exhaled a messy stream of smoke, then pushed the papers back to Will again. "I think about this."

"Good," Will said. "It's a good opportunity for your town. A good source of money."

"*Igen,*" the mayor said, nodding. "*Pálinka* before you go? I'm sorry my English."

"Your English is very good," Annie said, smiling.

"We'd love some *pálinka*," Will said.

The mayor left the room and returned with three small glasses and a bottle of pear liqueur. They clinked glasses. Annie did her best to sip the liquid that was sweet and warm in her throat, thinking what an odd moment this was in the mayor's dim, sparely furnished house. She wondered if the mayor had children or a wife.

"Very good," Will said.

"How do you like our country?" the mayor asked.

"*Jól*, good. A good time to be here. Good opportunities."

The mayor nodded. "*Igen*. Many, many changes. Some good. Some not so good. Not good for old people."

"So I understand."

"Why?" Annie asked.

"No work, no money." The mayor made that universal gesture for cash, his thumb rubbing circles against two fingers. "Prices up. Pension down." He turned his thumb up, then down. "You understand?"

Annie nodded. "And the Roma?"

The mayor made a spitting gesture.

"Gypsies? *Nem* good. A big *probléma* for Hungary."

Annie regretted asking the question. Will finished his drink, stood up and gave the mayor his card. The two men shook hands.

"Thank you very much. I look forward to doing business with you," Will said.

When they settled back in the car, Will said, "Now you see what I deal with."

She wanted to reach over to him and tell him that he should keep at it, but her heart held her back. She kept her hands in her lap. She couldn't lie to herself. Edward had helped her in that way. This trip to nowhere. It felt like a dead end. "I don't know how you do it," she said.

They rode in silence, the tires thrumming the road until Will fed a cassette into the tape player, his favorite compilation of classic rock songs: Allman Brothers live in concert; the Beatles; Led Zeppelin. She told herself to be patient. Success didn't happen overnight—whatever success meant. Edward was right: *Success is a phony word.* She sighed.

"What is it?" Will asked.

"Nothing."

She had run out of things to say. That was her problem. Their problem. This inability to find words to make things better. It was so much easier to say nothing. She felt the seductive pull of it. Stop speaking. Sink into quicksand. Become silent. Pretend things will be okay. Sink into silence as if it could protect her from the noise of life above and all around her. It was an old family habit, this silence. She leaned back in the seat, the music and the wheezing rush of the air conditioner meshing together. Silence was the phantom body in her family. Her sister's injury and, later, Greg's death in Florida. All those years drinking himself into silence, then falling to his end, a purposeful slip from a scaffold. He had waited until everyone had gone home. It was dark. They found him the following morning, his crumpled body. A stain of blood near his head. She disliked the word *suicide.* Sometimes she thought of it as liberation, his heart's release. But all of it was death in the end.

She sighed again.

"Maybe it will finally rain," she said, an effort to get out of the flooding in her mind as they approached the city. It was late afternoon and the beginning of rush hour. Clouds torn and heavy with rain amassed overhead.

"We'll be okay," Will said, squeezing her leg, but she didn't feel reassured. "We have to stay positive."

"It's getting harder. I'm having trouble breathing." She huffed in the car's weak, recycled air.

"Open your window. We're almost home. You'll feel better."

Will pumped the brakes and slowed to a near stop, inching along as feeder roads merged and became one avenue jammed with odorous Ladas. A bus cut in front of them. A Mercedes bullied its way between two lanes to reach the head of the line, where cars had stopped for a red light. A policeman standing on the side of the road walked out into the middle of traffic, stopped in front of their car, and pointed at Will, directing him to move off the road to a space in the breakdown lane behind a parked police car.

"Why's he pointing at us?"

"I have no idea," Will said. He eased out of the line and parked behind the police car as instructed.

"We weren't speeding," she said. "What's the problem?"

"I don't know." He rolled down his window.

The policeman walked over to Will's side.

"Do you speak English? We're American," Will said.

The officer shook his head. He walked to the front of the car and pointed.

"*Nem.*" The officer had a medium build, thin lips. He said something else, which Annie didn't understand but apparently Will did.

"We need those papers," Will said to her. "They're in the compartment."

Quickly and nervously, she handed Will the paper he had filled

out at the police station. Will gave them to the officer, who signaled
to a second officer sitting in the parked police car.

"What's the problem?" she asked again. "We haven't done
anything."

"Hold on."

The second officer came up to the window.

"You are American?" he said.

"Yes."

The officer strolled to the back, compared the numbers on the
plate with the papers in his hand, then resumed his position at the
open window again.

What did he want?

The officer leaned into the car to look at Annie.

"My wife," Will said. He said it again in Hungarian.

"Hello," Annie said, unable to force a smile. She felt scared,
not knowing the rules, not knowing how she should behave in this
context.

The officer nodded. She thought he appeared satisfied, yet he
surveyed their car once more, up and down, in and out, front and
back. Annie felt half-undressed, as if he were trying to strip them
of something. Finally, the man leaned in and returned the papers
to Will. Without looking at them again, the policeman stood back
and waved them on.

Oh, yes. They needed those papers. Once again, Stephen was
right.

Twenty-five

Burtz!" Leo said, pointing.

Annie followed him as he toddled after a lone pigeon on the walkway that circled the top of Castle Hill. And there it was: the spectacular view across the valley, reminding her why Will suggested Bernardo meet them up here. The view took in the entire flat side of Pest from this high vantage point. Below she could see Budapest's density and size, its possibility. Its immensity surprised her every time, spreading out like an ancient sea basin, sediments of centuries left behind, the present oozing into the horizon, simmering, active, mercurial, alive.

"Come on, Leo. Let's go see Daddy and his friends. This way." They crossed the cobblestone square.

Will stood at the entrance of the Hilton Hotel wearing his casual business attire: khaki pants, white Brooks Brothers shirt, no tie this morning, waiting for Bernardo to show up. She waved and he waved back, squinting at the sun, tilting his head up as if the sky might offer her husband insight. This wasn't just another meeting with Bernardo; this time Bernardo had specifically asked Will to bring her and Leo along for breakfast.

German tourists also gathered outside the hotel entrance, pointing at the old stone exterior. She watched them marveling as she had when she first arrived here. Stone walls and crooked gates charmed them as she had been charmed. But Budapest's premiere hotel needed an interior face-lift; its monastic origins and Gothic tower remained at odds with its dated seventies' decor inside. And with the brand-new hotel downtown, it had competition, a newer, uncomfortable concept for Hungary, the old communist mentality still hanging on.

She looked at her watch. Normally Bernardo was punctual, but today he was already ten minutes late. Will looked at her again, nodded toward the entrance door, and went in. She followed. Inside the dining area, brown carpeting, dark tables, and dim lighting made for a lackluster atmosphere. Where had Hungarians been these past five decades? Living in their minds, living in dreams, waiting for tomorrow with no money for repairs and no competition to spur them to make changes. It was inconceivable to an American, this waiting for tomorrow. She corrected herself—inconceivable to a *privileged* American. She'd been waiting less than a year for Will's business to pick up, and at this point she was barely holding on.

"You wish for breakfast?" the maître d' asked her. He was tall and lean, clothed all in black except for a red vest.

"*Igen*. May I take this with me?" She pointed to the jogger.

"*Igen*. At your pleasure."

She rolled the bike across the carpet to a table by the windows. In an unlit corner, two Hungarian businessmen smoked and sipped on cups of Hungary's thick coffee. One man had a noticeable paunch and bloated face. His companion was gaunt. Both wore black suits with the kind of sheen that comes from too much wear—maybe the only suits they owned.

She sat down beside Will, next to the big glass windows, and that hundred-mile view across the river and the flatlands of Pest. The maître d' positioned a high chair for Leo.

"I think they're former communist insiders trying to make it in the new world and not faring well," she said to Will, tilting her head toward the men in the corner.

He winked at her, bemused. "It's possible."

"It's not farfetched," she said. She saw suspicion in their grim, nervous eyes, as she had in the eyes of so many Hungarians as they inched their way toward a new and uncertain world of social democracy. More signs of it in their stained fingers—she couldn't stand the smell of their cigarettes. She pulled the high-chair straps around Leo's waist and handed him a bottle.

When would Hungry ban cigarettes from restaurants? she wondered. Pollution was a soaring problem in the city. Children who lived in Budapest had a 10 percent higher chance of developing asthma than those living in the countryside. It worried her. Was she risking Leo's health? They lived on the seventh floor, which, their doctor said, assured them of cleaner air. Again, she saw her mother standing at the kitchen sink in Maine, her silver hair pulled taut in an old-fashioned French bun: *But, Annie. What is it about Hungary?* Indeed.

"Change is hard," Will said, raising his hand to signal the waiter.

The maître d' leaned over their table, glancing in the direction of the jogger.

"Is it in the way?" Annie asked. She had parked the stroller next to the window.

"It is good."

"Coffee. Four, please," Will said, holding up four fingers. "Toast for the baby."

"Louds," Leo said, pointing out the picture window.

A stretch of clouds hovered over the Duna below, the river looking dull as a strip of pavement.

Bernardo stepped into the room, accompanied by Stephen Házy.

"Jesus. I couldn't find a parking space up here. It's like New York, for chrissake."

"Ordered coffee," Will said. "Next time I'll take you up on the funicular. Goes straight up the hill. That's what we took."

Bernardo laughed. "I bet Leo likes it. How you doing, fella?" Bernardo rubbed Leo's head.

"Louds," Leo said, pointing at the window.

"That's right, my boy. Can't wait for my little Bernie to meet you. You're gonna get along great."

"I believe you all have met before," Bernardo said. "Will's wife, Annie, and their son, Leo."

"Good to see you again," Stephen said, smiling at Annie. He sat in the chair opposite Will, reaching across the table to shake first Will's hand, then Annie's. "Feels like we're old friends already."

"Yes. It seems that way." She felt an initial rush of warmth toward him but checked herself. His face was the same as the one in

Edward's photo. There was no doubt. But what did that mean? So what if he altered his name—did that prove he murdered his wife?

"Stephen's got a place here on the river. Cost him nada. Absolutely nada, tell them," Bernardo said.

"It's all relative," Stephen said.

"Tell them what you paid for it."

Annie felt embarrassed by Bernardo's crass insistence, but she also felt a chill of recognition—the fact that he lived by the river fit Edward's story. But, then, what did that really signify? Plenty of people lived by the river. She and Will lived *near* the river. Across the table, she could smell the cigarette smoke on Stephen's clothing.

"I'm sure you paid next to nothing," Will said.

"Don't embarrass him," she said to Bernardo. She avoided Stephen's eyes, busying herself with utensils, Leo's napkin, and her water glass. Wanting to believe he wasn't what Mr. Weiss insisted he was, wanting to believe what she saw in front of her was a handsome, gentle man who lost his father in a horrendous tragedy, who had come back to reclaim his father's home.

"Louds!" Leo said, pointing to Stephen.

Stephen touched Leo's nose. "You're a funny, sweet kid."

"Come on. Tell them what you paid," Bernardo said.

"Around twenty thousand."

"Hear that?" Bernardo said, looking at Annie and Will.

Annie took her camera out of the jogger's back pocket and handed it to Leo. He loved gadgets. It would keep him absorbed while the adults talked.

"Kimrah," Leo said, walking his fingers over the buttons.

The maître d' returned with a pot of coffee and a basket of

croissants that he placed in the center of the table. He handed Annie a plate with toast for Leo, then began filling everyone's cups.

"Stephen is our man," Bernardo said, taking a croissant and tearing off a piece. "With his fluency, he can help us roll out this plan. We're talking millions over the next couple of years. Hear me out, Will. Don't close the door on me yet." Bernardo devoured the pastry and gave Annie his best I-know-I need-to-win-you-over smile.

She tried to be receptive to him, knowing he would see through any attempt she made to be fake. And she knew he wasn't all hot air. He actually had the money, a lot of money to get Will started. This is what private venture people did. They raised money and wrote checks. Her skin was humming. She cut the toast in half for Leo, who immediately began sucking on the bread.

Stephen crouched over the table, stirring in heaping spoonfuls of sugar, his head moving slowly over his cup of steaming coffee like someone just waking up or wrestling with a cold. He took a handkerchief out of his jacket and wiped his nose, shaking his head when Bernardo pushed the basket of croissants closer to him.

"Are you sick?" Annie asked Stephen.

"No. No. I have allergies." He fluttered his handkerchief as if to wave away the concern.

Bernardo started counting on his fingers, mentioning more figures, shifting to his get-down-to-business posture: hunching his shoulders, gesturing with his thick hands, his eyes sucking in everybody's body language, searching for clues. Annie recognized the behavior from their Fendix days. Bat around some jokes, get everybody feeling loose, practically lying on their backs showing their bellies, then lasso them and take them down.

"We're set up to bring in the cash now and that's what we want," Bernardo continued. Labor's cheap here. Hungarians are smart, aren't they Stephen? Will, I don't have to tell you the demand for cable and internet is insatiable worldwide. We get set up, save on labor costs—because they're the killer. Stephen's got the language—fluent in Hungarian, God bless him—and Will, you'll keep things flowing with your analytic mind."

Annie rubbed her eyes, using the temporary darkness to re-imagine Stephen with long hair. No question. He was the man in Mr. Weiss's picture. She wanted to grab Leo and run. Instead, she took a sip of her coffee and put a croissant on her plate, but she had no appetite.

"How long do you plan to stay here?" Will said to Stephen.

"Not sure. I don't have plans to leave, if that's what you're asking."

"Just curious." Will opened up a small jar of jam that was on the table and spread some on top of his croissant before biting into the pastry.

"I like it here," Stephen said.

"And you still have family here?" Will asked, probing.

"You're a man of questions this morning," Bernardo said to Will, obviously enjoying Will's interrogations.

Now she could see it: Stephen's greenish-gray eyes—even the soft-spoken way in which he laid out the facts—his Hungarian side as he put it. How could he show up like this? She felt that wrinkle of insanity, her mind trying to coordinate two opposing versions of who he was. Here he was in the center of their life. The timing was too perfect. Or was it a bizarre coincidence? Had he been watching them? Had he seen her visit Mr. Weiss? She felt hot despite the restaurant's air-conditioning, and though she heard Stephen respond to Will's question, Stephen's words didn't register.

"An uncle in the southern part of the country. I told Annie when I ran into her the other day."

Will's face rippled with surprise and Annie felt guilty for not having mentioned running into Stephen at the Bem József statue.

"It's a sad situation there, isn't it?" Will said. "The refugees are pouring in across the border."

"Yes. It's been a bloody massacre," Stephen said. "Americans, as usual, don't have a clue and don't want to hear about it—or help."

"What do you mean by that, bud?" Bernardo asked Stephen.

"You look at history. The '56 uprising here. A good example. Where were the Americans?"

"We should have stepped in," Will said.

"What do your parents say about it now?" Bernardo said. He finished his croissant and put another one on his plate.

"They don't. It killed my father. My mother suffers from depression. She checked out years ago."

That stopped everyone from speaking. Stephen looked down at the table, a terrible sadness passing across his face. He clenched his jaw. "My father killed himself. He couldn't take it."

"Stephen, man. I'm sorry. That's tragic," Bernardo said.

"Forgive me," Stephen said.

"It's terribly sad," Annie said, her clarity returning. "Terrible." She wondered if Mr. Weiss understood this about Stephen's family history. How it obviously informed everything Stephen did and why he had returned to Budapest, to right something that had gone horrifically wrong.

A waiter stopped in front of the table and carefully refilled their cups with coffee. Stephen spoke to the waiter in Hungarian. His words murmuring, soft as a secret. It's how the Hungarian language sounded to her: gentle, nonintrusive, quiet. The waiter left.

"There you go," Bernardo said, pointing to his new man. "He speaks the language. You're a rare breed, Stephen."

"Sorry. Don't mean to be a downer."

"Not to worry, my friend. We appreciate your honesty," Bernardo said.

Typical of Bernardo. He fawned on new people—as he had with Harrison—until he fired them. The favored person became the "it" man until the next anointed one came along. Will had managed to sidestep this pattern by keeping his distance.

Leo made a shushing sound with his lips, something he did when he was around Hungarian speakers.

"He speaks, too?" Stephen said, his eyes on her, sluggish in their movement.

"He's learned a few words from our babysitter."

"Stephen is our ticket to paradise," Bernardo said, overstating things as usual. "Our personnel manager speaks poor English and she's been prickly to deal with. I'm telling you the Fates served up Stephen on a silver platter."

Annie reached for her glass of water. Her throat felt sticky, her lungs constricted. It was too close and surreal, the reality of Stephen's sitting here, the possibility that she had fallen for a set of lies—but whose?

"You exaggerate. I'm not that special," Stephen said. "But I'm happy to help."

"Good," Bernardo said, looking around the table for everyone's affirmation.

Annie didn't say anything.

"Annie, you're looking extra spectacular today," Bernardo said, noticing how quiet she had become. "Did I tell you Eileen's flying over tomorrow?"

"Wonderful. Have her call me."She pushed the words out, her breath shaken. She understood that this was the reason Bernardo wanted her here for breakfast. He needed her to get his wife and kids on board. He needed Eileen to move here and would do whatever it took to make it happen.

She forced a polite smile to let Bernardo know that he couldn't win her over with fluffy compliments, and she forced herself to turn to Leo, happily preoccupied in his high chair, sucking on pieces of toast. She wanted to hide her face, but Bernardo was sharp, the sharpest when it came to reading people. Stephen / Van, whoever he was, was staring at her.

"She'll call you," Bernardo said, keeping his eyes on her.

"Perfect," Annie said, angling away from his gaze to cut Leo's toast into smaller and smaller triangles as if it were the essential task of the day. She had to find out where Stephen lived on the river. The man across from her was Mr. Weiss's son-in-law. No question. But that didn't explain all the rest. She felt tremors of panic. She wanted to throw up. She reached for her water glass and drained it, noticing once again, the two unhappy men at the table in the corner. They could be old-time informers, bricks, like their building super, torturers, murderers, spies—people who appeared normal, nondescript, a little rundown. Like Stephen.

Bernardo turned to Stephen. "What do you like about living here?"

"Oh, I don't know. It's easy. You can sort of disappear if you want to."

A surge of tension swept through her body. She straightened her back to shake it off.

"But you've lived here before?" Bernardo said.

"No. I visited my cousin a few times." Stephen lifted his chin, then winked at Annie, letting her know he knew they had talked about this, too.

"But you're from Jersey, that right? Not Boston," Bernardo said.

"Originally from Jersey."

"Large Hungarian community there," Will said.

"That's right," Stephen said.

Bernardo's cell phone rang.

"Excuse me, folks. It's Eileen." He walked away from the table to answer it.

"Will has cousins from Jersey," Annie said, probing.

"Distant cousins," Will said. "Where's your place here?"

Stephen hesitated. "I live by the river."

"On the Pest or Buda side?" she said, finding her voice again. She sensed Stephen's discomfort. Then, as if he had made up his mind about something, he said, "Pest. I'll have you all over for drinks. You'll like the view."

Bernardo flipped shut his phone and walked back to their circle. "Shall we go? Women. Can't live without 'em, right?"

"Everything okay?" she asked Bernardo.

"Last-minute jitters."

"You want me to drive?" Will asked.

"I'll drive. I need to get used to this place," Bernardo said. "Ready to go?"

"I'll get the check. This won't take a minute," Will said, lifting his finger to attract the waiter. "I'll meet you two outside."

Stephen stood and reached out his hand to her. "Nice to see you again, Annie."

Despite her unease, she took his hand, warm and firm as the first time.

"Nice seeing you, too."

The waiter returned with the bill, took Will's Visa card, and left. She waited until Bernardo and Stephen had walked outside.

"Will, it's him." She lowered her voice and surveyed the room. The two men in the corner were gone, too. "Stephen is Edward's son-in-law. You have to hear me on this. I saw his photo in Edward's apartment. There's no question. I told you Edward thinks Stephen killed his daughter. I'm freaking out. He could be dangerous. I don't think you should go."

"Calm down. Edward's an angry, miserable man. He needs someone to blame. He's not well. I'll be back in a few hours. I'll be with Bernardo and the mayor."

She flinched. She was beginning to hate the word *mayor*.

"But I saw the photo. There's no question, Will."

"That doesn't prove anything. Slow down, Annie." He reached across the table and squeezed her hand. "Nothing's going to happen. Not with Bernardo and me. We'll talk when I get back. It's a few hours away. You know where it is. Same mayor."

"Why is he showing up in our lives? What if he's been following us?"

"You're sounding paranoid. It's a small world here. You know that. Especially among expats."

She understood what he meant, the expat community was tiny and circled back on itself all the time—like those American women she met at the luncheon—but this felt different.

The waiter returned. Will put his card away and stood. He looked out the window. "I'll be fine," he said. "Don't worry. We'll talk when I get home. Leo, give Daddy a hug." He bent down to kiss the baby. Annie felt paralyzed. She didn't want to move.

"Listen to me, Annie. You need to calm down. Nothing is going to happen. Let's go. We'll discuss all this when I get back. They're waiting."

They walked back out to the courtyard, jogger and Leo in tow.

"Eileen's on her way. She's excited about seeing you," Bernardo called to her. "Be good, Leo!"

Stephen dropped his cigarette on the cobblestone, mashing it with his sandal. Only a week or so ago, she thought his sandals made him seem European or hip. Now she thought they looked weird, out of sync with the times.

The three men headed across the courtyard, their backs to her now. Bernardo was in the middle. Short and husky, it was almost comical the way he strutted between them, his body bobbing like a wrestler warming up. Will seemed to glide. It's what drew people to him, this smoothness he possessed, a secret well of calmness that soothed others in his presence. But this quality also made it hard for people to read him sometimes—including her.

Struggling against a kind of panic vibrating in her ribs, she shook her arms to quiet her body and pointed her son toward a flock of pigeons in the center of the square. An elderly lady was casting crumbs and it looked as if every pigeon on the hill had come for the meal. Leo responded, screeching delightedly as he headed toward the mass of birds.

She saw her husband and the two other men turn down a side street. One dash across the square with Leo in her arms, and she could run after him, yelling, Will, wait! Stop! No! She could call him now. Tell him not to go.

Or she could calm down. But how could she? It was too co-incidental, this meeting. All of it. She looked around for the two Hungarians from the restaurant. Maybe they were in on it, too? Maybe Stephen hired them to watch her. They were gone. So were the German tourists.

She was a mother. She had a child to protect, but if Stephen / Van murdered Mr. Weiss's daughter, then she had to help the old man. She had to do something. Too many people stood by and watched, and did nothing. What if she had called to her sister, screamed, Watch out, Tracy! Daddy's car is backing up! But she had been confused. Greg's ball sailed past and then Tracy was down.

Annie placed Leo in the jogger and fastened the safety belt. Running down the hill, Leo screeched with joy; he loved speed-ing. She felt crazy. Scared. The jogger accelerated, hastened by its own weight and gravity. Down, down, down to the flat side and the river, and Pest. She finally pulled back on the handle to slow it down.

Maybe there was an in-between—a way of helping Mr. Weiss without putting her family in danger. She had questions, so many things she still didn't know. Stephen Van Házy Howard. Which was it? Was Mr. Weiss's daughter's death an overdose? Too many pills? A mistake? What could Mr. Weiss prove? What did he have other than a gut feeling that may or may not be right? She stuttered her speed to a walk to catch her breath.

Higher in the sky, the sun inched upward through the haze. Another hot day in Budapest except that she knew now she had met and liked a possible murderer named Stephen Van Házy Howard. Normal, pleasant, agreeable, Mr. Weiss had said. Maybe the old man was right.

"Leo-lion," she said, making up her mind, "we're going to the embassy. Right now."

As she ran down the hill, the thought occurred to her that she should go to the American embassy to register her family. Isn't that what expats did to protect themselves? Leo screeched with joy; he loved speeding. She felt crazy. Scared. Anxious about Will in a car with a possible murderer. But, for once, knowing Bernardo was there gave her comfort.

After the embassy, she would call Mr. Weiss.

Twenty-six

The first week of September broke another heat record across Europe. By one o'clock in the afternoon, radiant heat shimmering off buildings and sidewalks pushed the air conditioner in the kitchen to its capacity. He knew he could go to a hotel for relief. A five-minute cab ride is all it would be. When Nan called, he would tell her that's what he would do. He didn't want her to worry.

Legs splayed, body sluggish, he sat on the couch. He'd over-worked the freezer, and now it barely functioned. Beside him on a small table, he sipped on tepid water. He thought about filling the tub with cold water—anything to relieve the discomfort of

intractable heat—but he decided he would not have the strength
to lift himself out.

Instead, he pointed his face toward the two standing fans and
the temperate mass of air emanating from them. The constant
blowing made him sleepy. Outside, a bike bell rang, the sound taking him back to his childhood. He saw the blue ice cream truck
coming down the street lined with triple-decker houses in his old
Boston neighborhood. He sat on the front stoop, the whole family
and neighborhood waiting for a breeze from the harbor a mile away.
His uncle and aunt lived on the second floor. When the truck came,
the grown-ups pooled their change and purchased pints of vanilla
ice cream for everyone to share. He could feel the wooden spoon
splintering on his tongue, a clean scratchy taste after he licked it dry.

On summer nights, hot as this day, he and his older sister
would take turns sleeping on his uncle's upstairs porch. The sounds
of the city faded with each passing hour, and every so often an actual breeze slithered in from Boston Harbor and found its way to
his little cot in the corner. Time was slow then. Slow as it was now.
The morning after, he'd wake up with tattoos of bug bites, yet he
loved sleeping there, exposed to the summer air, to every element.
Never had he felt so safe as on that porch. Sweet moments of for-
getting who he was, where he was. If that was a peek into eternity
or death where time didn't exist, he was ready.

Half-asleep, he heard a faint ringing, like something caught in
the fan blade. There it was again. The phone. The damn phone.

"Yes. Yes. All right."

He pushed himself up with a violent motion that propelled
him toward the door. Staggering, he grabbed at air, lurching to get

his hands on something to prevent a fall—but his hip hit the floor, and he ended up on his back looking at a water stain on the ceiling.

"*Christ.*"

The ringing stopped, then started again.

"Give me a moment," he yelled, out of breath. That he was lying on the cooler wooden floor surprised but didn't scare him. He wiggled his hands, his toes, neck. Amazing. God having another laugh. Everything still seemed to work.

Dumb luck. Like that time in France. Caught in the cross fire in Strasbourg. Trapped in a courtyard. His squad, part of the big drive in 1944; that blond kid from Kansas, sharing smokes, next second flying across mounds of rubble, leg and arms, blood every-where—not his blood, the kid's. One more lunge across the yard.

God!

Only time he called out for God.

Only time.

On the floor, he rolled onto his side and made an effort to lift himself. The skirmish stopped, a lucky moment, one in a billion of lucky moments. Dumb luck. When you're in a war, every day, hour, second that you're alive is dumb luck.

He clicked on his cell phone. "Yes?"

"Mr. Weiss? Are you all right?"

He pulled himself along the floor to the wall.

"Mr. Weiss?"

He leaned into the wall near the kitchen, heaving.

"Annie. What can I do for you?" His lungs seized on another breath.

"What happened? You sound terrible."

He brushed his shoulder. "I fell. It's not the first time." He didn't want her pity. "You called. What is it?"

"We met him again. Are you hurt?"

"What? No."

"Today. Stephen Házy. Van. He's the same man. I'm sure of it."

"I told you his name is Van."

"He calls himself Stephen. Stephen Házy. It's the same person in your photo. It's him, only his hair is shorter."

"A liar is a liar. Where is he?"

Her voice changed. "He said he grew up in New Jersey. Didn't you tell me that?"

His heart turned over. "Yes. I did." Reflexively, he touched his shoulder. It hurt.

"Mr. Weiss? Are you there? Will's with him now. They're at a business meeting."

"Where does he live? Did he tell you?"

"He bought a place by the river. He owns it. He even invited us over. I don't know the address. Not yet. I know I can get it. I'll get it for you."

"When was this?"

"Today. This morning. A few hours ago. We had breakfast. At the Hilton."

He listened. Leaning into the wall, he felt the air conditioner vibrating. "How did this come about? Where are you?"

"Will's old boss. Will's associate. Stephen is a translator for American businesses. It's a small community. I'm worried. What if he's been following us? I'm walking back from the embassy now. I registered. I'm with Leo."

"Tell me the truth. What did you think of him?"

She answered with her breath.

"Annie? You liked him. You don't believe me."

"I liked him. Yes. He's pleasant. Exactly like you said. I can't put it together. He changed his name. What are we going to do?" she asked.

"You're not going to do anything. Understand? Don't come here. Like I told you. Call me when you get his address. Nothing more. Give me your word." Sweat dripped down his sides. He listened but he didn't hear anything. She was breathing hard into the phone.

"Annie. Your word."

"Okay."

"Good." He slumped, the effort tired him. His shoulder ached, his body shuddered.

"When you get his address, call me. I'm here."

This was his second chance. He could prove that his daughter died of an overdose from her own prescription pills. He could smell the truth. He was getting close.

"Mr. Weiss? Are you there?"

"Annie. I'm tired. I'm going to hang up now, but I want to thank you. Thank you very much."

He ended the phone call. It would come to pass, he knew this even as he listened to his old thoughts winding back. How many times had he second-guessed himself? Exaggerating. Making things up. *You never trust anyone*, Sylvia had said. Maybe Sylvia was right. No. No more. Van made it seem as if Deborah, his Deborah, had unintentionally killed herself, an accident, an understandable, honest mistake. The insurance company implied the same thing. Both of them—insurance and Van—robbers, killers. Canceled his own insurance after that. He let the phone slide from his hand onto the couch.

And if Howard wanted to kill him, too?

He rubbed his shoulder again, raising his arm to check. He fought the insurance company, but in the end, the money went to the bastard. Bastards, all of them. They said he was her husband. Her rightful beneficiary. The coroner's opinion trumped all. A thick sweat worked like glue on his shirt and shorts as he let himself thump onto the hard sofa cushion.

He heard his voice speak out loud.

"Find the truth."

Twenty-seven

Will sprawled next to her on the living-room couch, both of them in their underwear. The large windows opened to occasional wisps of night air. Down the long, connecting hallway, Leo lay asleep in his crib. Annie lowered the sound of the television with the remote control and nestled a bottle of Hungarian beer between her legs.

"You have to register yourself," she told Will. "But I wrote your name on my form. I don't know why we didn't do this months ago. You're starting to believe me, aren't you?"

"There's something off about Stephen. No question. But that doesn't mean he's a murderer."

Maybe not, but she felt relieved that Will was home and safe—safer now that she had registered Leo and herself at the American embassy and at the very least put Will's name and address next to hers so that he was a known entity. The process was simple. She filled out a single sheet of paper. Afterward, she felt shielded by something larger than herself: the protection of her country. At the embassy, she wrote down her current and previous addresses, cell and fax numbers, primary contacts back in the States. The friendly American woman at the embassy desk took a photo of her and Leo's passports. She assured Annie it was a smart, good thing to do.

"You never know," the embassy woman said. She was a young postgrad from Iowa, in Budapest pursuing international studies.

"How long have you been here?" Annie asked her.

"Three months. Heading for Prague in the fall."

"Ah. Everyone wants to go to Prague."

"You been?"

"Not yet," Annie said.

Now, as she sat on the couch with Will, Annie sank into the luxury of safety. The apartment was quiet, toys and dishes put away for the night.

"Bernardo told a few bad jokes."

"Such as?"

"How many Hungarians does it take to screw an American?"

"How many?" Annie asked.

"One."

Annie smirked. "Not funny."

"Stephen thought it was. He loved it. 'Got any more, Steve?' Bernardo said. Stephen didn't like that. He said, 'That's Stephen with a *p-h*.'"

"Where was this?" Annie moved closer to Will on the couch.

"In the car, on the way to meet the mayor. Bernardo apologized, said, 'Stephen, I know how you feel, buddy. Can't stand it when people call me Bernie.' Then Bernardo asks if Stephen's involved with anyone."

"Why?"

"His way of kicking the tires. Never underestimate Bernardo. Find out what a man thinks about women and you'll know how he conducts business."

"Maybe there's truth in that." She took a long swig of the sweet beer. "That would make Bernardo untrustworthy. What did Stephen say?"

"He's seeing one woman, on occasion. Nothing serious. Then Bernardo wants to know what the woman is like."

"Brazen of him," Annie said. "But that's Bernardo."

Will shifted and put his arm around her.

"Stephen says: 'Pretty and too young.' Then Bernardo says: 'What's young? Eighteen? Sixteen?'"

Will looked out the window and waited for the sound of a car alarm to stop. Every night they heard these complicated alarms. Budapest had a high rate of car theft. Lucky for them, their car had not been stolen, thanks to the special lock they put on the wheel. They both listened as the car alarm went through a half-dozen shrill ditties.

"Those things will drive anyone nuts."

"What happened next?" Annie said, impatient to hear. She craved the truth about Stephen. Van. No. She couldn't call him Van.

"At one point, Bernardo says, 'Eileen and I married too young. Twenty. Maybe it was a mistake. You've never been married, right, Stephen?'"

Will paused to finish his beer.

"Stephen says: 'I was married. *Briefly*.'"

"Briefly. Oh my God, he admits he was married!" Annie said, sitting up.

"Here's the clincher, Annie. He said: 'She *died*.'"

"Oh my God."

"Bernardo changed the subject after that. Back to business. That's how he does it. He moves into the personal, then pulls back. I've seen him dance this way dozens of times. By the end of the day, Stephen and Bernardo were best buddies. That's how we got invited to his place tomorrow night."

"He'd already invited us at breakfast," Annie said.

"But Bernardo made it happen. He doesn't have a lot of time. He did his bonding ritual. He's anxious to see Stephen's place."

"Bernardo gets what he wants," she said. "Did he hire Stephen to be more than a translator?"

"No. He's kicking Házy's tires. Trying him out. Bernardo's smart that way. Wants to get to know him. I think Stephen is an odd duck, a loner, but—a murderer? That's something else. I don't think so."

"I don't know." She looked at the television—still on mute—and watched Lucille Ball and Desi Arnaz driving a white convertible the size of an airplane down a sunny California highway. America's fantasy land.

What would prove Edward right or wrong? She wanted to believe Edward wasn't crazy, but believing him changed everything. It meant Stephen or Van—the kind man who had offered to help them at the police station, the little boy who tragically lost his dad—was a criminal. A killer. No. She wasn't ready to believe that either. Maybe there was an alternative explanation. Something less black and white.

"Did you feel unsafe?" she asked him.

"Not at all. Maybe he had some problems back home and came here to escape or get away for a while. A lot of expats have stories like that. One could argue we came here to get away."

"Mr. Weiss lost a daughter. He's sick. He's in pain. Why would he come all this way?" she asked. "Why fabricate a murder story? That's extreme. What is the point of that?"

"He may honestly believe Stephen's a murderer and wants to get his daughter's money back, but what if he's wrong?"

"Oh, I can't believe it's about money. I don't want to believe that."

"Do you want to believe that the mayor we met sells sex in exchange for business favors?"

"What?"

LATER, IN BED, Will slept peacefully, as if he had come to terms with his perception of the situation with Bernardo, Stephen, and the mayor and was willing to ride it out, keep the door open, and finally seize the opportunity that had eluded him for these past eight, nine months. This was, after all, the primary reason they were here—so Will could have his business adventure. Was it fair to stop him from taking Bernardo's offer, as much as she disliked how it was adding up?

She reviewed everything Will told her: how a guest of the mayor's, a woman named Agnes, joined them for lunch. How the mayor introduced Agnes as his translator, but in fact she was also there to serve as an escort. How, during lunch, the mayor and Stephen had a short conversation in Hungarian that Will couldn't understand. On the car ride home, Stephen explained to them that Agnes was a gift from the mayor—sex, companionship, whatever they needed. The mayor also told Stephen that Hungarian tax collectors liked to show up unannounced and could shut down a business for weeks. Unless, of course, the Americans were willing to pay extra cash under the table for the tax collectors to leave them alone. The mayor offered Agnes as a way to repay the favor. Stephen and Bernardo laughed over this. They had no issue accepting this practice.

"They bonded around sex," Will had told her. "Look, I don't do business this way. But I can't control what they do with women. Bernardo's been having affairs for years. We know that."

And Bernardo had also offered Will a quarter-million-dollar salary. Incredible money, especially in Hungary. She looked across the narrow bedroom to the open window and the night. Will had told Bernardo he'd think about it.

It was such a different world out there. She couldn't believe these things happened. Yet they did. Here. Right in front of her.

Will told her that in the car Stephen had said, "Hungarians are traders. Money. Sex. Favors. They have a long history of it. It's how we've survived."

Traders or traitors, Annie thought, hearing Edward's sarcastic voice.

Apparently, Bernardo was talking a hundred-thousand-dollar salary for Stephen if he passed final muster. She wondered what Stephen got from his dead wife's insurance. If Will died, she would get a half million. They'd signed up for life insurance because of Leo, but the whole business was distasteful to her, a racket based on fear.

She shifted again on the hard platform bed, pressing closer to Will's chest. She could feel the light tapping of his heart. What would he decide? What if Bernardo's offer proved irresistible?

She heard the baby cough.

Leo coughed again, so she went down the long hall. In his crib, he lay on his back, plump and beautiful, his hair damp from the warm night. Sometimes he choked on his saliva. It was nothing more than that so she turned back, her foot kicking something hard under the crib.

Leo had found her camera and exposed the film, ruining the pictures she had taken that week. Ah, well. Photos, she could replace.

BACK IN BED, another car alarm started up outside—a high, whooping call and then a series of rapid beeps and short musical phrases, then back to whooping again. Finally it stopped. The only sound remaining came from their small fan on the sill blowing night air across her legs.

How could she stare at something and not see it? That first time that Stephen showed up on Edward's street. Next, he showed up at a business meeting with Will and Bernardo. Come on. She sat up. Too many coincidences. Was Stephen trying to win them over, win her over? Convince them the old man was wrong? She thought about the Jews who didn't believe what was happening in Germany in the 1930s, yet in retrospect, the signs had been everywhere. Will said it was like frogs—if you put a frog in water and slowly heat the water, the frog doesn't react, doesn't realize it's getting cooked. The thought distressed her: Was she like a frog slowly sinking into Hungary's soupy swamp of depression? Wasn't this the same thing as Jane's trailing-spouse syndrome, a slow acceptance of unpleasantries with emotional blindness setting in?

She lay back down. She'd come here to learn about herself, to see what happened when she stripped herself of her American culture.

Now she had to ask, what was left? Mr. Weiss was right—you can't escape yourself. But was he right about Stephen? She looked at the clock. Three in the morning. She turned on her side. Will would tell her to get some sleep. What would Rose advise? What would her neighbor do in this situation? She could call Rose and ask. Rose was the one who insisted they visit Edward in the first place, even though she knew he wouldn't like it.

That settled it. Annie needed to know, even if Edward didn't approve. She would go back, unannounced, look into the old man's face, and demand the truth. She rolled on her back and listened to the night sounds. Distant cars. Will's breath. She grew sleepy, her mind swaying in a sea of dreams. Something flickered, a flash of sunlight. She wanted to rip off the darkness.

She sat up gasping.

Twenty-eight

Early the next morning, Annie waited in a long line at the post office to mail the brown envelope addressed to Rose. In it, the letter she and Will had promised to send to the social worker.

Dear Birth Mother,

We wanted to share these three photos with you and to let you know how blessed we feel because of you. Our son is healthy, smart, beautiful, happy. There is no greater gift of life and love than what you have given us, no words to express the depth of gratitude in our hearts.

Leo sat in the jogger, flipping pages of his book on shapes and colors. Will stayed home to review Bernardo's contract. He told Bernardo he'd let him know either way at the end of ten days.

She was nervous but determined about visiting Edward one more time this afternoon, once Leo was asleep. Again, she found herself resorting to secrecy. She didn't mention her intention to Will.

Sleep-deprived, she wished she could push the hours ahead, see Edward now, but it was only nine o'clock, too early.

Annie and Will had written the letter for Leo's birth mother days ago, rearranging the words again and again. It wasn't possible to get them right. Giving up a child, handing him over to a strange couple as some kind of gift? The enormity of that act of courage was too large for words. But that was what it was: an act of courage, and faith.

Rose would forward the envelope to Calloway, who would send it on to the agency in North Carolina, which would pass it on to Leo's birth mother. Annie didn't know where his birth mother lived. Had she moved? What was her life like this whole last year? She would be twenty-one now.

Calloway didn't have the authority to do this, but she felt sure he would open the envelope before sending it on, his long, thin fingers unable to resist stroking the edges of Leo's photos.

At the post office, the line ahead of her did not move. The concept of service was a joke in this Eastern European country. None of the postal workers made eye contact with customers, or hurried or made an extra effort. The old communist posturing still ruled in a faded glory kind of way. Hilarious to watch when she didn't need to be anywhere, infuriating when she did. Today she had no place to go, only time to kill until evening when Agnes, the sex escort or companion—my God, was she living a crazy dream?—would pick them up at seven o'clock to go to Stephen's flat. Will said to think of Agnes as their chauffeur.

Leo kicked the metal footplate on the jogger. The narrow, windowless lobby with dusty floors smelled of human sweat and ink. Two weak fans barely stirred the air. At this rate, it would take an hour to mail one letter.

Leo kicked again. "Up, Momma," he said, stretching his arms toward her. An elderly woman near the front of the line motioned for Annie to come forward.

"Kicsi baba," the woman said. She pointed to Leo. A few others in line nodded in agreement.

"Köszönöm," she said. "Thank you." Annie moved to the front of the line, just as she had at the airport when she first arrived.

She gave her envelope to the postal worker, paid for the stamps, and smiled to the nice people in line on her way to the exit door. Outside, an explosion of sunshine disoriented her. She raised her arm to block the light—like that day, like her dream last night that was oh, so unbearably familiar to her: Tracy zigzagging on her bike, Greg aiming the ball, an aluminum flash like sunlight off the car, metal clanging, and Tracy tipping, sliding. Their mother's summer robe fluttering across the driveway. Tracy on the ground, quiet and still. The vision would never go away.

Leo put his hands over his eyes and started crying.

"Sorry, hon," she said, turning the jogger so that the sun was at his back.

She headed to the Parliament. Leo could play in the garden there and she had a hunch that the Roma sisters might be there, suspecting it was their regular turf. She had a peculiar curiosity to know where these children lived, as if knowing where they slept at night might convince her they would be okay.

At the Parliament, she sat on a bench watching Leo as he criss-crossed the narrow walkways between hedges of roses.

"Ower," Leo said.

Her hunch was soon realized: a thin-limbed girl jumped out from behind a hedge and handed her son a flower. A second girl appeared. Thrilled, Annie immediately recognized the two sisters and walked over to them.

"Do you speak English?" Annie spoke slowly.

Leo giggled.

The taller one shook her head and held out her hand for money. The younger girl copied her sister, shaking her open palm. They both had beautiful teeth, broad and white, the younger one with a small gap where a tooth was coming in on the side.

"Ow-er," Leo said, showing Annie the rose.

The older sister giggled and pushed her hand toward Annie again.

Annie took Leo's hand instead and said, "Name? What is your name?" She repeated the question in Hungarian, and waited for the Roma girls to decide whether to tell her. If she did, Annie would reward them with a dollar.

"Sigh-ra."

"Sigh-ra," Annie repeated.

The girl nodded, her long skirt sweeping her ankles. The younger one smiled.

"Sigh-ra. This is Leo. I'm Annie."

Sigh-ra opened her palm and shook it.

"Sit here. *Itt.*" Annie pointed to the bench and moved toward it, but Sigh-ra wasn't interested. She shook her palm again, her fawn-colored skin smooth and weathered. Annie gave both girls a dollar, wanting them to stay. Instead, Sigh-ra grabbed her sister's hand and began to skip away as if she knew she had won over Annie. Leo was smitten and started after them, shrieking, so Annie scooped him up into the jogger, snapped the safety belt in place, and followed them.

Sigh-ra turned it into a game of twirling, then stopping, the younger one in sync with her sister. Annie couldn't resist keeping pace, gently pursuing them, as if she were chasing an alternate reality of Tracy and herself in another life, another dream.

Leo laughed at every silly gesture that Sigh-ra made with her mouth and hands. Equally charmed by him, the sisters slowed and walked alongside him, just beyond his reach, enthralled by Leo's giggling and unfiltered delight. Listening to the children's laughter, Annie felt happy, too. Happier than she'd felt in months.

They turned down a boulevard, past a marketplace and narrower streets that look unkempt, with cracked sidewalks and buildings black with soot. Annie couldn't wait to see where the Roma girls lived, even as another part of her felt cautious, possibly rash for wandering into this unfamiliar section of town. So many people had warned her about Gypsies. Sigh-ra and her sister were children. Where was the harm? It was the middle of the day. People were out.

She followed the sisters to a grid of streets with few trees. Finally, the girls turned into an old building with a courtyard filled with a dozen dark-skinned children playing a game with stones. Barefoot toddlers. Children with dirt-dusted limbs. Mothers in skirts, like the woman who sold Annie a flower at Luigi's. Maybe this was where Sandor lived. Odd to think, after all these months Annie still didn't know.

A strange feeling of disquietude filled the courtyard. Unsure what to do, Annie quickly handed Sigh-ra an American twenty-dollar bill, the equivalent of a whole week's worth of groceries. A windfall of money. Was it wrong? She didn't know. Leo reached out his arms to get out of the jogger, wanting Annie to unbuckle him so he could follow the girls who had run into the middle of the large group of Roma children, all of whom had stopped what they were doing to stare. Now all the mothers and children in the courtyard—there were no men—had stopped to face her, lined up in a wall of defense.

"Nem," a woman called to Sigh-ra, shaking her finger at Annie, speaking in a rapid sing song chain of sentences Annie couldn't understand.

"We have to go, hon." She waved to the two sisters and guided the jogger back to the street, away from the women and children. Annie didn't need to understand their words. It was obvious that she and her son were not welcome there.

Twenty-nine

A persistent tapping on the door woke him. It wasn't Ivan's day.

"Mr. Weiss. It's Annie."

He lumbered to the door and unchained it, letting her in.

"What are you doing here? I told you—"

"Yes. I know," Annie said. "I need to talk to you."

"What is it?"

"Before I go to Stephen's tonight, you need to tell me the whole story."

"Van. I told you his name is Van. You have his address?"

"No. We're getting picked up. I have his phone number."

He slid the chain back on the track.

"Why didn't you call?"

And then he understood.

"You still don't believe me."

He scanned the room, taking in the dark curtains and the squint of light coming through, wondering when it would ever end. Why could he see things that others could not? He turned to her again. She stood taller, her shoulders in perfect alignment, and he could see she was intent, determined. She had pulled her hair back into a ponytail, which made her face look more angular.

"You accused a man of murder, Edward. I needed to talk to you about this in person, not on the phone."

He watched her inhale deeply, waited to hear what other excuse she would give him. Everyone had an excuse.

"You never told me what happened. No bullshit. Isn't that what you said? You owe me that."

She slid her hand into her back pocket and pulled out the business card.

"Here. You see? It's all here."

She pushed the card into his hand and he read the words for himself:

STEPHEN HÁZY

c. 36 1 438-5629

"Is this number real? Have you called him?"

His question made her pause. "No. I haven't. But he called Will, and Will's old boss has been in touch with him, and another American businessman from General Electric whom Will knows."

"I can call him right now." Edward reached for his cell phone and sat back down in the depression on the couch where he had fallen asleep after lunch.

"No, wait," Annie said. "What are you going to say? What if he asks how you got the number?"

"I won't tell him. I want to be sure it's him. If he picks up, I'll recognize his voice and I'll hang up."

"But your number and name will show up on his phone."

"I have no problem with that."

Edward began to punch in the numbers.

"But I do. Stop! He'll want to know how you got his number. Please think this through."

Edward stopped. She was right. He needed to remain calm with her. He didn't want to put her and Leo in further jeopardy. Yet reason kept dissolving in his head, the vortex of his emotions sucking everything into a blinding hole. As he clutched the business card, the tangible sensation of his daughter's killer in his hand made his chest hurt. He had a suffocating urge to dial Van's number, just once, so he could breathe. Then he had a thought.

"How about if you call him and ask for his address?"

"I never call him."

"Tell him you want the address to give to your babysitter. I'd think you'd want to do that, anyway, right? I'm not the bad guy, Annie. If someone murdered your son, what would you do? Can you answer that question? Of course you can't."

She took her phone and dialed the number, holding the phone between them so he could hear.

"You've reached Stephen Házy. Leave a message and I'll get back to you. Have a good day." The message continued in Hungarian and then the voice mail beeped. It was Howard. No doubt about it.

Annie spoke into the mouthpiece.

"Hi, Stephen. It's Annie. We're looking forward to seeing you tonight. I was wondering if you wouldn't mind giving me a quick call. I need your address to give to our babysitter. Thanks. Bye. See you soon."

She hung up.

"Van calling himself Stephen," Edward said, feeling an urge to spit. "Does he have your number? You didn't leave it with him."

"Yes. He has it." She pushed a stray hair off her face and looked hard at him. "My name and number will show up on his ID. And he called Will at the police station, remember? I told you about that. You don't trust anyone, do you? I came here in earnest, Edward. I need to understand what is going on."

Again, he heard Sylvia telling him to lower his voice.

"My daughter—Deborah—had a habit of picking losers."

"What do you mean by losers?" Annie asked, sitting down on the opposite end of the couch.

"Drug addicts. Hippie types. Boys who couldn't hold down jobs. Van was one more in a long line of them. His father committed suicide when he was a kid—a six-year-old kid. Said he heard the gunshot and found him. That tragedy was Van's calling card."

"I know about the suicide. He told me when we ran into each other. But he didn't tell me that he *found* his father. That *is* tragic. God, that's unthinkable," Annie said, taking hold of her ponytail and pulling on it. "You can see that, can't you?"

"Ran into him again?" he said, ignoring her question. He refused to get sucked into the quicksand of Van's victimhood. He was living with his own god-awful tragedies.

"I told you about this. I was coming to see you. He was waiting for a client. At the end of your street."

"And do you really believe he was waiting for a client?"

"I know he was. I saw the client. A man. They walked off together."

"You don't think it's an odd coincidence that he ran into you near my street?"

She took a deep breath, her shoulders rising. "I honestly don't know."

"How did you meet him the first time?" Edward asked.

"At Luigi's. It's where all the American expats go for Italian food. Will and I go there a lot. We met Stephen the day we met you." She bent her head away from him, thinking.

"Another coincidence?" Edward said.

"I don't know. I don't know. I think he was already at the restaurant when we arrived, but I can't say for sure. The restaurant isn't far from here. A business associate of Will's—someone from GE was having lunch with Stephen . . . Van, but now I don't know for certain. Maybe they were just having coffee. I don't know. The GE man introduced us. He said Stephen was working as a translator. Stephen gave us his card—that one," she said, pointing to the card in Edward's hand. "He offered to help. He was friendly. Nice, like you said. He called Will and showed up at the police station after Will's wallet was stolen."

Edward shook his head at the irony of it. "And how did he know what police station to meet you at?"

"Will probably told him when Stephen called to see if he could help. Will told him not to bother."

"I'd say it was another funny coincidence. Maybe he was following you. Did you consider that?" Edward asked.

"No. Of course I didn't. Why would he do that?"

She looked at the curtained windows.

"Maybe I should leave."

"Don't you see? That's how he operates. He helps. He slides in there like he did with Deborah. Am I right? Don't you see?" Edward stabbed the air with his finger. "Always an excuse. Bad childhoods. Victims. Tragedies. Who hasn't experienced something unforgivable? We're all victims of life."

"Maybe he came here to rectify his father's death," Annie said. "I'm not making an excuse for him. I'm just trying to understand."

"You think so? And what about my daughter's death? Who rectifies that? Why did you come here, Annie? I'll tell you why. You don't believe me." Edward readjusted his hip. His back ached. He didn't have the energy to explain himself to her. He was done with explaining. He had Van's phone number. "Whether you believe me is inconsequential, you understand? I know what I know." He drew in a long breath, surprised by how much effort it took.

"I didn't say I didn't believe you," Annie said, raising her voice. She straightened her back in defense. "I'm confused. You're telling me I'm in danger. You said he murdered your daughter. Now you're suggesting he's following me. I deserve to know the full story. You know I do."

He heard Sylvia telling him to calm down. *Don't raise your voice, Edward. You scare people.*

Edward remembered the day he met Van at Deborah's apartment in Boston.

"You want the full story? My daughter lived in a basement in Boston. A six-hundred-and-thirty-three-square-foot condo. Deborah called it a garden apartment. I gave her the down payment. If I hadn't . . ." He clenched his jaw. "If I hadn't helped her purchase that place, she would have come home. Van never would have followed her."

"You wanted to help her," Annie said.

Edward waved his hands. "Our house had too many stairs. Her MS had gotten worse. She was living in a wheelchair. She insisted on being independent."

"She sounds like you," Annie said. "What was Van doing?"

"Popping her pills, using her. What's he doing now?"

"He's a translator."

"So he says. Did he tell you he was living off her money? Did he tell you that?"

She leaned back, then leaned toward him again.

"No. He didn't."

"That's right. As soon as Deborah moved into her condo, he moved in with her. Next thing, they're married. A year later, she's dead. Know what her death certificate says? 'Asphyxia, multiple sclerosis.' It doesn't say opioid overdose. You understand? Insurance doesn't pay for overdoses. He did his research. He was careful to do it right."

Edward felt light-headed, the knot of rage pressing against his ribs. A truck honked long and loud outside. But when he looked at Annie's worried and confused face, he questioned whether she had the capacity to believe Van could murder someone.

He pushed himself to keep talking. "Translator? What's he translating?"

"He goes to business meetings. That's why he was at the breakfast yesterday."

Edward swallowed. "Did you see his eyes, Annie? My wife didn't want to believe me either. Can you blame her? Who wants to believe their daughter's been murdered by their son-in-law?" He sat up. "My daughter Nan—she's on the fence. She won't say either way. My friends in Florida tell me I'm grieving. Give it time, they say. What time?"

His eyes burned with tears.

"I want to understand," Annie said, moving closer to him on the couch.

"Look, Deborah was in a wheelchair for thirteen years. Her symptoms started at twenty-nine. Dizzy spells. Sudden falls. At first, I thought she was on drugs."

"Did she have a problem with that?"

"No. She wasn't on drugs. It was the early signs of her MS. Strangers on the street thought she was drunk—like your co-worker. Same issue. Before her diagnosis, one doctor told her to go out, have fun. Told her she was pretty and smart. 'Enjoy life,' he told her. She was insulted. She went out plenty. She loved life. That's how she met Van. She was volunteering at some drug rehab center, helping losers."

"Drug addiction doesn't mean you're a loser. It's a disease," Annie said. "I know about that, Edward."

"Look, Van's a loser, and so am I. I gave her money when she got sick. If I hadn't given her money every month, paid for her condo—"

"You can't keep second-guessing yourself like that."

"Sure I can. Aren't you second-guessing why you came to Hungary?"

Annie looked away, then met his gaze. "Yes. I am."

"All right, then. We agree on something. I like you when you're not lying to yourself."

She grimaced, pulling her knee to her chest.

"The truth is, Deborah framed everything in her perky, blind way. When she had to get a cane, she used to say to me, 'Dad, the cane distinguishes me. People get out of the way. They let me cut in line.' Always looking for positives, my Deborah. A bit like you."

He rubbed his forehead.

"Edward, we can stop," Annie said, her voice softening.

"Oh, no. We're going to finish this." He wiped the dry corners of his mouth. "All those years helping drug addicts, believing in losers. Where'd it come from? Maybe her mother. Why did you work with homeless men? What's the thrill in that?"

"I feel good helping people. I told you that."

"Why? What is it?"

He waited for her to answer. He could never understand what it was with Deborah. Why she put herself in jeopardy with life suckers. That's what they were.

"To offer hope, and I guess, honestly, I feel empowered by that. Like I matter. Like I'm not standing on the sidelines. I couldn't help my sister and brother, so I try to help others."

"My daughter spent the best years of her life thinking about others."

"She sounds like an amazing, caring person," Annie said.

Edward pushed himself up. "I've got to get some water."

"Let me get it," Annie said.

While she filled two glasses from the tap, he allowed himself to feel some satisfaction that she would leave here armed with the full story. Whatever she chose to believe about Van—that he was nice and suffering and all that bullshit—something else deep inside her would harbor doubts. He had what he needed to get to the bottom of Van's lies. He squeezed Van's business card against the palm of his hand and felt the thick paper softening from his sweat.

"Here you go," Annie said, handing him his glass. "I'm glad you got an air conditioner."

He drank the tepid water, spilling some on his pants.

"What medication was she taking?" Annie asked.

"Vicodin. It's a painkiller. You know it?"

"I've heard of it."

"It's no different from heroin, only more expensive. You have to keep upping the dose. Once she was in the wheelchair, I sent her money, direct deposit to her account. She told me not to, but I insisted. Sylvia—my wife—insisted, too. We were stupid. I should have made her come home. We could have built her a ramp. Bought one of those electric contraptions for stairways. I sold medical equipment, for chrissake. It would have cost us nothing!"

"She wanted her independence and you helped her with that," Annie said.

"No. I ruined her. She lived in that basement with a pill addict and a drinker—he liked his alcohol, too. Worse, he was a vampire living off her. What's a thirty-eight-year-old drug addict doing with a wheelchair-bound woman ten years his senior? She didn't care about conventions. I supported them both. Then Deborah began losing the use of her hands. She needed help eating and drinking. She said Van was her prince. He did the grocery shopping. Cooked. Fed her pills for her spasms and pain—had her money, a place to live, pills. Why not get married so he could get her life insurance, too?"

Annie shook her head. "I know you're going to get mad, but I have to ask you: Is it possible it was an accident? You truly think he planned it?"

Edward heaved a breath as he thought about Van—now calling

himself Stephen–walking into his Deborah's life the moment she was most vulnerable. "Yes. He saw an opportunity. What's there to understand? Why is this so difficult for people to comprehend? What else did he want except her money? Free rent. Pills. Life insurance. How many times do I have to say it? What could he possibly offer her—love? That's what Deborah said: 'love.'" The thought made Edward's stomach twist. "And what the hell is he doing with you, Annie?"

"Nothing. What do you mean?" She looked away, at the floor.

"Don't you think he knows you know me?"

"How would he know that?"

"Watching. I'll bet my life he's had his eye on this place."

"Why?"

"Because he knows I'm onto him."

"But we met him by accident at the restaurant. The expat world is tiny. It's easy to run into other Americans."

"That's right, and he's not stupid. He knows I'm here and that I'm not fooling around. He doesn't want you to believe what I'm telling you. He wants to get the word out that he's an upstanding, good man. He wants to get you on his side. It's not more complicated than that. I need a drink."

She started to get up again, but he stopped her.

"No. I'll get it. I have to move." He pushed himself from the couch and shuffled into the kitchen. It was coming together in his mind. A kid's puzzle. Ever since Van met Annie, he had been watching her. Saw Annie come over. Gets entangled in Will's business. Van invites them over to his place. Plays innocent.

At the kitchen sink, he placed a new glass under the tap and remembered how Deborah looked at him with her large blue eyes—her mother's eyes. Deborah had a flat forehead and small plump red lips, as if all the juice remaining in her life had flowed into her voice and mouth—and eyes. "Let me be me, Dad," she'd said to him. "Why do people assume that what they want for me is what I want for me?"

Deborah said Van was coming off years of drugs. "Got a bad start in life, Dad," she said. "His father came over from Hungary after the '56 uprising. Van heard the gunshot and found him *in the room, Dad. A little kid. Six years old. Can you imagine?*"

Really? Imagine it? Oh, yes he could. He'd fought in the war. Walked through the gates of Dachau hell. Deborah's naïveté drove him insane. Annie's, too. What about the Jews? Thousands of them were children with bad starts.

Everyone has to follow their own path in life, Dad. You know that.

Damn right. Leaning against the sink, Edward drank from his glass and refilled it once more. *Look, Dad. You'll just have to trust me on this one. I know it's hard to understand right now, but he loves me.* Who didn't? Deborah befriended everyone she met. She ran a circus of ne'er-do-wells beginning with the stray cat she brought home when she was three. Christ. She cried for a week when it died.

"This caring business," Edward shouted to Annie, turning toward her. "He cared so much, how come he killed her? How come he managed to give her too many pills? What's complicated about giving someone the right dose? He worked it out just right. You don't have to believe me, Annie, just get me the goddamn address!"

The familiar dizziness overtook him. He grabbed the edge of the countertop.

"Edward, is it your sugar?" Annie said, coming up beside him.

"It will pass."

He let her steer him back to the couch. She was small yet stronger than he expected when she grabbed his armpits and helped lower him to the couch. This time he lay back against the cushion, one leg stretched across the couch.

"The truth, Annie?" He looked up at her standing beside him. "He's a killer. Plain and simple. You like him? Don't be a fool like my daughter—like me. I should have stopped him. Van's a charmer. He crushed a few extra pills into my daughter's milkshakes over the course of several days until she couldn't wake up. It was too much for her system. Her MS was affecting her ability to swallow, so he crushed up the pills. A few too many is what he did."

"I'm trying to fathom it . . ."

"That's right."

He closed his eyes. He was exhausted. Once again, he saw Deborah wheeling down the long bowling alley of a hall to her garden. A large oak tree shaded a flagstone patio. He remembered the hanging plants—pink impatiens, sweet potato, and vinca vines cascading down a wooden fence.

"What's going to happen when things get rough?" he had asked Deborah.

A tall, thin man with shoulder-length hair stepped out onto the patio. He wore sandals and bent over to kiss his daughter on her lips.

"Van, this is my dad."

"Coming from work?" Edward said, knowing the instant he saw him that Van didn't have a job, was a drug user. A bloodsucker. A slouch with red-rimmed, glazed eyes in the middle of the day.

"*Dad. Don't start with the first degree.*"

"*Why don't I let you two spend some time together,*" Van said, turn-ing to the door. "*I can run a few errands and come back.*"

"*Don't be silly, honey. I told you what he was like.*" Deborah wheeled closer to the door, blocking Edward. "*You alienate everyone you meet, Dad. Why do you assume that what you want for me is what I want for me? Why? Why do you do this? Why?*"

"Why?" Edward said, opening his eyes. Annie was standing over him, her hand on his shoulder.

"You dozed off for a minute."

"What time is it?"

Old age and infancy. Not much difference between them. He looked at his watch. Two o'clock.

"I'm going to leave now," Annie said.

He sat up. "What time is the party?"

"Seven to nine. We're getting picked up at six forty-five."

"Call me when you get his address, will you do that?" He squeezed the business card curled inside his fist. The address was one of the remaining pieces of the puzzle, the one he needed and was about to get.

"Yes. I told you I would." She moved to the door. "You should register with the embassy. They can protect you."

He tried to soften his voice. "Thank you. Are you going home now? Where's Will? Where's your son?"

"He'll be home in a few hours. Leo's home wth the babysitter."

"Good. Be careful, Annie."

"I will." She glanced at the windows. "I can always call the police," she said, letting out an exasperated sigh. She walked over to the door.

Six feet away from him, he saw her youth, the years still ahead of her like a point in the horizon in one of his paintings. It made him ache for his daughter, for his wife.

"Thank you, Annie."

"Sure. See you, Edward."

As soon as she left, he got up to chain the door, then went over to the window and waited until he saw Annie reappear in the distance, jogging down the tree-lined sidewalk.

She was the only person in sight, though he knew that Van might be out there, hiding.

Watching her.

Watching him.

Thirty

The woman who was the mayor's so-called assistant wore a white blouse and bra so sheer her nipples pushed through like pebbles. It was the first thing Annie noticed when she got into the front seat of the Mercedes on the passenger's side, along with a powerful odor of cigarettes and lavender perfume.

"Hello. I am Agnes."

"Annie."

Agnes snuffed her cigarette in the ashtray, and held out her hand. "Pardon. I know Americans do not like smoking in cars."

Agnes's hand felt cool and dry from the car's air-conditioning.

"Nice to see you again, Agnes," Will said, sliding into the back.

"*Igen*. We are old friends already." She smiled into the rearview mirror. "I will tell you both that I am not used to driving in this city. These people are crazy, but I will drive slow for you. I like your dress. Very pretty," she said to Annie.

Annie had chosen a black sleeveless dress with a side slit, a favorite of Will's because he liked how the thin belt accentuated her small waist. "Thank you. What is the name of your perfume?" Annie said, exchanging compliments. "I like it."

"*Bibor*. It *eez* Hungarian for purple. You know it? It is popular now."

"Yes. I recognize it," Annie said.

"Thank you for driving," Will said.

"*Persze*. I am glad to drive for you. The police are very strict. You understand this? If you are drinking and driving, they will put you in jail. I will not drink tonight. But you can enjoy." She glanced again at Will in the rearview mirror, offering a broad lipsticky smile.

"Where is his place exactly?" Annie asked. Stephen had not returned her call. After she left Edward's, she thought of calling Stephen again, but she didn't want to sound urgent. Instead, she and Klara fed Leo an early dinner and waited for Will to get home and for Sandor to come over to help watch the baby for the night.

"Across the river, near the Erzsébet Bridge," Agnes said. "What you call Elizabeth Bridge."

"What is the name of the street and the number?" Annie asked. "I'd like to give my babysitter the address."

"*Persze*. Molnár utca 9. It is a small street, next to the river. It is fifteen minutes. Not far."

"Good. Thank you." In her lap, Annie felt the weight of her cell phone in her purse and wondered when would be the best time to call Edward. Despite what he told her only a few hours earlier, key questions remained unanswered. What if Edward's daughter had, in fact, died of an accidental overdose? Did that make Stephen responsible? What if Edward was right? The two questions orbited in her head like trapped flies.

"It is a beautiful night in Budapest, yes?" Agnes said, filling the quiet in the car.

"Gorgeous," Annie said, forcing herself to engage. She could feel Will sulking in the back seat. He had had enough of her talk of Edward and Stephen and told her as much while they were waiting outside for Agnes to pick them up.

"It's getting out of hand," Will had said, his face devoid of expression, his way of containing his annoyance. "No matter what I think about Stephen, no matter what Edward believes, hearsay doesn't make someone a murderer. It's his word against Stephen's. The fact that he's going by another name or even that he may be some kind of addict proves nothing. I'm not impressed with Stephen. I find him cloying, but this whole murder thing is taking it too far."

Now in the car, Annie stared out the window at the evening traffic and the darkening sky, lost in the dull clatter of her thoughts amid the honking sounds of the city until Agnes said, "There they are," and Annie spotted Eileen walking from the hotel to the car in a bright green fitted dress she remembered from Fendix days. Eileen's vibrant hair fell in long waves to her shoulders. Her curved figure and enormous breasts commanded attention, but much of that was because of the way she carried herself with pride and a sensual enjoyment of her body. Annie rolled down the window and waved.

"Eileen!"

"I'm relying on you to tell me everything," Eileen said, getting into the backseat. Bernardo slid in after her.

"What a great night, huh?" Bernardo said.

"Good weather for a change," Will said.

Eileen put her hand on Annie's shoulder.

"So good to see you here!" Annie said, twisting around to hold Eileen's hand. The car filled with the scent of wine and Eileen's perfume.

"Can you believe my husband is trying to drag me here? He's so enamored right now. I'm here to appease him. I can't get anything but glowing remarks out of him. I know it can't be all good. Nothing is. Right, Annie?"

"I suppose not," Annie said, not wanting to go there. "How was your flight?"

"Too damn long."

Annie laughed.

"Leave it to my wife to tell you what she thinks," Bernardo said.

"That's why we love her," Annie said.

"It's your job to convince her to stay," Bernardo said to Annie. "You, too, Agnes."

"*Persze,*" Agnes said to the rearview mirror. "Eileen, you ask me questions and I will answer for you."

"Have you slept yet?" Annie asked Eileen.

"Are you kidding? I'm all adrenaline right now. Adrenaline and wine."

Agnes laughed, then turned up the air conditioner. "Good. Then you will enjoy yourself."

"This city is a knockout at night, like a beautiful woman," Bernardo said as Agnes turned onto the road that ran alongside the river. "Look at it. Tell me that's not beautiful."

"Stunning," Annie said.

"Oh, here we go," Eileen said. "Everything is a woman to my husband. What's that bridge?"

"It is oldest bridge," Agnes said. "We call it Széchenyi lánchíd. *Lánchíd* is 'chain bridge' in Hungarian."

"Built in 1849," Will said. "It became a symbol for commerce, industrialism, and the future."

"It's an old future, yes?" Agnes said.

"Old future? Love that," Bernardo said. "Fuckin' love that."

"Watch your language," Eileen said.

The car turned and Agnes drove a block in from the river.

"Old city of illusions," Will said.

"Now what's that supposed to mean?" Bernardo said.

Annie knew exactly what Will meant.

"Not what it seems on the surface," Will said.

"*Igen,*" Agnes said. "Like Americans' smile, yes?"

"That hurts, Agnes," Bernardo said. "You don't like my smile?"

"*Persze.* I am sorry for my joke."

"Didn't you say Stephen lived on the river?" Annie said, feeling panicked that Edward, after all his talk, was mistaken and just plain wrong.

"Do not worry," Agnes said. "We park in back because it is safer. You will see the river from inside these buildings."

"Look at those art nouveau structures," Will said as Agnes backed into a parking space on the side street. "The architectural

movement swept across Europe around 1900 and erupted in Budapest during the building boom of the 1920s."

"Erupted?" Bernardo said. "That's choice."

"Pretty incredible to look at. See those ornate roofs and facades?" Will said, pointing. "Proof of better days."

"Yes. This is the Budap*esht* story," Agnes said. "You have studied it right, Will. I am impressed. This is true of many of our buildings. But this is changing." Agnes shut the motor off. "We are here."

"Is this Molnar we're parked on?" Annie asked Agnes. The dimly
lit road was narrow, more like an alleyway, behind the buildings.

"Yes. I write it down for you."

Everyone got out and waited on the sidewalk until Agnes joined
them, handing Annie a slip of paper with Stephen's address.

"Thank you."

"Who is this person we're seeing?" Eileen asked Annie. The two
women walked a few steps behind the others.

"Someone your husband is thinking of hiring."

"Do you know him? I have a million questions. Not tonight,
though. How about tomorrow for lunch? Just the two of us. Can
you meet me at the hotel? Bring Leo if you don't have someone
to watch him. That's another thing. Babysitters. How's the baby
doing?"

"Perfect. He's a joy. We have a wonderful babysitter. I'll be
happy to meet you at your hotel."

"That's a relief. I need to know about everything—schools, hous-
ing, and if my husband is out of his mind." She let out a big laugh.

"Absolutely. I'll give you names and places to contact. It's not
that complicated."

Ahead of them Agnes tripped on an uneven stone. Bernardo grabbed Agnes's elbow, then slipped his arm around her waist to help her regain her balance.

Eileen rolled her eyes at Annie and whispered to her: "Business as usual."

In the old days at Fendix, Annie liked pairing up with Eileen because of her candor and humor. Eileen let people know that she wasn't blind to her husband's flirtations. In that regard, she commanded respect from the other wives. But Annie wondered if Eileen knew how far he took those flirtations, like the woman he danced with at Club Z.

"Mysterious-looking place," Bernardo said, taking his hand from Agnes's arm and turning to wait for Eileen.

They passed underneath a twenty-foot arched doorway, then crossed a brick courtyard of a five-story building.

"This place makes me feel like a hobbit," Eileen said, laughing.

"What is hobbit?" Agnes asked.

"A small imaginary person," Eileen said.

"You Americans have interesting ideas," Agnes said.

The grand-size building had faded from years of neglect. The Budapest story, Annie thought. In a far corner, Annie noted the typical cluster of garbage cans and a few discarded ceramic pots of wilted plants, as if someone had tried but failed to get some greenery going.

Inside the building, a caged elevator hung from ropes dangling in the elevator's industrial-size open shaft. Will pushed the elevator call button.

"These old things make me nervous," Eileen said.

"It's an old future," Bernardo said, relishing the phrase once again.

"You don't worry," Agnes said, lighting up a cigarette. "It is not a problem."

"Made it through the war. Made it through '56. It'll be fine," Will said.

"Nineteen fifty-six. *Nem* good," Agnes said. "I wasn't born then. But it was terrible."

"How 'bout we lighten up this conversation a bit," Bernardo said. "We all know Hungarians suffered. So did the Jews, right, Will? But we have to live a little, enjoy ourselves." Bernardo put his arm around Eileen and squeezed her.

"Yes, that is the American way," Agnes said, walking into the elevator. "Top floor."

"Bernardo's way," Eileen said, throwing a look at the ceiling.

In the elevator, the cage rose slowly up the shaft, shuddering each time it passed another floor. Will stood across from Annie and gave her an affirming look, the warmth in his eyes returning.

"It's a good location, yes?" Agnes said. "A lot of people would like to live here on the Duna. Stephen is lucky. There is a lottery system for these buildings. But it is for Hungarians. Stephen must know someone."

"He paid cash," Bernardo said.

"His parents are Hungarian. That probably helped him," Annie said, bothered by the mention of cash, knowing full well where his cash had come from. Was she really going to a murderer's flat? Was Edward wrong? Losing a daughter and a wife could drive anyone over the edge. Edward told her the death certificate said death by asphyxiation and multiple sclerosis. It could have been an accidental death, a terrible convergence of circumstances. Again, her thoughts tangled in the same contradictions of dreary facts.

When the door opened at the top, they filed out and headed down a hallway lit by a single bulb hanging from the ceiling. The women's heels clattered, echoing in the stale air. Stephen must have heard them.

"Found it all right?" Stephen said, poking his head out the door at the end of the hallway. He immediately caught Annie's eye and smiled, then he turned to Agnes, greeting her in Hungarian. Agnes said something back to him and gave him a kiss.

"Just fine," Annie said. She thought Stephen looked handsome and was once again drawn in by his laid-back demeanor. He leaned over and kissed her gently on the cheek.

"Sorry I didn't get a chance to return your call. I was running around doing errands. It's 9 Molnar—."

"Thanks. Agnes gave it to me in the car," she said. Stephen's breath smelled of cigarettes and wine. He was dressed in brown pants, a white shirt with the sleeves rolled up, and sandals—his usual outfit, which worked for him, creating a casual confidence that remained appealing to her, except for his sandals, which bared his long, tanned toes and now struck her as boldly sexual.

"Good. Welcome, everyone," Stephen said, showing them in.

They entered a large but unfurnished living room. Across the room, floor-to-ceiling French doors opened onto a balcony and a startling view across the river to a white statue perched atop a cliff. The statue was flooded in footlights.

"Whoa, man, you underplayed the location," Bernardo said. "Imagine this place in Boston, Back Bay, overlooking the Charles? Jesus, man. You got a million-dollar view."

"Maybe more," Will said.

"For you Americans, yes," Agnes said. "Not for us."

"That's Gellért Hill," Stephen said, pointing. "I'm sure you know it, Will."

"Tallest hill in Buda," Will said.

Agnes looked startled, her eyes widening. "Will, I am impressed. You know a lot about my country."

"This place is impressive," Eileen said, crossing the large room. "Loving these herringbone floors."

"All the floors are like this here," Annie said. "These are especially nice."

"Where's the Bull's Blood?" Bernardo said, his voice clapping the air.

"It's all right here," Stephen said, leading them to a small table set up with crystal glasses, bottles of Bull's Blood, and *pálinka*—which the mayor had served Annie and Will—and Unicum, another Hungarian specialty liqueur.

"Shall we have some *pálinka*?" Stephen said, handing out a round of shot glasses filled with the clear, strong liquor.

"*Egészségünkre!*" Stephen said, throwing back a shot.

Bernardo and Will followed, emptying their glasses.

"What is that you say?" Bernardo said. "Eggs and shakes?"

"*Egészségünkre!* To our health!"

Eileen drained her glass. "Got to keep up with the boys," she said, grinning at Annie, who sipped slowly. The liquid was numbing her tongue.

"Bernardo?" Stephen said, tipping the bottle of *pálinka* as an invitation to refill his glass.

"Put her in and then let's have some of your Bull's Blood."

"What's Bull's Blood?" Eileen said.

"It is our famous wine. Egri Bikavér means 'bull's blood,'" Agnes said.

"Eger is the region where it's made," Will said. "There's a legend that says the wine gives you the strength of a bull."

"That's right," Agnes said. "Tell us the legend, Will."

"Some say the story dates back to an event that happened in the sixteenth century when a small band of Hungarian troops drank the local red wine and successfully fought back a large Turkish army."

"That's because we are a determined people," Agnes said.

"Yes, we are," Stephen said, guiding a glass of Bull's Blood into Annie's hand and taking her now-empty glass of *pálinka*.

"To Hungary. *Egészségünkre!*" Stephen said.

"And that unbelievable view," Bernardo said, drinking up.

They all headed onto the balcony to take in the full view. "You lucked out, man," Bernardo said.

"I was just reading about that statue," Will said, stepping onto the balcony next to Annie, who leaned against the wrought-iron railing to survey a grid of small streets leading to the river. It was a long way down and she pulled back, thinking of her brother.

"The statue's forty meters tall," Will said.

"Yes, I never get tired of her," Stephen said, joining the two men.

"Will, you are our history book tonight, yes?" Agnes said.

Bernardo guffawed, nodding. "Come on Eileen, join us."

"There's not enough room," Eileen said.

"Crowd in. Come on."

"What's the statue commemorating?" Annie asked. She stood wedged between Bernardo and Will, who put his arm around her.

"It is about the Soviet victory in Budapest," Agnes said, standing behind Annie.

Across the river and up the steep hill, the statue of a female flooded in foot lights held a palm leaf over her head like an offering to the heavens. In the night sky, two tiny stars appeared above the statue's head. Annie thought of the Bem József statue, how its arm was raised to the sky, too. She wondered if Greg were trying to go upward when he jumped. That was the odd thing about people's desires when they dove off buildings and bridges.

"We don't see this as victory," Agnes continued. "It is another occupation for us. The Russian occupation. We are always occupied. Now it's you, the Americans, who are trying."

"Sorry about that," Annie said.

Agnes smiled. "It is a joke. I love Americans."

The panoramic view from the balcony was mesmerizing. The river's dark face sparkled, reflecting the glittering lights on the Elizabeth Bridge, the one they had just crossed, and parallel to the quiet side street below, cars sped along the Duna leaving trails of red and white lights.

"The Russians liberated the Hungarians from the Germans in World War II," Will said. "But it wasn't freedom. Essentially, they went from one enslavement to another."

Annie felt dreamy, entranced by the view of the hill that staged these historic events. She gripped the thin iron railing and lifted her chin to catch a breeze from the river.

"What you can't see from here," Will said, "is the statue of St. Gellért for whom this hill is named." He pointed to the side of the hill. "It's below, behind there."

"Okay. Now I'm doubly impressed," Bernardo said.

"You know a lot," Stephen said, refilling everyone's glasses with more Bull's Blood.

"He likes his history," Annie said.

"Tell us more," Eileen said.

"Gellért was a Benedictine monk during the time of King Stephen I—he became a bishop in 1030. In 1046, he died a martyr. The Hungarian pagans threw him off the cliff or stoned him to death."

"Oh Lord," Eileen said. "Gruesome."

"Yes. Very sad," Agnes said.

"You look at the hill now and it seems unbelievable," Annie said, leaving the balcony to take in the rest of the apartment. The apartment was large for Budapest: three rooms, including the long, spacious living room on one end, sparsely furnished with a couch and two wooden chairs; an alcove kitchen; and a bedroom with a double bed at the other end.

"Folks, we need to celebrate the moment," Bernardo said. "You've got a damn nice place here, Stephen."

"It's really lovely," Annie said to Stephen, who had stepped back inside to join her. "How did you luck into it?" She guessed the ceilings were fourteen feet high.

"Not luck, Annie. You know I haven't been lucky. Right place. Right circumstances." He looked at her as if inviting her into his confessional, the one they had shared on the sidewalk and later at Bem József statue, before returning to the task of uncorking two more bottles of Egri Bikavér.

She took his bait, and said, "My husband told me about your wife. I'm so sorry."

Stephen smiled without light, but Annie noticed a subtle

change in his face, as if he had disappeared for a moment. The thought that he could be hiding something stabbed her in the chest. Why hadn't he told her about the death of his wife?

"I haven't been able to talk about it," Stephen said, as if he had heard her thoughts. "It's too fresh. Truth is, I'm here because of her."

"What do you mean?"

"She wanted to fulfill my—it doesn't matter anymore." He bowed his head and moved away to rejoin the others. Annie felt awkward and followed him, hoping he might tell her more.

"You see that," Agnes said, pointing diagonally across the river, the cigarette burning between her fingers. "That is the Gellért spa."

"I'd love to go to a spa," Eileen said.

"That one is the most famous one," Agnes said. "The queen of Netherlands stayed here on her wedding night. Now you are in Budapest, you must try it."

"I'm game," Bernardo said, draping his arm around Agnes. "You want to set it up for us?"

"He's always game," Eileen said, walking over to Bernardo, who removed his arm from Agnes and kissed Eileen hard on the lips. "I hear they swim naked there," he whispered to her so everyone could hear.

"Even better," Eileen said.

Annie drifted away from their banter. Eileen knew how to hold her own with Bernardo, but Annie still thought Bernardo was flaunting Agnes as if to say, If you don't move here, this is what's waiting for me. Annie moved around the apartment, sipping Bull's Blood, doing her best to admire the ceiling height and crown molding that had remained intact. Should she call Edward now, while everyone was laughing and chatting? There must be something here that would tell her who Stephen truly was, some indisputable clue. She thought of her brother, Greg, and wondered where he would be now, if he had lived. What city, what transient construction job, would he have found to keep him on the run? She glanced back at Stephen, who caught her eye and gave her a wistful smile, acknowledging this new disclosure of his dead wife between them. She felt sorry for him again—losing his wife, his father—and then she heard Edward's gravelly voice warning—*be careful, be careful*—echoing in her mind.

Everyone turned to the sound of knocking on Stephen's door.

"My neighbors. Marta and her grandmother, Olga," Stephen said, ushering two women into the living room. "I thought you would enjoy meeting them."

The younger one, Marta, greeted Stephen with a kiss on his lips. *"Szia,"* she said, using the familiar, colloquial greeting that sounded like "see ya." Annie thought it so typical of Hungary to adopt a greeting for hello that sounded like good-bye in America. It was yet another example of opposites embedded deep in the Hungarian psyche, where losers were winners and winners never won.

Marta appeared to be in her twenties—Stephen's girlfriend, Annie presumed. Both women had angular chins and bony frames. The elderly Olga wore a pink scarf around her neck that brightened the whole room, like a flag, Annie thought. Marta looked starved, her eyes blackened with eyeliner, her thin lips dark as Bull's Blood. Stephen went back to the kitchen to get more glasses.

"Marta is quite talented," Stephen said as he came back out. He handed glasses of Bull's Blood to the party newcomers. Annie wondered: Can you leave a country and become someone you are not?

He wants to get you on his side, she remembered Edward telling her.

Olga turned to Marta and spoke rapidly, then pointed a long, shaky finger at Annie and Eileen.

"I show you my jewelry? Maybe you American womens will like it?" Marta said. "I sell you."

"I love jewelry," Eileen said.

"Stephen, you get points for this," Bernardo said.

Stephen nodded, standing behind Marta, whispering something to her in Hungarian.

"I don't speak good English," Marta said. She kept shifting back and forth on her slim, long legs, glancing at Stephen for reassurance. He put his hand on one of her hips to reassure her. Marta was so thin her collarbone stood out, yet she exuded sensuality in her leotard-like miniskirt and blouse, with her small breasts, her ballerina's posture.

Annie felt a wave of claustrophobia crushing her head—too many glasses of wine on an empty stomach. What was she doing? Did Stephen plan on serving something more to eat, or did he intend for everyone to get flat-out drunk? She had a sudden need to splash water on her face. Turning, she headed down a short hall, searching for the washroom. In Hungary, this would be a room separate from the toilet room. It was the same in their flat. She thought it an odd arrangement when they first moved here, but now she preferred it over the American design.

From the small washroom that managed to accommodate a bathtub and sink, she could hear Eileen and Bernardo laughing about *pálinka*, their voices too loud, as if they were putting on a show. Annie had seen them perform like this at numerous Fendix parties, but even when they were heading toward drunk, they never completely lost control of themselves, and really, why did Annie care? She had her own self-control to worry about, the dull ache in her head was intensifying. Will was in his pontificating, professorial mode, taking in the surroundings and noting historical artifacts as he liked to do.

On the shelf above the sink, she found a container of aspirin from the States and next to it a liquid cough syrup in a plastic bottle. She opened the bottle and smelled it to confirm, then turned on the faucet and bent over to refresh the skin under her eyes. A small white oval pill lay wedged in a curl of the linoleum floor next to the tub. She picked it up and saw VICODIN stamped on one side of the tablet. Frightened, she placed the pill in her purse. She sat on the tub to calm her nerves, letting the water continue to run. What should she do?

She listened until she heard Stephen chuckling to something Bernardo said. Scared but determined, she dialed Edward's number.

"Edward, I'm here." She spoke softly, turning her back to the door.

"You have it?"

"It's 9 Molnár utca. On the river, just like he said." She spelled out the name of the street and explained that it was on a small back street. She spoke quickly, growing more terrified as the seconds passed. "The entrance is in the back. He's on the fifth floor at the end. Last apartment on the right."

Someone knocked on the door, startling her.

"Be right out!" Annie said, abruptly cutting off Edward without saying good-bye. Her heart was speeding.

She stood and splashed more water on her face. There was nothing else for her to do. Edward had everything he needed now. She almost felt relieved. Drying her face, she opened the door. Stephen stood in the small hallway, waiting for her.

Thirty-one

He checked the chain and the door locks and with a great sense of relief walked back into his bedroom. Annie had given him what he'd come here to get. Street address. Phone. Apartment number. A ten-minute cab ride. He sat down on the bed and traced the route on his city map.

Thank you, Annie. Thank you.

This was his chance. Now. Van was there. Annie and the others would be gone by the time he arrived. Now may not come again.

He heard faint sounds of a trolley making stops, starting up again, and the beeps and rush of cars heading for where? Parties on Saturday night. Dinners with friends. Tourists looking for action. Bars. Cafes. Clubs. Sex? It was all the same around the world.

Budapest. Boston. Humans. Day. Night. Moon. Stars. Animals.
Life. Death.

He took in the still night. The moment. The room. A finite
point in time and space; an intersection in the galaxy; a minuscule,
infinitesimal tick. A temperate night. The breeze lifted the bottom
of the window shade, a soft tapping noise each time. A sigh. He
shifted on the bed, sliding open the night table drawer, lifting the
gun out and holding it. Only good for close range, small and easy
to hide. He laid the gun on the bedsheet and went to the window
to look out, bending back a small section of the shade. At the end
of the street, he saw a cab turn down another road that led to a
maze of streets leading away from here. A month in this place. Long
enough. The wait. Waiting's what killed you in the war. He looked
at his watch. He would force himself to wait a few minutes longer.
The party would be over soon enough. Seven to nine is what Annie
had told him earlier. It was 9:20 p.m.

He returned to the bed and checked the gun once again as he
had so many times before, turning it over in his hands. Loaded.
Ready to go.

Thank you, Annie. Thank you.

A month or so ago he arrived.

This is here, the boy, Ivan, had said. *Welcome to your new home.*
Ivan had placed Edward's suitcase in the tiny elevator and up they
went to the second floor.

This is here.

That was the truth.

This was here: four thousand miles across the sea, far from the
graves of his dead daughter and wife, and yet no miles at all. They

were here, too. Sylvia beside him, shouting, *Edward, what is this? You're not going to live this way! What are you doing?*

Here.

He placed the gun in his pants pocket, then looked at his father's watch: 9:28 p.m.

Did he have everything? What else? He booked a room at the new hotel downtown. He sent for a cab. Soon it would be here.

Here. He surveyed the bedroom, turned off the bathroom light.

Before he left, Nan begged him not to go. What about his illness, his state of mind, his family? "What about *me*? Your daughter. I'm still here. I count."

"You count plenty. You have a *life*."

Nan had a partner, worked at a good hospital in Boston. His Nan and Sylvia, both dependable as rain. Not Deborah.

He took another peek out the living-room window at the empty street. He patted his other pocket. Wallet. Cash. Plenty of American cash.

"Nan, dear. You will be fine. That's how it is with you." Why? He didn't know. Born like that. Born gay, too. When she'd told him on the phone, she said, *You feel differently about me, now, don't you, Dad?*

No. No. He did not. He felt exactly the same. He shrugged at the memory of it. Surprised? Maybe. But she was a boyish child. He loved her. Nan was Nan. No. His feelings didn't change. Sylvia struggled with it. If they'd had a son, he might have struggled. Sylvia came around. Their daughter was their daughter. It made no difference.

Gay. What was that? It was an orientation. Isn't that what they called it? An orientation? What did that mean? Some kind of

position, like a boat tacking in the wind. Every human being had
an orientation, an attitude, a belief. Everyone crossed the waters of
life, one way or another.

He stood at the fan in the living room and let the breeze stream
through his shirt. It felt good. Then he turned it off and the air
conditioner, too, and listened to the silence.

For a moment he heard nothing.

Then their voices again. All of them, his family, streaming in
his ears.

I wanted to tell you.

Nan met her friend Patricia in the surgical unit at the hospital.
When Nan moved in with Patricia to share an apartment, he didn't
catch on until Nan spelled it out.

I'm gay, Dad.

The kids—they teach you a few things, more than a few things,
and some things you didn't want to know.

He picked up the photo of Deborah and removed it from the
frame. On the back of the picture, he wrote Nan's number, and
Josef's number in the States, then creased the photo and put it in
his pants pocket. Yes, Nan. You are here with me, too.

Funny. Both his kids needed to fix people. Maybe they got
it from their mother. Sylvia was always donating clothes or food
on the Jewish New Year and Hanukkah, delivering presents to
immigrant families from Russia. She didn't like to throw things
away. Something chipped? Cracked? A little glue worked magic,
she would say. She fixed everything, except her broken heart after
Deborah was killed.

Welcome to your new home, Ivan had said.

Home.

What was home? He didn't have a home. He was homeless. A homeless Jewish man. A homeless father. A homeless husband who used to have a wife. A homeless man who used to own a house in the 'burbs. Home was where his heart was. Oh. Yes.

Home was here, where his daughter's murderer walked and talked, lived and lied.

Was alive.

He went back to his night table drawer and removed the torn photo of Van. In the kitchen, he turned on the gas stove and held the photo over the blue flame. The flame grabbed the paper, sucked it up in a yellow flash before collapsing into ash. As it should be. He turned off the stove and went to the living room and took in the view of his easel and stack of paintings, the couch and TV, the curtains, the worn-down parquet floors as familiar to him as if he had lived here for years. He shook his head, settling the pieces of the puzzle in his mind.

Josef told him about the apartment fifty years ago. Five decades gone in a flash.

It was right after the war. Fall of '45. The liberation. Edward was twenty-six, an army lieutenant overseeing a small internment camp in Allied-occupied Austria, trying to keep peace among men and women grouped in cabins. He could still smell the flakes of paint, the air filled with crumbled leaves and dust, the odors mixing with the nearby woods. The Americans supplied food to those men and women from Slovakia and Hungary.

And Josef, the Hungarian first in line with a request. They all had requests. The women throwing themselves at Edward, desperate for food, offering sex for favors.

His unit was there to keep peace and order. That was the

American directive. But the whole system was not established, no structure, only desperation.

"I am Josef Szabo. I am Jewish like you. I speak your language. You see? I have training in research medicine. Please. You are Jew. You can help me get to America. I have a cousin in United States. Family. We help each other. I give you our family flat in Budapest. I speak English. *Parlez-vous français?* I speak French. I will not return to my country. You are Jew. You understand this. You must help me."

"You and everyone here—all six hundred of you. I don't need your flat."

"But I am Jew. And you are Jew. You cannot deny me America."

Josef was short, his chest thick as an oak tree, his eyes on fire.

They stood in the officer cabin—a plain, wood shed with a bed, a desk, a wooden floor, a pile of cigarette butts on the desktop. Edward chain-smoked then. He lit up a cigarette for himself and this Hungarian man.

Josef shook his head. "You give me America. I give you my family's flat. It is a promise." He took a pen, then tore a strip of cloth from his shirt, and wrote on it. He signed his name, wrote down the Budapest address, and his cousin's town in the States: Stow, Massachusetts.

Josef's handshake was firm, earnest—insistent—like Edward's grandfather who came from Russia, the old country. Maybe that was why Edward gave in. Josef reminded him of his grandfather, the peddler. The one who opened a grocery store in Boston. He couldn't say which of those things convinced him, but he got Josef on a ship to America.

"Don't forget my promise," Josef said on the day he left. Edward kept the piece of cloth in his duffel bag while he traveled around France, Austria, and Switzerland for eleven more months before returning to Massachusetts. He was American, a demigod in Europe after the war. What a feeling. He inhaled a long breath, remembering.

Outside, Edward heard a car alarm go off and begin its sequence of inane melodies. Whoop! Whoop! Doo-ah doo-ah. It chimed rhythmically like a giant, alien cicada in the Budapestian night. When the noise stopped, he unchained the door and leaned against the door frame until the mild dizziness subsided. This old geezer wasn't dead yet.

Edward looked down at himself and laughed. No wonder Annie took to him. He was a homeless, displaced American Jew in baggy pants, a wrinkled blazer. No different than those six hundred Hungarians and Slovakians in the Displaced Persons camp in 1945.

After the war, displaced persons like Josef were guests of the Allied armies. They were there to rehabilitate themselves. Get back into life. They had helped the Allies in some way. The Allies were charged with helping them return to their communities.

Edward rubbed his eyes. He was an old, displaced American man, wanting justice, wanting to set things right. He kept that piece of cloth with Josef's name and address in Budapest—this address. *Here.* 647 Károly utca. And Stow, Massachusetts. All of it on a torn piece of shirt that he kept for fifty years, stashed away in his drawer of valuables—a diamond tie clip from his grandfather, a pocket watch. His younger self, the one that existed back in 1945, didn't understand why he bothered to keep it, but his older self, the one looking at himself now, the one that existed even then, his older self must have foreseen the day he would need that piece of cloth. One day, a few months ago, he tracked down Josef in Stow, Massachusetts, the town where Josef's cousin gave Josef his start and where Josef and Rose remained to this day. Found his name in the Stow white pages. It was that easy.

"Because one day I will help you," Josef had said to him then. "You live on my promise. I am a good Hungarian. I don't like Nazis. I speak English. You see? My English is good. You will help me go to America."

Edward opened the door and stepped into the dark hallway, into shades of gray and brown. It was 9:26 p.m. The minutes were passing quickly. He needed to hurry now. This is what it came to: these moments you wonder about your whole life. And it is not what you had imagined.

Not at all.

Thirty-two

You okay?" Stephen said, standing in the hall. "I heard you talking." He looked intently at Annie, an expression of concern or suspicion, she couldn't tell.

"Yes, fine." She rushed her words, the lie catching in her throat. "I was checking in with my babysitter."

"Your son okay?"

"Yes. All is well. I didn't realize how late it was."

"Don't worry about the time. Come with me. I prepared some Hungarian sandwiches. I hope you like cheese and salami."

"I do."

She followed him down the hall, shaken that she was almost caught in the act of calling Edward.

"How long did you say you've lived here?" Annie asked, grasping for something to normalize their conversation. Her right toe was starting to ache. She wasn't used to wearing heels, or a dress for that matter. She straightened up and followed him into the kitchen.

"Less than a year."

"Not so long," she said, dissatisfied by his answer. Less than a year was vague. She wanted to know exactly how long, but she didn't want to raise his suspicions by asking again.

"No. But it feels like home."

In the kitchen, Stephen opened the refrigerator and began assembling the ingredients of the sandwiches on a small square table next to the window. The window offered another stunning view of the statue across the river.

"I started doing this earlier," he said, apologetically, "but I ran out of time."

She stood beside him and helped arrange the sandwiches in a circle on the platter. She wanted to bring up his wife again but wasn't sure how. "Are you planning to stay here permanently?"

"I think so."

Then she noticed on the windowsill a framed photo of Marta lying naked on a bed. It was embarrassing and irritating.

"She's a nice girl," Stephen said, gently putting Marta's photo facedown on the sill. He brushed a tendril of hair from Annie's face as if to tell her, It's okay. We're both embarrassed. Let's ignore it and carry on.

"I'm sure she is." Once again his intimate gesture unnerved her, his ability to be so familiar with her, and in response, she felt emboldened to ask more questions. "When did you two meet?"

"When I moved here. She's been a comfort. You know. After losing my wife."

"Your wife died young," Annie said, facing him. "Do you mind telling me what happened?"

"Multiple sclerosis."

"I didn't realize you could die from that."

"Yep."

Stephen finished his glass of wine and set the empty glass on the counter. "It is what it is. In the end, my wife couldn't feed herself. Truth is, she wanted to go—like your brother, like my father."

"No. My brother didn't want to go," Annie said. "He was depressed. And he was drinking."

"Well, my wife did. It was her wish, and it angers me because people don't understand that."

She could hear Edward yelling *bullshit*. "You mean society or your family?" Annie said, seeking clarification.

"She didn't want to live a compromised life in a wheelchair. That was not who she was."

Annie neatened the sandwiches on the platter, pushing them together so they overlapped like flower petals. What was Stephen saying? He was putting forth a totally different explanation for Deborah's death—not murder, not accidental overdose, but suicide—assisted suicide.

"Not many people consciously make that kind of decision," Annie said.

"You're not my wife."

"That was insensitive of me. I'm sorry."

"It's fine. I understand," he said, touching her bare arm. "I get upset about this. Sorry for what I said about your brother." He opened the refrigerator and pulled out a bottle of *pálinka*. "This stuff is great when it's cold."

In the other room, Eileen laughed gaily at something Bernardo said, and she could hear Will laughing as well.

"Deborah—my wife—she had a big laugh."

Stephen opened the *pálinka* and poured himself and Annie another glass. "She helped me in so many ways. I wanted to help her, if you understand what I mean."

"I'm not sure I do." She took a sip of the *pálinka* and it numbed her tongue again. She was too stunned to eat. Everything was beginning to sound like doublespeak. Help her how? Help her kill herself? Help her die, so he could collect the insurance and move here? Or simply help her die?

"How did she help you?" Annie said. She wanted to slow the fast currents of emotions flooding her thoughts.

"She wanted me to follow my dream of living here. She insisted on it. She believed in me when others didn't."

"She sounds like an extraordinary person. I don't think my brother knew what his dreams were."

"I'm sorry," Stephen said.

"Me, too," Annie said.

Stephen picked up the tray of sandwiches and took a decisive step toward the living room, but Annie put her hand on his arm to stop him. "Are you close to your wife's family?"

"Funny you should ask."

He paused at the burst of laughter coming from the other room—Eileen again.

"That's a conversation for another time. Come on. Let's join the fun. I don't want to be a downer. Marta's eager to show you her earrings."

She walked with him back into the living room, dissatisfied. He hadn't told her enough. The others were gathered around Marta's display of earrings, which she'd arranged on a cloth on the living-room floor. Only the grandmother was standing on the balcony now. The old woman looked exceedingly frail yet regal next to the iron railing. Annie, on the other hand, couldn't get her thoughts straight. If Deborah wanted to take her life, Stephen would have had to assist her because Deborah couldn't feed herself, at least according to what Stephen said. What would Edward say about that?

Bullshit. She could hear his deep voice as if he were standing beside her. *Deborah loved life. Always saw the positive in situations.*

Her ears started throbbing. Stephen admitted that he had helped kill his wife. Hadn't he?

"How about that *pálinka*?" Bernardo said to Stephen, holding out his glass. "Love the stuff."

"We are proud of our *pálinka*," Agnes said, freeing the bottle from Stephen's hand and pouring some into Bernardo's and then Eileen's empty glasses. "It is our Hungarian tradition of fruit brandy. Very strong to get drunk," she said, smiling. "We have festivals celebrating our *pálinka*."

Eileen was kneeling on the floor surveying the earrings, her tight green dress sliding up her thighs. Annie could see Eileen's black underwear, but no one seemed to care, certainly Eileen didn't.

"Please. Help yourself to some food, everyone," Stephen said.

Will came over to Annie and traced his finger on her lips. "You okay?"

"Not really." She whispered to him, "Do you think we can get everyone to leave soon?" She wanted to tell him that she had found a Vicodin tablet and that Stephen had just told her that his wife had killed herself and had asked Stephen to help her. Instead, she took Will's hand and squeezed it.

Stephen stopped in front of her and Will. "Another sandwich?" Will took one. "Appreciate it, Stephen."

"I appreciate your wife," Stephen said. "Annie, what do you think of Marta's earrings? They suit you. Elegant but not too overdone." Stephen spoke slowly, his voice drifting. "Marta is hoping to make connections with the American women here. Will told me you belong to the International Women's Association."

"Yes. I know a few women there." Annie chewed on her sandwich, wanting to hide from Stephen's ever-watchful eyes. He seemed to look through her and inside her. She didn't know how to meet his gaze or what to think of him anymore. She needed time to process her thoughts. He just flat-out told her his wife wanted to take her own life and that he helped her. Everything Edward told her would be correct, except through this different lens, it changed Stephen's intent. Didn't doctors perform euthanasia every day with morphine? Not officially. But out of compassion for their suffering patients? She knew they did.

Disturbed, she walked over to Marta and crouched down to peruse the earring display. She agreed with Stephen, the earrings— long strands of glittering beads—were elegant and whimsical, not overstated.

"These are lovely," Annie said to Marta. And she meant it. "I think the women at the IWA will love these. How much are you selling them for?"

"Twelve dollar," Marta said to Annie.

"She means twenty," Stephen said, moving closer. "Twenty and no change necessary. I'm her agent."

"I'm buying ten pairs to bring home as gifts," Eileen said. She pulled her hair back to show Annie her new earrings.

Bernardo came over and handed Marta two hundred-dollar bills. "American dollars okay?" he asked.

"Persze," Olga said, taking the large bills from her granddaughter and turning them over to make sure they were legitimate.

"Hungarians love American dollars," Stephen said. "The forint is pretty useless."

"How shall I meet American womens?" Marta asked Annie.

Annie lifted a pair of white strands and carefully threaded the silver wires through her pierced ears. "What is your phone number, Marta?" Annie said. "I'll call you."

Marta looked at Stephen.

"I use Stephen's phone and call you, yes?"

"Fine," Annie said. "Stephen has our number."

"Right here in my phone," Stephen said, tapping his pocket. His throat was flushed, his gray-green eyes noticeably bloodshot in the low light.

Marta stood up and thanked Annie and Eileen for the sale. Stephen raised his arm. "This calls for some Unicum!" Stephen went back over to the table with their empty glasses and opened the bulb-shaped bottle.

"Very expensive," Agnes said, coming over to Annie. "This is a most special drink for us."

"You can't get it anywhere else, only in Hungary," Stephen said. He filled new glasses with the dark liqueur. "Come on, everyone. Bernardo, Eileen."

Eileen reached for the glass of Unicum and lost her footing. Bernardo grabbed her and gave her a kiss, the two looking more glued together than ever. Annie decided she would never understand their combative relationship. She looked over at Agnes and wondered what she thought of this drunken collection of Americans. And Stephen? Was he pining for his dead wife? Relieved? Overjoyed? He certainly had moved on pretty quickly. But who was she to judge? What did she really know about his situation? What would she do if Will asked her to do the same if he were in Deborah's situation? It was upsetting to contemplate and deepened her increasingly dour mood, and it was approaching ten o'clock. She wanted to leave.

A warm breeze from the balcony brought in a faint musty smell of the Duna, the current floating up from an underlayer of dirt and stones. Below, on the street, a car alarm went off, a long trill and then a series of different beeps, alarms, chirps, and sirenlike melodies echoing, repeating. Budapest's night call, its nursery jingle: *Watch out! Beware! Run away!*

"We ought to be taking off soon," Will said, tapping his watch.

"One more on the balcony!" Stephen said, holding up the bottle of Unicum and filling a tray full of shot glasses—passing them to Bernardo and Will, and offering one to Marta's grandmother, who deferred, and went to sit in a chair by the table with the crystal glasses, clenching the two hundred-dollar bills in her fist. Annie wondered if the crystal glasses had been a wedding present.

"I'm cooked," Eileen said, taking the shot glass from Stephen and smelling it. "This stuff makes you feel weird."

"It's hallucinatory," Bernardo said.

"Think unique for Unicum," Stephen said.

"No more for me. I've had too much," Annie said. Her thoughts were swimming like a school of fish, taking reverse turns every time a new ripple of information passed through her brain. She couldn't keep up with herself.

Marta gathered up the remaining earrings and put them in a cloth purse, then joined the rest of the group on the balcony.

"Last one," Bernardo said, slurring his words, holding out his empty shot glass, "and we'll call it a night."

Thirty-three

Edward locked the door to Josef's apartment and started toward the elevator, past the open stairway. A meager bulb lit the way. He stopped to listen. In the building of mostly older folks, he could hear the distant humming of televisions and radios through floors and ceilings. He headed down the hall, running his hand along the wall to help his balance, until he reached the elevator to take him down.

Outside, engulfed by the humid air, he waited by the panel of buzzers, the blazer he'd worn on the plane hanging loosely over his upper body, an unwelcome reminder that he'd lost more weight. He could feel his thirst returning in the back of his throat. He swallowed.

Come on. He looked down the street for the cab.

Now it was 9:52. Late for him. Typically, he would have changed into his pajamas by now, settled on the couch to read and nod off. Annie's call gave him a surge of energy.

The taxi flicked its light. Edward raised his hand. His back stiff from arthritis, his eyes semiblind in the glare of the headlights, he bent forward and eased into the back of the cab.

"You speak English?"

"Yes. Where do you go?"

Edward handed him Howard's address, written on a piece of paper in block letters.

"You know where this is?"

The driver, a middle-age man, took the paper from him, nodding. "*Persze.* Near Duna."

"Good. How much in American dollars?"

"Three dollars."

"Get there quickly." Edward handed him a ten-dollar bill.

The movement of the cab jostled Edward's knees, his hips, and the memory of Deborah calling him the day before she died: *Dad, please call me . . .* Something in her voice not sounding right, but he didn't pay it enough attention. Was it the drugs? Her MS making her slur her speech? She didn't answer when he called back a few hours later. Why hadn't he called her again? Anger? He was still too angry at her for marrying a creep.

He deserved this nightmare and dry-swallowed the poison of self-hate. There was the call from Howard the next morning, telling him he'd found Deborah gone, in her bed. He thought she was sleeping, he'd told Edward. "She'd been sleeping a lot in the past few days. We were planning to go to Nassau. Maybe it was too much for her," Howard said.

"Don't let anyone take her before I get there." Edward hung up and was in the car, racing to Deborah's, the pain exploding in his stomach, ready to strangle Van with his own hands.

When Edward walked in, he told the police he wanted an autopsy. But it wasn't under his jurisdiction. Howard was her husband, her health care proxy. Howard refused.

"No autopsy. It's not what Deborah wanted," he said, showing the police and Edward the written DNR directive: do not resuscitate. "She was squeamish about that sort of thing," Howard said. "She wanted to be cremated, her ashes buried—not the traditional Jewish way—but that is what she wanted. She didn't want to take up space. It's all here," Howard said, shaking the papers.

Death by asphyxiation, multiple sclerosis. His daughter in ashes. Edward made a mess of it. He should have followed his instincts and insisted on the autopsy despite Deborah's wishes, and Sylvia's. Nan didn't try to interfere.

In the backseat of the cab, Edward placed one hand in his lap, the other on the car door handle. Alongside the Duna, the cab stopped at a traffic light. All around him, the city was alive and thoroughly disinterested in Edward's existence. Fifty years later, a piece of cloth, a priceless exchange in Austria after the war, and Josef Szabo's name and number in a telephone directory in Stow, Massachusetts. It was too unbelievable to be true, but there it was: Josef Szabo living three towns away from Edward and Sylvia, Deborah and Nan. For how long? Decades. All those years.

"This is Edward Weiss, the American—"

"Yes. It's you," Josef had said. "Not a day I forget you and what you did for me. What can I do for you, Edward?"

"Do you still have your place in Budapest?"

Fifty years after a war.

"Yes. Of course. It needs a little fixing up, but everything works. Do you need it? A place to stay? It's yours. It's waiting for you."

In the cab, driving along the river, his heart pummeled his ribs, demanding to be let out of its prison. Edward looked across a city glistening with lights, the old Chain Bridge draped in glitter, a sparkling white necklace. He was thirsty, his tongue pulling for liquid. He forced himself to swallow. *It's yours*, Josef had said. After all those years.

After the funeral director came and took his daughter away, Edward returned home to Sylvia, who began her death spiral, eventually leaving him, then leaving this earth. He told Sylvia he wanted to call the police, insist on an investigation, but Sylvia told him to stop. *Let her go in peace, Edward. Let her be.* Now he was taking a cab to the cockroach who took his daughter's life. He could never let it go.

Was he dreaming this?

The driver crossed Elizabeth Bridge. Edward watched a sightseeing ferry floating in the middle of the river, its oblong shape moving toward the docking station tethered to the bank. He spotted a fisherman smoking a cigarette under the bridge. Through the open windows, he breathed in a blossoming smell of river water and putrid car exhaust; the night's moist heat throbbed in his ears. He would make it. He'd made it through the war.

And here they were. The building set back inside a courtyard as Annie described it. Edward put one foot on the cobbled surface and struggled to lift himself. The driver took his arm and helped him out.

"Thank you."

Edward waited under the archway for the sound of the cab

departing, like wind fading, and then came the silence. He took his first steps into the courtyard. He would make it. He looked down at his feet. Sylvia was always telling him, *Slow down, Edward. Why do you rush so? What's the hurry?* His heart ached for Sylvia, her breasts warm and soft against his chest.

Life whipped by like a storm. Gone in an instant. His daughter. His wife. Everything.

He inched across the courtyard, familiar as the ones he crossed in the war. Shots banging into walls, stonework cracking. He was trapped in the open air, running for the rubble, calling on God. *God help me*, he had said then. God. He almost said it now in the quiet, late darkness. Not a sound in the night courtyard. He once told Nan waiting made you crazy. Battles knocked out crazy thoughts. She knew. Nan battled for her patients every day.

Inside the building, the heavy iron doors folded back and he stepped into a large cage of an elevator. Garbage in the entryway. Rotting odors to keep you away. But he wouldn't stay away. When Nan told him that Howard had moved to Budapest, he knew he had to follow. He couldn't let the killer go.

The cage ratcheted up, nicking the walls when it passed another floor. He leaned against the metal ribs to keep himself steady against thirst, against dizziness. The cage halted, settled in, and opened up.

Down the hallway to the end. On the right, facing the river, Annie said.

He moved along the wall, using it for support. The bulb cast a flickering light, the glare turning the walls yellow, scratching like sand in his eyes. He stopped midway, rubbing them to see. It had been days since he'd been out. Blood swelled in his head, his ears. He listened. Behind him, the cage started rattling its way down to the ground. He continued along the hall. Finally, he stood outside Howard's door.

He put his hand on the door knob. The knob turned easily. He released it. This was the moment. Here. He almost wept. This wouldn't do. He wiped his eyes and pulled the gun out of his pocket, unlocked the safety, and slipped it back into his pants. He turned the knob again and opened the door.

Thirty-four

Stephen stood with his back to the railing and raised his glass. "To this beautiful night, *egészségünkre!*"

"Eggs and shakes!" Bernardo said. "Stephen, thank you for your hospitality."

They all raised their glasses of Unicum, Annie included, though her glass was empty.

"His name is Van Howard!" Edward's deep voice penetrated the room. Annie pivoted. Stunned. What was he doing here? Edward appeared in the middle of the living room and not her imagination, walking toward them. He had combed his hair. He wore a light blazer and matching pants. He was moving toward the middle of the living room, toward the balcony, one hand in his pants pocket. And except for the sheen of sweat on his face, he almost looked like a different man.

"What the hell—how'd you get here?" Stephen said.

"That's not important," Edward said. "Though you didn't make it easy to find you."

"You kicked me out, remember?"

"Yes, regrettably, I do."

Edward stopped to catch his breath and steady himself, surveying the group bunched together on the balcony. "My daughter is dead because of that man," Edward said, raising his left arm toward Stephen. "Annie, I'm sorry. He let his gaze find her, his dark eyes scarred with pain. "I thought you'd be gone by now."

"I don't understand," Stephen said. "Oh, wait. I see. The call to your babysitter, Annie?" Stephen bowed toward her, sweeping his hand in an arc toward Edward.

Annie froze, caught in her lie. She didn't know what to say.

"Funny. You didn't mention you knew my wife's father," Stephen said.

"Is that a problem?" Will said, taking Annie's hand.

"She had no idea I was coming," Edward said.

Annie could hear the dryness in Edward's voice.

"Edward, are you all right?" Annie said. Once again, he became the tired, beaten old man she had grown to know in the past month.

"First-name basis. Interesting," Stephen said.

"Van, come on," Edward said, taking another step toward the balcony. "You know she knows me. You've been following her."

"Edward, that's a crazy thing to say. You don't look well," Stephen said, his voice fading. "Are you sick?"

"Too sick to wait any longer," Edward said, his eyes catching Annie's again as he approached the threshold of the balcony.

He was steps away from her. She wanted to link her arm in his and steady him, tell him to sit down, but she knew better. The gesture would agitate him.

"Wait for what?" Stephen said.

"The truth," Edward said, his breath stuttering. "How you murdered my daughter." He spat out the words, one at a time.

"Seems we're interrupting something we don't need to be a part of," Bernardo said, attempting to take charge. He guided Eileen past Edward and headed toward the door.

"I told you he's insane," Stephen said to everyone and no one.

Edward kept his eyes on Stephen. "We'll see about that."

"We're all leaving together," Bernardo said from across the room. "Agnes, you ready to take us all home?"

For once Annie appreciated Bernardo's skill at assessing a situation and his effort to control it by asking a perfectly reasonable question.

"Let's go," Will said. He pressed his palm into the small of her back, but Annie became inert, as if she had forgotten how to move, and then she remembered and took a step toward the living room.

"Tell them!" Edward said, shouting.

"You hear how crazy this man is?" Stephen said. "He's mad."

Where the night air had felt fluid and warm only a few moments ago, humming with gaiety and banter, the living room had turned stale and rigid. Annie's sense of consciousness teetered and dislodged from her body. The only part of her that she could still feel was Will's hand on her back. And then she was next to Edward, so close she could smell the burned-toast odor of his sweat.

"Edward, what's going on?"

"I couldn't wait, Annie."

"Wait for what, Annie?" Stephen called to her. "What's this about?"

"We should go," Will said, his fingers slipping from her back and finding her hand.

She didn't want to answer Stephen. She felt guilty, a traitor, her heart prickling with remorse. She heard the pleading in Stephen's voice, the injured spirit wanting something from her that she couldn't give because she was confused. Scared. What was happening? She couldn't fathom why Edward was here, now, at this party. He never once mentioned his intention of coming tonight. But here he was. She regretted calling Edward and lying to Stephen.

"I'm not sure . . ." Her jaw felt pinned together.

"Explain this to me," Stephen said, his voice barking at her.

"She has nothing to explain," Edward said. "She had no idea I was coming tonight. This was my idea."

She and Will joined Bernardo, Eileen, and Agnes at the door.

"Ready?" Bernardo said, keeping his voice low.

"I need to stay," Annie said

"*Egészségünkre!*" Stephen said, calling to the group, raising his glass of Unicum and draining it. "Agnes, take the old man with you. Get him out of here. He's psychotic. Agnes, drive him home, will you? Drive them all home. I'll pay you double."

"With my daughter's money that you stole?" Edward said. He was on the balcony now, facing Stephen, the white statue lit up on the hill behind them. Marta hovered next to Stephen, her long arms limp at her side.

"We cannot all fit," Agnes said. "I can come back. That is no problem." Agnes sucked hard on her cigarette and blew a harsh stream of smoke at the ceiling, all protocol of polite smoking manners gone.

"No problem?" Stephen said, guffawing. "I think this old man is a fucking problem."

"We'll grab a cab," Bernardo said. "Stephen, thank you for having us all here."

"No. Go with Agnes," Will said. "We'll take a cab."

"We can all fit," Eileen said, insisting.

Annie felt herself becoming one organism with the others, all of them conjoined by the growing crisis on the balcony.

"You go," Annie said. "I can't." This was her fault. She had to make sure things would be okay. She couldn't leave the undertow of tension between Edward and Stephen pulling on her. She needed to hear what they had to say.

"Not a problem, Agnes? That's funny," Stephen said, again waving the bottle of Unicum in the air. Marta ran over to her grandmother, who was still seated in the chair by the table with the crystal glasses.

"You know this man? Do you want us to wait for you?" Eileen said to Annie.

"Yes. We know him. It's okay. Don't wait," Annie said, appreciating Eileen's gesture. She couldn't begin to explain what she knew or didn't know, her mind flying back and forth between Edward and Stephen, or Van. It wasn't good. She knew that. She needed to see what Edward would do now that he was on the balcony looking frail and stooped, his whole body at a slant next to Stephen, who was drunk yet robust and tall. The contrast between the two men was alarming to her.

"This man killed my daughter with her medication. He murdered her with her own pills."

"You're crazy," Stephen said. "This isn't happening."

"Stephen, do you want me to come back?" Agnes said, opening the door.

"His name is Van Howard," Edward said. "He's been lying to all of you. You know how he bought this place? My daughter's life insurance. He killed her and ran off with her money."

"It was her gift to me," Stephen said.

"You stole it from her." Edward groaned and clutched his chest.

"This is nuts," Bernardo said.

"Call an ambulance," Will said to Agnes. "Hurry."

"Edward, are you okay?" Annie said. Behind her, she heard Agnes speaking in Hungarian and recognized the word for police. "Edward!" Annie said. She started toward the balcony but stopped midway.

Something atmospheric was enveloping them all, something heavier than the summer's dark heat, louder than the noise of traffic rising from below, something more odorous than their sweat-laced bodies, Eileen's perfume, or the drift of Agnes's cigarette smoke. Annie's feet ached as she stood in her high heels, immobilized, watching Edward's body trembling.

"Edward, you need to sit down. Stephen, can you help him?" Annie said, taking a tentative step closer. But Stephen ignored her.

"Don't fall for it," Stephen said. "Annie, tell him what I told you tonight."

"Tell me yourself," Edward said, his voice straining. "This is between me and you. Leave her out of this." Edward leaned back against the railing for support.

"Your precious daughter wanted to die."

"Jesus," Bernardo said. "This is unbelievable."

"The ambulance will be coming," Agnes said, her words urgent, on the verge of panic.

"You're lying," Edward said to Stephen. "Nothing worse than a liar. Deborah called me the night before she died. Something was wrong."

"She wasn't feeling well," Stephen said. "Maybe she was calling to say good-bye."

"Good-bye to what?" Edward coughed abruptly.

"Annie, this is your fault," Stephen said, taking a swig of the Unicum straight from the bottle. "Why did you tell him to come here?"

"She didn't," Edward said. "Forgive me, Annie. One day you'll understand." Edward turned toward her and she saw the grief in his eyes, and the love.

"It's okay, Edward," she said.

"It's not okay," Stephen said. "He's insane. He's been dogging me ever since my wife died. He hated me from the first time we met. Tell Annie that. Go on."

"I knew you were trouble. Now tell me the truth, God damn it!" Edward choked on his breath. "Tell me what happened to my daughter."

"I will never tell you what happened. You don't deserve it," Stephen said.

"My daughter deserves it." Edward's voice was hoarse. He

coughed again. "You murdered her with pills," Edward said. "It wasn't an accident."

The two men's voices stabbed the night with their accusing words ripping away pent-up emotions, the air enveloping them toxic with anger. Where was the nice Stephen that she thought she knew, and was Edward in his right mind?

"She wanted to die," Stephen said. "You can't face that. It was inevitable. Do you understand?" Stephen lobbed the bottle of Unicum over the side of the railing. "Your daughter wanted to die. She asked me to help her."

The bottle smashing below sounded like a truck backfiring.

"My daughter wasn't sick enough to die."

"What do you want from me?" Stephen barked at Edward.

"Truth. She didn't want to die. Deborah loved life."

Marta screamed.

"Jesus. He has a gun! Get out, everyone," Bernardo said, his words flinging across the room like small stones.

"What the fuck. Is it loaded? Is it real?" Stephen raised his arms and spread them out like a vulture's wings. "Deborah was dying a slow death. I spared her years of pain. I let it happen sooner than she expected. Okay? Is that enough truth for you, American army man?"

"You bastard!" Edward said. "Did you hear that, Annie?"

"Good thing we didn't get that autopsy," Stephen said, laughing, taunting Edward. "You and your stupid truth? Where were all the great American heroes when my father needed you? Tell me about that truth!"

Edward swayed forward, then listed back again, holding on to the railing with one hand.

"Edward, please put the gun down," Annie said, but he was beyond her reach and words. He was untouchable. The footsteps of the others, except for Will, who remained at her side, thundered down the common hallway toward the elevator.

"You murdered my daughter. You stole her life!" Edward said, his voice breaking.

Marta shrieked.

"Shut up, Marta, will you? Shut the fuck up." Stephen shouted something in Hungarian.

"Annie, come on," Will gripped her arm.

"I can't . . ."

Outside she heard sirens. She knew the police would be there in a minute or less.

"Deborah hated her disease," Stephen said, half-lowering his arms. "I put her out of her misery. You don't want to hear that. You never will. Now leave me the fuck alone."

Annie and Will both moved toward Edward as the old man started to fold forward, but Stephen grabbed the gun from Edward's limp hand and shot Edward twice, the hideous explosions causing Edward's body to jerk.

"Stephen, what are you doing?" Annie shrieked. "Stop! Oh my God! Stop!"

She started again toward Edward, slumped in a pile on the balcony, but Stephen swirled toward her, waving the gun. "Shut up, Annie. Get back. You saw what he did. He tried to kill me."

"I know. It's okay. Put the gun down, please," Annie said.

"Stephen, put the gun down," Will said.

"Shut the fuck up. It's not okay." He pointed the gun at Will. "He came here to kill me. It was self-defense."

"Stephen, please," Annie said, pleading.

"You saw it with your own eyes. Look!" Stephen pressed the small gun to his head, shouted something in Hungarian, and shot himself, the loud pop a terrifying and final sound as Stephen lurched backward into the railing and collapsed onto Edward, lying on the balcony floor, the backside of his blazer soaked in dark blood.

Annie crouched down to hide from what she had seen, her arms helmeting her head inside a bubble of time that felt like the rest of her life, until she was yanked back by a sharp pang in her calves and toes, and the oceanic sound of traffic outside, and the continuous scream that wasn't Marta, but a siren, and a scattering of Hungarian men in dark uniforms filling the room and the familiar faces of Agnes, Bernardo, and Eileen standing over her and Will. Both Edward and Stephen lay motionless beneath a steady stream of red and white strobe lights crisscrossing the living room and ceiling from the street below, and then the flashing ribbons stopped.

It was over.

Thirty-five

*T*hat *night*—because that was how she would always think of Edward's death—Annie and Will returned home in the darkest hour before dawn, sleepwalking, in shock. Grieving. In the vestibule, they passed the familiar stink of garbage bins and the super's apartment door with the number 1 on it, shut and silent. She saw a pale light from a television flickering under the door.

The elevator on the top floor opened to a view of their bald neighbor's beer cans lined up on the mat, two grocery bags stuffed with a week's worth of trash: chicken bones, fruit rinds, old bread, juice bottles—rotting smells rising everywhere.

"Jesus," Will said, fitting the key in their door.

They walked into the quiet, clean oasis of their apartment and Leo's room. They had Klara to thank for that.

A gentle nightlight glowed in the hallway. Annie could hear the television down the hall in the living room where Klara and Sandor had fallen asleep on the couch. Will had called them from the police station. Never had Leo's room felt as safe as in this moment when she stood over his crib and simply stared at his face, the sleeping baby surrounded by his stuffed animals and the sweetness of life, because life held that possibility and it was embodied right here in front of her, in their child.

It was her favorite room because of the views, especially at night when the castle on the hill, illuminated by spotlights, shone like a full moon. Will took her in his arms. She leaned into him, the feeling of safety flowing through her like water satiating a terrible thirst. Her small family was intact.

She looked out the window to Castle Hill and wrapped her arms around Will's waist to combat the sensation of her body losing gravity, the horrible images of death pummeling inside her head. In this tranquil moment with Will, she remembered the sounds of thudding footfalls approaching, loud voices and electronic noises and a handful of policemen bursting into Stephen's living room. Was it exactly after the last shot fired? During? Just before Annie was shielding her own head with bent wrists and elbows to fend against another horror she did not want to see? She'd witnessed enough already when Stephen fired two shots and Edward fell to the floor.

At Stephen's apartment, a policeman directed her next to the table with the crystal glasses. Agnes appeared. And then Bernardo and Eileen, Marta and Olga—everyone huddled together trying to make sense of the insensible. Will was by her side.

The police would not let her approach Edward, but Annie wanted to touch him, kneel by his side, place his head on her lap, give him back his body's dignity. "Van killed him," she said. "We saw him do it." But the police would not let her approach the crime scene.

A young officer pointed to the balcony, speaking quickly to Agnes in the soft tones of the Hungarian language.

Will said, "Van Howard is his name. He also goes by Stephen Házy. We saw him shoot Edward twice."

"*Igen.*" Agnes touched Annie. "The policeman wants to know if you know him."

Annie started to move toward Edward again, but a young officer blocked her.

"*Itt!*" the policeman said sharply to Agnes in Hungarian.

"Please obey them," Agnes said to Annie.

Two medics carried stretchers to the balcony.

Annie saw that Edward's mouth was open in a distorted *O*, a dark spot around his crotch, a pool of blood oozing from his stomach area, his eyes staring at something only he could see. Stephen was twisted on his side. Thank God she couldn't see his face.

But something else happened in those moments of gunshots. As she inhaled the bitter odor of the gun, and in the confusion of lights and police and medics, and Hungarian words she couldn't understand, she thought she smelled, too, the sunbaked odor of tar on the driveway where her brother, Greg, lifted his knee and aimed the ball at the chalked white circle on the blacktop. She felt her legs remembering the skip-step she took toward the circle. She'd wanted to catch the ball, to be part of the game. So she started for the chalked circle, hearing Greg shout, *Annie! Get out of the way!* She saw the ball flying toward Tracy on her bike. Annie heard a thump of metal and saw the edge of the white line, and she remembered how she couldn't move, paralyzed on the blacktop as her brother shook Tracy, lying on the ground, trying to rouse her; she did not hear his frantic words, she did not hear anything.

She burst into tears in Leo's room.

"Annie, Annie," Will said, placing his hands gently on her shoulders. She shook her head.

Dear Mr. Weiss.

She couldn't erase the image of Stephen's angry smile provoking Edward. *Good thing we didn't get that autopsy.*

How long would she hear those hideous words and gunshots? How long would she see Stephen pointing the gun at her and at Will?

Annie felt her body's fluids pulsing through her legs and arms. Why did Stephen point the gun at them? Edward was right. Stephen was an angry, homicidal man.

In the car ride to the police station close to midnight, the roads were still crowded, the sidewalks busy with couples dressed for late dinners and club hopping. This city didn't sleep. This was no slouch of a town. It's what seduced Annie when she and Will first came, and Will decided that yes, he could do it, he could quit his job. Only now she knew: what they had seen on the surface of these streets and hills with their quaint, backward time-warped ways was not at all what breathed beneath. The police car merged onto the fast avenue along the river.

She hadn't penetrated the city's veneer, but she saw that trying to get inside this country had been her attempt to get inside herself.

The police car drove past an intersection crowded with twenty-somethings, a Budapestian girl in black boots with thick heels stepping off a curb, crossing in front of the car. The car swerved out of the way and kept moving alongside the river, where small and midsize boats inched down the dark waterway, the Duna, the liquid beast that swallowed secrets of time and death.

Edward and Stephen both dead. There were no winners here.

AFTER SANDOR WOKE Klara on the couch and took her home, Annie and Will, exhausted but unable to sleep, made love in a way they hadn't in months, with a sense of gratitude and purpose, and sadness, clinging to each other like flood victims grabbing hold of deep-rooted trees, as if Edward's death confirmed that life was worth living, more than they ever imagined. She tried to erase the image of Edward's lifeless body on the balcony, to see him alive once again in Josef's apartment, vibrant with complaints. Fighting. Difficult and irascible, appalled by love's injustices. But the lifeless image hung in her mind like a limp flag. She hoped time would bleach it out, make it fade and disappear.

"It wasn't in vain, coming here, was it?" she said to Will as they lay in bed, her eyes sore from crying. "He'd still be alive if I hadn't told him the address. They both would be."

"You gave him what he was looking for. He got answers. He would have persisted with or without you, Annie. Have no doubt about that. It's why he came here. To find out the truth. He told you that."

"You think he got his answer?"

"Absolutely," Will said. "I do."

She pulled Will closer, skin to skin, and shutting her eyes, she saw the blinding spark of sunlight from the car's metal fender. Tracy didn't have a choice. She was a victim of fate wedged between their father's car backing up and Greg's errant ball, yet Greg blamed himself and carried the burden of her family's despair.

Maybe they were all victims of fate.

Thirty-six

A year later, on the anniversary of *that night* in early September, Annie went for a jog around a small pond in the woods near her parents' house in Portland, Maine. Her legs were flying on their own through the familiar path under the pine trees. Annie was the mother of two now, ever since the hour before dawn on *that night* in Budapest when she and Will conceived Gracie—naming their daughter in honor of her brother, Greg. Now Leo had a baby sister asleep in a bassinet on their grandparents' deck in the backyard. Tracy was visiting, too, on this Labor Day Sunday, her older sister in a wheelchair, her head ensconced in a helmet from years of seizures and medications, a dependent child in a mature woman's body. Annie fought against feeling pity for her sister. Edward was right. Pity didn't help. It took life away.

She wished Greg were here. If only he were alive and able to hear the truth that it wasn't his fault. It wasn't his fault. She put her hand to her chest and inhaled the minty scent of pine trees that ringed the pond and whose veil of thin, dry needles softened the trail under her feet.

The day after Edward died, Nan arrived in Budapest with her partner, Patricia. They stayed at the Kempinski Hotel and brought Edward back to Massachusetts to bury him next to Deborah and Sylvia.

Annie tried to imagine Edward's frame of mind, taking a gun with him across the ocean. Why the gun? Did he believe that Stephen would try to kill him, too?

"He refused to listen to me," Nan had told Annie in the hotel lobby. "I told him not to come here." Nan was pretty in an androgynous way, with her crew-cut hair and man-tailored shirt and pants. She had her father's intelligent, quick eyes. "He wouldn't listen to anybody. That was my dad," Nan said, resigned but not embittered. "That includes you, Annie. And that's why we loved him."

Annie hugged Nan and promised to stay in touch.

That night, Annie called Rose from the police station and learned that neither Rose nor Josef had any idea about the gun, only that Edward needed a place, and was trying to find his son-in-law and didn't want anyone to know about it.

"I should never have given him the address," Annie said to Rose.

"It is not your responsibility," Rose said.

"Isn't it?"

"No, Annie," Rose said. "We are not responsible for the choices Edward made."

According to the lawyer Will hired to translate the police documents for them, Stephen was drunk and also high on Vicodin. His death was ruled a suicide, Edward's a homicide.

The lawyer also helped the police understand that Annie and Will, Bernardo and Eileen, Agnes and Marta and her grandmother—none of them—had committed any wrongdoing.

"Annie!" Will called to her at the end of the running path. "Are you coming?"

"One more round, okay?"

Will was smiling more since their return to the States. He had accepted a job in Boston with a small start-up called AllConnect. The company created software that allowed businesses to send out emails in the form of newsletters. Annie was still trying to understand the excitement Will felt about the internet, its power to reach out to the world. He still believed that telecommunications had the potential to curb wars. She doubted that. Humans destroyed the most promising things.

"The applications are endless," Will told her. "We're only seeing the beginning of it."

"Perhaps," she said.

And everyone—all the big papers and news networks—was talking about China now. How it was much bigger than the Eastern European gold rush. Hungary was a blip, a mosquito compared to behemoth China. Bernardo, too, had abandoned Hungary, but he had not given up on trying to recruit Will to his latest scheme in Hong Kong—a city Bernardo avowed was Manhattan on steroids. She was no longer annoyed by Will's old boss and would forever maintain a soft spot for Bernardo and Eileen because of what they endured together on that fateful night and, most important, because they and Agnes had waited at the elevator and directed the police back to Stephen's apartment and, who knows, maybe they had saved her and Will's life. Maybe Stephen had turned the gun on himself when he saw the police at the door, choosing suicide for his final escape.

Still, Annie had stood her ground when she told Will if they didn't leave Budapest *now*, once everything was settled with Edward, she was going to leave without him. Within ten days, they had packed up thirteen bags of luggage and returned to Boston, to a rental apartment near the Route 128 technology corridor.

Two months after that, Will accepted the job with AllConnect, and a month later they bought a new modest, contemporary home in Concord, forty minutes outside of Boston, rushing back into home ownership before the rising real-estate market shot out of their reach. Even Josef and Rose were talking about selling their water-stained house for much more than what Annie would have believed possible. But, as her father liked to say, "A house is worth what the market will pay for it," and the real-estate market in the last year had turned volcanic, with people buying up wrecks, then knocking them down and replacing them with McMansions everywhere, a new emblem of prosperity, one more way to prove that too much was never enough. During that time, Annie was going through her morning bouts of nausea in the new house—unborn Gracie asserting herself.

A breeze gusted through the tops of the trees as Annie rounded the small pond again. It had been weird seeing their former house painted green when she took Leo to visit Rose and Josef in their old neighborhood. She agreed with Rose: she didn't like the change in color. Rose's house remained unchanged except for a pair of Edward's paintings that Nan had given them, which now hung in their front hallway. Nan gave one to Annie and Will as well—a landscape with dark smudges of blue-gray mountains and a thin streak of lemon-yellow horizon, which Annie interpreted as hope rising above.

"We have life and we have death," Josef said, patting her shoulder. "Right now it's your job to enjoy your life."

"I'm trying."

"You Americans. Trying? What's trying? You can do better than that. Come on, Leo. What do you say in Hungarian?"

"*Jó napot kívánunk!* Good day!" Leo said, shaking his auburn curls and giggling.

"Hungarian is in him," Josef said.

Annie could thank Klara and Sandor for that. All those hours they cared for Leo. Now the young couple were living together in a four-hundred-square-foot flat in Pest, expecting a child of their own. Klara said they lived near the Roma. "You will be happy to know this," she wrote to Annie in a letter.

Persze. Annie wondered what the two Roma sisters were doing on this warm September day, guessing they were plucking flowers as usual at the Parliament and selling them. She wished she could have done more for them than hand out American cash. There were too many things to fix in the world.

A BREEZE CROSSED the path, ruffling the pond water's silver-blue surface. How she missed Edward on this anniversary day. She felt it in her chest.

"I was thinking about Edward," Annie said, slowing down to

walk with Will, who was waiting for her. "I don't blame him for wanting to know the truth. But the gun. Why did he have to have a gun? It shows he had harmful intentions. There's no justification for that, is there? If only I hadn't given him the address."

"If only the road to hell weren't paved with good intentions," Will said. "If only someone hadn't stolen my wallet, or murdered Edward's daughter, or accidentally hit your sister with a baseball. If only," Will said. "None of it is good. And if someone killed our child, what would you do, Annie? What would I do? I'm a peaceful guy, but I think there's a good chance I might get a gun."

"It didn't solve anything. It didn't bring his daughter back," Annie said. She heard the whine in her voice because the thought of someone killing her child was too much to contemplate.

"He said he wanted the truth," Will said. "I'm guessing he thought the gun would force Stephen to tell him, and it did."

She scuffed the path, dissatisfied with that answer, her sneakers kicking up tiny pebbles as they emerged from the trail onto the sidewalk leading back to her parents' house. The sidewalk was lined with sycamore trees, distinctive for their mottled, exfoliating bark. As a child, she stored strips of the thin bark in a shoe box and wrote wishes on them. *I wish Tracy would get better.* When she graduated high school and was packing up for college, she threw the shoe box away because the strips had crumbled, and Tracy's health had gotten worse. Where was the justice in that?

The road to wisdom was a long one.

Thankfully, Mr. Calloway had stopped contacting them. It had been around this time when he last wrote, wrapping up any future obligations they had with him.

Dear Mr. and Mrs. Gordon:

As promised, I passed on your materials to little Leo's birth mother. This completes our agreement. If you are ever so inclined, I hope you will drop me a line from time to time and let me know how you and the little guy are faring.

Sincerely,

John Calloway

At the heart of it, she understood that Calloway was likely someone who didn't get enough praise for what he did in his life. But that wasn't her burden to carry. She had two children to raise.

How much had she had contributed to Edward's death, or to Stephen's death, or Greg's? What was her fault? What wasn't? Who was responsible for how things turned out? Some questions didn't have answers. Instead, they left permanent stains on her heart.

As for Stephen Házy, aka Van Howard, she couldn't say for certain that he had followed her. She was inclined to believe Edward's version of the story because of the coincidental meetings—at Luigi's, on the street near Edward's flat, and at the Bem József statue, where she had stopped with Leo. Even Stephen's uninvited appearance at the police station might have been planned. Was it kindness or manipulation, or both? As time passed, she wondered how thin was the line that divided good from bad. Stephen had lied. He was a murderer. And yet, she couldn't ignore that he had also been kind to her, which in some ways made it even worse. Deborah's criminal overdose was Stephen's ticket back to reclaim his father's home. And what did it buy him? Multiple deaths.

How had she allowed herself to be so convincingly deceived? Could she really blame it on the fact that she was a woman feeling estranged in a stranger's land?

Annie knit her fingers in Will's, and in response, he stopped to kiss her before they returned to her parents' house, one of a dozen stately brick estates gracing the street.

Only one question continued to claw at her: did Edward intend to kill Stephen?

She wanted to believe he had brought the gun across the ocean to scare his son-in-law into making a confession, as Will had said, and not harm him. She needed to trust in the ultimate goodness in humanity. She yearned to believe that Edward hadn't deceived her or set her up. He hadn't sought them out, after all. He had told her again and again to stay away. But in his insistence to hunt down the truth, hadn't he also crossed a critical line? Hadn't he put her and Will and the others in lethal jeopardy? In his defense, he didn't realize that they would still be there at Stephen's. The party had run long, after all.

If she had been in Edward's position, how far would she have gone to make things right?

She didn't know.

What she did know was that Edward and Deborah, Tracy and Greg, and Stephen, and all those lives shattered on European shores during and after the wars, and on an asphalt driveway in America— those lives whose truths had disappeared into a vault of eternity beyond her reach—were not gone or silenced. She could hear them calling.

Acknowledgments

Many thanks to my Hungarian friends for life, Laszlo Szotyory and Szófia Székely, who taught me so much about a different way of being when I lived in Budapest for a year, in 1994, and to George Hazy, who introduced me to Hungary's beautiful city on the Danube.

Throughout the writing of this novel and its many revisions, I turned to those who understood and helped: Susan Henderson, Caroline Leavitt, Patry Francis, Barbara Shapiro, Risa Miller, Deb Henry, Dawn Tripp, Tish Cohen, Robin Slick, Billie Hinton, Joyce Norman, Daphne Kalotay, and my dear friends at Book Pregnant and ePubs and Pen names.

Thank you to Emma Sweeney, my brilliant agent, who saw the promise of a book early on, and to everyone at the agency for making things happen behind the scenes. Emma also brought me to Chuck Adams, extraordinary editor at Algonquin Books and wonderful human being. To the outstanding Algonquin team— Brooke Csuka, Betsy Gleick, Jude Grant, Brunson Hoole, Debra Linn, Michael McKenzie, Lauren Moseley, Craig Popelars, Ashley Mason, Elisabeth Scharlatt, and everyone else—your incredible devotion to books is inspiring and necessary to a free world. It's an honor to be one of your authors.

I gained a deeper understanding of WWII, the holocaust, and Hungarian Jews during the 1940s from talking to generous individuals, many gone now, who took time to share some of their experiences with me—from the horrors in Europe to their harrowing journeys to get to America, where they subsequently prospered and thrived. Thank you: Hannah Entell; George Friedmann; Marika Barnett; Joel T. Klein, PhD; and Bob Berger.

Eternal thanks to my father, Melvin H. Brilliant, also gone now many years, for his WWII service in the US Army's Rainbow Division, and for his part in helping to liberate Dachau concentration camp. Though he refused to see himself as any kind of hero, I view him differently. His memories helped guide this book.

Thank you to Mom, my sisters and brother, for keeping it real, and to my in-laws and extended family members for your talents and diverse perspectives. And to Tina Cherry, founder of the Louis D. Brown Peace Institute, for her incredible heart and wisdom.

To our son, thank you for teaching me more than I ever imagined about life.

To my husband, Barr, thank you for believing in my work, for your genius insights, and for walking beside me all these years, with love.

Strangers in Budapest

Hidden Among Us:
An essay by Jessica Keener

Questions for Discussion

Hidden Among Us

An essay by Jessica Keener

In the winter of 1993, I moved to Budapest with my husband, our six-month-old son, our dog, and seventeen overstuffed suitcases. We had been living in Atlanta for several years. I don't know if there is a best time for making a change in one's life, but I was in my late thirties and felt an urgency about time passing. I was especially fearful of having regrets at the end of my life. The arrival of our son, whom we adopted at four days old, intensified these feelings.

One of my dreams after graduate school was to live overseas, someplace in Europe—maybe Italy or France. Budapest never crossed my mind back then. But Eastern Europe was in the news a lot in the nineties. Budapest and Prague were "it" cities, and

Americans were streaming over to have a look at countries long hidden behind Russia's Iron Curtain. A few years prior, a Hungaian American friend of ours urged us to meet him in Budapest so he could show us around. We visited his cousins in the countryside, ate homemade goulash, drank Hungarian beer in tiny dark bars downtown, and ordered room service at our hotel because it was ridiculously cheap.

I loved traveling to landmark cities in Europe (Paris, Rome, Vienna, Madrid), but Budapest got under my skin in a different way. I was unnerved and haunted by its convoluted history. And my response felt more personal because of my own family history. I was Jewish. My grandparents came from neighboring Ukraine and Poland. My father had fought in World War II as part of the army's 42nd Rainbow Division and had, along with the U.S. Seventh Army, liberated Dachau concentration camp in Munich on April 29, 1945. He witnessed thousands of corpses lying stacked in open train cars. As a child I had carried my father's war story inside me.

I wondered if the ghosts of my Jewish ancestors were nudging me toward Budapest in some way.

The city also reminded me of Boston, where I grew up. Budapest had the Danube running through it, while Boston had the Charles. Budapest was gorgeous and gritty, the poor cousin of grand, polished Vienna. Boston was charming and smart, but quaint compared to its behemoth neighbor: New York. And Budapest was rife with narrow back streets and stairways that cut through the city's hills like the neighborhoods I'd walked in Boston. I was intensely, almost compulsively drawn to this familiar yet strange city. My husband and I visited Budapest a second time the following year, and that was when we made the decision to relocate.

When I boarded the plane with our babe in my arms to meet my husband, who had gone ahead to secure an apartment, I had no clear plans. No job. My husband had a few business ideas. I knew I could write anywhere. We had some savings and our American optimism. Whatever unfolded would surely be okay.

Our year in Budapest was much more difficult than I expected it to be. From the first month of our arrival, I experienced a deep loneliness I was never able to shake. Calling it homesickness was an understatement. I wanted our son to know his grandparents. I craved having conversations in my own language. The things that had seemed intriguing as a visitor—the dirty streets, the lack of retail options and services, the vacant synagogues, the bullet holes defacing old buildings—were constant reminders of the country's long economic hardship, its isolation from the world, its history of violence.

Increasingly, I felt as if I were trapped inside Dickens's *Great Expectations*. Once-stunning mansions sagged behind overgrown bushes and vines. I could see outlines of Budapest's former grandeur, but so much had been worn away by wars and government takeovers.

At the same time, Budapest ignited a seed that had lain dormant inside me—about who I was as an American and as a Jew and what it meant to feel safe.

My response to Budapest also struck me as shamefully egocentric and naïve. As tattered as the city appeared on the outside, something else was waking up and demanding attention from its deeper inner core. I was stunned by how vibrant the city was despite its soiled appearance. The place was teeming with millions—the sidewalks overflowed with young and old, couples and families.

Yet, until my first visit, I'd never given this elegant but frayed city a thought. This was a country that gave the world Liszt, produced chess and math wizards, designed distinctive porcelain and lace, and was saturated in Gypsy lore. But something had gone wrong, terribly wrong. I wanted to understand what and, most of all, why.

After a year, we returned to the States and resettled in Boston. For a long time, I didn't know how to make sense of my Budapest experience. Hungarians were both friendly and reserved, the culture complex and layered, full of contradictions. What had I learned that I could pass on to others? What greater meaning did it hold?

Over the next decade, two disturbing encounters led me to synthesize my overseas experience and write *Strangers in Budapest*. The first was in 2002, when I wrote a magazine article about the tragic death of a teenage boy who was innocently caught in a street gang's crossfire. Ironically, this young man from Boston was on his way to a "teens against gun violence" meeting the afternoon the bullet struck him in the head. In writing this story, I interviewed his mother, a remarkable woman who started a foundation in her son's name, the Louis D. Brown Peace Institute, to help families deal with the rage and depression that come with the loss of a loved one from a violent death. I wondered how Louis's mother could absorb something so horrific and channel her grief into something so affirming and healing for others.

In the second encounter, I learned that my neighbor's daughter had died an unexpected, untimely death. The mother suspected foul play by the daughter's boyfriend. Though the police looked into the matter, nothing came of it, and the case was closed. The mother considered delving further, but she didn't have the heart for it, ultimately knowing it couldn't bring her daughter back to life.

During both encounters, I remember asking myself: What would I do? As a mother, the question was almost too painful to imagine, but it served up the final piece of a larger puzzle my subconscious had been trying to fit together concerning so many things: my time in Budapest, violence and wrongful deaths, my father's experience at Dachau, and how far I would go to protect my child or rectify a crime.

I began to see how we are all survivors of violence in some way or another—either personally or historically—though I had never thought about myself from that perspective. I began to see that we can choose how we respond to violence's devastating impact. Will we hate or forgive? Rage or love? That was when I knew Budapest in the mid-1990s offered an ideal time and setting for my American characters, who are wrestling with grief and its lethal consequences.

When she arrives in Budapest, my protagonist, Annie Gordon, is initially seduced by a city trying to free itself from decades of secrecy and repression. She has come with her husband and their newly adopted baby to support her husband's business ventures. But she soon grows restless. The city's dark side unhinges her own repressed memory of an accident she witnessed as a child and couldn't stop.

Annie is also someone who needs to help others, especially people broken by life. So when she meets Edward Weiss, an ailing expat and World War II veteran, she quickly entangles herself in his desperate search for a man he says murdered his daughter. What she doesn't realize is how far Edward is willing to go to uncover the truth about his daughter's death. In accepting Annie's help, Edward prods her to take responsibility for her own choices, as they hurtle toward the story's final, defiant act.

Questions for Discussion

1. In *Strangers in Budapest*, the city of Budapest seems to function as another character in the story. What are some of the characteristics of this Eastern European city that helped shape Annie's experience there? Do you think the story would have unfolded differently if it had been set in Philadelphia? What does the idea of a place functioning as a character mean to you?

2. When Annie meets Edward, something about the old man takes hold of her and her relationship with him quickly grows intense—with Edward provoking Annie to let down her guard. Annie's husband, Will, tells her not to get involved. Why do you think Annie ignores Will's warnings to stay out of Edward's problems?

3. The Holocaust and the plight of the Jews in Europe during World War II is woven into the novel. Annie is not Jewish, but her husband is, and so is Edward, who fought in the war and helped liberate Dachau. In what ways do you think Judaism influences the story?

4. What are your thoughts about Annie's attraction (or is it the opposite?) to Will's former boss, Bernardo? Do you think she wishes Will would share Bernardo's boldness in approaching life?

5. From the outside, Annie appears "normal," yet something about her feels off center, as though she is yearning to break free. Why do you think Annie disdains offers to help her integrate into the American expat community? Do you see a pattern in her behavior, in the idea of actively staying away from people and places that are like herself?

6. In the novel, the Gypsies are almost like phantoms floating around the fringes of the city, appearing in the middle of things but never really being a part of anything. Why do you think Annie becomes obsessed with them? Do you think they represent some part of Annie? If so, what?

7. How did you feel about Annie's relationship with Stephen? Do you think she was attracted to him or repulsed by him? Or was it both?

8. Can you see yourself moving to another country as Annie and Will do with their young son? Annie seemed to be trying to escape from something, while Will was looking to embrace something new. Of the two, which do you think had the stronger motivation, and, in the end, the stronger will?

9. There seemed to be a kind of inevitability to the way Edward's and Stephen's stories played out, but without Annie's role in their lives it's likely that none of it would have happened. Do you feel that Annie made the right decisions? If so, why? If not, why not?

10. What do you think Annie and Will's relationship will be once they are away from Budapest and back home in America? Do you think the marriage will survive? Why, or why not?